Louisa Heaton lives on Hayling Island, Hampshire, with her husband, four children and a small zoo. She has worked in various roles in the health industry—most recently four years as a community first responder, answering 999 calls. When not writing Louisa enjoys other creative pursuits, including reading, quilting and patchwork—usually instead of the things she *ought* to be doing!

Fiona McArthur is an Australian midwife who lives in the country and loves to dream. Writing Medical Romance gives Fiona the scope to write about all the wonderful aspects of romance, adventure and medicine, and the midwifery she feels so passionate about. When she's not catching babies, Fiona and her husband Ian are off to meet new people, see new places and have wonderful adventures. Drop in and say hi at Fiona's website: fionamcarthurauthor.com.

NURSE'S NIGHT BEFORE VALENTINE'S

LOUISA HEATON

OFF-LIMITS TEMPTATION FOR DR DAY

FIONA McARTHUR

MILLS & BOON

First published in Great Britain 2026
by Mills & Boon, an imprint of HarperCollins*Publishers* Ltd,
1 London Bridge Street, London, SE1 9GF

www.harpercollins.co.uk

HarperCollins*Publishers* Macken House, 39/40 Mayor Street Upper,
Dublin 1, D01 C9W8, Ireland

Nurse's Night Before Valentine's © 2026 Louisa Heaton

Off-Limits Temptation for Dr Day © 2026 Fiona McArthur

ISBN: 978-0-263-41980-1

01/26

NURSE'S NIGHT BEFORE VALENTINE'S

LOUISA HEATON

MILLS & BOON

To anyone who doesn't need a Valentine's Day
to celebrate their love xxx

CHAPTER ONE

AUNTY MORAG HAD said Cass was trying to escape again by choosing a job on the most isolated western island of Scotland.

Cass had disagreed. 'Far from it. I'm just expanding my horizons.'

'You're running again. Why not just stay here? Make a life here?'

It isn't that simple, she'd thought as she placed her bags in the boot of her trusty Beetle car, which was only held together by rust. Make a life? She'd never been given the opportunity to settle and make a life anywhere. Anytime she'd ever thought she could, she'd had her heart ripped out. It was easier to keep moving. But she'd pasted on a wide, fake smile in the hopes of reassuring her aunt as she'd turned to give the much older woman—her only family—a hug goodbye.

'I'll be back before you know it,' she promised her aunt.

'Aye. And then where will you run to next?'

Aunty Morag had been the only mainstay in Cass's life. An anchor point that she could return to whenever she needed. A place where Cass knew she would never be turned away. Her aunt had lived in Lochgilphead for all of her life. Her cottage was located on the outskirts of Loch Gilp. It was isolated. Quiet. The perfect place to hide and lick wounds. The *only* place where Cass had never felt judged. The only place she'd ever felt *wanted* after being kicked out by her parents when she was sixteen years old. Pregnant and afraid.

Morag had been the only one to care. To go looking for her. To wrap her arms around her and give her a place to stay.

Cass had thought that she'd be okay. That they'd both be okay, but then she'd given birth and her heart had been broken again and it had become too painful to stay in the place of her broken dreams. So she'd fled Morag's nest to go to university and then again to work in various GP surgeries as a locum practice nurse, but she'd always returned to rest and recuperate and gather herself before she left yet again. Sometimes for weeks. Sometimes for months. But never more than that. Never a year. Never long enough for people to get too close, for other people to potentially break her heart and ruin her defenses.

'I don't know what I'll do when you're no longer here,' Cass had said once to her aunt as they'd sipped on mugs of cocoa one cold winter's evening. Winds howled outside of the cottage, wailing like the ghosts of her past.

'Don't you worry, lass. This home will always be here for you, even if I can't be.'

Cass hoped so. Aunt Morag's place was where she'd been living when Daniel had been born. It was where all her memories of him were kept. Like a time capsule. That's what kept bringing her back. To fill herself back up on him. To pull his things from the shoebox beneath her bed and hold them, to inhale his scent. A scent that had faded with time.

It had only been a week since her last posting, so when the Lark Agency had called her to say that there was a practice nurse position on the Isle of Gulray, west of Islay, to cover a short maternity leave, she'd jumped at the chance, even more so when she'd heard that she'd be a hell of a lot more than just a simple practice nurse.

The Isle of Gulray was home to just a few hundred people and many of those were unable to make it to the practice, living on the distant edges of the isle, away from the one village practice. Cass would not only be a practice nurse but would also take on the role of a district nurse.

What a challenge! When she'd trained as a nurse, she'd completed a placement with the district nursing team and loved it, so the opportunity to visit people in their homes and care for them there, as well as have her own clinic at the practice...? It seemed too good to turn down and a huge step forward for her career and curriculum vitae.

And now she and her Beetle were on the ferry in mid-January, chugging away towards the isle. Seagulls were crying overhead as cold winds gusted at her on the ferry railing, finding their way through all the gaps in her clothes to raise goosebumps on her skin.

She could see the isle in the distance, a green hill in an otherwise empty horizon, her home for the next few months. Her gaze also fell to the people around her. A couple was bickering over something, the woman looking hurt, the man drawn and hung-over. Cass felt glad she didn't have to deal with anything like that. A partner disappointing her. She knew that pain. Further on was a small family. A mother appearing tired and exhausted as she chased two small toddlers who looked like they could be twins, whilst the father tapped away at something on his phone.

She found other people's family dynamics fascinating. For a long time, she'd thought that her own parents were normal. That every child grew up feeling like they needed to keep their parents happy because there'd be hell to pay if they didn't. That every child grew up walking on eggshells in fear of their overreactions and anger. That every child took care of their own needs and was self-sufficient, because parents need never do more for their kids than put some food on the table at the end of the day. To discover that other families had not been like this was fascinating to her. But also deeply saddening, when she realized all that she had missed out on.

There was a couple standing at the ferry's railing: a guy who stood with a much older woman. His mother, maybe? She had flaxen, almost silver hair whose soft curls billowed in the wind, compared to his darker, short style. They had the same eyes, though hers had more laughter lines and the shape of her face was softer. The woman was looking lovingly at the isle, whereas the son looked only at his mother with what seemed like sadness and pain that made the line of his jaw hard. Something about her was hurting him and Cass recognized that pain and felt her heart harden. Caring for others, loving others only hurt you in the end.

It was best in this life to be alone.

Cass's gaze left them and she looked back out to sea. She hated that she was so empathic. That she was so tuned in to others' emotions and upset, due, no doubt, to always having to be aware of her parents' emotions and moods in order to survive. It had become a safety mechanism as a child, but as an adult? It was a millstone that she proudly carried, knowing it was also a shield that protected her from more hurt.

They passed a small fishing boat, bobbing up and down from the bow wave of their ferry, and she watched the lone occupant haul in his nets for a while and wondered what the fisherman's life was like. Was it all a solitary one, or did he go home to a big, boisterous family that worried for him all the time he was at sea?

'Ladies and gentlemen, this is the captain speaking. As we approach the beautiful Isle of Gulray, might I ask all passengers that are arriving with their vehicles to please make their way down to the vehicle deck and prepare for disembarkation.'

That was her. Cass gave the isle one last look and headed on down the steps that would take her to her car. The vehicle deck was solidly packed with cars, vans, trucks and one or two motorhomes, and she wondered how many of these people were visitors and how many might actually become her patients in the weeks to come. There was always something so exciting at starting somewhere new, meeting people and getting to know them. Not too much disclosure, obviously, but enough to make them feel comfortable with her. Enough to make them feel welcomed and safe, but not so much that she'd ever be devastated to leave them behind. Gulray was temporary, like everyplace else she'd been. And temporary was best, so that she didn't have time to get attached to anything or anyone. And also so that no one got attached to *her*.

Cass felt the ferry slow. A horn sounded and then sunlight filled the vehicle deck as the bow opened up, the ramp lowering and vehicles in front of her beginning to move forward. She turned on her engine and awaited her turn and soon she was driving off the ferry and back onto dry land. The port was quite small and her satnav indicated that she needed to drive two miles north towards the village of Kilmarrin, the residential heart of the island.

She passed many fields filled with sheep, one or two with horses, as the narrow roads dipped and curved, taking her past isolated cottages and trees that would be beautiful in summer. At one point she drove through a tree tunnel, what pale sunlight there was flickering through the sparse canopy overhead, as the car ascended a small hill. When she hit the top, the trees disappeared and the sprawling vista ahead showed her the village of Kilmarrin, nestled in a valley. It looked perfect and she couldn't quite believe that she was going to get to live and work here for a little while. She'd managed to secure a small one-bedroom cottage that wasn't too costly, but still within the village. Her satnav told her that she would reach her destination in three minutes.

Kilmarrin was small and perfectly formed. Pictures online had showed it at its best in summer with grey stone cottages, brimming with flowers and blooms that hung over low stone garden walls. Today, in mid-January, it looked a little greyer, but still quite pretty. There was a small inn called the Puffin's Nest, a general store, a post office, with a clock tower in the centre of the high street. Cass turned left there and then right into Pendock Lane and then she was pulling up outside of her cottage.

It was beautiful. Even more so than in the website pictures she'd viewed online when she'd accepted the posting. She got out of her car and looked at it for a moment, before pulling her one case from the boot and locking it. A white cat that had been sleeping on the small wooden bench in her front garden lifted its head to look at her as she opened the squeaky gate.

'Hey, puss.'

The cat gave her a slow blink and sniffed the air as if to test her, then seemingly decided that she wasn't all that interesting after all and returned to its sleep. Cass wondered who the cat belonged to, then pulled the piece of paper out of her pocket that had the combination to the key box bolted to the wall by the front door. Once she'd released the keys, she pushed the door open and stepped inside.

This was now home.

For a little while at least.

Dr Lachlan Finlay was just saying goodbye to his first patient of the day when the receptionist, June, who everyone affectionately called Junebug, rapped her knuckles on his door and poked her head round.

'The new nurse is here!'

He looked up and breathed a sigh of relief. Thank God! The agency had struggled to fill the position for months and Lachie had been working more hours than he should. He was exhausted. What with his patients and Ronan and his mum, he'd been kept ultra-busy. So much so that Nic, his nurse, had offered to return until her due date, if he needed, but he'd stopped that suggestion even before she'd reached the end of the sentence. *No. Absolutely not. You need to go rest and get ready for that bairn.* She'd had some raised blood pressure, so he was not going to make her work and be responsible for her giving birth early, or getting sick with eclampsia or anything. Not when they were so far from emergency treatment. And besides, her husband, Matt, had gotten some time off work and they deserved some time alone together, just the two of them, before the bairn came.

He'd not had high hopes when he'd contacted the Lark Agency for a locum nurse. Not many nurses would want to come this far west to an isolated isle when they had the options of choosing something far more exciting in a thriving city with nightlife. And so when the agency said they'd found someone—a Cassandra Wallace—a quiet yet warm nurse with a vast array of experience and dependable, he'd pictured a middle-aged woman. Maybe someone divorced? With adult kids that she would talk about fondly? A steadying influence whom his island patients would like in an instant, with her natural maternal charm. n short, just what he needed. And though he'd been told she was coming, he'd not wanted to believe it until she actually got here. He'd been let down before.

'At last! Where is she?'

'She's in the staff room—I made her a mug of tea.'

'What's she like?'

Junebug smiled. 'She seems nice! Young, though. Younger than I was expecting.'

Young? Oh. Well, he got that wrong, then. 'I'll go say hello.'

'Okay. Oh, I had George Stewart on the phone a minute ago—needs a repeat prescription for his pain meds and wonders if you could drop them off for him.'

Lachie nodded. 'Add it to my lunchtime list.'

'You're a hen.' Junebug smiled and bustled back to reception, which was calling her with a ringing phone. He heard her answer. 'Kilmarrin Surgery... Oh hello, love.'

Lachie headed to the staff room, ready to say hi, hello

and welcome and get the new nurse situated quickly. The quicker, the better. But he stopped in his tracks at the doorway when he saw her.

She was definitely younger than him. Late twenties, perhaps? Chestnut hair swept up into a clip, dark brown eyes that were large and almond shaped. And *beautiful*. Oh, so incredibly beautiful! Alarmed by his visceral reaction to her, he cleared his throat and hoped that his pause in the doorway hadn't been too noticeable.

'Cassandra Wallace?'

She looked up at him as if she recognised him from somewhere, was struggling perhaps to place him, but then a beaming smile crossed her face. 'Cass, yes.' She stood quickly. Pumped his hand. Sending tingles of delight up his arm. 'You're the guy from the ferry.'

'I'm sorry?' He was confused.

'Yesterday? You were on the ferry. I saw you there, I think.'

Ah. Yes. He'd come back from the mainland after taking his mother to see a specialist. They'd made a weekend of it. Despite it being the New Year, his old university friend, Dr Radha Barti, had offered to see Lachie's mum in her Saturday morning clinic and then they'd returned to the island yesterday, so that the trip wasn't too much for his mum. He'd not told anyone about her diagnosis. Not yet. Though Radha would officially send a letter to the surgery to go on his mum's file and Cass would soon learn of it, because he would be asking her to look after his family as part of her role.

He nodded. 'I'm Lachlan Finlay, the GP here at the surgery.' He realised they were still holding hands and with a quick laugh he let go, realising that strangely he felt nervous for some reason and his skin still tingled from her touch. 'Are you all settled in? Find someplace local?'

'Pendock Lane. I've rented a small cottage.'

'That's near me. You're one street over.' There were only so many places available to rent in Kilmarrin, so he shouldn't have been surprised she was so close. 'Garrett Cowper rents a place over there—are you renting from him?'

'Mr Cowper? Yes.' She nodded.

'Oh! Our gardens back onto one another's, then. So we're neighbours.'

She continued to give him her polite smile. 'Looks like it.'

'Well, I guess we'd better get you orientated! Thank you so much for taking up the post—we've struggled to find someone willing to come this far out. Do you have family with you?'

'No. It's just me.' She looked awkward for a moment, but it didn't last, the light in her eyes returning quickly.

He wondered at it. What had that awkwardness implied? He liked to think that he was good at reading people. Understanding the unspoken. But maybe a lot of that came from the fact that he already knew so much about everybody here on Gulray, he could make a good, educated guess at what was wrong. Cass was an enigma. An unknown. And that was intriguing to him. 'Okay. Marlene at the Lark Agency says you're already familiar with the computer system?'

Cass nodded.

'Great. I'll show you around. Obviously you know where the kettle is. Did Junebug give you a key to a locker?'

'Junebug?' Cass raised an amused eyebrow.

He laughed. 'We all call her that. First name is June, second name is Crane.'

Cass looked puzzled.

'Crane fly? Daddy-long-legs? It's a bug, so...' He trailed off, realising how lame it sounded now he had to spell it out. He smiled awkwardly.

'Junebug. Okay.'

He realised, explaining it, how silly the nickname now seemed. But the way her smile lit up her face did strange, unsettling things to his insides, which was quite disconcerting! Her eyes gleamed, her smile wide and generous, and he knew instantly that his patients would love her. She had a quality, a warmth to her smile that he just knew would work wonders at making people open up. It was disarming. The kind of smile that could draw him in, too, and he was never going to allow that to happen. He had no room, nor time, for attraction. So, bristling slightly, he led her back out into the hallway and tapped in a code to let them into a small room. 'Stock cupboard, obviously. You'll find most things in here. June orders anything we get low on. Code to get in is four-six-eight-nine.'

'Okay.'

'This is our procedure room. We do ultrasounds here. Small ops. Lumps and bumps, you get the idea. It's a jack-of-all-trades room that we need here on Gulray.'

Despite the smallness of the room, it had some modern equipment, including the latest ultrasound machine, which he was very proud of.

'Perfect.' She smiled.

'And this is your room.' He swept the door open wide, revealing a standard examination room. A bed, with a lamp attached to the wall at the foot end. Opposite, a desk and chair, with a computer and printer. On the shelf above, a blood pressure cuff and a selection of blood vials in purple, light blue and gold, and a range of needles, including butterfly wing needles. There was a fridge where they kept certain vaccinations and above it a cupboard. 'You'll find bandages and dressings in there, I believe. It's how Nic had it, but feel free to change it to your preference whilst you're here.'

'Thanks.'

'There's a go-bag in the stock cupboard, along with our rapid-response bag, which contains oxygen and a defibrillator, all the usual. When you have a moment, feel free to take a good look around and familiarise yourself with everything.'

'It all seems pretty standard.'

'Now, you're aware that you'll be expected to visit people in the community who live on the far side of Gulray in the more isolated areas? One or two are housebound.'

'Absolutely! I'm looking forward to it.'

She most definitely was. He could see it in the gleam of her eyes. An excitement at the thought of it. It was a huge responsibility and one of the many reasons he'd struggled to fill the position since Nic left. Not a lot of nurses wanted that responsibility, or others didn't have their own vehicles and simply hadn't been suitable. 'And I'll also ask if you could take on *my* family as your patients, whilst you're here. Nic usually did.'

'Of course, if that's what the previous nurse did. Anything I should be aware of?'

He thought of how he'd felt to sit in Radha's room on the mainland and hear her confirm that his mother's forgetfulness and uncertain mood swings were not from old age but most definitely from Alzheimer's. To be on the other side of the desk, not as a patient, but as a concerned family member, hearing a diagnosis of something that had no cure was hard. That she would experience an inexorable decline in which his mother would lose who she was and who everyone else was, memory by memory. Basically, his mother was going to die soon, but he was going to do everything he could to make sure that that road she travelled on went on for miles. 'Well, my son, Ronan—he's five—he occasionally has asthma, but it's all under control. And my mother, Kathleen, she, er...' He didn't want to say it. If he told someone, it made it real, but Cass would have to know. 'She's just been diagnosed with Alzheimer's. That's where we were coming back from. On the ferry. We'd been to see a consultant.'

Her face went solemn and she nodded. 'I understand. I'm sorry.' She paused, almost as if she were having a moment of silent reflection, before she asked, 'And...you?'

'Me?'

'Will I be looking after you?'

He smiled. Laughed. 'I guess so, but thankfully I'm healthy as a horse.'

'That's good to know.'

'Aye.' It was. Because he didn't need any extra worries in his life.

He had enough to deal with.

'You must be the new nurse?' said Mrs Palmer as she shuffled into Cass's new examination room.

'Yes. My name's Cass. Pleased to meet you.'

'Short for Cassie?'

'Cassandra.'

'Oh, that's a beautiful name.'

'Thanks. You're here for a COPD review?' COPD stood for Chronic Obstructive Pulmonary Disease, which was basically an issue with the lungs and respiratory system. It was important to steer the patient back on track. Cass had a full clinic today and she wanted to make a good impression on Dr Finlay. Plus, she didn't like to give away too many personal details to patients. They were her job, not friends to pass the time of day away with.

'I am.'

'Okay, so how have you been since you were last here? Any episodes of breathlessness or wheezing?'

'Only the usual, going upstairs and the like.'

Cass nodded and read Mrs Palmer's notes from her previous visit. Her COPD seemed quite stable, though she'd been admitted to hospital, early December of the previous year, when she'd contracted the flu and needed oxygen assistance.

'And is it better or worse since your admission into hospital?'

'Initially it was hard, when I first came home. I got breathless quite quickly, but since Christmas, I've been quite good. Going out every day and getting fresh air. Trying to keep up with my walking. I've got a little dog, see, and he needs his walks.'

Cass smiled and nodded. 'Okay, I'm just going to place this on your finger to assess your oxygen saturations, and are you okay if I listen to your chest?'

'Aye, of course.'

Her oxygen saturations came back as expected. Eighty-eight. A normal person without COPD could expect anything from ninety-four to ninety-eight and Mrs Palmer's chest sounded exactly as she'd expected it to sound. 'I can hear a little wheeze there, Mrs Palmer.'

'Una.'

'Una.' Cass smiled. Her saturations were at a normal level for Una. 'Can you show me how you use your inhaler?'

Una demonstrated perfectly, so that was good. 'You're not a smoker and you said you walk your dog? How often?'

'I try for twice a day. Once in the morning and once in the afternoon. If it's not raining, of course.'

'And you've had all your vaccinations... How's your appetite? Eating well? Hydrating?'

'Does tea count?'

Cass laughed. 'Of course!'

'Well, lots of tea. I make a fine brew. You ought to pop round one day and test it. I could make my famous shortbread for you to try.'

'That's very kind of you.'

'Maybe sometime this week?'

Oh, she actually meant it! Cass instantly felt herself pull back. 'I've got a lot of unpacking to do,' she said, which was a lie. Mr Cowper's cottage had come fully furnished. Cass had arrived on the island with one small suitcase and that was all.

'Of course. Well, maybe I could drop some in for you? You're on Pendock Lane, aren't you?'

Cass was a little alarmed that her patient knew, but of course this was a small community and everyone knew everyone. Maybe she'd been spotted on the ferry as a new strange face? Maybe Mr Cowper had told someone that he was renting out to the new nurse? News travelled fast, clearly.

'You don't have to go to any trouble and I'm going to be out a lot.'

'No trouble at all!'

This was getting away from her. Getting personal again. Next thing she knew Una would want inviting in for tea and a chat and asking all sorts of personal questions! 'You're, er, taking all your medications with no problems?'

'Oh yes. Like clockwork.'

'And you have support? Family?'

'Four strapping boys.' Una smiled. 'I see you don't have a ring on your wedding finger! Maybe I should introduce you to my Colin? He's a good lad. Kind. Generous. Loving. Lives local, I could drop in a good word, like.'

'I'm, er, not looking for a relationship right now, thanks, though I'm sure he's lovely.'

'Pretty thing like you…you need someone to hold you close and keep you warm on an island like this.' She leaned in. 'Nothing like a strong pair of arms to keep you safe, eh?'

CHAPTER TWO

HE'D NEVER NEEDED to consult Nic, the previous practice nurse, about his *own* health. As Lachie had explained to Cass, he'd always been healthy, which was a bonus when you lived on such an isolated island like this, where if you needed surgery or emergency treatment, you had to go to the mainland.

Like Meghan. Only it hadn't happened quickly enough for her, and his wife had died. If they'd been on the mainland, who knew? Maybe she'd still be here. Still be his wife and a mother to their son.

Of course he'd thought of leaving the island. What if it happened again? To Ronan? His mother? But his mother didn't want to leave this place and Lachie had so desperately wanted her in his son's life that he'd stayed, too.

There was only so much he *could do* on Gulray. He did minor procedures as much as he could, but if someone needed something more complicated, then they had to travel to one of the larger hospitals in Argyle.

But the idea that *Cass* would be his nurse for anything? His brain helpfully provided him with the image of sitting on the edge of an examination bed, unbuttoning his shirt so that she could press a stethoscope to his chest. All the while she gazed softly into his eyes, which made his heart rate increase, which was ridiculous because he was a grown man and grown men didn't have instant crushes.

Or did they?

He'd not felt like this in…well, for as long as he could remember! Gulray got tourists, but new people coming to the island and staying? That didn't happen very often and so he was used to all the usual faces and besides, they were all his patients. It would be unethical to even think about having a relationship with one of them, and he wasn't looking for that anyway. He'd been married. He'd been a husband and now he was a widower and he didn't need the complication of other people in his life, or more labels.

But Cass? She was *temporary*. She wasn't staying. She probably had her own doctor back home, wherever that was. Had he asked her? He couldn't remember asking her. Was that rude? He'd make sure to show he was interested in her the next time they got the opportunity to chat.

And besides, his awareness of her beauty didn't matter. He had a son and his mother to worry about. And everyone else on this island. Cass was here to help him out for a few weeks. Nothing more. Like a mayfly, she'd be gone before he knew it.

'Hattie?' he called.

His next patient was Hattie McIlroy. Mid-forties, she was a knitwear designer and always arrived at the surgery wrapped up in whatever new creations she'd designed. Today she wore a blue beanie hat, a wrap around her neck that had a bright colour fade from red, to orange, to yellow, and fingerless gloves in a soft grey, speckled with neon brights.

'Hi, Lachie, how are you?' Everyone knew each other so well, they all called each other by their first names. He couldn't remember the last time anyone called him 'Doctor'.

'I'm good, Hattie, thanks. Is your Declan well?' Her husband had been struggling with a bad knee and Lachie had begun giving him steroid injections as Declan wanted to avoid having to go to the mainland for a surgery.

'As good as can be expected. The injections are helping.'

'That's great. Take a seat and tell me how I can help you today.'

'Well, I've been having these pains.' She rubbed her upper gastric area, just beneath her ribs. 'They come and they go, mainly after I've eaten, and yesterday, they doubled me over, they were that bad. I couldn't even touch my knitting, I was in that much discomfort.'

He nodded. 'And how is it today?'

'It's eased off some, but I still feel really sore.'

'Any nausea?'

'A little.'

'And you say this happens after you eat?'

'Aye.'

'What did you eat yesterday that caused such a bad reaction?'

'Well, every Sunday morning, Declan and I like to have a fry up for our breakfast—eggs, bacon, sausages, fried bread, all that good stuff.'

He smiled. 'Fatty foods. And when you've had these pains before, can you remember what you'd eaten beforehand?'

'No, not really. Maybe pancakes, I think?'

It could be any number of things causing her problem.

He needed to narrow it down, but he had his suspicions. 'Can I have a feel of your tummy?'

'Of course.'

'Do you want me to get a chaperone?'

'Oh, you're all right. I trust you.'

He waited for her to clamber up onto the examination bed and began to palpate her abdomen. He couldn't feel anything unusual. Her abdomen was soft, though she did say she felt a little tender in the upper right part of her stomach. He nodded and helped her back up and when they were sat back at the desk, he shared his thoughts.

'Well, there are a number of things for us to consider and check out. One, it could be gallbladder related. You felt tender on examination over that area and the fact that you had intense pains after fatty foods makes me suspect that this could be the answer. However, you had bread in that fried breakfast and you also had pains when you made pancakes and so this could also be a gluten issue. So we'll need to do a blood test to check for coeliac disease.' Coeliacs would mean an autoimmune condition, where the body reacted violently to the presence of gluten and began to attack its own tissues.

'And the other one?'

'Well, I could do a quick ultrasound of your gallbladder, see if we could spot any stones, and I could also refer you to a doctor on the mainland for a more thorough workup if your bloods come back consistent with a gallbladder issue.'

Hattie nodded. 'And when could we do that?'

'We can do the bloods and ultrasound right now.'

'All right. Let's do it.'

He did the bloods first, taking the vials needed to be

sent off to the lab on the mainland. Every day a courier came and collected the samples and took them back via ferry to the hospital that did their testing, and the results were sent back via the computer to Lachie's system at the surgery. The coeliac disease test would take a little longer than the others, but they'd get answers quite quickly.

In the meantime, he took Hattie through to the ultrasound room. 'Take a seat and I'll just get our new nurse to come and chaperone.'

'It's all right.'

'It's policy, Hats. You're going to be lifting up your top and exposing yourself.'

'Nothing you haven't seen before.' She smiled.

He smiled right back. Maybe, but it had always been with a chaperone. His earlier palpation of her abdomen had been done *over* her clothes. This was different and it protected them both. 'I'll go get Cass, our new nurse. Introduce you.'

He headed to Cass's room, grateful that her door was open, the standard signal that stated she had no patient with her at that moment.

Tapping notes into her computer, she wasn't aware of him standing in the doorway. He noted her hands. They were beautiful. Dainty. He imagined them trailing down his chest... *Stop thinking about her damn hands!*

'Hey, can I borrow you for a moment?'

Cass turned, smiling widely. 'Of course.'

'Need a chaperone for an ultrasound. Hattie McIlroy, query gallbladder issue.'

He was aware of her following him as he led her towards the procedure room. 'Hats? This is Cass. Cass, Hattie McIlroy.'

The two women shook hands and exchanged pleasantries as he readied the machine and brought it over.

Cass helped Hattie lie down and asked her to raise her top, whilst Cass tucked in some blue paper around Hattie's top to stop it from getting covered with the transducer gel he would need to put on Hattie's skin both to help it move more easily and to help conduct the imaging.

'Okay, let's take a look here. All you should feel is some pressure as I move the scanner around.' Ultrasounds were a wonderful tool to look for the presence of gallbladder stones, or inflammation within the organ, which might indicate cholecystitis. He could also look for thickening of the gallbladder walls or look for build-up of fluids, or polyps. Hattie's bile ducts looked clear, which was good, but he could clearly see some stone deposits within the gallbladder itself, and though this scan would go off to a radiologist to be checked as well, Lachie knew he needed to refer his patient to a consultant specialist. 'You've got stones, as I suspected. Four that I can see, though there may be some smaller ones that aren't showing up. The pain you experienced could have been a stone passing, or something getting blocked, though I don't see any evidence of a block today.' He stopped scanning and Cass stepped forward to use the blue paper to wipe away as much of the gel as she could. Then she helped Hattie back into a sitting position.

He smiled his thanks at her. 'I'm going to send off your bloods and this scan will go through to the hospital and I'm going to refer you to a gastroenterologist for further assessment.'

'Does this mean surgery?'

'Not always. But if you're having the symptoms that you described experiencing yesterday, then surgery may be suggested.'

Hattie sighed, clearly disconcerted by the news. 'I'd hoped for something a little less serious.'

He understood that. When his mother had begun to experience forgetfulness, he'd just put it down to a blip and ignored it. But those blips had become something he could no longer ignore. He'd tried talking to her about it, explained his concerns, but even she'd been in denial. However, when she'd nearly burned her house down because she'd put some eggs on to boil and forgot about them, filling her cottage with smoke, they'd both known they couldn't ignore it. Things like that were scary and so he'd gotten in carers in the meantime.

He'd considered moving her in with him and Ronan, but what if Ronan got hurt accidentally? He could never forgive himself, and so he'd let her stay in her home. As they lived on the same street, just a couple of houses apart, he could still keep a close eye on her. There was a care home on Gulray, but it did not cater for dementia, and the idea of having to move her back to the mainland… Well, that was an option he knew she wouldn't like. She loved Gulray. Had made her home here with Lachie's father. His grave was here on the island. Plus he had to think of his son. Ronan was happy in his school and there were only twelve kids in his class. If he had to move to the mainland to be near his mother in a nursing home, he'd lose it all and Ronan would get lost in a class that had thirty kids or more, and he wanted Ronan to enjoy Gulray for as long as possible.

'You should hear from the hospital in a couple of weeks regarding an appointment, but sometimes the waiting list time can be quite long. Or you could go private if you prefer.'

'And how long would that take?'

'A week or two. They're usually very good at seeing you quicker.'

Hattie sighed. 'I don't know. You pay into a system your whole life and then when you need it...' She shook her head. 'I might see how long the wait is and if it's too long, then I might pay to go private.'

'Well, if you do, let me know and I can do the referral, but if you get any more pains like you have recently, then give me a call. And probably best to stay away from fried or fatty foods in the meantime.'

'I will. Thanks, Lachie. You, too, Cass, is it?'

Cass nodded. 'Take care, Hattie.'

When Hattie was gone, he turned to Cass. 'Thanks for that.'

She smiled warmly at him. 'No problem.'

They stared at each other for a moment, smiling, then felt the awkwardness of the moment rise. 'Well, I'd, er, better go. Just give me a call if you need me,' she said.

He nodded and watched her go, admiring her figure then shaking his head, berating himself for even noticing. What was he doing? She was here to do a *job* and so was he! So she was attractive, so what? He was not going to let himself get involved with anyone; his life was complicated enough.

Lachie headed back to his own consultation room and typed up his notes and forwarded the referral to a gastroenterologist for Hattie.

Best to keep his mind on the job.

* * *

By home time that evening, Cass had received four invitations. One to Kirk McDonald's house to meet his wife, who was apparently the spitting image of Cass; one for coffee and cake at All the Tea teahouse by a lovely old lady called Jenna Ripley; one to join the Kilmarrin book club—*we're reading a romantasy next!*; and one to join a knit-and-natter group, because apparently they had some good natter and would get her up to speed on island news in a jiffy.

She'd made vague noises to all of them, but had been polite and explained that she still had a lot of unpacking to do, even though the truth was all she wanted to do at the end of the day was to go home, cook herself something to eat and stay in and watch television.

It had always worked for her before. That way she avoided getting too close to anyone, or allowing people to ask her personal questions she didn't want to answer, and she stayed out of any spotlight. She was just on the island to do a job. That was it. Get in. Get out. Don't make attachments. Socialising with colleagues always led to complications, like friendships, and she didn't want any of those. She just wanted to do her work and get paid and leave.

So when there was a rap at her door, just as she was switching off the computer to go home, and Dr Lachlan Finlay put his head around the door, she was ready to turn down any invitation that might be coming her way. Lachie was a good-looking man. Her age. Probably married anyway. A guy that looked like that? His wife was a lucky woman. But that didn't stop her from noticing. She'd felt a physical attraction to him the second she'd seen him on the ferry.

'How was your first day?'

'Oh, it was good, thank you! How was yours?' She realised after she asked that it was a stupid question. Dr Finlay had not just had a first day at work. *She* had. *Am I nervous? Why does he make me feel that way?*

Earlier, when she'd chaperoned for him, she'd barely said a thing to him or Hattie. It was like she was being tested or assessed, even though she knew logically that it wasn't the case. He'd needed a chaperone. She was available. That was it. Maybe previously the chaperone, without the nurse Nic there, had had to be Junebug from reception? He was probably grateful to have an actual nurse now!

Lachie laughed. 'It was fine. How many home-cooked meals have you been offered so far?'

Cass laughed, too. 'Just the one. Kirk McDonald suggested I go to his house for a meal cooked by his wife, who apparently I'm the spitting image of.'

Lachie tilted his head, thinking. 'Maybe. You have less wrinkles.'

'At my age, good!'

'Well, we thought we'd throw you a special welcome for your first day. It's curry night at the Puffin's Nest and everyone's going. You could meet Ronan, my son, though I often am the first to leave as I have to get him home in time for bed, so I won't be there all that long.'

She wondered if his son looked like him. But if he did have a son, then that meant there was a mother somewhere, but he'd not mentioned her. She'd not considered that before, as she'd been distracted. Was he divorced? The thought that he might be was worrying; perhaps he was available. She didn't need that complication.

This was just the sort of thing she normally avoided. But it sounded like something they'd organised just for her. And other people were already going! It would be awkward if the guest of honour didn't actually show, wouldn't it? She didn't want to be seen as rude or ungrateful and maybe she wouldn't have to stay that long if he was going to leave early because of his son, anyway.

And besides, it wasn't like it was a date or anything. It wasn't going to be just her and Dr Finlay. Others would be there. And she wouldn't have to go home and cook and then wash up afterwards. 'I do like a curry.'

'Great! We'll meet you there at six and I promise you can be home early, if you need.'

'Okay. Sounds good,' she said, even though she felt like she'd hate every minute and be clock-watching. But in this instance, it wasn't something she could turn down. Not without offending everyone who just wanted to welcome her. 'I'll see you all there.'

CHAPTER THREE

'DON'T FILL UP on the fizz, Ronan. I want you to eat your curry,' Lachie said to his son as he reached for his lemonade yet again.

'I'm thirsty.'

'I know, but we're waiting for my new nurse to get here, then we'll order food.'

It was just after six and Cass hadn't arrived yet. Was something holding her up? Or was she doing that fashionably late thing? Either way, he still wasn't sure if his offer for her to join them had been a welcome invitation. He'd noted how she'd automatically glanced at the exit the second he'd asked.

Junebug sat opposite him. Next to her was Nic, his previous nurse, who was looking very well and very pregnant now at thirty-six weeks, and her husband, Matt. And next to him was Agnes, the healthcare assistant who worked at the surgery on a part-time basis. She would soon be leaving, too, having gained a place at university in Edinburgh to study adult nursing.

They all knew each other so well, but everything was changing. Agnes leaving in September. Nic was becoming a mum to her first baby. Cass… Lachie wasn't great with changes like these. Everyone else moving on, whereas he had to stay the same. He felt left behind. Their change tilted his world and made him uncomfortable. It was why he'd invited Cass here tonight. Technically, it wasn't really a welcome meal for her first day. The team always met at the Puffin's Nest on a Monday and he'd wanted her to feel a part of them quickly.

The doors swung open, bringing with it a chill wind that whipped in icy swirls around their feet. And then Cass appeared, eyes scanning the interior, wrapped in a coat and oversized butter-yellow scarf. Lachie stood and raised a hand to signal where they were, at the table beside the open fire that was crackling away nicely beside them.

Cass made the universal signal that indicated she would grab a drink at the bar and then join them in a moment and he nodded, smiling, before sitting back down and watching her speak to the barman. She had a nice easy manner to her. He saw the way Mack, the barman, looked back at her. Alert. Straightening to make himself look taller. Clearly interested in this beautiful newcomer. Mack looked like he was flirting and strangely Lachie felt a twinge of envy that he had to push down and try to ignore.

Nic swivelled around to look, then turned back, smiling at him. 'She's pretty. Single?'

Lachie shrugged. 'Why would I know that?'

'I don't know. Did she come to Gulray alone?'

'Aye.'

'Single, then. Interesting.'

'Why'd you say it like that?'

Nic shrugged. 'Well, a single, attractive woman your age who moves to the island might be an object of interest for a single, attractive man like yourself.'

'Knock it off, Nic,' said Matt, smiling. 'Leave the poor guy alone.'

'I'm just saying, is all,' she answered innocently, taking a sip from her orange juice and rubbing at her belly. 'Ooh, shift that foot, will you?'

'Baby kicking you?' Lachie asked.

'Mmm.'

'See? Even the baby disagrees with you trying to matchmake, so stop it when she gets here, please. I want her to feel welcomed. Not like she's being sized up.'

Nic made a zipping motion over her lips as Cass arrived at the table, holding what looked like a gin and tonic. 'Hi! I'm Nic, you're my replacement! There's a seat next to Lachie.' She smiled.

Cass shook her hand and Lachie became extremely aware of her as she settled into the seat next to him. She'd sprayed herself with some sort of perfume that was doing crazy things to his senses and suited her perfectly. 'Cass? This is my son, Ronan, Junebug you know. This is Matt, Nic's husband, and at the end there we have Agnes, who's our HCA, but she won't be at the practice until Thursday and Friday.'

Agnes reached over the table to shake her hand. 'Pleased to meet you. I hope to be you one day.'

'Oh?' Cass looked confused.

'A nurse. I'm off to uni this September.'

'Oh! Well, that's great! Good luck with your future studies.'

Cass removed her scarf and coat.

'Say hello to Cass, Ronan.'

His son leaned forward and gave a shy wave.

Cass smiled and waved back. 'Pleased to meet you.'

'Right, my son is starving to death, so shall we order?' Lachie said, knowing he also had to get his son home and bathed before this night was over.

His question was met by a resounding yes from all at the table.

'Sorry I got here late. When I opened the door to come here, a white cat ran inside my house and I had to catch it and let it back out.'

Lachie groaned. 'White cat with a tartan collar?'

Cass nodded. 'You know it?'

'Unfortunately. That's our cat. Frosty.' He leaned in. 'I apologise for the unimaginative name, but I let Ronan name her, so...' He shrugged. 'She goes in everybody's house. Sorry for the bother.'

'Oh, she was nae bother, not really. Just wanted to curl up on the couch, to be fair. I almost let her, but didn't know how long I'd be out.'

She smiled warmly at him and he wasn't sure how he felt, knowing his cat was making itself at home in *her* home.

'You're very kind, thank you.' He reached for his pint and took a sip. Nic was watching them both with amusement and he frowned.

Matt went to the bar with all their orders and they sat back to wait. Nic was holding court on how she'd been feeling recently, the nesting instinct, the heartburn, the not being able to sleep and the slow and steady creep of Braxton Hicks contractions that she'd been experiencing the last few days. She rubbed at her abdomen. Happy. Content. The picture of impending motherhood.

Cass seemed to be looking at Nic with a strange smile.

Lachie remembered when Meghan had been in the latter stages of her pregnancy with Ronan. She'd felt huge. Ponderous. Aching for the time when she would no longer have to carry her large baby through the sweltering, midge-ridden heat of summer. Worrying about her stretch marks and whether she'd drunk too much indigestion remedy. How he'd sit beside her on the bed or the couch, trying to soothe her woes, massaging her feet and ankles, telling her she was beautiful, that he was proud of her, that he couldn't wait to be a father and parent their child with her. If she'd have known how little time she had left, would she still have complained? But like anyone else in their late twenties, Meghan had believed she still had her whole life ahead of her. Sixty years or more, when in fact she'd only had one.

When the curries arrived—chicken korma for Nic and Ronan, tikka masala for the rest of them—they all tucked in with gusto.

'This is amazing!' said Cass, as if she'd never tried a good curry in her life.

He felt inordinately pleased that she liked it. 'Have you tried the naan?' He passed over the basket that contained slices of garlic and herbed naan that he knew the chef made himself and she took a piece.

'Thanks.' She tore off a strip and used it to soak up some sauce, popping it into her mouth and making a satisfied sound. 'I can see why you chose here.'

Nic made a sound and pulled a face. 'It is good, but to be fair, we don't really have that many options. *Ooh*.'

'You okay?' Lachie asked.

'Aye, I'm fine, the baby's just… Oof! Wow, that hurt.'

'Baby kicking?' asked her husband.

'No. This is more like a cramp.' She looked up at Lachie and met his gaze, a silent message passing between them.

'Braxton Hicks starting to hurt?'

Nic nodded.

'Could be a sign of something starting early. Maybe you should get home? Get some rest? I could come and check on you in a few hours if you wanted?'

'I think that's a good idea. Sorry to bail on your welcome dinner, Cass.'

'That's okay. You need to take care of yourself first.'

Nic nodded and struggled to her feet. 'I'm going to call my midwife, Jane,' Nic said. 'They tell you to eat curry, don't they? To get things started?'

'I don't think two mouthfuls of korma is strong enough, love,' said Matt with a smile.

Nic smiled, then apologised again to everyone for disrupting their night and promised to keep them all updated, before leaving with her husband.

Cass had hated that she felt so envious of Nic as they'd sat in the pub. Her gaze had been drawn to Nic's enormous belly and the way she kept stroking it, and she'd thought how happy the other woman looked as she'd laughed and joked with Matt. Like she was enjoying every minute of being pregnant. Secure and safe and loved. It had been so far from her own experience of carrying a child that she'd felt so envious!

Nic, hopefully, had a whole new life ahead of her as a mother. Looking forward to her new role, a role that Cass sometimes felt had never been hers to have. Not for long, anyway. Mere days. And though Daniel had made her heart swell with her love for him, their life together had been all too short and painful.

'Are you not hungry?' Lachie asked, noticing that she hadn't eaten a bite for a few minutes now that the other nurse had left.

She hadn't realised she'd drifted away, wallowing in memories past. 'Oh! I am. Sorry, I got lost for a moment there.' Cass blushed and spooned a mouthful of curry and fluffy white basmati rice into her mouth to show that everything was fine. Even though it wasn't. She suddenly ached for Daniel, for his little face and the way he'd felt in her arms. The way he'd snuggled into her chest that one time she'd been allowed to hold him and she had breathed in the scent of his hair and held him close, before realising that there was something terribly wrong. Your hopes, your dreams, your world, could change in an instant. 'I hope Nic's okay. She said she has a midwife?'

'Mmm, Jane. She holds a monthly clinic at the surgery, but mostly she just goes to patients' houses.'

'She couldn't join us tonight?'

'She was out on a home visit.'

'And she delivers the babies at home?'

'Sometimes. But if someone has a high-risk pregnancy they often go to the mainland to be delivered in a hospital.'

'What if it's an unexpected emergency?'

She saw him suck in a breath and his eyes darkened. 'Then we call the air ambulance. It's all we can do living this far out without a proper hospital. But most new mums don't take the risk and go to the mainland anyway.'

She nodded, guessing that was just what people did. They adapted to situations. She'd read somewhere that there was a place called Svalbard in Norway, where all mothers were encouraged to leave the island a month before their due date, so they could give birth safely as the hospital did not have the facilities to handle childbirth. It was similar here.

'Was Ronan born here on the island?' Lachie's son was sweet. Golden haired compared to his dad's dark hair. Blue eyed compared to his dad's chocolate brown.

Lachie smiled and nodded. 'He was. His mum, Meghan, had an easy pregnancy with him and though it was our first, she was allowed to have a home birth.'

'And it all went well?'

He continued to nod, smiling as his mind went back in time, and she liked the way his eyes lit up when he was talking about his son. 'It did! No complications. We were very lucky.' But then his eyes darkened again and she didn't know why.

'And Meghan? Is she at home?' Perhaps there was a reason as to why she wasn't here tonight. But she'd like to meet the woman that had married this man and carried his child.

Lachie glanced at his son, but Ronan wasn't listening to the adults. He leaned in and spoke quietly. 'She passed when Ronan was a baby.'

Cass sucked in a breath, awkward and mortified that she'd just innocently stumbled into a painful memory for him. 'I'm so sorry!'

'No, it's okay. You didn't know.'

'May I ask how she…?' Her voice trailed off, unable to say the final word, knowing that grief had touched this man as it had touched her, though in a different way. Lachie had lost his wife and the mother of his child, and Cass had lost her much-loved son.

'Brain aneurysm. It was sudden, no one knew of it beforehand, there'd been no symptoms.' He kept his voice low so that Ronan didn't hear. He clearly didn't want to upset his son by talking about his mum.

Her heart ached for him. Cass knew grief. Knew the pain of it intimately. How it marked you. Never left you.

Haunted you.

'I'm sorry,' she said again, her appetite for her curry waning.

He smiled. 'You carry on, don't you? There's no choice in that matter.'

'Aye.' Cass couldn't remember much about the days that followed Daniel's passing. She knew she'd slept a lot. Languishing in a darkened bedroom, barely eating. Barely drinking. Only emerging for the dreadful day that was the funeral. Aunty Morag got a doctor out who gave her pills—she knew that much—and somehow she started going out on walks, slowly returning to life. But the actual minutes? The hours? The nights without him? The time she must have put away his things into the shoe-box? The tags from his wrists and ankles? The Babygro he'd been wearing? The vest? The scratch mittens? A small teddy? She'd blanked those out. And she didn't want to remember.

What in those dark days after his own loss did Lachie not want to remember?

'Well, we'd better make a move. Got to get this wee laddie bathed and into bed for school in the morning.'

She nodded. Good. They could end this. 'Of course. Nice to meet you, Ronan.'

'Nice to meet you, too!' He gave her a smile and in

the firelight, she could see his freckles across the brow of his nose. He was cute. Cheeky looking.

She watched as Lachie helped Ronan into his coat. Watched the careful way he made sure his son was all wrapped up properly so that the cold wouldn't touch him. The way Lachie ruffled his son's hair before pulling a woolly hat over it. The little details that spoke of a father's love for his son. It was nice to see. A father loving his son. Her son's father had wanted nothing to do with either of them.

Lachie and Ronan stepped out into a squalling gale, by the sound of things.

'I ought to be going, too,' Junebug said, standing. 'I'll walk out with you. So how was your first day?'

She forced a smile. 'Good, thanks!'

'Aww, that's great to hear. We've missed having a nurse. You're a welcome sight, believe me.'

Cass gasped as they stepped back outside into the bitter wind. Scotland in January was freezing, but out here on a remote island it seemed worse! The skies were darker. Fat droplets of rain were beginning to fall. Droplets that could become sleet if it got any colder. She wrapped her long yellow scarf tighter around her neck.

'I noticed you've got Lachie's mum on your home visit list tomorrow.'

'I do?'

'Kathleen Finlay? Aye, she's his mother. Lovely woman. You make sure to tell her I said hi. We've not seen her in the surgery for a while.'

And of course Cass knew why. Lachie had said she'd just been diagnosed with Alzheimer's. Maybe Junebug didn't know that yet. 'I will.'

'Well, this is me.' Junebug stopped at the gate to a cottage two doors down from the Puffin's Nest.

'You live here?' Warm yellow light exuded from behind drawn curtains.

'Aye. We're all quite close in these parts. You have far to go?'

'My car's just there. I know it's not far, but heard the weather might take a turn, so…' She pointed out her yellow Beetle, which sat beneath a street lamp. The rusty patches made it look like it had some sort of plague, but it had never let her down and she loved it.

'Then I'll see you tomorrow.'

'Aye. Sleep well.'

A downpour greeted Cass when she left Kilmarrin surgery to begin her first ever home visits on Gulray. She'd not brought an umbrella and so she ran out to her car as fast as she could, unlocked the door and jumped into the driver's seat with a sigh of relief. Phew! Her uniform trousers were wet and her coat she put in the passenger seat so she could stay a little drier until she reached the house of Lachie's mother. Technically, she could have walked the distance. It wasn't that far—only a street away, but the rain was torrential and the skies above were grey and thunderous with no sign of a break, so car it was.

Parking outside, Cass shrugged into her coat again and pulled the hood up over her head. Then she grabbed her bag and got out of her car as quickly as she could, hurrying up the narrow pathway to the front door, where she knocked briskly.

A young woman answered the door, dressed in a purple polo shirt with a care company logo on it and dark trousers.

'Hi. I'm Cass, the new nurse from the surgery.'

'Oh, aye, come on in! I'm Siobhan.' Siobhan stepped back to let her in and Cass gave her a smile as she entered the house. 'Kathleen's in the front room, just through here.'

Cass followed her into the cottage. It was neatly decorated and clean and the hallway had a side table filled with family photos in silver frames. She saw pictures of Lachie in a university gown as a much younger man, holding a scroll, and there were many, many pictures of a young boy. Lachie? Or Ronan? *Maybe a mix of the two.* And then there was a wedding picture. Lachie, without his short beard. Stood proudly next to his beautiful bride. They looked the perfect couple and she felt glad that Lachie had managed to find happiness, even if it was just for a short time.

Kathleen Finlay was sat on the sofa, looking through a photo album. Behind her were patchwork cushions made out of hexagons and what looked like a handmade quilt over the back of the couch.

'Hello, Mrs Finlay! My name's Cass and I'm your new nurse.'

Kathleen looked up. 'You work with my boy?'

'Lachlan? Yes, I do. I started yesterday, in fact.'

'He's a good lad. Looks after his mother.'

She smiled. 'That's great to hear. How have you been feeling? The surgery was told you had a bit of a bad day yesterday.'

Kathleen looked blank. 'Did I?'

Siobhan sat down next to her. 'You remember? You said your foot was hurting you?'

'No, dear, I don't think so.'

'Well, shall I take a look at it for you?' Cass suggested. Sometimes it was difficult to know when an Alzheimer's patient, or anyone suffering from dementia, really, was in pain or discomfort. Their brains sometimes didn't register the pain and conditions and situations could get missed unless caregivers kept a vigilant eye. The patient very often couldn't say, or remember, what was wrong.

'If you want.'

Cass got Kathleen into a comfortable position on the couch and then she lifted her leg, resting it on her lap. 'I'm just going to move your ankle and foot a little. Will you tell me if anything hurts?'

Kathleen nodded.

She began to rotate Kathleen's ankle, carefully watching Kathleen's face for any sign of pain or discomfort. There were one or two twitches on her face and she frowned, but it was hard to pinpoint which movement actually caused it. 'Can I remove your slipper and your sock?'

'Why?'

'So I can see if you have any bruising or injury.'

'If you want to. I just hope my feet don't smell.'

Cass smiled, removing the slipper first and laying it on the floor and then carefully removing the sock. Kathleen had a visible bunion, but no cuts or bruising on the top of the foot that she could see. She tilted her head to look at the underside of the foot and saw something sticking out of it. A piece of thread. She thought again of the handmade cushions and quilt.

'Kathleen, did you make these?' she asked and pointed.

Kathleen smiled. 'I did! I made this when my Lachie was small, so he had an extra blanket for his bed to keep him warm.' She stroked the quilt as if she were rather fond of it.

'And have you been sewing recently?'

Siobhan nodded. 'We do it most afternoons. She likes to paper piece hexies. Why?'

'Well, my lovely, I think you have a sewing needle in your foot.'

Siobhan looked horrified. 'Oh my gosh! We did lose a needle—we looked all over for it! Oh, Kathleen, I'm so sorry!'

'It's all right. Accidents happen,' Cass said. 'But it's going to need to be removed.'

'Can you do it here?' Siobhan asked.

'Dr Finlay really ought to be the one to do it. I know he's your son, but if the needle is in two pieces he'll need to administer anaesthetic to draw it out. It is quite close to the surface of your skin though, and it looks like it's in one piece, so he should be able to just pull it out.'

'And you can't do that?'

Cass shook her head. 'I can't take the risk in case it is broken. I'll give the surgery a call. See if he's free.' She knew from when she looked at the appointments this morning that Lachie had only two patients. Maybe he'd seen them both already and could come straight around? She hoped so, as Kathleen needed this needle out of her foot.

'Surgery, can I help you?' Junebug answered the phone.

'Hi, June, it's Cass, I'm at Kathleen Finlay's house. She appears to have a sewing needle embedded in her foot and I'm going to need Lachie to help get it out. Could we check her tetanus status as well and ask him if he's free?'

'I believe he's just finished up with Jed Simpson. I'll let him know. Hang on a moment, love.'

Cass examined Kathleen's foot even more as she waited, checking for any other sign of injury, but could see none. And the thread was right there—it would be so easy to just pull it out! But if that needle had snapped, or was bent in some way...plus Kathleen would need her tetanus shot administered, if it was necessary. And that meant Lachie had to come. Not only to remove the foreign body, but also to bring the injection.

'Is my Lachie coming?' Kathleen asked, her face brightening.

'Hopefully.' Cass smiled.

June could be heard picking up the phone. 'He's on his way.'

'Thank you.' She ended the call and looked up at her patient. 'I think you're going to have to be more careful in future.'

'I'm always careful,' Kathleen said. 'I pride myself on it. Never put a foot wrong my whole life. They say if you take care of yourself, then...' Her voice faltered and she looked confused. 'How does that end? If you take care of yourself, then...'

'You can take care of others?' Cass suggested.

'That's it!' Kathleen beamed. 'You are a pretty thing, aren't you. I can't think who you remind me of. I should introduce you to my lad, Lachie. I think you'd like him.'

'I do like him, Kathleen. He's very nice.'

'He is. But I'm biased. I would say that, wouldn't I? You'd make a nice couple if he wasn't already married.'

Cass simply smiled. There was no point in correcting Kathleen that she no longer had a beautiful daughter-in-law. At this moment, her head was in a different space to everyone else and that was fine. It was always just best to agree when dealing with patients who were experiencing memory loss, but not everyone understood that. She could remember one patient she had with dementia who kept struggling to remember that her mum was dead, and her partner would keep reminding her, upsetting her and making her grieve over and over again. The partner felt that if he could just get her to understand and remember, she wouldn't keep asking for her mum, and it took Cass months to convince her patient's partner otherwise. That patient was in full-time care when she left and non-verbal, but she often wondered about them. That was the thing with never staying in one place for too long: you never got to see the end of people's stories.

Ten minutes later, Lachie arrived and Cass still had Kathleen's foot on her lap.

Lachie knelt down to examine his mum's foot. 'I see what you mean. Good spot, Cass. Honestly, Mum! What will we do with you, eh?'

Kathleen leaned forward and pressed her palm to her son's face.

Clearly mother loved son and son loved mother.

Cass felt jealous. How many times had she yearned for a single show of affection from her own mother? Or her father? How many times had she wished she could have just called them up to have a normal conversation? In which there was clear affection between them? Because it had never happened and they'd kicked her out at sixteen, with nowhere to go until her Aunty Morag had kindly taken her in. Her aunt had become her soft place to fall and she was the one to love her the way a mother should. But it still hurt. She still felt that empty space in her heart where her real mother should have been.

'Okay, Mum, I'm going to inject a little anaesthetic here so that you don't feel anything as I take this needle out, okay?'

Kathleen nodded.

'Sit back and relax, Kathleen. Imagine you're on the beach in a recliner,' Cass suggested.

Lachie's mum chuckled. 'All right.'

'Can you hold her foot steady for me?' Lachie asked.

'Of course.' Cass positioned his mum's foot so that he could clearly see what he was doing, but also in a grip that, if Kathleen flinched at the needle, she wouldn't move too much.

Lachie used an alcohol swab to clean the foot around the puncture first of all and then injected a small amount of anaesthetic. 'How's that, Mum?'

'I didn't feel anything.'

He smiled. 'That's good.'

Cass watched as he palpated the sole of his mother's foot, feeling for the needle. 'I think it's still in one piece, but I guess we'll find out in a minute.' He muttered to himself. 'Okay, let's see if we can get it out, shall we?'

'What are you doing down there?' Kathleen asked.

'You've got a needle in your foot, Mum. We're getting it out,' he said gently.

'Oh! Well, good luck.'

Cass smiled at the older woman and stroked the top of her foot reassuringly. 'It'll be out in a jiffy, Kathleen.'

'That's good. Are you helping him, Meghan?'

Cass noted the confusion. Obviously seeing her here with Lachlan had made her get confused over who she was for a moment. But no reason to correct her. 'I am.'

Lachie made a small incision around the puncture wound, to allow him to use tweezers to grab the end of the needle where the eye was. 'Okay, I'm going to try and pull it out now. Can you hold her foot firmly for me, please?'

Cass nodded and watched with amazement as Lachie slowly retrieved the sewing needle that was thankfully all in one piece. 'Well done!'

He looked up at her and smiled. 'Thank you.' He dabbed at the underside of his mum's foot with a gauze pad.

'What was her tetanus status?'

'She should be all covered for another few years yet.'

'Okay. Kathleen? I think we'll need to prescribe you some antibiotics, just in case.' She looked over at Siobhan, the carer. 'You'll be able to collect them from the pharmacy by the end of the day?'

Siobhan nodded. 'Of course. I'll update her care instructions and medicine chart so that all the carers know about the extra tablets.'

'Perfect.' Cass took the dressings from her bag and began to wrap Kathleen's foot.

They said goodbye to everyone and left Kathleen's cottage.

Standing outside with Lachie, she was grateful for him to be able to come straight out. 'Thank you for coming.'

Lachie smiled. 'No problem. I guess that means you've met all my family now. I'm, er, sorry she called you Meghan.'

'Oh, that's okay. I understand.'

'You both have long brown hair, similar looks—she just gets confused a lot lately.'

'Don't worry about it.' She'd thought Meghan had looked gorgeous in the wedding photograph, so to be compared to such a beauty was a compliment, really. Did Lachie see the similarity?

'So, you have one more house call to make?' he asked.

'Er, yes, a Douglas Parker?'

'He's a sheep farmer on the far side of Gulray. Fancy some company? I've completed my list for today.' He looked a little dismayed, or even maybe a little embarrassed, after his visit to his mum's. Maybe he was upset that she was losing her memory. Maybe he was upset that she'd been confused with his wife? Or maybe, he was just a little lonely? But he'd helped her out and one favour deserved another.

'Sure.' She would hopefully be able to take his mind off of Kathleen.

They took her car. It was a rusty old thing. More rust than paint and he was a bit dubious getting inside it, but Cass had laughed and promised him that though the outside looked questionable, the engine was sound.

'I'm going to have to believe you,' he'd said with a laugh.

He was still surprised at how his mother's diagnosis was affecting him. He'd suspected Alzheimer's for some time, but having it confirmed had made it different and to see how quickly her mind faltered in the space of ten minutes still had the power to rock his foundations. He'd dealt with Alzheimer's patients before—of course he had—

but it was different when it was *your own mother* and you knew that neurons were dying every day and piece by piece, memory by memory, he would slowly lose her. The shell of her would still be present, but everything that made her his mother, everything that made her Ronan's grandmother, would eventually slip away. Hearing her forget what they were doing in removing the needle and that slip about Cass being Meghan... Was the disease advancing quicker than he'd like to admit? He'd been telling himself for some time that she was just in the early stages, but Radha had suspected differently. The meds the consultant had prescribed could not stop the disease progressing, but they could slow it, hopefully.

'Are you okay?' Cass asked, glancing at him as she drove through the rain, windscreen wipers struggling to cope with the deluge.

He sighed and nodded. 'Aye. It's just difficult to see her like that, you know?' How long did he have? How long until she didn't know who he was at all?

'I know. But she's still here. You've still got her in your life, even if her memory is foggy. Some people don't even have that,' she said, sounding rueful.

'I know. We're lucky, but it doesn't feel that way, sometimes.' He could feel himself losing his mum. Which was easiest, to lose someone fast and unexpectedly, like he had with Meghan? Or to slowly watch someone decline over months and years, knowing you couldn't do a damn thing about it?

'I guess all you can do is make sure you spend as much time together as you can.'

'I know.' He was quiet for a while as she drove them through the country lanes. He looked out over the fields he knew so well, across at the farmhouses dotted in the distance. He needed to soak all this up, too, because one day he and Ronan wouldn't live here anymore.

'So, Douglas Parker. What do I need to know?'

He was grateful for the change in conversation. 'Good guy. Grandad to Agnes, our HCA. Born and bred farmer. Hard-working, riddled with arthritis now. On statins. Type two diabetic with one heck of a foot ulcer.'

'Which I need to dress each day?'

'You got it. He'd been keeping it clean and I've been going about two, sometimes three times a week to do it, but he cleaned out his sheep barn and somehow got an infection in it, so he's been needing re-dressing each day. It's deep. Near the bone.'

'Poor guy.' She glanced at him and as with every time she did it, he felt something. Like an exciting feeling that grew with every look.

'Yeah. He's a workhorse, so if this gets worse, I don't know how he's going to cope with it.'

She nodded. 'Left here?'

'Aye and then take the next right. Looks like a mud track, but it takes you directly to the farm.'

She drove through fields of sheep, still thick with their coats, as they stood in the rain, nibbling on the grass. 'Who shears them when it's needed?'

'Who do you think?' Lachie raised an amused eyebrow at her. Douglas did.

'Wow. I've not even met the guy and already I'm impressed by him. Hardy stock out here.'

'We have to be.'

Cass seemed to ponder on his comment. 'When your

wife got sick…you must have had to wait for emergency transport.'

He glanced at her as she pulled to a stop outside of Doug Parker's farmhouse. 'Aye. It didn't get here in time and there was nothing I could do. Not with all my training, not with all my knowledge. I just had to sit and watch her slip away.'

The pain felt fresh with every retelling.

Her voice was low as she looked at him. 'That must have been awful.'

'Aye.' He sniffed and ran his hands through his dark hair, letting out a breath. 'So, shall we do this?'

He had to push his grief back into the shadows. He'd done it so many times now it was easy enough. He didn't need anyone feeling pity or sympathy for him. They just needed to do their job here and go. Be the nurse and doctor Doug Parker needed them to be until Nic came back and he could say goodbye to Cass, too.

'Aye.'

CHAPTER FOUR

By the end of that first week, Lachie felt like Cass had fitted into the surgery so well, he felt like he'd worked with her and known her for years. Feedback from patients that he saw out and about was that she was great. Warm, affectionate, a good listener, skilled—he couldn't have asked for more. A pity that she was only temporary. But today was meant for happier things, because he'd received a call first thing and he was out today, visiting his latest and newest patient on Gulray.

'Want to hold him?' Nic asked, cradling her newborn son, who had arrived screaming into the world last night, healthy and hearty, delivered safely by Jane, the island midwife.

'I'd love to.' He held out his arms and accepted the baby into them. 'You forget they start out this small!'

'Small?' Nic scoffed. 'You did hear he was eight pounds? My downstairs feels like a bomb's gone off in it and probably looks that way, too.' She looked up at Matt and laughed. 'You did'nae hear that bit, okay?'

Matt bent to kiss her forehead and there was a knock at their door. He went to answer it.

Lachie slowly rocked the baby, remembering Ronan at that age.

'Hello,' he said. 'Welcome to the world, little one.'

'Hi. I hope I'm not disturbing you?'

Lachie looked up, brightening even more at hearing Cass's voice. 'No, no. Just here getting cuddles.'

Cass was holding a gift bag that she passed to Nic.

'It's for you. A specially formulated postpartum bath soak. It's meant to aid the healing process.'

Nic accepted it happily. 'Fabulous! Thank you so much—you didn't have to get me anything.'

'It's nothing,' she added, looking a little embarrassed. 'And the baby's birth is the talk of the island.' Cass smiled, coming over to sit by Lachie and gaze at the bairn.

He felt her sink into the seat next to him and inhaled the soft scent of her. Something stirred within him and he had to distract himself. 'Want to hold him?'

Lachie saw a look of such intense want and need fill her eyes as she nodded and he passed the baby over. Cass took him, her face filling with adoration and awe, a smile creeping across and lighting up her face in a way he had not yet seen.

'Hello, little one. What's your name?'

'Daniel,' Nic said proudly. 'Daniel Joseph McClintock.'

Cass looked up sharply, her smile faltering slightly, before she looked back down and smiled, almost as if she were near to tears. 'Hello, Daniel,' she whispered.

He watched carefully as her gaze took in all the baby's features as he slept in her arms. The little button nose. The pink lips. The chubby cheeks.

Cass pressed her lips together and then half laughed, half cried. At least that was what it sounded like. Holding this baby was doing something to her, but what? Did she yearn for a baby of her own? Or did Daniel remind her of a baby she'd held before and couldn't see because she was here, so far away from home? That had to be it! She was missing her own family. She probably had nieces or nephews that she missed terribly. Surreptitiously he passed her a handkerchief that he kept in his pocket and she laughed, embarrassed to take it, but dabbed at her eyes nonetheless.

'Sorry! I don't know what came over me!'

Lachie looked at Nic, who was simply happy to see her son had moved someone to tears. Of course it was a happy occasion. Things like this affected people. Just because they were medics didn't mean that they had no emotions. Just because they had to hide them often didn't mean that they didn't feel *intensely*. So when they did have the opportunity to feel openly, those emotions could be overwhelming without the usual barrier there to hold them back.

'He's beautiful,' Cass said before looking up at Nic. 'And he's well?'

'He's perfect,' said Matt. 'Can I get anybody a drink?'

Cass shook her head and so did Lachie.

For a moment he and Cass sat side by side, gazing at baby Daniel. It reminded him of when he and Meghan would sit and gaze at Ronan as a baby. Like they couldn't quite believe he was theirs. Meg had said that babies were the perfect time waster and he'd agreed, because those first few days had passed in a blur of awe and adoration. Where they'd just stared at him in his cot whilst he slept, or gazed at him in their arms, marvelling at his perfection. This little child that they'd made. There was absolutely nothing like that moment.

Baby Daniel began to snuffle and waken, blinking his eyes open and gazing up at Cass.

'Looks like someone's getting ready for his next feed,' Nic said.

Cass stood up and passed him over. 'Is there anything I can do whilst I'm here? I'm not the greatest cook, but I can do laundry or cleaning. Put me to work, what do you need?'

'Och, we can'nae ask you to do anything like that!' Matt said. 'You being here is enough.'

'If you're at a loose end I'm calling in on Mum,' Lachie said, the words out of his mouth before he'd even realised he was about to ask her to join him. Inwardly, he felt surprised that he'd asked and he tried to style it out, even though he realised she would probably turn him down. Why would she want to spend some of her weekend off with one of her patients? 'But, you know, you don't have to. You've probably got loads to do.'

Cass was looking at him carefully, but then she surprised him by saying she would be happy to.

'Oh. Right. Well, good. That's great!' He glanced over at Nic, who was giving him her smile that said she could see right through him. He frowned at her and shook his head a little to tell her it wasn't what she was thinking. 'Well, we'll be off, then. Let you get this little one fed and remember, if you need anything, give me a ring.'

'That goes for me, too,' Cass added.

'Thank you both for coming.' Nic smiled, already beginning to unbutton her top to feed her son.

'Take care.'

Cass was glad to be outside in the cold morning air. It was a special kind of cold out here in Gulray. The air fresh and clean, the slight aroma of a storm-washed sea. She knew that if she went beachcombing right now, she would find all sorts washed up on the beaches. Driftwood, seaweed. Maybe sea glass and white slivers of cuttlefish. There was just something invigorating about the air and it helped clear away the shock she'd felt at hearing that Nic had named her son *Daniel*.

It had been a weird, emotional moment. Sitting there, holding that newborn baby boy, staring at his beautiful face and hearing that his name was Daniel. The same as her own son, who she'd lost years ago. It had transported her back to the past. Sitting in a hospital bed, sore from birth, holding him in her arms. *I'm going to call you Daniel. Do you like that? I think it's a good name.* And Daniel had yawned in that moment and stretched his little arms out above his head and given a gassy, pink-gummed smile, because she'd just fed him whilst she'd thought on names. It had been such a perfect moment after months and months of stress and upset with her family. To forget the past just for a little while and dream of the future. His and hers.

She'd been just sixteen. Was she still considered a child herself, now that she'd had a baby of her own? She'd managed a few perfect hours with him. Showing him off to Aunty Morag, her only visitor, and then bedding down for the night, only to wake some time later with a feeling that something was terribly wrong. And it had been. The moment her world had fallen into turmoil and upset once again.

As they'd rushed Daniel off to emergency surgery, she'd cried herself into exhaustion all night long, wondering just what on earth she'd done so wrong to deserve such horrible things to keep befalling her. Why had her life always had to be a constant heartache and struggle?

'Where's Ronan?'

'He's at a friend's house. Apparently a new computer game has come out that's the in thing. They have to build a zoo and run it, or something, I'm not sure, but I've got a free day today, until this evening when he comes back.'

'That must be nice? A free day?'

'Well, aye. Listen, speaking of free days, this is the weekend. Are you really sure you want to spend it hanging around with me and one of your patients?'

'Actually, yes. I do,' she said, surprising herself. She didn't want to be alone right now. She was always alone and right now, in the turmoil of her feelings about Nic's baby's name, she felt like she wanted some company. Because if she went home to think about it, she'd just sit and stew and that was never good. And though normally she liked being alone, the prospect of a choice between loneliness and Lachie meant that Lachie, despite her dangerous attraction to him, would win every time.

'How's her foot doing?'

'All good, thanks. I said I'd pop in before going to see Doug Parker and re-dress his ulcer as I'm on call this weekend.'

'Do you still think it's getting worse?'

'Aye. Well, you saw it for yourself the other day. Transport is arriving Monday to take him into Argyle on the mainland and get a proper assessment, but I think he might lose his foot.' He shook his head. 'Listen to us. Our days off and we still talk about work. Let's talk about you,' he said as they began walking in the direction of his mother's. 'What do you like to do when you're *not* working?'

'Oh, I'm not that interesting,' Cass said, sticking to her tried-and-tested method of not letting anyone know her enough to get beyond her walls. 'Tell me about you.'

Lachie gave her a look. 'Nice try. I'm sure you know more than enough about me already. I want to know about *you*.'

'Why?' she asked. She wasn't used to people wanting to know about her like this. No one had ever taken an interest like this before. Not even her parents. They'd never known her favourite colour, or what she liked to do, whether she liked music or who her friends were. They'd only ever been interested in themselves.

'Hmm, deflection again. Are you hiding a terrible secret? Are you a spy?'

Cass laughed. 'What could there possibly be on Gulray for me to spy on?'

He smiled. 'Good point. So massive secret it is, then. Okay, I won't pry. Clearly you don't want me to.'

As she followed him up the garden path towards his mother's front door, Cass felt something that she'd never felt before when deflecting. She felt *guilty*. A strange sensation. Like she owed him some sort of explanation. She felt like she ought to give him something. A snippet of her to show…what exactly? That she wasn't being rude? Or unfriendly? What was it about Lachie that made her want to share something? Maybe it was because she knew he was a fellow traveller? That they'd both been affected by grief and trauma? She just strongly felt that it would be bad to keep brushing his interest off.

'I'm sorry. I'm not good at sharing. It's just… I've learned to keep people at arm's length.'

He turned to look at her. Saw something in her eyes that told him she wasn't just being a jerk. 'Hey, it's okay. I shouldn't have tried to pry—you don't have to say anything. Just because the whole island knows my situation and I'm so used to living in a place where everyone knows everyone else's business… You're not used to that. It shouldn't have to be the same for you, so…' He held up his hands as if in surrender. 'My apologies.'

'Lachie…' She reached out with her hand, placing it on his arm briefly, then withdrawing as if he was too hot to touch. Because he was. She'd felt it. The second her hand touched his arm and he'd made eye contact with her. 'I've just been through some things and… I just don't talk about them, that's all.'

He nodded. 'It's fine, I understand.'

He was being so kind about it, but she still felt like she should share *something*. 'How about I tell you something that's easy… Let's see… I like pink! And I've never been abroad, or even left Scotland for that matter, and my favourite food is the butterscotch mousse my Aunty Morag makes and I once broke my nose trying to do the crow pose in yoga and…' She trailed off as she realised he was smiling at her, eyes twinkling in delight. 'What?'

He reached up and gently tapped on the tip of her nose. His touch was electric, shocking her into silence. 'It looks great…considering.'

And then he blushed and it was the greatest thing she had ever seen since coming to Gulray. Realising that he had touched her like that. It had been an intimate thing to do. Standing so close. Staring into one another's eyes.

It was incredibly disconcerting. She'd not been in a single relationship since Tommy. Very rarely had she had a date and even then, she'd had to be persuaded into those. She could remember each and every one. Waiting for the moment in which she could excuse herself and scurry home again. Feeling uncomfortable. Afraid of what her date might want from her. Something she couldn't give. So to be standing here with Lachie, her heart thumping madly, her pulse racing…

'Thank you,' she said. Breaking her nose like that, when she'd been trying to heal her mind, had been the last straw when it happened. So many people had tried to give her advice on how best to take her mind off her grief. Go walking, they said. Exercise, they said. But she'd not wanted to go out. She'd not wanted to see everyone else carrying on with their lives, smiling, laughing, like her own world hadn't ended. But after lying in bed for days, doing some sort of exercise seemed like something she could attempt. She used to do yoga. She'd always enjoyed it before and she figured she'd just do some of the old moves she'd learned before. And so she did. Downward dog. Child's pose. Warrior one. Warrior two. Crow's pose.

And crash. Face-planting into the floor of her bedroom.

She'd cried for hours and kept checking her appearance in the mirror, convinced she'd look awful for the rest of her days, and that life was out to get her, but the doctor at the hospital had straightened it for her—very painful—and now it was barely noticeable. But every time she looked in a mirror now and saw the almost miniscule misalignment, it reminded her of that moment. Crying during her yoga practice, attempting the crow pose and falling forward onto her face, blood everywhere, crying even more, salty tears, snot and blood mixing together into one horrendous mess as she'd sat in A&E with a bag of frozen peas on her face.

She blushed. 'Have you ever done something stupid like that?'

'I once gave myself a concussion when I hit a post with my head, trying to save a goal. I had to be carried off the field on a stretcher and over forty people saw me throw up when I realised I was bleeding.'

'Is that true, or are you just trying to make me feel better?' she asked with a smile.

'Both. Perfectly true. Ask anyone.'

She smirked. 'You threw up at the sight of blood? Aren't you a doctor?'

'Hey, I can deal with anyone else's! Amputations, degloving injuries—I've seen them in my time, but when it comes to my *own* blood? That's a whole other ball game. No pun intended.'

'Thank you. For making me feel better.' She gave him a playful nudge with her elbow.

'Anytime.' He winked and nudged her back.

'Och, I could tell you loads of stories about this one!' said Kathleen, Lachie's mother with a sparkle of mischief in her eyes. 'How much time have you got?'

Cass laughed. 'Tell me your favourite.'

'Oh well, let's see now… Oh yes! I've got one. There was this one day when he was a wee bairn and in the middle of potty-training—'

'Mum, please—keep it clean!'

Kathleen cackled. 'I am, that's what the story is about! Hush now, don't interrupt! So, I was on the phone, speaking to a live radio show about a song request or something. They did it back in those days and as I'm talking, young Lachie here was sat on his potty and he stood up and shouted—loud enough for everyone to hear— "Mummy, can you clean my bum-bum?"'

Cass laughed. 'He didn't!'

'He did! Oh, bless his little heart. I blushed so much, but everyone was so sweet about it and it makes a good story, doesn't it?'

'It certainly does.' Cass looked at him, eyes sparkling, and he loved that she was enjoying the mishaps of his youth. He liked her hearing them. Loved seeing the way his mother opened up to her and liked her, too.

Yes. I definitely like her.

This was her day off! And she was spending it with a patient and that told him something about her. Maybe she wasn't great at sharing personal things and wanted to keep something of herself hidden, but he was getting to know her, whether she realised it or not. She was loving watching the interaction between himself and his mother. Almost like she was fascinated by it. Maybe she'd not had a great relationship with her own? Or maybe her mother had passed young? Whatever it was, he could see she was lapping up theirs and he was happy that he could make her smile. He could sense a great sadness in Cass. A reserve. Like she was a small island in a vast ocean and though she yearned for connection and people, she stopped anyone from landing on her shore. Or maybe it was simply a wall? She surrounded herself with it and kept herself isolated, as if it protected her. But was it keeping everyone else out, or keeping her a prisoner? He knew this mindset. He'd lived it. Still did to some degree.

Well, he would respect her boundaries. He understood having those. Getting too close allowed you to be hurt.

Lachie made them all a tea and when he came back into the living room, his mother was asking Cass a question.

'Is your family back on the mainland, then, Cass?'

'Aye. My Aunty Morag lives in Lochgilphead. In a small village by Loch Gilp. Well, just outside of it really. It's a little isolated, but it's home.'

'And your parents?'

Cass suddenly looked uncomfortable. 'They're in Paisley, near Glasgow.'

'How come you didn't live with them?'

'Okay, I think that's enough questions, Mum!' Lachie said, laying down the tray of mugs and a plate of biscuits, not wanting to stray into unwanted territory. 'We're not interrogating anyone.'

'I was just asking a simple question, dear.'

'You were *prying*, Mother.'

'Am I not to know anything about your new girlfriend?'

Girlfriend? He flushed madly. 'This is Cass, Mum, remember? The new nurse at the surgery?'

His mum looked confused for a minute. 'Och! Of course I know that!'

Cass looked at him gratefully and he sat down beside her on the couch and passed her the plate of biscuits. She took a shortbread. Good choice.

'What about you, Kathleen? Where did you grow up?' Cass asked, expertly changing the subject and diverting again, he noticed. He didn't blame her at all.

'I've lived here forever, dear! Ever since I can remember.'

Lachie glanced at Cass and shook his head. That wasn't true. 'Actually, Mum was born in Edinburgh, and when she met my father, who was a fisherman, they moved to the Isle of Gulray, and lived here since. My father died when I was twelve,' he added quietly.

'Oh. I'm sorry to hear that.'

'He got injured. Caught his hand on a hook and it became infected. He got septic and went into organ failure. It was fast and I don't think he knew too much of what was going on at the end.'

'A silly little cut. Just a silly little cut,' his mum repeated.

'I wanted to understand what had happened to my dad. It was why I became a doctor.' He could still remember the confusion of that time. Remembered his dad coming home with his hand all bandaged up, saying it was just a scratch, that he didn't need to go to the doctors and initially he'd seemed fine. But then his dad hadn't felt well one night. Went to bed, saying he just needed to sleep. By morning? His dad was gone.

It had seemed almost impossible that something like that could happen so fast and he'd needed to make sense of it. Becoming a doctor after that had just seemed like the next step to make, to try to ensure that something like that didn't happen to anyone else. And so he'd chosen to practice on the island that had been his home for years, when the outgoing doctor retired back to the mainland, because people on isolated islands very often dismissed their health worries as something simple. Anything to avoid having to be evacuated off the island. No one wanted to cause a fuss. His dad had not wanted to cause a fuss and he'd died because of it.

'I always wanted to be a nurse, even when I was little,' Cass said, her gaze far off, as if she were looking into the past. 'They seemed like they were kind people. Caring for you and making sure you were all right. I wanted to be that. Someone who held your hand through a tough time, or gave you a hug.' She laughed to herself.

Lachie tried to interpret what he could from the valuable snippet of herself that she'd shared. She lived with her aunt and not her parents and had dreamed of being a nurse because she'd wanted kindness in her life. Caring. Had her parents not been affectionate? Or worse than that? Something…cruel, perhaps? And she'd been sent to live with her aunt? He wanted to ask her. To know. But he also did not want to pry. She would tell him when she felt ready. When she felt like she could trust him fully. Would she ever? It wasn't like she was going to be here long. Only a few months. Maybe she thought there was no point to letting any of them in? Perhaps that was why she did the work she did—locum nursing—so that she never stayed in a place long enough to form connections? He ached at sensing her loneliness. She'd been alone for a long time; he just knew it. And he knew what that isolation could do to a human soul, no matter how much you told yourself that you were fine.

'Well, I for one am glad you became a nurse,' he said, meaning it. Because if she hadn't? Then he would never have had the chance to know her.

'Thanks. I like travelling to new places and meeting new people. And this job in particular I was very happy about— getting to go to people's homes? It's new and exciting.'

He smiled at her, aware, even if she wasn't, that she had a tiny crumb of shortcake caught on her upper lip. It drew his gaze to her mouth and he must have been staring because she caught him looking. 'You've got a, er...' He tapped at his own lip to indicate there was something there and she blushed beautifully as she realised and *heavens above*, licked it away with her tongue, sending a wave of desire crashing through him. He looked away, feeling like he'd witnessed something he shouldn't, which was ridiculous.

'Is it gone?'

He nodded, briefly unable to speak as he struggled to get his body under control. Now where the hell had that come from? He'd not felt longing and desire for another woman since Meghan. He'd shut himself down completely in that way, concentrating on being a good doctor, a good father, a good son. But there was something about Cass that stirred him and it wasn't altogether welcome. He'd accepted the fact that there probably wouldn't be another woman in his life. Not until Ronan was much older anyway and they'd moved back to the mainland, but even then, he'd assumed he'd be stuck in his ways. So to experience it with Cass, his nurse, his locum nurse *who wouldn't even be staying on the island*, was terrible timing! Or maybe he was only attracted to her because he knew she was unavailable? Did that somehow make her safe? Unlikely to hurt him?

On the back foot, suddenly discomfited, he necked the rest of his tea in one go, burning his mouth slightly, and stood up. 'Well, I'd better go and see Doug, get that done.'

Cass stood, too. 'Of course. I've taken up too much of your time, I ought to make a move, too.'

He nodded. 'Doing anything nice?'

'I thought I'd explore the island a little. Can you recommend anything?'

'There's plenty of places. I guess it depends on what you're interested in.' *And as I don't really know what you're like, because you don't want to tell me, kind of makes it difficult to suggest anything.*

He realised the unkind thought immediately. It wasn't her fault she wanted to remain private and it most certainly wasn't her fault that he was attracted to her. He hoped the tone of his voice hadn't implied how irritated he now felt with himself.

'Nature? Trails? A good beach?'

'In Scotland? In the middle of winter?'

She smiled and laughed a little. 'Too much?'

'There's Asmund's Tor,' Kathleen said. 'Over to the west of the island. Used to be an old fort there, I think, but wild birds nest in it now.'

'Sounds perfect,' she said.

'Lachie can drop you off on the way to Doug's place and pick you up afterwards.'

Damn it, Mum!

'Oh, I can get there myself, it's nae bother,' Cass said.

But he wouldn't hear of it. Attracted to her he may not want to be, but he could still be a gentleman about it. 'No, it's fine. I can drop you there, like Mum said. It's hard to find and not very well signposted, if at all.'

'Well, if it's not a problem…?'

'Of course not. Why would it be?'

Lachie was strangely quiet in the car as he drove them through the narrower roads out of Kilmarrin. She kept glancing at him, trying to see if everything was all right. Maybe it was seeing his mum's memory fluctuate? 'I thought your mum was on good form. Happy.'

'Aye. She has her moments, of course, but today seems a good day.'

'I hope you weren't offended when she called me your girlfriend.'

Now it was his turn to glance at her, laughing awkwardly. 'Of course not! Patients with Alzheimer's get confused, it's not their fault.'

'Exactly. And she didn't call me Meghan by mistake this time, so technically, I've been downgraded from your wife.' She tried to inject a moment of humour into the situation. But she did find herself wondering what it might feel like to be someone's wife. To have been chosen by someone. To be loved. Adored. For someone to have said *I want you for the rest of my life.*

But Lachie didn't respond, slowing for a small stone bridge and concentrating on that.

'You have a wonderful relationship with her. It's nice that you've had each other all these years.' Seeing Lachie and his mother interact, it was clear that they loved each other very much. She was happy for him that he'd had that. Maybe it would help cushion the blows that Alzheimer's would continue to cause as the disease progressed, and allow him to look back with fondness in those moments that became dark.

'Thank you. We are close.'

'You must have gotten closer after your father passed.'

'Aye. I guess we did.'

There was an awkward silence for a moment. Cass found herself reaching for something to discuss. Something had changed and she didn't know what. But she knew she didn't like this sense of discord she could feel. How to correct it? She wasn't very good at knowing the answer to the ripples of discontent that entered her life. She always found herself floundering. Never quite knowing the right thing to say or do. Which was why getting close to people was so difficult.

'Were you not close to your parents?' Lachie asked out of the blue.

She gazed at him as he drove, wondering how best to answer. To misdirect with a question of her own? Avoid answering at all? Allow the silence to exist?

But Cass realised, suddenly and surprisingly, that she didn't want to take any of those options with him. She was right. Something had changed between them. He'd changed her. Spending time with him. Learning about him and what he'd been through. Seeing him with his friends and his family. And already she felt like maybe she could trust him with a truth about her past. 'No. Not really. I had a difficult childhood.'

'How so?'

Should she say more? Blurt everything out? Would it make this moment feel better if she did? She wasn't after sympathy or pity. But when had she ever told anyone her story? And could she tell it here? On a small island, where he'd already told her that everyone knew everything about everybody?

But Lachie didn't strike her as a gossip. He was a doctor; he held people's secrets and confidentiality as his job! Surely she could trust him with a little about herself?

Yet it was scary to imagine what it might be like if she opened the floodgates. So maybe, perhaps, it might be better to stand at the dam and take just one of her fingers out of the holes and allow a small trickle to get out? Just a bit couldn't hurt, could it? 'My parents should never have become parents. They didn't have it in them to look after children. They were too selfish and narcissistic.'

It was only a small piece of information, but now that she'd said it, she felt open. Bare. Naked and vulnerable, like she wanted to take it back, like she wanted to gather that piece of information back in and pretend like it had never been said. But she couldn't take it back and now she felt scared, and suddenly it was like the floodgates wanted to burst all the way open and she should just give in and tell him everything! And before she knew it? She was crying. Crying so hard he had to stop the car and once again pass her a handkerchief.

Cass cried even more. How many times would this man see her cry? And how many handkerchiefs did he have, for crying out loud?

'I'm sorry, I don't normally cry like this. I don't know where it's coming from.'

But she did know. It was being vulnerable. It was Nic's baby. Holding him. Being reminded once again of all that she had lost. All that she had never had. Babies were a promise of the future and when they were taken from you... Sometimes she could go weeks or months not being hit by these random moments of grief. But today? It was hitting her hard.

'Sounds like you needed it. Like maybe you've been bottling stuff up inside for maybe too long and it needed to get out.'

Perhaps he was right. Perhaps she wasn't softening after all? She'd not formed a special bond with *him* per se; it was just everything from her past building up in the pressure cooker of her brain. Pressure always needed an outlet. It was a relief to know it wasn't him. That this was just her and it probably would have come out no matter where she was.

She laughed and nodded, sniffed and wiped her nose. *I must look a right sight!* 'I'm sorry. I'm fine now. Honestly, you must think you've employed a madwoman.'

'I don't think that at all.'

'You're very kind.' She dabbed at her eyes one final time, folding and refolding the handkerchief. She looked at it in her hands. 'I'll get this washed by the way. Actually, that reminds me, I think I still have that other one you gave me at Nic's house.'

'It's fine, don't worry about it. I have plenty. You keep them. Looks like you might need them more than me,' he said with a smile, trying to brighten the mood.

She appreciated it his kindness. He hadn't judged her. He'd just accepted her tears. Made her feel a little less embarrassed. Lachie was a good man. She looked out of the window and realised that they were at Asmund's Tor. They were parked in a very small car park and a gravel path seemed to wind its way up the tor towards the top, where there appeared to be some sort of ruins. Thankfully the rain had stopped and though there was a little bit of low mist, the weather didn't seem too bad now. Purple spots of heather peeked out among grey rocks.

'We're here? Thanks for dropping me off. I'll let you get on.' She made to get out of the car.

'Are you sure you're okay? I don't want to leave you here alone. Do you want company?'

She did want him to stay with her. She didn't want to

be alone right now. She was always alone. Always dealing with everything all by herself. It might be nice to have some company for a change. But he had a job to do. 'What about Doug?'

'I can call him and tell him I'll be a little late.'

But she couldn't do that. 'No. That's not fair on him, he's waiting for you. You go. I'll be all right.' Maybe being alone would give her some time to gather herself again?

'You're sure? If you ever need an ear, I'm a good listener.'

Cass smiled. 'I'm sure.' She clambered from the car and got out, pulling her coat closer around her. 'The fresh air and a decent walk is just what I need.' Exercise. Fresh air. That was what most people prescribed.

'All right. Well, I won't be long. Once I've dressed his foot, I'll come back and join you.'

She nodded and closed the car door. 'Drive safe.'

'Watch your footing. It can be slippery up there.'

'I'll be fine.'

Lachie was glad in the knowledge that Doug would be going to the mainland tomorrow about his diabetic foot ulcer. It was most definitely not getting better and he feared the worst. Doug admitted to not being the best diabetic patient and was eating things he shouldn't, so Lachie hoped he wouldn't blame himself or get depressed if serious measures had to be taken. But with Doug taken care of and no other house calls to make, Lachie headed back to Asmund's Tor, hoping he'd find a brighter and happier Cass. He'd hated leaving her behind, sensing that she had so much more she could have said. That she was still holding back. But she'd insisted and so he'd left, hating every second that took him away from her, out alone in that desolate spot.

Should he press her for more? Maybe she'd feel better for getting it all out, whatever it was. *But what if hearing her story only ends up pulling me in even closer?* The problem was, he knew he liked her. He was attracted to her and the more time they spent together, the more they shared, the more he found himself stealing secret glances at her, the more he'd be at risk when she left. Because she would leave. There was no doubt about it and she would move on someplace else and he and Ronan and everyone else would be left behind. It was always hard for those left behind.

I need to remember my place. I'm just her boss. That's all I can be.

Parking his car, he got out and began heading up the darkly stoned gravel path, his feet crunching away with every step, and began to head up towards the ruins. Steeling himself. Telling himself to create that barrier again, to take a step back and create that distance.

Asmund's Tor was named after a Viking leader that had once settled on Gulray many hundreds of years ago. The settlement was built all around this area, but Asmund's home sat atop the hill, the legend went, so that he could see his enemies approach from all directions. It was the one place on the island high enough where you could see the sea in whichever direction you looked. In later years, a stone fort was built there by an English king who had used Gulray as a lookout point for invaders also.

Lachie wondered if Cass could see him coming up the hill. He couldn't see her, but maybe she was on the far

side. It would be best if he could just find her, admire
the view politely for a little bit and then take her home.
Leave her be. Get on with his own life and see her on
their next day at work.

There'd been no other cars in the car park, so he knew
they were up here alone and for a moment he imagined
them as being the only two people alive in the world.
Strangely, he found himself smiling at that and then he
felt guilty, thinking of his mother and Ronan, and be-
rated himself, because of course he'd want them there,
too! And wasn't he supposed to be creating a distance?
He'd certainly not meant to imagine himself as he and
Cass alone in the world.

'Cass?' he called when he reached the top, looking
around through the ruins, trying to see where she might be.

'I'm over here!'

He turned in the direction of her voice and passed by a
part of the ruins that had some stone steps still embedded
into the earth. Suddenly he saw Cass sat at the bottom of
the steps, holding her right arm as if it were hurt. Alarm
filled him in an instant. All prior thoughts to keep a distance and be professional went right out of the window.

'Are you all right?' He rushed to be by her side, his
heart pounding as he thought of her sitting up here alone,
stranded, in pain, whilst he'd sat in Doug's warm, dry
home, discussing blood sugar control.

'You were right. It's slippery up here. I took a tumble
on these steps and hit my elbow.'

'How bad is it?'

'It's not broken, just sore—I think it took the brunt of
my fall.' She winced. 'It might be bleeding.'

'Let's get you back to the car to take a closer look.'

* * *

When she'd taken the tumble and then sat there, waiting for Lachie to come back, it had just felt that life was taking yet another pot-shot at her. Sitting there alone allowed her to wallow in some pretty deep thoughts about how everything for her always seemed to go wrong. She couldn't even take a walk without getting hurt! And she'd realised that being alone was not helping her, that she would continue to be alone if she didn't start letting people in! It would continue to feel this horrible!

But hearing Lachie's voice carry over the tor had made her sit up straighter, had made her hope, feel *better*, which made her further question her decision to remain alone.

Seeing him come running down the steps, she found herself both fearing for his safety, too, as well as feeling happy he was by her side.

But getting close to someone, allowing someone in, still felt risky. Old habits die hard. He was a spider and the web he'd spun was made of kindness and comfort. But if she allowed herself to settle in those beautiful silk lines, would she end up more vulnerable than ever? Her silence all these years had kept her safe from more emotional pain. Kept her at a distance from other people's drama. It was like a plaster cast for her heart

Was she ready to risk letting him in? Was she ready to risk her heart? Knowing that she would be leaving this place and leaving him, his son, Kathleen and all the other patients behind?

When they reached his car, he opened her door for her and helped her gently inside, his touch light and protective: *Mind your head.* Then he opened the boot of his vehicle to grab his go-bag and got into the driver's seat. 'Can you get your coat off?'

'I think so.' But getting your coat off in a car was hard enough, without the added burden of a painful elbow. Movement made her wince and she could already feel the stiffness and bruising that she would have tomorrow.

'Here, let me help.' He took hold of her right sleeve cuff and held it so she could pull her arm free. When she did, she could see that coat sleeve had indeed split from the impact on the stone and her top's sleeve was bloodied and stained.

'Ouch.'

'Ouch indeed. Hold still, let me have a look.' He put on some gloves and slowly rolled up her sleeve. He was as gentle as if he were handling something incredibly fragile and didn't want to break it any more than it already was.

She stared at his face as he worked the fabric up her arm. He looked concerned and worried, a frown causing a small rut between his brows, his eyes darkening as the wound revealed itself. Her stomach had butterflies in it just watching him.

'Is it bad?'

'You've split the skin. You must have landed hard.'

'Maybe a little,' she said, trying to downplay it.

He smiled. 'Medics. We're the worst patients of all. How's the pain?'

'Manageable.'

He met her gaze. 'On a scale of one to ten?'

'Two,' she said, meaning four. It really did hurt, but that was because she'd not only hit the bone, but had also hit the elbow joint. It felt jarred and it was going to be stiff tomorrow; she knew that for sure.

'It's going to need a stitch or two. We could do that here if you could hold your phone light on the area.'

'What about glue?'

'I have that, too, but the position of the cut would need a stitch, or every time you bend your arm, you'd pop that glue open.'

She nodded. Made sense. 'Okay. Stitches, then.'

'All right.'

With her free arm, she activated the light on her mobile phone and shone it at her right elbow as he worked.

Lachie cleaned the area with saline, wiped it with gauze and then injected a small solution of local anaesthetic. 'You're lucky that the go-bag contains all that we need.'

'Benefit of being a doc on an isolated island, I guess,' she said.

He smiled, looking up at her. 'Numb yet?'

Meeting his gaze like that, in the close confines of the car, was making those butterflies in her stomach swirl around as if they were in a typhoon. It was disconcerting and yet hypnotic and she wanted to stare into his eyes for ages. Her gaze had dropped to his mouth. His lips. She wondered what it might feel like to kiss him…

She started. 'I think so.' What a wonderful thing local anaesthetic was, she thought. How it numbed you. She could have done with that in her past. A numbing agent to take away all the pain she'd ever experienced, at the hands of her parents, when the boy she'd thought loved her dumped her when he'd discovered she was pregnant. Losing Daniel…

If only there were an anaesthetic you could take that would remove all of that so quickly. Like in seconds.

Maybe that's why people drink sometimes. Or take drugs. It numbs the pain.

'Ready?' Lachie asked.

She nodded.

'Two stitches should do it.'

He was quick and adept, knotting each stitch and moving onto the next, and it was easily done within a minute. He tied off the thread, snipping it with scissors, and then he swabbed it with iodine, placed a gauze square there and wrapped up her arm with a bandage.

'There you go.' He smiled, letting go.

'Thank you.' She tested her arm, moving it this way and that, content that she'd still be able to use it for clinic tomorrow.

'You're welcome. I guess I'd better get you home so you can get that top in some cold water to get the blood out.'

It was torn. She'd probably throw it out. 'Thanks.'

The drive away from Asmund's Tor was much better than the drive *towards* it. Conversation flowed and she didn't feel icky about the fact that she'd told him something of herself previously. She'd kept it vague, thankfully, so there'd been no judgement. And he'd had no idea of the way her thoughts and feelings had tumbled over one another as she'd tried to work out how she felt about him. Just now, in the car, as he'd tended her wound and she'd stared at him, wondering what it might be like to kiss him, it had been alarming. She couldn't allow that to happen, no matter how much she kept thinking about it.

She would not tell Lachie anything else and as long as she kept conversations focused on work, or his family, or island living, then she figured she'd be able to get through the next couple of weeks here easily. It was too easy here to imagine something more. And that made it all the more dangerous the longer she stayed.

She was just here to do her job and she had to remember that.

And then she could go home.

And start up again someplace else.

Alone.

Just how she liked it.

CHAPTER FIVE

WITHIN A COUPLE of weeks, Cass felt like she'd truly begun to settle in to island life. She'd been to a few curry nights at the Puffin's Nest, revelling in feeling a part of something special and she'd met most people on the island, either in clinic, in their homes or out and about when she'd try to take a daily walk, if the Scottish winter weather allowed. She'd gotten into a rhythm that suited her here. Her stitches were out and her elbow had healed nicely, though there was a bright pink line marked upon her skin that would remind her always of this place. It saddened her, she realised, that she would have to leave one day.

She'd joined the book club and she was devouring a rather fantastical pirate romantasy book. She'd also had opportunity to work with Agnes, the HCA, a couple of times and instantly knew that the young girl had all the makings of a fabulous nurse. And now she was about to perform a check-up on Peter, the husband of Jane, the island's midwife.

He'd had a bit of a fall just over a week ago and had been on crutches after being taken to the mainland for a knee surgery. He was in her clinic to have his staples out.

'Morning, Peter, how are you doing?'

'Och, not too bad, thanks.'

'How's the knee feeling?' She noted that he wasn't on crutches anymore, but had graduated to just a sturdy walking stick. That was a good sign.

'Brand new.'

She waited for him to settle onto the examination bed and then, when he was ready, asked for permission to lift up his thankfully loose jogging bottoms to expose his knee. There was still had a gauze pad taped to it and she noted there was no sign of any fluid leakage coming through.

'Okay, let's see what's under this, then, shall we? How have you been coping since the surgery?'

'Not bad, I guess. It's been frustrating not being able to do all the things I want to do. I'd like to be out in the garden, but I've not been able to kneel or anything, so I've felt quite restricted to just standing and putting things in seed trays.'

'Isn't it early to be growing anything?'

'Most things, yes, but there are a few things you can sow right now and I've a sturdy greenhouse that Doug Parker helped me build a few years ago.'

With the gauze pad off, she turned on the lamp and aimed it at his knee to take a closer look. The surgical site had healed really well. Only a small amount of redness, but that was where the new skin was growing. There was no sign of infection at all.

'This looks good! Are you happy for me to remove the staples?'

'I don't know, will it hurt?'

'You might feel a bit of pinching.'

'Maybe I should have taken a wee dram before coming, then?'

She laughed. 'At nine thirty in the morning?'

'Go on, then. Should I bite down on me stick?'

Cass smiled. 'You'll be fine.' She pulled the instrument table over towards her and placed the small cardboard kidney dish onto the bed beside Peter's knee. It contained an instrument called a staple extractor. It looked like a nail clipper, but had a mechanism that would grip each staple and release it from the wound. 'Happy for me to begin?'

'Aye.'

Cass decided to use her age-old trick of distraction therapy. 'How's your wife, Jane?'

'She's good. She tells me you've joined the book club?'

Clip one.

'Yes, I have. You didn't join us at the meeting. Are you not reading it, then?'

'I read the blurb on the back. It's not for me. I prefer books steeped in a bit more reality. Grittier stuff, crime, you know?'

Clip two.

'I like crime, too. I read a decent one a while back, can't remember the author, but it was set in the Hebrides. Quite dark, really, but you really felt the sense of isolation.'

Clip three.

'So you read a horrifying crime novel set on a remote Scottish island and then decided to move to one?'

Clip four.

Cass smiled, then laughed. 'I guess. What does that say about me, eh? Last one.'

She checked the wound once more and, happy that everything was good, asked him to flex and move his leg. 'How does that feel?'

'Aye, lass, it's good.'

'Excellent and you didn't need the stick.'

'You had a gentle touch. So is that it, then?'

She nodded. 'Have you got an appointment to have a check-up with your surgeon?'

'Aye, It's in a few weeks.'

'Good, he should be happy with it and sign you off, but if you have any problems in the meantime, then you know where to come.'

'I do.'

She rolled his jogger leg back down and helped him off the bed and walked him to the door. When she opened it, she saw Nic in the waiting room, her baby buggy at her side. Daniel was crying.

Alarm filled her instantly. She quickly said her good-byes to Peter and when he'd left she hurried over. 'Is everything all right?'

She smiled, but looked harassed. 'Aye, he's fine. It's me. I've got redness and a fever. Think it's mastitis, but I just want Lachie to take a look.' She moved the buggy back and forth, back and forth to try to calm her son. 'But he won't stop crying because I can't feed him very well. And I try and try but he just won't latch on because he keeps crying!' Tears came to Nic's eyes and she tried to wipe them away, but it was too late. The floodgates had opened.

Cass ached for her. She knew what it felt like to have your breasts fill with milk and have no one to take it away.

Behind Cass, Lachie's door opened and he called Nic's name.

Cass turned back to her. 'I've got twenty minutes before my next appointment. Want me to look after Daniel, whilst you get checked out?'

Nic looked relieved. 'Would you? I'll only be five minutes, I'm sure.'

'I could chaperone?'

'No, it's fine. But if you wouldn't mind taking him? I promise I won't be long, but I really could do with five minutes of quiet.'

'Of course, no problem.'

As Nic went in to see Lachie, Cass scooped the crying, wailing baby Daniel from his buggy and held him to her shoulder, gently swaying and patting him on the back, trying her best to soothe him, cooing and making gentle, soft sounds. She could feel the tension in his small, furious body, but as she held him, he relaxed a little.

Maybe he sensed someone who was calmer, but he quietened and sniffed.

Junebug on reception smiled at her. 'You've got the touch.'

Cass smiled, enjoying the feel of holding a baby once again. The smell and feel of him. Warm milk. A hot little body, the way his tiny fists rubbed against his red gums and the little noises he made as he snuffled, his anger calming. She began to walk him away from the main reception. Just down the corridor, towards her room. Just for a moment alone.

For her and a baby boy called Daniel.

And for a brief moment, she was transported back to holding her own son in the hospital. Inhaling the scent of him from the top of his head. Feeling the way he snuggled into her and thinking to herself that it had all been worth it. All the upset, the way his father had deserted them both, labour, delivery, the way her parents had re-acted to news of the pregnancy. It was all worth it, for this moment of utter joy.

So many people had said she wasn't ready. That she was too young. Maybe she had been both of those things, but that hadn't lessened the love she'd felt for her son and she'd known, in that moment, that she would do anything for him. Go to the ends of the earth to protect him, and that overwhelming parental love had made her wonder how her own parents could have been so cruel to *her*? Had they never felt this love that she was feeling? How could they have held her in their arms and felt anything else *but this*?

It had been a long time since she'd held a baby. Oh, she saw babies in clinics sometimes, but it was always as patients. She didn't get these opportunities to just hold and be in the moment. They were precious. Amazing. There was something special about holding a child in your arms.

Cass wondered if she'd ever get the chance to hold a baby of her own again? She'd not dated for god only knew how long, not venturing beyond friendship with anyone, even if they made it that far. Most people had been acquaintances. Colleagues. They were *friendly,* but had they been true friends? So dating, being roman-tic, trusting any guy enough to want to be with him inti-mately was…not likely. Where would she find someone she could trust? Who would be warm and kind and trust-worthy? Someone who she knew, without a doubt, would have her back? Who would love her the way she often hoped one day to be loved? To go through a pregnancy with? To endure sleepless nights and spit-ups and colic? Tommy, her own son's father, had not been ready for that kind of commitment.

Behind her, she heard Lachie's door open and Nic thanking him for his help. The other nurse's face lit up when she saw Cass and Daniel in the corridor.

'You got him to stop crying? Thank you!' She neared them and gazed at her son with such love, gently stroking her finger against his cheek.

Baby Daniel was now snoozing, exhausted, no doubt, from his crying.

'How did it go?' Cass whispered, not willing to wake up the baby.

'Mastitis, as suspected.'

'Ouch. Sorry.'

'It happens, right?'

'It does.' Cass had it once, too. Remembered the fluey feeling, the fever, the aches. But most of all, how painful it had been to experience it when she'd no longer had her son to feed.

'You look like you have the magic touch,' Lachie said, smiling at her.

She smiled back at him. Inordinately pleased by his compliment. 'Oh, it's nothing. He was probably just tired.'

'Take the compliment. You look like you've done this before,' he insisted.

She blushed. She didn't want anyone to know about her own son. Not here. 'You handle a lot of babies as a nurse.' Cass gently passed baby Daniel back to his own mother, who walked him back to his buggy and laid him down in it. Cass fought the yearning to hold him some more.

'Now, go and get some rest,' Lachie ordered Nic. 'Sleep when he does.'

Nic smiled, thanked them and was gone.

Cass's arms suddenly felt very empty and the wrench

of it burned tears into the backs of her eyes. But she forced them away with a large, false smile. 'Okay, who's up for a giant mug of tea?'

That weekend, Lachie was at his mother's house with Ronan, who was sat at a table doing a jigsaw puzzle. He often popped round when he could, sometimes cooked a meal for them all. Tonight they had an extra guest coming because he'd invited Cass to join them.

The invite had been intentional. He was very much aware that she was here alone, with no family or friends, and he didn't want her to feel as isolated as the island that they walked upon. It wasn't a hardship to cook for one extra mouth and besides, he enjoyed her company. Very much. And if he was honest with himself, the invite was as much for him as it was for her.

Lately Lachie had begun to feel extremely lonely. And Cass intrigued him. Pulled at him. And he thought about her often. But he reminded himself that he was only inviting her as a friend. That was all! You could respect a professional boundary and maintain an emotional distance without being a jerk. She had no one here and it wasn't like he was inviting her out on a date. A meal for two. His son would be there. His mother. Cass's patients.

Plus, he was great at keeping himself busy and looking happy for everyone else's benefit and he did enjoy his work as a doctor and his role as a father and a son, but every night, after Ronan was in bed and he sat alone in his cottage, he'd found himself yearning for something more. For someone to talk to. Someone to laugh with. To watch a movie with. To revel in someone else's company. A woman's company.

He had plenty of friends, both male and female, but they were all patients and that wasn't the type of companionship he was yearning for. Lachie was missing having someone to be with who wasn't officially on his patient list. Someone to just enjoy spending time with.

The fact that his bed seemed vast and empty lately did not come into it. The fact that he remembered the wonder of waking on a weekend morning and the simple joy of lazing in bed with someone, reading the paper, having a coffee and breakfast, and maybe sometimes for that lazy moment to turn into something else, did not come into it, either. The fact that when he thought of those things, he also thought of Cass was just him being human. Right?

And being human meant extending invites to people whom he thought might be lonely, too. There was nothing wrong in two lonely people spending time with one another, if that was all it was.

And so he'd invited Cass.

Plus, he told himself in moments of doubt after issuing the invite, he knew how much Cass enjoyed his mother's company. And just how much his mum loved Cass. The invite worked for them all, quite frankly.

His warmth for her came naturally—she made it easy to like her, even if she did put up walls. Honestly? She was a bit of a mystery, but that just intrigued him more. He'd not thought of how irritating it could be to know everything about someone, living here on Gulray. Where was the intrigue? The opportunity to find out and learn about someone, through a conversation? That was what he yearned for, to know more about her—that was all. Nothing wrong in asking for as much as she was willing to tell him. And simply an evening to just, well…

see her smile and laugh and know that he had somehow caused her to have those warm feelings inside. Feelings that would make him smile and want to see her again. Feel less alone for a little while.

He wasn't looking for anything romantic. Just for some adult conversation with someone who was intriguing to him. And in return he and his small family would provide companionship and warmth to her, too. She seemed to like it and so it had to be a good thing, right? Inviting her around? They were just friends.

And though he yearned for more, the idea of actually pursuing it was terrifying. You put your heart on the line getting involved with someone. You never knew when they just wouldn't be there anymore. Look at Meghan. Gone too soon.

A knock at the front door had him opening it and welcoming Cass inside.

She looked amazing in simple blue jeans and a white cabled fisherman's style jumper. For the first time, he saw her with her hair down, flowing over one shoulder. A rich brunette colour with hints of warm reds. He kissed her on the cheek as a greeting and invited her in. She had a bottle of wine in one hand and a covered tray in the other.

'I come bearing gifts!'

'Excellent. Come on in!' He closed the door and followed her through the living space, where she said hello to his mother and Ronan briefly before heading into the kitchen and placing her things on the table.

Removing the cover, she revealed a traybake. 'I'm not a great cook, as I said, but these I can do. Flapjacks!'

'Awesome. Thanks.'

'Only four ingredients, so even I can't get it wrong.'

'I'm sure they taste amazing.'

She smiled, warmed by his compliment. 'Something smells good. What's for dinner?'

'Just a hotpot.'

'Can I help with anything?'

'No, no. You're the guest. Why don't you join the others and I'll bring you a drink? What do you fancy?'

'Just a tea would be great.'

'Coming right up.'

He watched her go into the living room and sit down beside Ronan and engage with him as he tried to work on his jigsaw. There was no doubt about it; she made him feel good inside. She genuinely seemed interested in Ronan and laughed with him and encouraged him as he worked. His son seemed to be telling Cass about a story he'd heard in school today, and Lachie almost burned his fingers holding onto a teabag for too long, as he got distracted watching them. Shaking his head, he took her tea through and sat on the couch opposite.

'So, how's your day been?'

'It's been good, I think. Though I did wake up to a stranger in my bed.'

What?

He wasn't sure how to respond to that! His mum and his son were listening! Surely that wasn't a good topic of conversation to—

'Your cat, Frosty! There she was at the end of my bed, purring away.'

He laughed, much relieved. But there'd been a moment after the shock. A flare of what—jealousy? Impossible! But the image was there in his head now. Imagining her waking up. Her gorgeous hair spread out over her pillow.

Her naked shoulder, perhaps revealed by the duvet… 'I'm sorry. How did she get in?' *And how could I?* He felt himself blush at the forbidden thought.

'I left the small window in the kitchen open overnight. She must have jumped in through there.'

'I'll have a word with her.' Lachie smiled, feeling stupidly jealous of a cat.

'She's nae bother, honestly. It was kind of nice, once I'd got over the shock of feeling something move on my bed.'

'She must have scared you for a moment?'

She nodded. 'But then she purred and let me stroke her and all was well with the world again.'

Lachie could imagine lying in her bed and being stroked by her.

Where are all these thoughts coming from?

'I used to have a cat,' Kathleen, his mother, said.

Cass turned to smile. 'You did? What was its name?'

'When I was a child. I think we adopted him, he was a stray and we called him Haggis. Big ol' lumpy thing he was, a bit straggly, but he was ours. Arrived one day out of the blue and disappeared the same way.'

'You don't know what happened to him?'

His mum shook her head. 'My mammy told me he'd gone to a farm, but I think that was her way of telling me that he'd died, as she didn't want me to be upset.'

Cass smiled. 'Did you never get another?'

'No. My daddy wasn't too fond of cats. Said they made him sneeze, but that didn't stop ol' Haggis from settling on his lap! I think there's a picture, somewhere of him… Lachie, be a dear and find it for me.'

'It's in your album, Mum, beside you on the table.'

His mum hefted over a large photo album and began leafing through. 'Here! Here he is, look.'

Cass excused herself from Ronan and went to sit by his mother.

Cass felt enamoured by the memories contained within the album. It was not something her own parents had. They'd never been ones to take photos, or even try to make memories, which was why Cass didn't have many pictures of herself growing up. There was one she'd found, of herself as a baby in her mother's arms. Her grandmother had taken the photo, by all accounts, which was why it existed. She lay in her mother's arms and was clearly crying or screaming the place down and her mother was giving a grudging smile to the camera. It spoke volumes about her family. Her mum had once told her that they couldn't afford a child when she came along and she'd wanted to abort, but that Cass's father had convinced her to keep the baby. And all her life, she'd grown up feeling like she was an inconvenience and if she could just stay out of their way and not cause trouble, then they'd all simply rub along together just fine. No wonder she went looking for love with Tommy. She'd been desperate for any show of affection by the time she ran into him.

'And this one is when Lachie was about five years old, I think!'

Cass smiled. 'Love the haircut.'

Lachie laughed. 'Yeah, it was a bold choice, wasn't it?'

In the picture, Lachie's hair was much lighter than it was now. It almost looked blonde, shaped in a wedged bowl cut. Clearly it was some sort of school photograph and he was missing a front tooth.

'Here's Haggis! Bless him. I loved that cat.'

Haggis did look like a wild, feral thing that had some-how been tamed reluctantly. He had clumps of fur miss-ing, possibly from fights, and scrapes and a large piece missing from his left ear. But there he was, curled up on a much younger Kathleen's lap.

'I can see how much you look like one another in that picture, Kathleen.'

'Oh yes. He was the spit of me, wasn't he? Looks more like his father now.'

'Is there a picture of him in there?' Cass asked.

'Yes. Here.' Kathleen pointed at a black-and-white pic-ture. A group of men standing on a dock, in waterproofs. She pointed at the man in the middle of the picture and Cass gasped at the similarity between Lachie and his dad. It looked like Lachie himself! Only the beard on his fa-ther was a little thicker and longer.

'Wow.'

'He was a lovely man. You would have liked him, Cass.'

'I'm sure I would.'

'We lost him much too soon. A piece of my heart went with him.'

Cass knew how it felt to lose someone too soon. Dan-iel had died days old—but he'd had a whole potential life ahead of him. But he had died and now? She had spent a lifetime of not talking about him. But she wanted to let Kathleen know—and Lachie—that it was all right to talk about Lachie's father and bring him back to life. Because maybe, by hearing their stories of someone they'd lost, she could feel braver about one day sharing her own?

'Tell me about him. What was his name?'

Kathleen smiled and looked dreamy. 'James. But everyone called him Jamie. I met him in Edinburgh, where I lived at the time. He was there with friends on some sort of break and we met at a dance and what can I say? He swept me off my feet.'

Cass smiled, trying to imagine it. 'Was he romantic, then?'

'Och, he was a big ol' softy! Not that he showed it to his friends, mind. But with me? He was different. We could talk and talk and never had a single awkward silence between us in all the years of our marriage.'

'Lachie said you moved to Gulray?'

'It was where the good fishing was and he had to make a living to support his growing family. We used to sit on this very couch and he'd sit next to me and rest his hand on my bump when I was carrying Lachie...' Kathleen looked to Cass.

She was in the spot. Where Lachie's father had sat.

'Was he a good father? Did he change nappies?'

'Oh, aye! When he was here! More often than not he was out to sea, but when he came home? He loved nothing more than just spending time with us all.'

There were unshed tears in Kathleen's eyes and Cass felt guilty for making them appear by pursuing her own line of questioning. But it had felt so lovely to hear the memories. To learn a little more about their wonderful family. To know that Kathleen had struck lucky with her first love, even if Cass hadn't. That she'd had a good family and a good husband who'd stuck around for his kid and cherished him.

It was so alien to her own experience. She felt envious of it. Imagining how different her life might have turned out if she'd had good, loving parents. If Tommy had stuck around. If Daniel hadn't died. Where would she be right now? Because she didn't think she'd be here—that was for certain.

'I'm about to serve,' Lachie said. 'Ronan? Go wash up, please.'

'Okay.' Ronan placed one last piece into his puzzle and then got to his feet and disappeared to the kitchen to wash his hands.

'Let me help you,' Cass said, taking the album from Kathleen, closing it and placing it on the table and then helping the older woman into the kitchen.

When they were all ready at the table, Lachie placed a large, heated pot on a griddle in the centre, along with some dishes filled with broccoli, peas, carrots and a small dish of dinner buns. 'Did you make those?' Cass asked.

'I did.'

'Wow.' He really was a man of many talents! Doctor, father, cook. What couldn't he do? Where were his faults? There had to be something.

'Maybe you should try one before you get too impressed,' he said with a smile.

'Lachie is known here for making bread that could break your teeth,' Kathleen said with a smile. 'But God loves a trier.'

Cass smiled and took one, trying to give it a squeeze and acknowledging that yes, Kathleen could be right. And as her dentist was on the mainland, maybe it might be too risky to try and eat it. She politely placed it back down on her side plate. She noticed Lachie smiling at her and she laughed. 'Sorry.'

'Don't worry. We can use them later to hold down the tarpaulin out back if we get another storm.'

Cass chuckled at his self-deprecating joke. 'You might need them for that. Did I hear we might be getting another storm as we head into next week?'

'Just another Scottish day,' he said.

'It's your birthday soon, isn't it, laddie?' Kathleen asked Ronan.

Ronan shook his head. 'My birthday is near Christmas.'

'Then what is it that happens in February? I know it's important.'

Lachie reached for his mother's hand. 'It's your wedding anniversary, Mum. On Valentine's Day.'

'Oh, right. Of course! Can't believe I forgot that for a moment.'

Cass smiled. 'You got married on Valentine's?'

The older woman nodded. 'Aye. The weather was blowing a hooley on that day. There's a picture somewhere of Jamie trying to hold the skirt on my wedding dress down.'

'Like Marilyn Monroe?' Cass asked.

Kathleen laughed. 'A bit, aye! Oh, those were the days.'

'Did you have a honeymoon?'

'We had a weekend away on the Isle of Skye. Oh, it was beautiful! What about you, dear? Have you got a fella?'

Cass felt her gaze go to Lachie in an instant, but shook her head. 'No time for any of that. I'm always working.'

'That's no way to live, pretty little thing like you. I keep telling Lachie that he needs to find a mother for his wee laddie again, but he says the same thing! Always working. Never any time. You have to *make* time if you want to be happy.'

'I am happy, Mum,' Lachie said.

'And what about your wee boy, eh?' Kathleen clucked and turned to her food.

'I'd like to have a mummy,' said Ronan into the sudden quiet.

Cass caught Lachie's gaze and gave him a sympathetic smile. He seemingly had so much compared to her. A wonderful mother, despite her health. An amazing son. But they still had a hole in their lives. Did anyone have a perfect situation? Did people who seemed to have everything—spouses, children, parents, friends—did they still feel like something was missing?

Cass worked hard so that she didn't notice how alone she was. She had no partner. No child. No family, except Morag, whom she didn't often see, except for in-between jobs. Apart from that? She was alone. She didn't even really consider herself to have friends. They were colleagues. Associates. And she'd always thought herself fine with that. It was her lot in life, the cards she'd been dealt. But since spending time here with Lachie and his family and this close-knit community, she'd begun to realise just how much she didn't have. And how much she wanted. But there was no point to even wanting them, because she wasn't staying here long. She'd be leaving soon. There was no point in getting attached to these people, here on this island, because she wouldn't be coming back.

Would Ronan ever get another mummy? She hoped so. He was sweet and Lachie was...well, Lachie was the kind of man that was easy to like. She hoped that one day he would find happiness. She tried to imagine it for him, but instead of creating this faceless female in her mind, her imagination placed *her* in the role. Holding hands with him. Kissing him. Doing things together as a family. And then her brain went one crazy step further and she could see herself sat on a picnic blanket at the top of Asmund's Tor, Lachie beside her, Ronan off playing with a kite and Cass was sat there, rubbing at her pregnant stomach!

And then sadness came, because she knew that would never happen and someone else would get that role. That kind of happiness would never be for her.

Cass cleared her throat and abruptly brought herself back to reality by choking on her mouthful of food and having to reach for her water.

'Are you all right?' Lachie asked across from her.

Embarrassed, she coughed and spluttered, dabbing at her mouth with a napkin and managing to squeak out, 'I'm fine. I'm good.'

'You didn't try to eat one of my dinner buns, did you?'

She laughed, her voice returning. Strengthening. 'No. Just went down the wrong pipe.'

The rest of dinner, they chatted about ordinary, everyday things and Cass began to forget about the choking episode and relaxed into feeling a part of their family for the evening. Time passed quickly in their welcoming, easygoing, happy company. After dinner they played a board game, but Kathleen kept forgetting the rules, or when it was her turn, and they were all laughing and gently teasing and it was a wonderful evening. It was clear to see their love and connection and she'd felt so happy to be a part of it. Around 8:00 p.m., the night carer arrived to help Kathleen get changed and ready for bed, so they bid her goodnight and left her cottage.

Outside, in the cold February air, Cass pulled her coat closer about her body and did up the zip. 'Thank you for inviting me out this evening. I had a really good time,' she said. It had been wonderful and just what she'd needed.

'It was our pleasure. Mum really likes having you around.'

And you? she wanted to ask him. *Do* you *like having me around?* But she didn't. She clamped her lips shut because Ronan was there, even if he was yawning and clearly ready to be getting into bed himself.

She was reluctant to leave them all just yet. Surely the night didn't have to end so soon? The time had gone so quickly.

'Walk you home?' Lachie asked.

She nodded, smiling. 'Thanks.'

As they walked down the lane, she realised how nice it felt. Walking with a man and a boy. Almost like if they were a family. How she envied Lachie! The evening had revealed him to have had a lovely clan and though he'd lost his father much too soon, his mother had more than made up for the loss. It was clear they had been very close. Lachie had been loved and supported and encouraged—so different to her own upbringing and he most certainly had not been kicked out of the family home!

'You know, I envy you,' she said as they walked.

'Why?'

'Your mother…she's amazing. I can tell you were very happy as a child.'

'She is and I was. To be losing her this way, to the dementia, seems harsh and cruel, when she's given me so much of herself. I want to spend as much time as I can with her, whilst she still knows who I am. Who Ronan is.'

'She enjoys having her grandson around, too. It lights her up when you're both there. I sometimes wish my parents had lit up like that for me. It might have made all the difference in my life.' If she'd have felt loved by them, then maybe she wouldn't have run into Tommy's arms at the first show of affection. Affection she'd mistaken for love.

'You said before, about your family, that your mum and dad shouldn't have been parents,' he said quietly. Ronan was walking ahead of them slightly, not really listening.

She shook her head. It was so easy to talk to him about this! She felt like she could talk about them with him, knowing it would go no further. 'No. They weren't emotionally equipped for it, nor did they have the bandwidth. Couldn't see beyond their own needs and I was just this child who quickly learned how to take care of herself.'

'I'm sorry. Were you an only child?'

'Aye. They said they learned their mistake having me.'

Lachie frowned. 'Sounds harsh.'

'It was the only mode they had. I grew up feeling so alone, desperate for love and one day, I thought I'd found it, but I was wrong. Because I didn't know what love was meant to feel like, or look like and it just ended up being another bad relationship. So to spend time with you guys, like I did tonight…well, that's special to me. You're all so warm and inviting and kind. It's a revelation and… makes me feel envious of what I should have had.' She should have felt odd telling him all of this. But she didn't.

'I'm sorry that happened to you. I really am,' Lachie said, reaching out to touch the small of her back. Just a gesture. Small. Innocent, really. But her heart thudded with warmth and appreciation for the fact that he *saw her*. That he understood her pain and empathised with it.

'This is me,' she said, standing outside of her cottage.

Did they really have to say goodnight? Couldn't she just enjoy being with them a little longer? No. Ronan was yawning. He needed to get home. She couldn't be the selfish one now.

'Aye. Good to see there's no sign of Frosty.'

She smiled. 'He could be inside for all we know.'

'Want me to wait whilst you check?'

Cass shook her head, even though that would have been nice. She could have found his cat and carried him out and placed him in Lachie's arms and they might have a moment, where they would be close and she would brush against him and there'd be a flare of...what? She was good at misreading signals.

'He's fine. He's a good snuggler.' She laughed.

'That he is.' Lachie looked unsure as to how to end their evening.

They were just colleagues. He'd invited her to share a meal with his family. It was what friends did. Nice friends. But she wanted him to know that she'd appreciated him inviting her into his family, if only for the night. Wanted to show him how much it had meant. So she stepped forward and kissed him on the cheek. Brief. Innocent. Even if inside it felt to her as if it were charged with something more. A wanting. A need to belong. A desire for this kind, clever and handsome man who was her boss. A line she couldn't cross, no matter what. But the heat had flared in that moment and she knew she was dealing with a spark that could turn into a blaze. She paused and then stepped away. Reluctantly. 'Thanks for this evening. I really enjoyed it.'

He looked at her. 'Me, too.'

'I'll see you at work.'

'Aye. Sleep well.'

She watched him back away down the path, almost as if he didn't want to tear his gaze away from her, but then he stumbled on a stone edging the path, arms wheeling madly, before he steadied himself with a hand on the low stone wall and laughed, embarrassed.

She laughed back at him, amused, thinking how his clumsiness had only made him even cuter. Cass gave him a little wave and watched Lachie and Ronan until they were out of sight and then, with reluctance, she turned to go inside her empty cottage.

Alone, once again.

Cass used to value her alone time. It had always kept her safe and protected from others.

But for some reason, here on Gulray, she didn't like it at all anymore.

After Lachie had put his son to bed, he stood for a moment in his living room and stared at the empty room. It was neat. Tidy. Family pictures up on the mantelpiece and on a side table by the television. Pictures of Meghan, mostly, so that his son didn't forget his mother's face.

He picked one up and stared at it.

Lachie knew he would never forget her, or what it had felt like to be with her. The way she had made him feel. But tonight, he'd realised that being with Cass made him feel good, too. Like he wanted to spend more time with her. He loved listening to her speak. Being in her company. He sensed a soul hungry for something more but afraid to have it, and he wanted, deep in his own soul, to be the one that somehow helped her get what she needed from life, even if that didn't involve him.

He missed having someone to just chat with. Especially now that his mother was losing parts of herself. He felt that with Cass, he could talk to her about that and how that made him feel, the way he would have shared it with Meghan. He'd been keeping so much of himself to himself lately. It was difficult being the island's doctor, because who was he supposed to talk to about his worries?

Having Cass here was…balm to his soul. He'd been alone for so long, and Cass gave him the hope that one day he wouldn't be. It made him feel a little guilty that he could feel that. He'd always thought he would be loyal and true to Meghan until the day he died, but here he was, wanting to spend time with another woman. Did it mean he loved Meghan any the less? No. He didn't think so. But he almost felt like he was somehow cheating on her memory by enjoying another woman's company. And he didn't want to confuse Ronan. He'd explained Cass was there tonight at his grandmother's house because Cass had nobody to spend time with on the island and how it was a nice thing to do. To offer her some company, but honestly? He'd had an ulterior motive.

He'd been the lonely one.

The one who'd fed his own selfish needs.

Was that wrong, when he honestly felt like he'd also helped her? Did it matter at all, if it helped them both?

Walking home tonight, it was like he was part of a proper family group again. That Cass had taken his wife's role. Someone to walk by *his* side again.

Lachie missed being a part of a couple.

He missed being married.

He missed being truly happy.

CHAPTER SIX

'MORNING, EVERYONE!' CASS SAID as she entered the staff room the next morning, shaking off her umbrella in the sink and then peeling off her coat. 'What a day! It's pelting it down!'

'Typical February weather,' said Junebug.

'You're telling me.' She draped her jacket around a chair in the hopes that it would dry off by the end of the day, then she saw Lachie do a double-take as he walked by in the hallway.

'Ah, Cass. Do you have a minute?'

'Of course.' She followed him to his consulting room. 'What's up?'

'I've heard from Argyle General Hospital regarding Doug Parker. Unfortunately the decision was made to amputate his foot.'

'Oh, poor Doug! Do we know how he's holding up?'

'I've just got off the phone with Agnes. He's giving them all hell over there, apparently.' Lachie smiled. 'And he's raring to get home. Reckons he'll be able to carry on working with crutches, but Agnes and her family are trying to arrange for some sort of support on the farm, until he's properly up and about.'

'When is he coming home?'

'No date yet, but she says she'll let us know the second she hears.'

'Okay, well, thanks for letting me know.'

'No problem.'

'Was that all?'

'Aye, well, actually... I just wanted to thank you for last night. I had a great time.'

She blushed. 'So did I.'

She'd lain awake in bed afterwards with a huge smile on her face just thinking about the evening. How nice it had felt to be welcomed in by his family and how much she'd enjoyed the walk home and dropping a kiss onto his cheek. She'd not wanted the evening to end at all! She'd even—shockingly—lain there imagining what it might feel like to put roots down here! To settle. Maybe buy a place. But she'd quickly disavowed herself of that because what would she do? She was here nursing as a locum until Nic returned to work after having baby Daniel. *If* she returned. She might decide to be a stay-at-home mum and then Cass could... *Wow. This place, Gulray, the people on it, Lachie, Ronan, Kathleen, her patients, they are all changing me.*

And how terrifying was that? Because if she did put down roots, if she did stay, then she would eventually tell everyone about her own baby Daniel. Lachie already knew a bit about her parents. What would he say when he learned the rest? About Tommy? About being kicked out? About her son? Would she be able to let the people around her in? Would she let them heal her even more? Or would she be like Doug Parker? Resistant to help and stubborn till the end?

Lachie was looking at her, still smiling, still looking

like he had something else to say but the words were caught in his throat.

There was so much she wanted to say, too, but she wasn't sure she'd be able to say it eloquently enough— just what it meant to her that he'd welcomed her the way he had. To the job, to the island, to his family. To curry nights on Mondays and meals with his mother and son. For trusting her to take on patients he'd cared for for years in their own homes. But also for keeping her confidences. Especially on a small island such as this.

'Lachie, I—'

But before she could say anything else, they heard footsteps come running down the corridor and Junebug appeared behind her. 'There's been an accident!'

'Where?' Lachie asked.

'On the coastal road, near Glencarrig. Two cars in a head-on collision.'

Cass turned to look at Lachie. There were no ambulances on Gulray. Just them. 'What do we do?'

He looked straight at her. 'We attend. Is the air ambulance on its way?'

'Control called and said it's been dispatched, but it won't get here for another half hour. The voluntary fire team are being assembled, but you two are on your own until then.'

'Then let's go!'

'How far is Glencarrig from here?' Cass asked as she put the go-bags, oxygen and emergency defibrillator into the boot of his car.

'About seven minutes away by car, but in these conditions, maybe a little longer.'

It was still raining heavily and if the accident had occurred in the stretch of road he suspected it might have, then they could be about to walk into a devastating event. The coastal road meandered gently along the isle, but just before the small settlement known as Glencarrig, where maybe a hundred people lived, there was a sharp, blind turn. If you weren't familiar with it, then it would be easy enough to come off the road and into a ditch.

But this was a head-on collision between two cars, so who had hit whom? And which of his patients was he about to find? Thankfully, he'd not been called out to many road traffic accidents in his career here on Gulray, but on the occasions he had, they'd been thankfully minor. Most of his emergency call-outs were for lacerations or farm accidents—one of the worst when Doug Parker had once gotten crushed against a barn by an amorous cow and broke a few ribs and punctured a lung. The old-timer had certainly had his fair share of trouble.

'Ready?'

Cass nodded, her face full of apprehension. 'You're going to have to tell me how to perform emergency triage. I've never done anything like that before.'

As they drove towards the crash site, he began to fill her in on their priorities. 'Your first instinct will be to dash in and check on the victims of the crash, but we must fight that and ensure the scene is safe for us to work in. If the crash happened right on the bend, then we're going to have to put out cones and hazard lights to stop anyone else on the road hitting us before we can work.'

'Of course. I didn't think of that.'

'We'll need to be aware of environmental hazards, too. All this water on the roads is a skid risk, there could be fuel leaks from the car, risks of ignition. We'll want to put on our high-vis vests and helmets. They're in the boot of the car.' He glanced at her and saw the terrified look on her face. Wanting to reassure her, he reached out and briefly grabbed her hand with his, squeezing it tight. 'Don't worry. We'll be okay.'

She nodded quickly.

Reluctantly, he let go. He needed both hands for driving and he needed to concentrate, so that they didn't end up in an accident themselves! And holding her hand had been distracting in many ways he couldn't give time to think about right now. He hoped this wasn't a serious accident. He hoped that the worst they'd find was a couple of cases of whiplash and a calm discussion about swapping details of car insurance. The desire to drive fast and get there quickly was also an impulse he had to fight, as he needed to get them there in one piece and he had no legal right to speed.

They passed the road sign for Glencarrig, carried on through the small village and out the other side and as they neared the site of the accident, he saw through the blur of rain on his windscreen two vehicles crumpled into one another, right on that dangerous corner. His stomach dropped with dread. Onlookers had gathered—no doubt to try to help, but they were all in the road, huddled under umbrellas and were at risk themselves.

Parking the car, they got out and after opening the boot, donned the PPE that they'd need to operate this site safely. 'Can you get people off the road? If they want to help, they can put out the traffic cones and hazard lights, but establish a boundary and keep them out.'

Cass nodded and darted off into the rain as Lachie

grabbed the medical equipment he might need. He recognised one of the cars and he was trying to remain calm, telling himself that maybe it was a coincidence? Maybe it was just a tourist that had the exact same car as the person he suspected it belonged to and that maybe she was safe at home, in the warm and dry, blissfully unaware of the dread beating of his heart?

As he approached, he assessed the scene. He saw no telltale rainbow effect in the slick of the road, which might indicate a fuel spill. There was no smoke coming out of either car, so he didn't think there was a risk of fire, and Cass had established a safe perimeter and was running to join him. He headed for the car he recognised as it was closest. He would analyse and triage each of the passengers and drivers in each vehicle and decide who to treat first until the air ambulance arrived in… He glanced at his watch. In the next twenty minutes?

The red hatchback with the Gulray Wildlife Reservation sticker that he recognised in the side window belonged to Nic, and he could see her mop of blonde hair inside, mixed with red. The engine block of her car was crushed and there were cracks across her windscreen from the impact of the two vehicles. He saw someone beside her—Matt, who looked unconscious.

'Check his airway,' he instructed Cass, who'd returned to join him, breathless and pale, as he pulled open the driver's door to assess Nic.

Nic was conscious, but confused and in pain. Though she was wearing her seat belt, she might have hit her head on the side window as her car had spun from the collision. Opposite, Cass pulled open Matt's door.

'He's breathing! Oh my God! The baby!'

He glanced in the back seat and saw that little baby Daniel was strapped into his car seat, crying. Lachie had been aware of the noise, but a crying baby was a good sign. It meant airway; it meant consciousness.

'Check him over.' He laid a hand on Nic's arm. 'Don't turn your head. Run it down for me.'

'They were on the wrong side of the road! They—'

'*Nic*. Tell me what hurts. What are your injuries?'

'Right. Right. Is Daniel okay?'

'Cass is checking him now. Tell me about you.'

'I need to know that Daniel is okay!'

Lachie looked to the back seat, at Cass detaching the baby seat from the belt and lifting it from the car. 'She's checking him, Nic.' He knew she wouldn't be able to concentrate until she heard about her son. Of course Daniel was her first thought. Ronan would be his if he'd been in a similar accident. And so, he performed a quick primary survey. She was using her arms without pain. Her legs shifted without her crying out. The only injury he could see was a laceration to her head, but that didn't mean there weren't any internal injuries.

'I need you to keep still for me,' he said, placing a cervical collar around her neck, then he rushed to the other side of the vehicle to do the same for Matt. It would keep his airway safe until backup got there.

'Matt? Matt, are you okay?' Nic called out, now unable to turn her head.

'Hold his hand for me. I just need to check the other car.' Lachie glanced over at Cass on the side of the road. She'd pulled baby Daniel from his car seat and was checking him over, so he could only go by the cursory glance at her face. She looked frightened but relieved and so he could only assume that Daniel was fine. But he needed her help.

'Pass Daniel to Mary! I need you,' he instructed.

He'd seen Mary Connors standing there. She was a woman in her sixties who lived in Glencarrig. She had many grandchildren and he could trust her to look after the baby whilst Cass helped him on scene. He waved to get Mary's attention, and the older woman took Daniel from Cass's arms.

Cass ran over to him as he assessed the people in the other car. He'd never seen them before. Tourists to the island? Visitors? But the car was an older model and more compacted by the crash. An older couple was inside. A man driving. A female passenger. The man had lots of chest pain and was struggling to breathe and the woman seemed confused and frightened.

'Check the woman,' he said, sending Cass to the far side of the vehicle.

It was still pouring with rain, which wasn't making the situation any easier, but he managed to get out of the man that his name was Richard and that he had asthma.

It made him think of Ronan. Of his struggles with the condition. 'Is it controlled?'

'Yes, but my chest hurts.' *Could be from the seat belt compression during the crash*, he thought. *Could be his asthma. Could be a heart issue caused by the stress and shock.*

'Anything else hurt?'

'My back and my neck.'

At that moment, Lachie became aware of another sound. Something that he couldn't quite pinpoint, and then he realised it was a helicopter, looking for a place to land. *The air ambulance! Thank God!*

They'd made good time. Had they been able to fly around the storm? Or through it? Either way, they would have backup soon enough. Another doctor at least. The downdraught from the helicopter was incredibly strong as it passed over them.

'I'm going to put a collar around your neck. It's probably just whiplash, but we can't be too careful. What's your wife's name?' He'd heard Cass asking the older woman her name, but had just gotten nonsense from her.

'Thea. Her name's Thea. Is she all right?'

'A little confused. Did she bump her head?' Cass asked.

'I don't know.'

Lachie had begun to attach an adult mask to the oxygen and now he placed the mask over Richard's face to help his breathing. 'How are we doing, Cass?'

'I don't know. She might have concussion.'

'She'd begun to talk strangely right before the collision. I'd turned to look at her and that's when I lost control,' Richard said.

Lachie frowned. '*Before* the crash? You're sure?'

'She said she had a headache and then she went all weird.'

A stroke? It was a real possibility. 'Are either of you on any medication? Any medical history I need to know about?'

'I'm on blood thinners. Thea takes statins and a thyroid medication.'

Probably levothyroxine. But he couldn't assume. He passed a cervical collar to Cass to put on Thea. 'Stay with them. Keep them talking. I'm going back to Nic and Matt.'

'Okay.' Cass nodded.

He could see that she was frightened, but she was holding it together for him and he was incredibly proud of her in that moment. She'd probably never imagined a situation like this when she'd accepted the posting to Gulray. It was one thing to see patients in clinic, or in their homes to change a dressing or perform a blood test—quite another to have to attend a road traffic accident and be a first responder. To see people bleeding from head wounds, or trapped in their cars. Now he heard sirens. The single fire engine that came from Kilmarrin was operated by a small team of volunteers made up of two local police officers, two farmers, George from the baker's shop and Al, who also volunteered on the lifeboats.

Lachie could feel his own heartbeat slowing, could feel the stress of the situation now being shared by others. The fire crew would have taken longer to assemble, having to wait for everyone to get to the station, but he was glad they were here now. They would stabilise the vehicles, take care of clearing the roads afterwards. They would make the scene safe. The two police officers on crew would also be able to take any witness statements.

They didn't need the fire crew often, but when they did, it worked and Lachie was most grateful for their assistance.

Nic was crying when he got back to her, shivering and shaking as the shock of the accident set in. Matt was coming round, but seemed woozy and confused.

'You're going to be okay. Just hold still.' He turned to update the helicopter team, sharing his primary assessment of Nic, Matt, baby Daniel, Richard and Thea. As the air ambulance team set to work, he turned, looking for Cass, and saw her under Mary Connors's umbrella with baby Daniel in her arms, smiling and cooing. He breathed a sigh of relief that the baby seemed to be okay.

He waved to catch her attention and she headed over. 'Can you show Nic that her son is fine?'

'Of course.'

Lachie held Nic's hand for reassurance as Cass showed the other woman that her baby was doing all right, then he laid a hand on Cass's shoulder to gently suggest that she stand off to the side, whilst everyone else worked, keeping the baby safe.

'I should call Nic's family. Or Matt's. Do you have their numbers?' she asked.

'M-Matt doesn't have any f-family. We're it. And my parents are in Arbroath for a w-wedding,' Nic said, shivering still from the shock and adrenaline of the accident. Her teeth were chattering.

'We're going to want to take you all in to the hospital on the mainland,' said the doctor from the air ambulance. 'I don't think there are any serious injuries here, but it's just in case.'

Nic had tears appear in her eyes. 'Who will look after Daniel?'

'I will,' said Cass, stepping forward. 'I can take care of him until your parents get back.'

'Thank you!' Nic cried.

Lachie smiled, relieved. He would have offered himself, but with Ronan and his own mother to take care of, he wasn't sure he could take care of Daniel, too. He was grateful to Cass for stepping up and he had to admit, she did look like she knew what she was doing. Clearly she was no stranger to holding babies. She looked at home doing it. She looked happy holding him. Content. He had a flashback to when Cass visited Nic after the birth and how she'd held Daniel and cried and he'd passed her his handkerchief. He realised, in that moment and now, she'd looked different.

Like a mother.

Whole. Despite the tears. Like this was what she wanted—needed—more than anything. The longing in her eyes, sated.

There was a story there. He was sure of it.

'You should go sit with him in the car. Get out of the rain,' he said, reaching for the baby bag from the back of Nic's car and draping it over Cass's shoulder.

It seemed an age before Lachie joined her in his car. But an age in which she could stare down at this beautiful baby boy and enjoy holding him and caring for him, just the two of them. How long had it been since she'd sat with a baby on her lap facing her, playing peekaboo or clapping his little pudgy hands? Marvelling at the softness of his skin and watching with joy and happiness as he finally fell asleep in her arms?

This moment, despite its origins, was perfect and it filled a hole in her heart that she'd been desperately trying to ignore for years.

Silently she watched as Nic, Matt, Richard and Thea were taken away to the mainland for proper checks as the fire crew team unblocked the Glencarrig road. Then she saw Lachie walking towards the car, Daniel's car seat in hand, spent and exhausted as the last of the rain finished for the day. He looked wet and tired and her heart ached for him.

He opened the back passenger door to install the car seat and looked over at Daniel sleeping. 'He okay?'

'Aye. He's good,' she said with a smile. 'Is it all done now?'

'Aye. Everyone's gone off for checks. Matt will probably be kept in for longer than Nic, because of losing consciousness, and I have strong hopes that Richard will be okay, but Thea? I think she was having a stroke just before the accident.'

'Oh no. Poor thing. I hope she's okay.'

'I'll call the hospital later for an update. We should get you and the little one back. Don't worry about your afternoon clinic. I'll see your patients.'

'There were only one or two. Nothing major.'

He nodded. 'Want to pass him over, so I can get him strapped in?'

'Sure.' She didn't really want to let him go. Or wake him. She was finding it difficult to share him. He seemed so at peace after the drama of this morning. But she passed him over and Lachie got him strapped in safely.

'Are you staying in the back with him?'

She nodded.

Lachie got in the driving seat and slowly did a three-point turn and began driving back to Kilmarrin.

If her own son had lived, he would not be a baby anymore, of course. He'd be a strapping teenager. No doubt a tall lad and beginning to become his own person. All she'd had with him were the first few days of his life and she'd replayed those few hours when she'd thought he was fine, over and over in her mind. Had there been

signs of what was to come? If she'd had her nursing training by then, would she have noticed his hypoxia earlier?
The first weeks, after he'd died, were the biggest blur,
though, thankfully. So to get moments like these, where
she could just spend time with a baby, was precious, because she knew how fleeting it could be. Nic and Matt
had been lucky today that no harm had come to their son,
because if it had, they would never have forgiven themselves, even though the accident had not been their fault.

'I've called Nic's parents and they're on their way back.
Reckon they'll be back by late this evening. They want
to call in at the hospital to see Nic and Matt first. Then
they're going to travel back to Gulray on the ferry.'

'That's fine. I don't mind looking after Daniel until
then.'

He nodded, glancing at her in the rear-view mirror.
'You have a fine bond. A way with bairns.'

She smiled, feeling happy at his compliment. 'I enjoy
babies.'

'You ever thought to have one of your own?'

She sucked in a sharp breath, unable to look up at him
and meet his gaze now. She was thirty years old. She'd
spent the last thirteen years missing her son like crazy.
Thinking of him every day. She'd had one of her own.
And lost him. 'Doesn't everybody?'

'I guess everybody considers it at one point.'

She looked up at him. 'Do you ever think that one day
you could give Ronan a brother or sister?'

Lachie laughed. 'I'd have to meet someone pretty
damn special before that could happen. And on Gulray?
My options are limited.' He paused. 'Honestly? I'm not
sure I could be ever ready for that. Inviting someone new

into Ronan's life? Replacing his mother? I think we'd have to leave the island for that to happen.'

'Does he remember her?'

'No. He was still very much a baby when she passed.'

'It must have been difficult,' she said, thinking of the days she'd endured after her own son had passed. The level of her grief and the feelings of loneliness had been incredibly hard to bear, even with Aunty Morag's support. She couldn't imagine losing a loved one, but also having to take care of a baby. 'You had family to help you?'

'My mother and Meghan's parents were amazing. I wasn't functioning very well and they took on a lot of Ronan's care in those early days. Taking turns and making sure I ate and encouraging me to spend time with my son.'

She envied him again. Even in grief. That his family rallied around him. She'd had one phone call from her parents—their main message being it was probably for the best. And that now she'd be able to carry on with her life. They'd not even visited. Had never mentioned him afterwards.

Their cruel, uncaring words had been the final severing of her ties to them and she hadn't spoken to them since. No birthday or Christmas contact. Nothing. She could hardly bring herself to believe that she was even related to them anymore and that was fine now. She'd had to do it and it had taken her many years to do so. The millstone that had been her familial pain hanging around her neck was gone and they couldn't hurt her anymore. She'd moved on from the pain they'd caused her.

'I'm glad you had them to support you. And Nic will

have her family to support her and Matt. Do you think Richard and Thea have people?'

'I don't know. But I'll certainly keep in contact with them and check in on them in the days to come.'

'You're a good man,' she said, locking eyes with him through the rear-view mirror.

'Thanks. And I couldn't have gotten through this morning without you by my side. I'm glad you came to us, Cass.'

She felt her heart thud at his words. Felt colour bloom in her cheeks. She was glad she was here, too. Here on Gulray and here with him. She looked back down at the sleeping baby Daniel. His chubby cheeks. His innocent bliss, oblivious to all the drama that had surrounded him this morning. Thank goodness that he was too young to be traumatised by today's events. His parents would be. They'd remember it forever more. But Daniel? He'd only hear of it and have no memories of it. That was a good thing for him, because memories could be painful. They'd taught her that many times.

'Are we heading back to the surgery?'

'Aye. Is that okay? Or would you like me to drop you off with the baby at home?'

'No. I think the surgery is probably best. That way we can all keep an eye on him and I'm sure Junebug will love the opportunity to spoil him rotten, if we get patients.'

Lachie smiled knowingly. 'She will at that.'

They drove for a few minutes more and eventually arrived back at the Kilmarrin surgery. Cass lifted Daniel in his car seat from the back of the car and draped his bag of essentials over her shoulder as she waited for Lachie to grab the go-bag from the boot. Together, tired and spent, they passed through the doors of the surgery together.

Junebug stood up from behind the reception desk. 'Oh, my loves! You're back. How was it? Wait? Whose is that wee bairn?'

'Nic and Matt's. They were in the crash,' Lachie said. 'Hopefully just minor injuries but they're being taken to the mainland for checks anyway, as Matt lost consciousness and Nic had a nasty laceration.'

Junebug gasped, her hands covering her mouth. 'Oh, the poor things! And the little one, is he okay?'

'He's been checked over by the paramedics and cleared. We said we'd look after him for the day, until Nic's parents get here tonight,' Cass said.

'Och, well, we can do that, can't we? All right. You two settle in—I'll pop the kettle on and make you both a brew. You must be shattered. I'm sure I can rustle up some cake or biscuits, too.'

'There's no need to go to any trouble,' Cass said.

'Oh, there is! Look at you both! You go get the wee bairn settled. Has he got milk or do you need me to go fetch some?'

'There's a bottle in his bag with expressed milk for his next feed, but if you could fetch enough to get me through the rest of today, that'd be great.'

'No problem. I'll take the mobile with me, so if someone rings through I'll be able to answer the phone, but I'll only be a couple of minutes. Now you both go rest. Put your feet up. Let me make you a cuppa.'

Cass felt love and appreciation for the way Junebug took care of them for the next few hours. The older woman bustled about her and baby Daniel like a busy bee, ready with a smile and a pair of warm, welcoming arms to hold the baby each time she went to the bathroom and when she had to see Greta Jamison with a suspected urinary tract infection.

Thankfully the surgery did not have a busy day. But it gave Cass time to sit and do stock orders and catch up on her admin tasks whilst Daniel slept. But the best times were when Daniel was awake and needed cuddling and holding. Those were the moments in which she felt a true peace in her heart. And as she gazed into his soft baby blues, she pondered on how much she'd changed since being here.

'Need a hand?'

She looked up from bouncing Daniel on her lap to see Lachie in her doorway and she smiled. 'I'm all good. Unless you're here for cuddles, of course. Baby cuddles,' she added with a blush.

'I think it's my turn. Come here, wee man.' And he lifted Daniel from her grip and held him against his shoulder. 'I've barely heard a peep from him all day.'

'He's a good baby. Very content.'

'Took the baby formula okay?'

'He was good with the bottle and between me and June, he's not had the opportunity to cry about being here.'

'She misses her grandson, I think.'

'She told me. Reuben.'

'It's difficult for her with him living down in Cardiff.'

'Mmm.'

He glanced at her. 'You've enjoyed babysitting, too. I can see it in your face.'

'Is it that obvious?'

'A little.' He smiled at her, swinging back and forth,

tapping Daniel's back until he let out a huge burp and deposited a small amount of baby milk onto Lachie's shoulder.

'Oh my! Stay there,' she said, grabbing for a muslin square and standing close to him to dab it away and clean his top. As she pressed at his shoulder, wiping away the milk, she was looking at Daniel, speaking to him in a sing-song voice as the baby boy mouthed Lachie's jumper. But then she looked up and met Lachie's gaze, and the mixture of being so close to him, touching him and gazing into his eyes was a very alarming experience.

She became so acutely aware of him, his masculinity, his stature and strength. She could feel his muscle through his clothes and she became aware of him in such a way that the dabs she was making to his top slowed, until just a wet patch remained. 'There. That will have to do,' she said, backing away, aware of her desire at that moment for much more. Alarmed by its intensity.

'Do you have nephews or nieces?'

'No. Why?' She fidgeted with the muslin, folding and refolding it.

'You just seem to know what to do.'

'Oh. I've just met a lot of babies in clinic.'

'That must be it. By the way, I called the hospital about Nic and Matt. They've been given the all-clear generally, but they're keeping Matt in for one more night, due to his concussion.'

'I'm glad there weren't more serious injuries.' She really was. Things like this in life just happened. Car accidents in the rain. A sudden stroke. Undiagnosed co-arctation of the aorta. You couldn't prepare for them and you would never be ready. Nic and Matt deserved

every happiness. They had each other. They had supportive parents. A beautiful baby boy. They deserved their
charmed life to continue on as such. It's what she would
have hoped for herself, having already suffered so much
trauma, but no, still the world had taken from her. It had
taken her first love, her family, her home and her son.
And afraid that it would continue to take from her, she
struggled to make connections.

And here life was showing her what she was missing
and what it would take from her when she left. Here she
yearned for what she didn't have, and being in this small
room with Lachie and baby Daniel was a glimmer of gold
in a world full of grey.

'They were lucky. Richard, the other driver? Not so
much.'

She looked up. 'What happened?'

'His wife, Thea. She'd had a devastating stroke, as I
suspected. She's been taken to surgery to have the brain
bleed stopped, but it's not looking good.'

Cass felt sorrow instantly for the older woman. 'Poor
Thea.'

Daniel chose that moment to begin his protestations,
drawing her attention back to him, and she reached for
him and Lachie passed the baby over.

It felt good to have the little boy back in her arms, but
for how much longer? Nic's parents would come to collect him eventually.

'He probably needs changing,' she stated.

'Want help?'

'That's all right, but you can stay if you want? I was
just about to grab something to eat.'

'Perfect. I'll go grab my lunch box from the fridge.'

* * *

Once Daniel had been changed and fed, he quickly fell back to sleep. Cass had made him a makeshift nest on her examination bed, surrounding him with pillows, and she stood over him like a protective guard, unable, it seemed, to tear her gaze away.

There was something about the way she looked at Daniel that spoke of an inner pain, and Lachie yearned to ask her about it, but didn't want to appear intrusive. Her whole demeanour had changed and the way she kept wanting to just check on him… Adjusting his blanket. Laying a hand upon his chest as if checking his breathing. Maybe she was just being conscientious? The little boy had been in a car accident this morning and she was probably just being careful and keeping an extra eye, but it felt more personal somehow. Like she was missing someone. But who?

'Come and eat your lunch,' he suggested. 'You need to keep fuelled up, too—you've had a stressful day.'

'I'm okay. I like watching him sleep.'

'Cass? Doctor's orders. You've had nothing since breakfast and possibly a biscuit from Junebug. You need to look after yourself, too.'

She turned to smile at him, acknowledging that he was probably right, and he felt much better when she finally sat next to him by her desk, even if she did keep glancing over each time Daniel snuffled or made a noise in his sleep. Cass opened her lunch box to reveal sandwiches, a strangely flavoured yogurt and a small bunch of grapes.

He, on the other hand, had made himself quite a grand salad, with cold new potatoes, chickpeas, boiled egg and a dressing of tahini and sweet chili sauce. He speared his fork into it and took a bite. 'Mmm. Just what I needed.'

Cass took a bite of her beef and horseradish and then nodded. 'Wow. I'd not realised how hungry I actually was,' she said, wolfing the first triangle of bread down.

'There have been times when I've forgotten to eat. Looking after Mum or Ronan. Have you ever done that?'

Her eyes darkened. 'Once or twice.'

'What kept you so busy you forgot to eat?' he asked good-naturedly.

'Oh, you know. Working.'

She wasn't telling him the truth. Work was a cop-out. He could tell by her tone and body language. He was getting good at reading her now. Why did she feel like she couldn't tell him the truth? Why did she continue to hide parts of herself away? She was entitled to her privacy, of course, but he'd hoped that he'd demonstrated that he was someone to keep her secrets. She'd already mentioned the issues with her parents, but he sensed there was more to the story.

'And the real reason?' he prompted.

Daniel's arms lifted suddenly and he moaned in his sleep and Cass leapt to her feet, face full of concern and he just knew.

It was because of a child.

Without a shadow of a doubt. But what child? Whose child? He didn't think it was a patient's. This was much closer to her, more personal. A member of her family? A close friend's? But she'd not mentioned friends ever. He sensed she was very much alone. Walled in by some pain or hurt that made her reluctant to trust him with her truth.

'What was their name?' he asked quietly. Maybe if he

just gently asked? Maybe if he showed no judgement? Then maybe she might tell him.

Cass took a sip of water from her bottle and looked at him. 'It doesn't matter.'

So she wasn't going to tell him. Okay. He had to respect that. Even if he still felt hurt that she couldn't confide in him. 'All right, so will you tell me one other thing, then?'

She sighed. Resigned. 'Like what?'

'Like how anyone can eat a toffee-and-hazelnut yogurt? I mean, what shop did you even *buy* that in?' He grinned, knowing he had to lighten the mood.

Cass laughed, grateful to him, he could see. She'd thought he was going to ask something else that was personal. 'The greengrocer's in Kilmarrin. They also do a lemon-cheesecake yogurt, for those with a sweet tooth.'

He smiled back at her, pointing his fork. 'I shall keep that in mind.'

CHAPTER SEVEN

AS THE DAY dwindled to its end, Cass decided that there was no point in staying at the surgery anymore and that she might as well get back home to her cottage with baby Daniel. She envisioned a wonderful evening of just the two of them. She could feed him. Bathe him. She'd never even gotten to give her own son his first bath, so that would be nice. So she was smiling when there was a knock at her surgery door.

'Come in!'

The door opened and there was Junebug. 'Ruth and Marcus are here, love.'

Ruth and Marcus? Cass was puzzled. She didn't have any patients on her clinic list. Her day was over. And then she realised, with a shadow that passed over her heart like a storm cloud. 'Nic's parents?'

Junebug nodded and opened her door wide to admit them.

An older couple came in and smiles filled their faces at seeing baby Daniel happily burbling away in Cass's arms.

'Thank you so much for looking after him!' Ruth said, reaching for her grandson and lifting him away from her.

Of course Cass had to give him up. She had no claim

on the baby. He was their grandson and her babysitting duty was officially over with their arrival.

'No problem at all,' she said, her arms painfully empty once again. 'He was a pleasure.' She reached out for one last piece of contact, to adjust his blanket.

'He was a good boy and he wasn't hurt at all?'

'No. He was protected by his rear-facing car seat very well. Both Lachie and I have monitored him all day and there have been no ill effects and he was checked by the paramedics, too, of course.'

Ruth was stroking the top of the baby's head and pressing kisses to his hair. 'Bless him, the wee mite.'

'You've made good time. I wasn't expecting you until later this evening.' Part of her had actually hoped that they would be delayed. Stuck in traffic, or deciding to stay at the hospital with Nic and Matt for longer. That she'd receive a call asking if it wasn't an imposition to ask her to look after him for the night.

'Oh well, Nic told us to come here first. That Daniel was her priority and she was fine and that she wanted her son with family.'

'Understandable,' Cass said. She'd have done the same, if she'd had a mother and a father that would have worried about her.

'We'll take him home with us. We've got a travel cot he can sleep in. Nic and Matt think they'll be sent home tomorrow, but we don't mind doing the night shift.'

'Of course.'

Why did she feel like she was going to cry? Why did it feel like her tears were threatening to fall? Bravely she tried to hold them back by gathering Daniel's things. His bib, the muslin square she'd used to mop up the milk from

Lachie's shoulder. A soft toy. His nappies and wipes and skin cream.

When she turned to hand them over, she saw Lachie appear in the doorway.

'Ruth. Marcus.' He greeted them both, kissing Ruth on each cheek and shaking Marcus's hand.

'Lachie! Oh, bless you! Thank you so much for taking care of my precious girl. Such a frightening call to receive when you're so far away.'

Cass was grateful that the attention was on Lachie right now. It gave her a moment, unnoticed, to breathe deep, gather herself and force back those tears. Why was she even getting upset? It wasn't like she was losing her own son again! This was a friend's baby. A colleague's baby. He just happened to have the same name as her son and it was only right that he went back to his true family. To his loving grandparents. Or maybe she was upset because this, like everything else on Gulray, just kept helping to remind her how little she actually had in her life. No mother to comfort her. No grandparents to rally round. Just stoic Aunty Morag.

I've never had community. No village helped me with my son.

When all the small talk was done, Marcus took the baby bag from Cass, thanked her once again and then he and Ruth left. She heard Daniel give a cute little baby sneeze as he went and it made her smile. She'd always loved baby sneezes.

Lachie turned to look at her and frowned. 'You okay?'

Were her eyes red? 'It's just been a long day.'

'I don't mean that. I mean whatever it is that's going on inside of you that you won't let out. I'm not asking you to tell me what it is, Cass. I respect that you want to keep your private life to yourself, but I just need to know that you're going to be okay.'

The softness of his voice, the timbre of it, was so caring and kind and full of consideration that the tears she'd fought so hard to push back broke through the dam and suddenly she was crying and sobbing, sinking into her chair by her desk and feeling absolutely mortified that she'd broken down like this. And not in a cute, lone-tear-down-the-cheek way. But a full-on snot-ridden, hiccuping, red-eyed bawl.

Cass became aware of Lachie softly closing her door for privacy and then he knelt beside her and passed her a tissue from the box on her desk. She blew her nose and wiped her eyes and gave a sardonic laugh at the ridiculousness of it all.

'I'm sorry,' she said eventually, when she was able to talk. 'I don't know where that all came from.'

'I do,' he said softly. 'From that dark place inside, where you've been keeping your emotions prisoner for probably far too long.'

She gave another laugh. Short. Sharp. 'And how do you know things like that?'

'Do you know how many patients I've had break down like that in my consulting room? It's not usually from something acute. But from pain they've kept hidden inside for ages and then someday some small thing comes along and it's the last straw. Their tether breaks and the floodgates open.'

He was looking at her with such empathy, such kindness. Passing her fresh tissues when the one she'd used initially had begun to break apart.

He made her feel like it was okay. He made her feel like she could tell him anything. And why not? He'd not told anyone about what she'd said about her parents. And doctors were good with confidentiality. Lachie was good. And something inside of her that she couldn't quite define told her that she needed to share with him what pained her.

'I'm a mother, Lachie,' she said quietly. Her voice wobbling on the word *mother*. A word that held such power, such strength, but one that she never usually allowed herself to utter. To admit to anyone. Most places she worked saw her only as a nurse. As a single woman who hadn't yet tried to settle down or have time for a relationship. Maybe they saw her as someone's daughter. But none of them would have known she was a mother.

Was.

Her gaze met his to see his reaction. She could see he was confused. Maybe he had questions. But rather than asking them, he just knelt there, quietly, waiting for her to say more, as if he knew this was going to hurt her to say.

'I had a son and his name was Daniel.' Her voice broke on his name. As if by saying it, it released all the pain and emotion all over again. Admitting him out loud made him exist again, but if he existed, then so did the hurt. The grief.

A sob escaped her and suddenly Lachie was holding her, his strong arms around her, holding her close as she wept into his shoulder and she could hear him making soothing noises, stroking her hair, telling her it was okay.

It took a while for her to catch her breath. Knowing now that the dam had broken, that she could tell him everything. It didn't matter anymore and with Lachie?

Her son did not deserve to be kept a secret. And as good as it felt to be in Lachie's protective arms, she knew she needed to tell him everything.

'I was sixteen years old when I discovered I was pregnant,' she began.

Lachie pulled up another chair and sat beside her, his hand holding hers for support.

'My parents were appalled. Ashamed. They kicked me out of the house when they found out. I was only two months gone. Personally I think it was just an easy excuse as I'd been made to feel like a burden forever anyway. I found myself on the streets, not knowing what was going to happen to me, until my Aunt Morag found me. She'd been called by a neighbour across the road who'd heard my parents yelling at me and slamming the door. My aunt was worried about me. She'd been through a similar thing when she was young and so she took me in. Gave me a roof over my head.' She paused to take in a deep breath. 'The baby's father, Tommy, he didn't want anything to do with me. Even said the baby probably wasn't his, which was a lie. He was the only person I'd slept with. Searching for love in all the wrong places, I turned to a guy who I thought loved me, when all he wanted was a little fun. Anyway, I moved to Lochgilphead and awaited the birth there.

'Aunty Morag wouldn't let me stay idle, though. She made me sit my exams at a college nearby. Got my GCSEs, so I could go to university at some point in the future. My pregnancy was fine. Normal. And when I went into labour, Aunty Morag sat by my side and watched me deliver Daniel into this world.'

Lachie smiled. 'Do you have a picture of him?'

Her heart skipped a beat. Yes, she did. She pulled out her mobile phone and scrolled to a picture of her holding him in the hospital.

Lachie's smile broadened at the photo.

Her smile in the photo had been broad, too. Until everything went wrong.

'Everything seemed fine to begin with. But ten hours after he was born, his breathing changed. His lips went blue and he became floppy and he got rushed away by the doctors for scans and tests. They poked and prodded him, took bloods, placed him on oxygen in the Special Care Baby Unit and told me that he had a coarctation of his aorta.' A coarctation was a narrowing of the aorta.

'Were they able to fix it?' Lachie asked.

Cass nodded. 'But they also discovered some other anomalies with his heart. It wasn't pumping as well as it should and I was told that he would probably need multiple surgeries as he grew.'

'That must have been terrifying for you.'

'Aye. He was the sweetest little thing. Blonde haired. Blue eyed. An angel on earth. I watched him all the time. Spent every moment with him that I could, but his heart couldn't take the strain of the surgery and he went into heart failure and he died. Barely two days old. No one could possibly describe the pain you feel on seeing such a tiny coffin. Or how empty your arms feel when they're gone.'

'Oh, Cass!' He squeezed her hand tight and then he was pulling her up into his arms and just holding her for such a long time.

It felt so good to be held by him. Safe. Protected. Cherished.

She felt glad that she'd told him. Glad that he knew. But letting go, even a little bit, released the torrent; everything else came flooding out with it and she began to cry for everything. Her lost childhood. Feeling so alone. Sitting shivering in a park waiting for Aunty Morag to arrive. Being driven to Lochgilphead and given more love and attention than she'd ever received in her life to date. Being scared of the future. Being afraid of labour and birth. If she'd be a good mum. And then finally the contractions in a hospital. Aunty Morag holding her hand and telling her she could do it. Sucking on that gas and air, being terrified of the strange waves of pain that coursed through every atom of her body. Giving birth. Being torn. Having stitches. Holding her baby boy...

Thinking that the worst was over.

Believing that the hardest part was behind her now.

Being wrong.

The funeral.

The goodbyes.

The knowing she had to carry on with her life, when all she wanted to do was hide under the duvet and cry. Aunty Morag forcing her out every day on walks she didn't want to take. Going to college to become a nurse. Keeping herself apart from others because she felt like her pain was an open wound and she didn't want to get it infected by other people and their drama. Getting her first job, making her barriers stronger.

Keeping out the world.

Keeping out people.

Keeping out the pain.

All of it. All that she'd kept cooped up for so long came rushing out in his arms and she cried and she cried and

Lachie held her tight. Stroking her back. Stroking her hair. Soothing her, until her chest stopped heaving from her breaths. Until her tears dried on her cheeks and they just stood there. Holding one another.

Breathing.

Lachie's heart *ached* for Cass. He understood her grief. Her pain. Her distress. He'd lost someone special, too, when he'd lost Meghan. But he knew he could never understand the pain of losing *a child*. A baby, really. And he didn't want to imagine how it might feel to lose Ronan. There'd been times, of course, when Ronan's asthma had become unstable, and to watch his own son gasp for breath and struggle to breathe was painful enough. To lose him completely? To never hear his voice again? Or smell his hair? Or feel his arms around his neck? He simply couldn't imagine the pain that would cause, or even if he would have the internal courage and strength to get over such a loss.

Cass had. And she'd gotten up and continued to function as a human being. Caring for others. Putting herself last. Finding a smile every day.

'I'm in awe of you,' he said quietly, whispering into the top of her hair, which was soft and silky beneath his lips. 'And you are strong. Amazing. I can't even begin to imagine...' He closed his eyes briefly, then reopened them. 'Thank you for telling me.'

She lifted her head to look at him then, and there was a moment in which their eyes met—hers, a little red still. All wept out. Gazing up at him with gratitude and thanks and...something else. A yearning. A desire.

He felt it, too. Her soft body against the length of his.

The heat of having her close and now aware of just how pressed together they were. How alone and unwatched they were in this little room. How anything could happen, now that both of their guards were down.

Lachie wanted to kiss her. Her lips were pale pink. Lush. Full. Parted as she looked at him. The logical part of his brain told him that now was *not* the time to kiss her! To take advantage whilst she was emotionally vulnerable was wrong. But the rest of him wanted to so much! When else would there be the time? They were always working, or he was with Ronan or his mother and…

Without thinking, he raised his hand slowly and used his thumb to brush over her parted lips.

He could sense her little intake of breath as she tilted her face into his hand, her eyes closing slowly. Blinking softly. Opening again, her pupils dilating at meeting his gaze.

'Cass, I…' He'd not kissed another woman since Meghan. He'd stayed true to her memory and he'd been fighting his attraction to Cass for all this time and yet here they were! Alone! Together! And this was a moment! Could he kiss her? *Should* he?

His body felt alive. More alive than it had felt for ages. Like he'd been sleepwalking through life and now he'd been jolted awake and aware, just for her. His pulse thrummed in his ears. Blood was speeding around his body like it was in a Grand Prix.

Would it hurt *either* of them to do this?

Would it *complicate* matters to do this?

She swallowed and where his hand was upon her neck, he felt the movement in her throat, could feel the pounding of her pulse there and he just couldn't help himself. It was Cass! And he felt so emotionally connected to her right now.

He narrowed the gap between them. Brought his face close to hers. Pressed his forehead to hers as they gazed into each other's eyes. His fingers were buried in her hair now and he could feel her warm breath upon his own mouth, could feel the intense yearning of his lips, that desire to connect.

He realised that they were softly swaying together. Almost like there was music somewhere. But the only melody was them and the tune was perfect.

Lachie could hold back no longer and he closed his eyes and pressed his lips to hers. Fireworks were going off in his body, electricity rippling across his skin and every nerve ending. Heat exploded in his groin as she moved softly against him, brushing against where he was most tender, and his body cried out for connection.

Her hands pulled him closer and she made a soft sound in her throat that fuelled the fire within him. Cass was the oxygen. His reason to breathe.

And it all felt so right.

So perfect.

Like this was meant to be. Like it had been ordained from the first moment that they'd met, when he'd first seen her standing in his staff room here. Dark brown hair swept up into a clip. Large brown eyes. Her soft smile. Her beauty. And that visceral reaction he'd had to first meeting her.

He should have known it would come to this. He had *tried* to keep his distance. Tried to be professional. Tried to welcome her just as he had every other member of staff he had ever worked with. Treat her like everyone else.

He should have known that with her it was always going to be an impossibility.

* * *

The next day that Cass walked into work, Junebug was busy adjusting a small bust of Cupid on her desk that was festooned with red hearts. 'What's that all for?'

Junebug turned and smiled. 'It's nearly Valentine's Day! Got to show the love!'

Valentine's Day.

Normally, Cass let that day pass without even worrying about it. It surely never had anything to do with her. She and Cupid's arrows had long since acknowledged that they would never meet. She was always happy for others to celebrate, if that was their thing, but she'd always go home and spend the night exactly how she wanted it.

Alone.

But yesterday she and Lachie had kissed and it hadn't been a kiss that friends share. That kiss had been... She sighed, feeling the warm glow wash over her at the memory of it. At how reliving it had kept her awake most of the night. How it made her smile just to think of it. How it had ended because there'd been a knock at her surgery door from Agnes and they'd leapt apart from one another like two naughty teenagers caught necking behind the bike sheds! How she'd bustled away and hurried home as Lachie had gone to help Agnes. She'd known it was cowardly. But she'd needed the fresh air.

Now she looked at the hearts and thought about Valentine's and wondered what that meant for her and Lachie.

I mean, it's not like we announced we are in a relationshi, or anything.

It was just one kiss.

One perfect, butterfly-inducing, heart-racing kiss.

She'd never been kissed like that before. Oh, she'd had

kisses with Tommy—of course she had—but looking back on them now, compared to Lachie's kiss, she could see that they were miles apart in technique and how they had made her feel. She and Tommy had been so young. Only sixteen. They were each other's first kisses, which was cute and everything, but it was just something they'd done. Cass had read more feelings into them than there had been, simply because she'd been so lonely and desperate for affection, but now that she looked back on it, poor Tommy hadn't been that great a kisser. Not compared to Lachie. Lachie's kiss had been heartfelt. Tender. Passionate. There'd been no innocence in that kiss. Instead, there'd been intent and desire and wonder. *Hunger.* Her whole body had come alive in response to it; she'd been greedy for more and to feel his arousal pressed up against her as their lips and tongues had danced had been a powerful thrill. A drug that she could easily become addicted to.

But what did it mean? She'd not had chance to speak to him after Agnes's interruption. She'd burbled some excuses, made noises about having to leave and how she'd see him tomorrow. She'd headed home and soaked in the bath and had thought about texting him, but she didn't want to seem too eager. Because what if it had just been a spur-of-the-moment thing for him? A crazy impulse that he regretted? She had no idea if there'd been other women for him since his wife died. They had to *work together.* She didn't want to make this awkward. She didn't want to read something into it that wasn't there. Because she did that and look at how devastated she'd felt when she'd realised that all of the feelings and all of the needs had been hers and hers alone?

'Well, the decorations look lovely. You're doing a great job,' she said, heading down to her consultation room.

'Love always puts a smile on people's faces!' Junebug called after her with a hearty chuckle.

Cass smiled. Maybe she was right. But love was scary. Love meant surrender. Love meant being vulnerable. Love meant that you could be hurt and she *didn't want* any of those things. Passion? Desire? Lust? Those were exciting. And perhaps they were safer than love? If Lachie wanted a sort of friends-with-benefits thing, would she be up for that? Possibly. He excited her. Stirred her blood with a heat that burned when she was with him.

Entering her consultation room, she switched on the computer and got her room ready. Then she went and made herself a mug of tea. As the kettle boiled, she heard voices out in the corridor and then Lachie was there, smiling, a little cautious as if he didn't know what to expect.

'Good morning, Cass. How are you?'

She smiled back at him, her heart accelerating at seeing him there. 'I'm good.' And she really was. Letting out all that emotion yesterday? It made her feel lighter than she'd ever been. Her soul unburdened and free. It was an amazing feeling and she wanted to keep it.

'How are you?' she asked, nervously, half expecting him to explain that yesterday was a mistake and could they forget about it? And how she'd smile and nod and say *of course!* Even if it would hurt.

He nodded. 'I'm good.' Lachie looked behind him to make sure they were on their own and then walked up to her, close but not touching. 'Are we…okay, after yesterday?'

Her gaze dropped to his lips. She couldn't help it. Felt

her blood pound once again at being this close to him. 'I am. Are you?'

His smile brightened his face. 'I am now that I know that you are.' Another glimpse behind him and he reached out, curling one finger around one of hers. 'I was worried it might be a little awkward, seeing as we didn't get to speak properly after.'

His finger around hers was causing all kinds of wonderful sensations and flashbacks to the kiss that made her want to pull him towards her once again and feel the press of his hard body against hers. But they weren't in the privacy of the consulting room here. They were in the staff room and anyone could come in at any moment. She would have to restrain herself. 'We're adults. We can be adult about it.'

Lachie smiled and nodded, gazing down at their fingers entwined together. As if he, too, were thinking of yesterday. Thinking of *more*.

It was exciting. This secret they shared, just the two of them.

'Hey, you two, I've got some heart streamers left over. Do either of you want them put up in your rooms?' Junebug said, walking in behind them.

Cass let go of Lachie's finger and beamed a smile at June. 'That would be great, thanks.'

Cindy Grey, a patient that Lachie had known for five years, ever since she'd moved to the island, sat down in front of him, looking nervous.

'What can I do for you, Cindy?'

'I want to be tested for the breast cancer gene. My mother died of it a few years ago, my aunt, Mum's sister, has had it twice, my older sister has just been diagnosed with it and it was suggested by her oncologist that the rest of us get tested, too, in case it's a genetic link.'

Lachie nodded. 'I'm sorry to hear about your mum, aunt and sister. How is she doing right now?'

'On her fourth round of chemo. She's hoping for surgery soon to remove the tumour.'

'And your mum passed from this?'

'Yes. It metastasised.'

'And your aunt?'

'First time she was diagnosed at the age I am now. She fought it and thought she was clear, but then it reoccurred and it's spread. I'm sure I'm fine, but I want to know my risks. I have two daughters and I need to know.'

He understood that. Cancer was a frightening thing, but doing genetic testing for the BRCA1 and BRCA2 genes themselves could take a psychological toll. 'Have you spoken to anyone about it?'

'I have online therapy and I've talked to my therapist about it for some months and I've finally decided that I do want to know. In case I have to do anything about it.'

He knew what she meant. Preventative surgeries. But they weren't there yet. 'Apart from your mum and sister, have there been any other cancers in the family?'

'My dad had prostate cancer, but he lived with that for many years.'

'And he's passed?'

'Yes. Two years ago.'

'And what age were your mother and sister when they contracted breast cancer?'

'Mum was fifty-eight and Laurie was forty. I'm thirty-nine, I want to see my daughters grow up and be healthy enough that I can enjoy their lives and be around for any grandchildren that may come along.'

He nodded, pulling up the Manchester Scoring System to assess her risk and began to input the data. Cindy scored above fifteen, the criteria for referring her to a specialist genetic clinic. 'I'll certainly make that referral for you.'

'Thank you, Lachie. I know it's scary, but I think anything worth it in the long run is worth taking the risk for and knowing for sure, don't you think?'

He nodded. Absolutely. He understood her impulse and need for knowledge. The not knowing would drive her mad and she'd always be anxious, constantly monitoring herself for any lump or pain or discomfort. If she could take positive action to keep herself safe, then maybe she'd feel better about her own future and that of her daughters.

After he'd waved Cindy goodbye, he thought about his own mother and her diagnosis of Alzheimer's. It was something he could test for, if he wanted to. At least to see if he carried the gene, but he'd decided not to. What good would it do him? He couldn't cut parts of himself away to reduce the risk and if his results were positive, then he'd worry so much for Ronan and what was the point in that? Lachie wanted to look to the future. He wanted to be positive and optimistic and he liked feeling good. The way Cass had made him feel yesterday. That was exciting and thrilling.

And those were the kinds of feelings he was happy to pursue.

Anything worth it in the long run is worth taking the risk for.

Could he do that? Could he be brave enough to take

the risk of being with Cass? If she even wanted him, that was. She wasn't going to be staying here forever. And if he allowed himself to feel the things he wanted to feel with her and then she left, never to be seen again, could he deal with that?

Or should he just hope, in vain, that his feelings would be strong enough to persuade her stay? He'd spent so long throwing himself into looking after his mother and his son, he never considered the possibility of love for himself again, and for a time he'd believed that if he just loved them enough, then nothing would happen to them.

But he knew now that that was impossible. His mum would get worse. He would lose her at some point. And when Ronan grew up, he'd move away and start his own life and then where would Lachie be? Alone.

So…maybe this thing with Cass might be worth pursuing. If she felt the same way…? Then maybe they could enjoy a short time together, because if he could accept that he'd lost his wife, was going to lose his mum and that he'd have to let go of Ronan, perhaps he could get his head around losing Cass, too? If he knew it was going to end, then he could prepare himself for it and be more accepting of it when she walked away?

The kiss had been explosive. It had been everything. Reminding him of what it was like to be with someone. She'd met him, heartbeat for heartbeat. Her response telling him that she felt the same way as he did. And then this morning, with his finger curled around hers, the way she'd looked at him had made him want to do all sorts of pleasurable things and it was all he could do to not think about her non-stop.

She knew his situation. She knew her own and the parameters of why she was here on the island and yet she'd kissed him back. What did she want from this? A fling? Simply some fun? Or did she hope for more?

Maybe, if he made it clear that this was just temporary, a comfort to both of them in the time that they had, then maybe she'd be up for it, too?

As morning clinic finished and Cass was just replacing the blue paper on the examination bed, Lachie appeared in her doorway. 'Got a minute?'

She straightened, happy to see him. 'Sure.'

He came in and closed the door behind him, making her heart pound in anticipation. And then he was stepping up to her, cradling her face and kissing her. Kissing her like he'd thought about it all morning. Kissing her like he could not go another minute without doing so.

His touch sent shivers of delight through her. His lips on hers igniting a fire that was almost impossible to douse.

But they were at work and eventually they broke apart.

Lachie smiled at her. 'How are you?'

She smiled, feeling all warm and fuzzy inside. 'I'm good. You?'

'Great.' He kissed her again. 'With you like this, I feel amazing. You make me feel unstoppable.'

Cass laughed. 'Well, that's awesome, because when you're kissing me, I don't want you to stop.'

He smiled, but then he paused and took a step back.

That step back told her that something was about to change. Had she done it again? Allowed her feelings to run off for someone, believing it was something more than it was? Was she about to be disappointed again?

'We need parameters, Cass. We need to know what we're doing here.'

Of course they did. It was sensible. Lachie came as part of a package deal.

'This. You.' He reached forward and took her hand in his. 'I don't want it to stop. I love how you make me feel alive again and it's fun, but I need to know…is that what this is? Just fun? Because you're only here on Gulray temporarily and I need to know where to draw the line with my feelings.' He laughed to himself. 'Because I can do temporary, if that's what you need. If you need to draw a line under us when you go, I think I can do that. But if you want something else…' He laughed. 'You're the most amazing person I think I've ever met in a long time and you're making me feel all these crazy things, but if you're going to leave in a few weeks, then I need to let my heart know, so that I don't go and do something crazy…' He paused, flushed red. 'Like fall in love with you. Because my heart can't take another beating. I can't deal with another loss, if I allow that to happen. So, we either stop this right now. Or we're just temporary and fun. Or…we're not.'

Wow. Cass almost took a step back herself. *Fall in love with her?* No. No, she couldn't let that happen. Because she would be leaving Gulray. She would be the one that would have to pack up and leave. Find the strength to walk away and it was much easier to do that, if you didn't have any strong connections. Or feelings for someone. 'We're just having fun, Lachie. Aren't we?'

He nodded, smiling. 'Yes, but… I'm not really a casual man. I don't do flings or one-night stands. I've always been the kind of guy that looks to create something long term and if I need to change that, to know in my heart that it's short term and temporary, then tell me now, because Valentine's is coming up, too, and I've always been a bit of a romantic.'

She loved that he was being honest with her. Warning her that he could fall hard and fall fast. And she loved that they were adult enough to talk about and define what they were doing, so that neither of them got hurt.

'I'm not casual, either. I fall hard and I fall quick, but… I'm not someone that can trust what they're experiencing is real. I always read far too much into it, so, for now, could we just be fun? I don't want this to end, but I know that *it will* and whilst we have this connection, then we should enjoy it for what it is. Just that and no more.'

He nodded. Smiled. 'Okay. Okay! So temporary, then! We both know that there's an end to this.'

'Yes. If that's all right?' She wanted to tell him otherwise. She wanted to tell him that she could easily fall in love with him and *want to stay*, but she was so terrified of getting it wrong. Of reading something into a relationship that wasn't there on his part. And even if it was there and she stayed on Gulray and uprooted her tiny life from Lochgilphead, what if it all went wrong? And Lachie realised after he'd gotten everything that he wanted from her, he no longer wanted her at all? Because that was her reality. That was what she was used to and she didn't think she could stand to be rejected by him.

'So…no hearts and flowers on Valentine's Day, then? No card declaring myself to be madly in love with you?'

She laughed, trying to show that she wasn't hurting inside. Wasn't *afraid*. 'Flowers might be nice.'

'Got you.' He stared at her for a moment and then

he narrowed the gap between them and was kissing her madly. Like she was his air and he was hers. The press of his lips on hers, every point of contact that they had, was *everything*. And just when she thought she wouldn't be able to breathe, he broke away from her and left the room.

And she felt awful that he'd gone.

Temporary. She wanted temporary. It wasn't until she said it that he'd realised he'd hoped for more, but if this was all she could give him, then he would have to deal with that. He knew it would be difficult to force his mind into a new way of thinking, but he would do it just to be with her, and he would somehow tell himself that it was enough.

But it hurt him that they couldn't be more. But he should have realised, right from the start, that those he loved never stayed.

As they left the surgery together at the end of the day, Lachie's mobile phone rang. Pulling it from his pocket, he saw that it was Siobhan, his mum's carer.

'Hi, Siobhan. Everything okay?'

'Physically, your mum's fine, but I've just got here and I don't know, she seems upset. The house is a mess! I don't suppose you could pop in on your way home?'

He felt his hope for some adult time with Cass fade. 'Sure. I'll be right there.'

'Okay, thanks.'

Siobhan rang off and Cass was looking at him. 'Everything okay?'

'Issue with Mum.'

'Oh no. Can I help in any way?'

'Would you mind picking up Ronan from after-school

club and taking him home? I'd rather he didn't see his granny upset.'

'Of course I will.'

'I'll call the school, let them know that you'll be there to pick him up instead of me.'

'Okay.'

'Know the place?'

Cass smiled. 'I do. Now go. Go see your mum and I hope she's okay.'

He thanked her and then as he walked to his mum's cottage he dialled through to the school and told them about the new pickup. Hopefully, the issue with his mum would be simple, but he was beginning to wonder if she needed carers full-time. Right now, she had four visits a day and one overnight, but that meant there were short periods in the day when she was alone. Maybe that all needed to change?

He arrived at his mum's cottage and could already hear his mother from outside, yelling about something. When he got inside, he saw that contents had been pulled out of drawers, and the photos that had always been so lovingly lined up on the mantelpiece were scattered across the floor, as if thrown.

Siobhan was in the kitchen with his mum,who seemed tearful and stand-offish, arm out, palm up, warding Siobhan off from getting closer.

Lachie looked to Siobhan, then back at his mum. 'Mum? What's going on?'

'Jamie! Where have you been?'

Jamie. His dad. 'Mum? Mum, look at me. It's Lachie.'

His mum frowned at him and she looked confused, like she didn't recognise him. 'Who are you?'

'It's Lachie, Mum. I'm here.' He tried to approach, but clearly she was terrified and backed away, so he stopped.

'No! Lachie's little! Jamie, why didn't you answer the phone? I've been calling and calling!'

Who had she been dialling? It wasn't like his dad had had a work phone out on the boat and he'd died way before mobile phones were a thing. He made a note to check his mum's phone bill later, to see if he needed to apologise to anyone.

'He's out on the boat, Mum. Remember? He's gone fishing, like he does every day and sometimes he's gone for a long time.'

Her fevered gaze switched back to him.

'They said he was dead!'

His stomach dropped. 'What? No. No, that's not true. Listen, do you think he wants to see you like this when he gets home? Do you think he wants to see his house look like this? And you all upset? Why don't we go in the living room and get you settled on a chair, okay? And then me and Siobhan will clear the place up a bit.'

She calmed down a little. 'And make me a brew?'

He nodded in response. 'Yes. We'll make a brew and get you one of your favourite biscuits, how does that sound?'

'And then Jamie will come home?'

It broke his heart to see her like this. Knowing that he was losing her, memory by memory. 'Yes, then he'll come home, much later, though, probably after you've had a sleep.' This was classic sundowning. It could happen to patients with dementia. Confusion and agitation increasing in the late afternoons or evening.

She allowed him then to take her hand and slowly,

gently, he guided her back to her chair. She was shivering and shaking. Clearly she had gotten really worked up. How many times would he have to do this?

Lachie guided her over to her favourite chair and got her settled, pulling a blanket over her lap and asking Siobhan to make the tea. He sat and held his mother's hand, stroking it, noting how thin her skin had become. How friable. How prominent the veins. Her nails needed trimming. He'd ask Siobhan to do that later.

He looked up at his mum and smiled. He was losing her to this disease. He'd lost Meghan quickly and now he was losing his mother slowly. He wasn't sure which was worse. But if his mum was getting violent outbursts, would it be safe to bring Ronan to see her? What if she flipped out on him? He was only young; it would terrify him. Upset him and he needed to protect his son from any of that.

Or maybe it was time to consider putting his mum into a home. Accepting her situation. Accepting his own limitations.

Accepting that he needed to focus on building a bright future for his son and possibly moving to the mainland, sooner than he'd expected, even though the idea of leaving Gulray broke his heart.

CHAPTER EIGHT

'CASSIE!' RONAN RAN right into her arms at school pickup. Laughing, she scooped him up and swung him around in the air, before putting him down again.

'Oof! You're getting bigger. Did you grow since I last saw you?'

Ronan laughed. 'Dad says I grow bigger every night.'

'I think that might be true. Do you think you're like bamboo?' She knelt down to face him and said in a whisper. 'If we're really quiet, do you think we could actually hear your bones growing?'

Ronan looked intrigued and listened hard. 'Can't hear nothing!'

Cass sighed, like she was truly disappointed. 'Oh well! Just a normal human being like the rest of us. Ready to go home?' She held out her hand and he took it.

'Yeah! Where's my dad?'

'He had to go see Granny.'

'Oh. Dad says Granny's got something wrong with her memories. That they get all mixed up.'

'That's right.' She didn't want to explain too much. She had no idea of how much Ronan understood his granny's condition, or how Lachie had chosen to explain it and it wasn't her place to say more. 'So, what did you do at school today?'

'Er, we had carpet time and were read a story and then we did some PE in the hall with the bars and benches and things and then we did some painting and played outside and then Miss Dale let us play in the music room.'

'Wow! Sounds exhausting! Are you tired?'

'No!' he answered brightly. 'But I am hungry! What's for dinner?'

She laughed. 'I don't know. We'll have to see what your dad's got in the fridge when we get home.'

'Can I have biscuits?'

'Hmm, I don't want you to spoil your appetite.'

'Just one?' he whined.

Cass smiled down at him. 'Maybe a small one. If you're good and get changed when we get in.'

'Okay!' Ronan skipped happily by her side, chatting all the way home, holding her hand.

If felt good to be walking him home. She'd never picked a kid up from school. Never walked one home in her entire life and she liked it. Liked the way it made her feel. Like she was a mum and this was what it felt like. She'd seen others do it, obviously. Watched streams of parents and their children issue from school gates as she was driving home herself and often felt envious. And yet here she was. With Lachie's wonderful son and with what was happening between his father and herself, it was all too easy to pretend that actually Ronan was *her* son and they were a family.

But she knew she was only pretending. Borrowing a child. Borrowing another family. If Daniel had lived, she'd have done this. She'd have settled somewhere and Daniel would have skipped home from school with her every day. She'd have had these chats with him. Holding his hand to cross the road. Looking both ways to watch for cars. Having certain things pointed out to her that took his fancy. Being asked about biscuits before dinner. Maybe he'd have wanted to invite some friends over? Maybe she'd have a whole house full of children running around? Who knew how different her life could have looked if he'd survived?

Unlocking the cottage with the key Lachie gave her, she let Ronan in and was instantly greeted by Frosty the cat, who weaved between her legs, clearly happy that she was at this house, too. Once she'd dusted the white fur off of her navy trousers, she hung up Ronan's book bag on his peg and asked him to go upstairs and get changed and whilst he did, she headed into the kitchen and switched on the kettle. She would make a tea and maybe enjoy a biscuit herself, too. After all, she had no idea how long Lachie would be and she was hungry.

As if manifesting him, her mobile rang and she saw his name. 'Hey, how's it going with your mum?'

'She got a bit confused and upset. It's taking some time to calm her down and now I need to clear up. I know it's an imposition, but could you get Ronan something to eat? I'll be home as quickly as I can.'

'It's no imposition at all. Ronan and I are having a great time. You do what you have to do and get your mum settled. We're all good here, okay?' She meant it, too. She was loving spending time with his son. And the longer she stayed? The less time she had to spend alone at home.

'Thanks, Cass. You're sure? I know it's asking a bit much.'

'Absolutely!' she said with a wide smile. 'Take care of your mum. I've got this end.'

'You're the best.'

His compliment brightened her heart. Gave her warm and tingly feelings inside.

'So are you.'

It took him a long time to fix his mum's house and return things to their natural place. A couple of photo frames had shattered and were beyond repair, so he made a mental note to get her new ones and in the meantime he just propped the photos up in place against an ornament. Then, as he had no rush to get home, he cooked his mum something and decided to stay and eat with her, wanting to spend as much quality time as he could with her. Clearly today she was struggling with time and place and it wasn't until they were eating that she seemed to recognise him again.

'You're a good boy, Lachie.'

He smiled. 'What I am is all down to how you raised me, Mum. You did a great job.'

'You made it easy for me.'

He stayed and watched some television with her and then with the night carer's help, they got her ready for bed. Lachie sat and read to her until her breathing became soft and regular and then he kissed her on the forehead and crept downstairs.

It was only eight thirty and he'd probably missed Ronan's bedtime, unless the little tyke had somehow persuaded Cass that his bedtime was much later. 'Call me if there's a problem,' he said to his mum's night nurse.

'Of course. Don't you worry about us. You go home and get some rest yourself.'

He walked home and quietly slid his key into the lock, not wanting to wake Ronan if by any chance he was asleep. The table lamp in the hallway was on, but everywhere else was in darkness. Removing his coat, he hung it over the banister and slipped off his shoes, before silently climbing the stairs and heading for Ronan's room. Maybe Cass was in there reading her son a story?

But he couldn't hear any voices, only his son's white noise machine that he liked to have on. Ronan's bedroom door was ajar and he stepped into the darkness, letting his eyes adjust to the dim light and then felt his heart fill with joy when he saw Ronan and Cass fast asleep in bed, with Cass curled around him, on top of the covers.

For a moment he just stared down at them both, feeling love in his heart for the sight of the two of them. This was what Ronan missed out on. A mother figure who would fall asleep with him at night. Someone other than his father. So that he enjoyed the presence of two parents and not one and didn't feel like the odd kid out at school. He knew that Ronan was the only kid on Gulray his age who didn't have a mother and he knew that he missed that. So this? This was something special, even if it was only temporary.

How would Ronan feel when Cass was no longer around?

Should he wake her? It was probably the best thing to do, even though he wanted nothing more than to clamber onto the bed and join them. Even though there was no room left. But he felt like she'd already done far more for him today than she ought to have done, considering their relationship.

He crept forward and laid a hand softly on Cass's shoulder. 'Hey,' he whispered.

Her beautiful eyes blinked open in the dark and the first thing she did was check that Ronan was still asleep, then she turned and looked at Lachie, all sleepy and smiley. 'Hey.' Cass sat up, rubbing at her eyes. 'Sorry. I didn't realise I was that tired.'

He took her hand and led her from the bedroom, pulling his son's door closed behind him, then he turned towards her in the dark. 'I'm sorry I was late.'

'No problem. How was your mum?'

'Confused, but I think she's okay now.' It felt good to be standing there with her. The comfort of her hand in his. Someone to console him after the drama.

She smiled. 'Good. I saved you some food. You hungry?'

He shook his head. Not for food, no. 'I ate at Mum's. But thank you anyway.'

'Oh, okay.'

What was it about standing here with her in the dark? In his own home? Staring into her eyes? Why did he suddenly feel afraid of his feelings here? Because the last woman he'd kissed in this house was his own wife? And he was only a few feet from the bedroom that they had once shared?

Cass seemed to sense his uncertainty and she simply slipped her arm through his and led him downstairs.

Downstairs, in the light, seemed much safer and he pulled her into his arms in the lounge and began to kiss her. 'I've missed you.'

'You were only gone a few hours,' she said softly, kissing him back.

'Too long. We never know how much time we can be together. Every second counts.'

Cass laughed, exposing her throat, and he took the moment to trail his lips along it, tasting her, breathing her in, allowing his senses to fill with her. It was dizzying. He felt almost drunk with her delicious scent.

He felt her pull his shirt from his trousers and then her hands were upon his hot skin and they felt so good. He, in turn, needed to touch her and so he began to explore beneath her top, pulling it free, feeling the softness of her skin, the smoothness that so aroused him as he inhaled her gentle perfume and allowed his hands to caress her breasts through her bra, feeling her nipples form into soft peaks as he rubbed his thumbs over them and she moaned, pulling his lips back to hers.

He could lose himself in her. He knew this. He was like a starved man being offered a table groaning with the finest desserts. There was so much. It was overwhelming to his senses and he wanted everything at once, but also to go slow and savour every delicious bite.

And then they were moving somehow, staggering over to the couch, unable to let each other go, and they tumbled backwards with a laugh and a giggle, slumping into the cushions. Cass clapped a hand over her mouth to be quieter and he pulled it away and kissed her some more, his arousal pressing into her as he crushed her body with his. This wasn't enough. He needed more.

Somehow clothes began to be undone. Removed. His head was dizzy with delight and desire. He felt her hand reach for him, embrace the length of him and he moaned with pleasure and felt himself truly come alive for the first time in a very long time.

How long had it been? Years since a woman's touch had inflamed him. The last time had been with Meghan and now it was with Cass and he thought he might feel guilty, but the feeling of guilt never came. All that mattered was her and her alone.

He slipped into her and she gasped, pulling him closer and somehow, maybe someone kicked out, but a lamp by their feet got knocked off a table, not that he cared in that moment as he moved above her, both of them breathing heavily, both of them—

'Dad? Are you home?' a voice called from the top of the stairs.

Lachie and Cass broke apart so quickly! Lachie stood up and zipped up his trousers and pressed his arousal down as Cass sat up and straightened her clothes, buttoning them up and clearing her throat and trying to act normal, grabbing at the lamp and straightening it, and then reaching for a magazine on the side table and pulling it open, pretending to be engrossed in an article as he hurried to the base of the stairs.

'Yes. I am. Go back to sleep, you've school in the morning.'

'Can I have a kiss goodnight?'

He let out a breath. What had he been thinking! With his son in the house! Imagine if Ronan had come down the stairs and caught them in flagrante? 'Of course.' He hurried upstairs and settled his son back to sleep, thanking every god that there was, that his son had not crept downstairs and caught him with Cass. It had been stupid to start something here.

As he sat there in the dark, watching another person that he loved fall to sleep, he realised that he and Cass needed to be careful. He had a son to think about here, too, and he knew Ronan loved Cass and would be upset when she left the island, so no point in letting his son think that she might stay.

Because she wasn't staying. She would leave.

And he needed to guard his heart in readiness for that.

Cass waited patiently for Lachie to come back down the stairs and when he did, she already had her coat on, signalling that she was going to leave. It was for the best. No need to let a little boy get a hope for a mummy that wouldn't be staying.

'I had a wonderful night,' she said, meaning it. And it had been the best night. Spending time with Ronan? Feeling like a mum again? She'd forgotten how wonderful it felt. How being with Lachie's son had made her remember a part of herself that she'd shut off many years ago. And then, just a few moments ago, a glimpse of what it might be like to be with Lachie. They would have great fun together, if given the chance.

But she'd be leaving soon. Nic hadn't planned a long maternity leave. She'd told Lachie, before she had her baby, that she would want to return to work quickly, and Cass had to remember that fact. Her time was almost up here. And they'd been foolish to do what they did.

'Sorry we got interrupted.'

Cass nodded and smiled. *Yeah*. 'But probably a very timely reminder that it's not just us we have to think about. That we need to be careful.'

'Mmm. Yes. Very wise.'

Cass did love Ronan. Damn it, she loved Lachie's mother, too! His whole family. This community! This tiny island. And Lachie? *I could so easily fall for him, too.* But she couldn't allow herself the privilege of that. Because she would need to sail away from here and start again someplace else and try to make herself forget how Lachie and Ronan and everyone else here made her feel!

'Well, have a good evening. Get some rest,' she said.

'You, too.'

She looked at him with longing. It was so hard to go when all she wanted was to stay and finish what they'd started. But they couldn't mess around here. He had a son to think about and she needed to think of Ronan, too. No matter how much she loved spending time with that little boy, she was going to leave him behind as well and the more she spent time with them, the harder it would be to walk away. She didn't want to hurt the little boy.

Time to go back to my empty cottage! Where I'm all alone.

She'd always thought that being alone had served her well. It had seemed logical and easier than anything else. But here she doubted the truth of that ethos.

They'd agreed to just fun and that was good, right? Fun equalled temporary. Fun equalled no one getting hurt when that fun had to end. They were being sensible.

And that was how it was going to need to be.

Cass kissed him quickly on the cheek and then left, walking away from his home, telling herself to not look back until his home was out of sight.

Agnes, their HCA, was Cass's first patient the next morning. She came in, looking sheepish and smiled a hello.

'Agnes! What can I do for you?'

The young girl placed a hand at her throat and when she spoke in a light voice that was almost indiscernible as sound, Cass learned that Agnes had been to a music concert on the mainland the night before and had now lost her voice.

Cass smiled. 'Oh my gosh, you poor thing! Was it a good concert?'

Agnes smiled and gave her two thumbs up. 'But I screamed and sang so much, I've lost my voice and I've got clinic soon,' she said, her voice, like a strained whisper.

'You've probably just overused it, or strained your larynx. Let me take a look at you.' Cass performed basic observations on Agnes. She had no obvious signs of illness and her breathing wasn't affected. She had no wheeziness and no stridor—a high-pitched breath sound caused by troubled air flow. Using her pen light, she examined the back of Agnes's throat. There was no redness, no swelling that she could see and no post-nasal drip. Palpation of her friend's neck revealed no swelling on the lymph nodes and no tenderness or masses that shouldn't be there. Her physical assessment looked good. 'Say "ee" for me.'

'Ee.'

'Say "ah".'

'Ah.'

They both came out like a breath.

Cass smiled at her. 'I think this is just a simple case of vocal fatigue. You did too much. Best thing to do is rest, try not to whisper as that just strains the vocal cords more, and have plenty of fluids. If you're overly worried, you could try steam inhalation, but I think good old-fashioned rest is what's required here.'

'Okay. Thanks. I guess I should have known that having fun will always come with a price, huh?'

Cass looked at her. Thinking about the fun that she and Lachie were having. Maybe it did? Even though she kept telling herself that she wasn't letting her feelings get involved, look at how hard it had been to leave Lachie's last night. It reminded her of the importance of keeping what they were doing as casual. Or maybe to stop it altogether? Was that the wisest course?

She forced a bright smile, pressed a finger to her lips. 'Rest your voice.'

Agnes gave her a hug, mimed a thank you and left.

Cass is just on the other side of this wall.

Lachie stared at the wall separating their two rooms even though he was meant to be reading Jed Simpson's patient notes in front of him before calling him in. Jed was a carer for his dad and so he felt an affinity with the man.

This was silly. This was crazy! He was a grown man, about to turn forty years old on his next birthday, and all he could do was sit there like a teenage boy dreaming about the girl next door! He'd lain awake most of the night, too, reliving that moment when they'd both fallen onto the couch and begun to pull at each other's clothes. What it had felt like. What he was going to do if they hadn't been interrupted by Ronan getting out of bed and calling from the top of the stairs. Had knocking over that lamp woken him? If they'd been more careful, would they have gotten to finish what they started? And if they had?

Would he still be telling himself that temporary fun was good enough for him?

Lachie sighed. Then stood and gazed out of the surgery window, out across the swoop of green fields and up to the rise of the hill beyond. At the dots of white that indicated sheep grazing on the grass. At a couple on the high rise, walking hand in hand, gazing at one another's faces. God, he'd missed that kind of connection! And to think he might have had it with Cass? His feelings weren't fun. For her they were serious; he could feel it, and he knew he was screwed.

I need to control myself. Accept what is and just move on.

Slumping back into his seat, he stared hard at the patient notes, reminding himself of Jed's medical history, then called the man through.

Jed came into his room with his hand wrapped in a towel.

'Jed! Good to see you. What's happened there, then?'

'Och, bit of an accident.' Jed began to unravel the tea towel and as he got closer to his own hand, more and more blood began to show through the cloth. He winced as he unravelled the last bit to reveal a clean slice right across his palm.

Lachie sucked in a breath. It was going to need cleaning and stitches. He got up and opened his cupboard where he kept gauze pads, saline washes, suture kits and all the paraphernalia he'd need to attend to the wound. 'How'd it happen?'

Jed shrugged. 'Och, you know… I was in the kitchen, mishandled a knife and before you know it, my hand looked like this. Can you fix it?'

Lachie washed his hands and put on some gloves before examining the wound more intently. Thankfully, most of the blood had slowed to a slight oozing, but the positioning of the laceration was odd. Right across from under the man's index finger, across the palm to just under his little, pinkie finger. 'How exactly did you slice this?'

'I was cutting through a crusty bread roll. Trying to open up one of those longer ones, you know, the ones for sausages and hot dogs, that kind of thing?'

Lachie nodded, dabbing at the wound with gauze.

'The knife went straight through. Wasn't as crusty as I thought.'

The one good thing about being a GP was that you got to know your patients well. You built a relationship with them over time and one of the benefits, or maybe in this case, one of the truths of this relationship, was that you could get a sense when a patient wasn't being fully honest. And Lachie could hear the way that Jed was speaking that he was trying to hide something. It was in his voice. The tone of it. The way he was trying to present his version of events as the truth, when clearly something else had happened. But what? The cut was too high on the palm if he'd been holding a bread roll the way Jed said.

Jed, like him, had an elderly parent that he cared for. But Jed's father was a paranoid schizophrenic. Mr Simpson senior was usually harmless and he was generally stable on his medications, but on occasion there could be a flare-up.

'Okay. You're sure that's what happened? Because this looks like a defensive wound to me.' He looked up at Jed's face, saw the man's cheeks colour and then Jed looked away.

'He didn't mean it, Lachie, okay? It was an accident,' Jed said quietly.

'If you're in danger…or at risk in any way, then I need to be concerned.'

'I'm not in danger. He missed a couple of his tablets, but he's back on them. I stood and watched him take them this morning. He was very apologetic when he realised.'

'Even so, I think I'd like to call round and see him. Just to review him, okay?'

Jed nodded.

'Okay, well, this seems to be a clean cut. Can you move all of your fingers for me? Good. And you can feel me touching you here? And here? What about here?' He wanted to make sure that the knife had not gone through any tendons or nerves. But Jed could feel and move everything fine. 'Okay, good. We'll get you stitched up.' It worried him, seeing what had happened to Jed, especially so close after seeing how his own mother had lost control. Smashing things. Being aggressive. She couldn't help it and nor could Jed's father, but it made him wonder if maybe he was blinded by how close he was to his mother's case? Was he dismissing her episode too easily? Was he making excuses for her behaviour, the way Jed had? Did he need to be seriously thinking of putting her in a long-term facility sooner, rather than later? But if he did, it would mean moving her to the mainland. There were no dementia care homes on Gulray.

When Jed was stitched up and sent on his way, he popped his head into Cass's room. 'Got a minute?'

'Sure. What's up?' She was restocking her supply cupboard. Loading it up with dressings.

There were lots of things he wanted to say, but he knew he needed to keep this business. 'It's about Mum. I wondered if you'd go and see her and give me your honest opinion about whether you think she ought to move permanently into a long-term facility.'

Cass looked surprised. 'I'm not qualified to make that sort of decision, Lachie.'

'I know, it's just… I fear I'm too close. Go see her. Talk to her carers. Let me know what you think. As a nurse.'

She thought for a moment, then nodded.

'Hello, Kathleen, my love! How are you?' Cass held both of Kathleen's hands in hers, as a greeting, sitting by her side.

Kathleen looked at her a little blankly. 'Do I know you?'

'My name's Cass and I'm a nurse. I work with your son, Lachie.'

Kathleen nodded, still looking vague. 'Oh.'

It was a difficult position for Cass to be in. She didn't want to tell Lachie what to do with his mother. Putting her in a home was a decision that family should make. But he'd asked for her professional opinion and as his good friend, she wanted to help. She knew he'd had trouble the other night, but he'd not really gone into specifics. She really liked Kathleen. Thought she was wonderful. But had to accept that Kathleen had some health issues.

Excusing herself to go and help the carer prepare medications, she entered the kitchen and spoke to Siobhan. 'How has she been lately?'

Siobhan sighed. 'She's getting worse. You see this sometimes. They can be stable in their condition for ages and then they suddenly go downhill. The other night was the first time I saw her petrified and frightened. She didn't know she was at home, or what year she was in. Or who Lachie was. She broke a couple of ornaments and picture frames because she threw them.'

Cass felt her heart break. For Kathleen. For Lachie. It must be so hard to lose his mother like this. She knew what it was like to have a mother that was physically there, but not mentally or emotionally present. It made you feel alone and adrift. But in Lachie's case, he'd had a good relationship with her before the disease. And Cass really wanted to help him if she could. He couldn't have her heart, but maybe he could have her counsel.

'And how has she been since?'

'Calmer, but she seems to be confused the majority of the time lately. Before, she could remember people, time and place, but lately? It's moved fast. I've not seen her lucid for days.'

'Do *you* think she needs full-time care?'

Siobhan shrugged. 'Possibly. We come in four times a day, but that's not long enough now. I try and stay as long as I can, before I have to go and see other patients, but that means there are times—thirty minutes, maybe an hour or so—in which she's alone and I'm not sure that's safe for her anymore. I turn off the oven and hob at the wall, so she can't cook or anything, but we never know what we're going to find when she's like this.'

Cass sighed. From this report, it seemed like the obvious solution was for Lachie to put his mother into care. To keep *her* safe, more than anything. But how would he feel hearing that? She thought that maybe he already knew what he had to do. He just needed someone else to tell him the same thing. 'You should speak to Lachie. Tell him what you've just told me.'

Siobhan nodded. 'I will. But he doesn't have to worry today, because I can stay until the next carer gets here.'

'Thank you.'

When Cass got back to the surgery, Junebug waved her over.

'Nic and Matt are here. In with Lachie. They want you to join them.'

She brightened. *Daniel.* 'They are? Oh, wonderful! How are they doing since the accident?'

'Well, they looked a little bruised still. Don't you just hate when bruises go that yellow-green colour? It's not pretty.'

'I guess it's not.' She headed towards Lachie's consultation room and knocked on the door.

'Come in!'

Opening the door, she strode inside, brightening at seeing Nic and Matt there, with baby Daniel in a pram. She wanted to go see Daniel. Look at him. Stroke his soft cheek. It had been too long since she'd last seen him. But Nic and Matt both got to their feet when they saw her.

'Cass! Thank you so much for helping us at the accident and taking care of Daniel! You have no idea how much I appreciated that!' Nic threw her arms around Cass and almost squeezed her to death.

Cass smiled broadly, laughing at Matt, who patiently waited his turn to give her a thankful and grateful hug. 'How are you both doing?'

'We're good. We're doing great. Things like that… they're a huge wake-up call.'

'I bet they are,' she said, finally getting a moment to look at baby Daniel. He was fast asleep, his chubby little hands curled up tightly either side of his head as he lay on his back beneath a pure white blanket. 'Bless him. Wish I could sleep like that.'

'Don't we all,' said Matt ruefully. 'We just need him to do that through the entire night and then we'll be laughing.'

She smiled at Matt, then back down at Daniel. She remembered very clearly the sleepless night she'd spent by her own son's bedside. Listening to every breath. Carefully watching every rise and fall of his chest. Listening to the heart monitor. Hoping for every beat. Panicking when the rhythm began to falter.

'I've been speaking to both Matt and Lachie and I've made a decision, Cass,' Nic said. 'About returning to work.'

Cass stood up and looked at her. Was this it, then? She wanted to come back early, maybe? Did that mean that Cass was going to have to leave Gulray *sooner* than expected? Her stomach dropped at the thought. She wasn't ready! Even though she knew it had to happen, she wasn't ready for it! Saying goodbye? 'Oh. Okay.'

'The accident was a huge wake-up call. Before I had Daniel, I was convinced that I wanted to return to my job as quickly as possible. That I wanted to do both. Maintain my job and be a mum. Have the best of both worlds. But then I had him and my thinking changed, even more so since the accident, since being away from Daniel, on the mainland, it made me realise how precious life is. How precious time is to be with your loved ones and I'll never get these early days and weeks and months with Daniel ever again and I want to cherish them. So what I want to do is be a stay-at-home mum. At least until Daniel goes to school and then I'll think again. But what do you say to staying on here in Kilmarrin and being the practice nurse on a permanent basis?'

Cass stared at her in shock. Her gaze flicking to Lachie, then back to Nic. Then Matt. The baby.

Lachie was looking hopeful that she'd say yes. Same as Nic. Same as Matt.

Stay?

Put down roots. Let these people finagle their way into her heart more than they already were? And then what? When Nic's son was five years old and started school,would she want her job back? After five years? Because by then, she'd be... *I don't know what I'd be.* And what would happen with Lachie if she stayed? She couldn't live with years of being his friend with benefits, because she knew herself. She fell hard and quick. Like him she'd dream of something long-term and permanent. Their hearts would become entrenched. Only to have to leave at the end. Because she'd feel that she had to, if Nic wanted to return. There might be no job for her here.

And yet...the possibilities were tempting still. She felt torn in two. One part of her wanting to hold back and protect herself and yes, keep running away, whereas another part of her was exhausted by all of that and wanted to stay. To put down those roots. To embrace all that Gulray, Lachie and the rest of the people had to offer. To see where things went with Lachie.

'I know you might already have another job lined up

for after this one,' Lachie continued. 'But we're seriously asking you to consider this proposal.'

She didn't have another job lined up after this one. She'd looked at the job postings on the Lark Agency website, but she'd not pressed Apply for any of them. At the time, she'd thought she still had time. But now? 'Can you give me a while to think about it?'

Cass saw Lachie's smile fade, his face harden, and a stab of guilt went right into her chest, but what could she do? She had to think this through and not make a snap decision. It was tempting to stay, of course it was, but how would she feel with that ticking clock all the time? It would be like Daniel's heart monitor. Knowing that every day that passed was another day less she would be here on Gulray. She'd never been anywhere long-term. She'd never let anyone get close.

And the possibility of having it all, *yet still losing it*, was terrifying.

Lachie was surprisingly child-free, as one of Ronan's friends had invited him to see a new pet puppy, and so he decided to take Cass out for dinner in the hopes of persuading her to stay.

'Let's go to the Puffin's Nest for something to eat.'

She'd agreed and now they were walking against a strong wind across to the pub where they had their usual Monday-evening curry nights.

The pub, like the surgery, was decorated with red and pink hearts in anticipation of Valentine's Day tomorrow and the pub was full of people they knew. Most raised a hand in acknowledgement or said hello, and Cindy Grey, sitting with her husband bought drinks for 'the good doctor and his nurse'.

Armed with their drinks, they settled into an alcove near the crackling fire and ordered neeps and tatties with a beef stew for Lachie and a lasagna and garlic bread for Cass.

He decided to circle his most pressing question with another. 'So, I never got to ask you earlier, but how did your visit with my mum go?'

Cass dabbed at her mouth with a napkin. 'There's clearly a difference in her memory since I first met her, but that doesn't mean she'll be that way all the time.'

'I know. This disease can come in waves.'

'I spoke to Siobhan. She knows more about your mum than I do and if it's a question of Kathleen's safety, then you must do what you think is right. I can't tell you what to do here, Lachie, and I wouldn't feel right doing it. It's not like I'm family.'

'No, you're not. But I feel like you are and I totally respect your personal and professional opinion.'

Cass looked uncomfortable at that. 'It's a progressive disease. There's going to be a time when your mum does need twenty-four-hour care to keep her safe and well and you're not going to be able to provide it. Your only question that *you* need to answer is whether you do that sooner or later.'

He nodded. He knew that, of course. 'What would you do?'

'I don't talk to my parents. I won't ever have to make that decision.'

'But if you had to?' he persisted.

Cass sighed. 'I can't decide for you, Lachie. And I won't. It wouldn't be right.'

'No. I'm sorry. I guess I was just hoping someone else would tell me what to do so that I don't feel guilty.'

She reached for his hand then. A comfort. Reassuring. 'I understand.' Then she let go quickly, realising that they were out in public, her cheeks flushing.

He felt his own cheeks colour. Neither of them needed gossip about themselves spreading like wildfire across the island. But it was a simple slip-up and could easily be explained away if anyone asked. Most knew about his mother. They all knew about Meghan.

'Have you thought any more about staying on?' When Nic and Matt had come into his room earlier that morning and explained their situation, he had to admit he wasn't all that surprised. Nic had said from the very beginning that she would always return to work quickly after her baby was born, but he knew, from experience, that minds could change and he'd seen how besotted Nic was with her newborn son. No wonder she didn't want to leave him. He'd felt the same way with Ronan. This precious bundle who seemed to change and grow with every minute. He'd not wanted to miss any of it! But with Meghan gone, he'd had to and there'd been many milestones he'd missed whilst out tending patients and putting other families before his own. You could never get those lost years back. Now his mum was losing memories and he might lose Cass, too. He could feel himself wavering between wanting her to stay and wanting her to just go so that he didn't live in any more uncertainty.

'I don't know. It's a big step.'

He could see the fear in her eyes. 'What's worrying

you about it?' He really wanted to know. Maybe it was something he could help with? Because he really wanted her to stay. His feelings for her were sometimes all he could think about. The idea that she might leave? So soon? Did not sit well with him. He loved Nic and he'd loved working with her, but it was different with Cass.

Cass was something else. Had *become* something else.

Someone important to him. And he'd already lost his wife. Was about to lose his mother. He didn't want to lose her, too. He thought that what they had could become incredibly special. If he could get her to stay, then maybe they could become something more?

'Five years is a long time.'

He nodded. 'Yes. But I'd be with you, every step of the way.'

'How would that look, exactly?'

Lachie leaned in. He didn't need them to be overheard. 'How it looks now. I want to be with you.'

'In what way?'

'In *that* way,' he said, smiling. 'I'd really like to see where it takes us.'

'You mean, in a committed relationship?'

He smiled. Nodded.

Why did she look so afraid?

'And what would happen at the end of those five years? When Nic wants her job back? Because I'd always feel like I'm filling in. Like I'm temporary, no matter how long I stay. It's what I've always been. I'd have nothing to do here on Gulray. I'd have to leave. I'd be *asked* to leave. Always feeling like I'm on borrowed time and not wanted anymore. Leave you. Ronan. The surgery. All the things I would fall in love with, because I know that's how my heart works and I'm not sure I'm strong enough to deal with any more heartbreak.'

'What if I left Gulray with you?'

'What?' She looked shocked.

'If my mum goes into care on the mainland, then I'd want to be able to see her. Often. And if she's on the mainland then maybe I should be, too. We wouldn't have to be apart.'

'You'd leave Gulray? But it's perfect here!'

'It's beautiful. And I do love it here. But it's not perfect.'

Cass stared back at him, her face a mask of fear and confusion.

'I do love it here and I love the people and I adore living in a small community. But my family's needs are requiring more than what the island can offer us. Meghan *died* here on Gulray because we had to wait for an emergency evacuation. It has no dementia care homes here to take care of my mother, and what if something happened to Ronan, too? Could I bear to sit and watch, the way I had to sit and watch when my wife died? I've been thinking about this for some time. I simply stayed because Mum was here and I wanted Ronan to have a female figure in his life, but maybe I've stayed too long? Maybe I should have moved straight away? Before you came to work at the surgery. But the thought that you might leave, too? This is why putting Mum into care is such a big decision, because if she's going, then so am I.'

He'd just never voiced it before. Never said it out loud, because who could he tell before? He'd been there for years; everyone was used to him. Everyone knew him and he didn't want to let them down.

'Gulray isn't the only small community. I could find a village practice somewhere. Settle down. Start a new life. But still have access to all those that I care about and know that they can be taken care of quickly if necessity demands it.'

'I had no idea you were thinking about that as an option.'

'I don't think I did, fully. Until Mum's situation got worse and...' He paused. 'Until you came and I had to think about how I'd feel if you left.'

'But what about Nic and Matt?'

'They'll be fine. They'll all be fine.'

'You really mean this?'

He nodded, looking directly into her eyes. 'I do.'

'But...we hardly know one another. What if it didn't work out? These things often don't. The first rush of feelings...they can't be trusted.'

'I know you enough and my heart tells me that I need to keep you in my life. If you'll stay.' This was important. He needed her.

Cass stared at him, looking more and more scared and then suddenly, she stood up. 'I, um...'

He waited for her to say something. He knew he'd said a lot and that she needed to process it all, but surely she could see that they could both have everything they'd ever wanted in life?

But he didn't get an answer, because she suddenly bolted from their table and shot out of the pub's door.

His jaw clenched as he realised he'd been given his answer.

She couldn't give him what he wanted. She was too scared to make the leap into a relationship with him. She was going to leave and leave him behind with a broken heart.

So there was nothing for him to do right now but accept that he had lost her, too.

He felt a physical pain in his chest. Like his heart was being wrenched right out of it. But what could he do? She'd walked away, just as he'd feared she might, and he had to accept that.

Maybe he was too much? He came as a package. She wasn't just getting into some simple relationship here. He had a son from a previous relationship. A dead wife. A mother with dementia. These were all very stressful things!

I'm asking for too much from her.

She had baggage, too. No relationship with her parents. No relationship with the father of her child. A bereavement. She'd lost her baby! Her life was filled with loss and she lived a transient life. What he was offering her was too strange, too big, too terrifying for her to accept.

Would it be possible to change her mind?

Did he need to move more slowly?

Was she even worth fighting for?

Yes! Of course she is! A thousand times yes!

So why was he still sitting in the pub? Staring at the crackling fire? He'd not been able to do anything about losing Meghan. That fight was over before he realised it and he'd had to sit impotently and watch her fade away.

But I could do something about Cass.

His gaze fell upon the paper hearts. The banner reminding him it was Valentine's Day tomorrow. You didn't need a special day to declare your love for someone. If you loved them, then you showed them every day. You fought for them. Protected them and gave them your all.

And I love Cass. I know I do. This is why this hurts.

Was he brave enough to risk fighting for her, knowing that she could still walk away? Was he willing to put his own heart on the line and fight for her?

He stared at the door.

And tried to think.

CHAPTER NINE

HE WALKED THROUGH the rain to her cottage. He'd wanted to run, but made himself walk, knowing he needed to gather his thoughts and think about how best to say what he needed to say. If after he'd said it, she walked away? Then he would know he had tried, but she was worth pursuing. Worth fighting for and he would not give up on their love so easily, just because she was scared of it.

He rapped his knuckles on her front door.

Cass opened it, tears pouring down her cheeks.

He stepped forward. 'No one has ever fought for you, have they? They've all just given up on you. I'm not like those others, Cass. I won't let you go without a fight.'

Frosty appeared, curling his way around Cass's legs as she stood there. 'I can't risk it,' she said. 'I can't risk having my heart broken all over again.'

'I would *never* break your heart,' he said, wincing as the rain began to fall more heavily. Big wet droplets falling from the sky and soaking him instantly. 'I would cherish it. Protect it. Love it. Love *you*.'

She met his gaze. 'Love?'

He smiled, rain pouring down his face, but he didn't care about that. All that mattered was her. 'You've never had true love, so maybe that's why you don't recognise it. Maybe that's why you're afraid of it. Because loving someone means making yourself vulnerable, doesn't it? But I do know true love. I've had it once before and I feel I have it again. With you.'

She nodded.

'Be vulnerable with me, Cass!' He paused for a moment. Knowing his next words needed to be said well. Heard clearly. 'I love you and I want to be with you. Always. Not just for five years. Not just for fun. I want us to be together properly. Committed.'

It was scary for him to say it, too. He'd only ever told one woman before that he loved her and it was in a situation a lot less fraught than this! Somehow, this time it felt more important.

'I don't know what to say.'

'Tell me you love me, too.' He laughed. 'That's usually a good response. But…only if you mean it, because if you do, then I'm going to be stepping over your threshold to kiss you and I'm going to track all this rain in.' A pause. 'But if you don't feel the same way, then tell me now and I'll—' he shrugged '—take my cat and leave.'

He could see a thousand thoughts and feelings play across her face. Shock. Confusion. Apprehension. Want. Desire. Hope. And in turn, he hoped that she could be brave enough to tell him the truth.

'I think…that I might love you, too.'

'*Think? Might*? I'm afraid I'm going to need solid reassurances before I step in and ruin your carpet.' He smiled ruefully, hoping the rain was making him look cute and not like a feral, drowned rat.

And then she smiled and it was like the sun came out and dried up all the rain. 'I love you, too,' she said.

Laughing. Gasping as he stepped forward to take her in his sodden arms.

She was warm and dry.

And so very beautiful.

He stroked her face, gazing into eyes he knew he would get to gaze into for as long as they both lived. A thought that made him very happy indeed.

And then he kissed her.

Kissed her with all the love in his heart and soul.

Kissed her until he felt her relax in his arms.

And then he closed the front door with a swipe of his leg.

EPILOGUE

'LOOK AT HIM! He's loving this,' Cass said, watching Ronan as he splashed in the edges of Loch Gilp, wearing his brand new bright red wellingtons that he'd been given by Aunty Morag.

The sun was shining and it was an unseasonably warm day for February, as she and Lachie sat on a picnic blanket, watching Ronan play by the water's edge.

She'd made a picnic. Aunty Morag would be joining them when she got back from her book group, and later on they were going to call in and see Kathleen. They'd managed to get her into a beautiful care home on the outskirts of Ardrishaig, close to Lochgilphead, where Lachie had managed to find a posting as GP.

Cass had been nursing there, too, but recently? She'd been away.

On maternity leave.

Their daughter, wrapped up nice and warm in a crocheted white blanket, nestled in her arms. Eilidh had been born six weeks ago, with Lachie by her side, safe and well, with no sign of the heart issues that had befallen Daniel.

Eilidh had brought Cass so much joy. From the first suspicion that she might be pregnant, all the way through the easy pregnancy, right through to the birth that had been over and done with in three hours. She would never forget her firstborn son and she would make sure to tell Eilidh that actually she had *two* older brothers. Ronan *and* Daniel.

Her life had become something amazing with Lachie by her side and she looked forward to their future.

Lachie reached into the picnic basket and pulled out a champagne bottle and two flutes of glass.

'I can't drink that. I'm breastfeeding,' she said with a smile.

'You don't need to drink a whole glass. Maybe just take a sip.'

Cass smiled. 'What are we celebrating?'

'Well, I know that a lot of couples do all their celebrating tomorrow. Telling their loved ones that they love them on Valentine's Day, but since meeting you, the evening before Valentine's is something I remember with particular fondness.'

Lachie popped the cork and bubbles fizzed over onto the grass before he could pour champagne into their two glasses.

'The day you first told me you loved me.'

Lachie nodded, passing her a glass. 'And the day you first told me you loved me and so in that tradition, I wanted to add something else special to our day before Valentine's.'

'Oh? What's that, then?' she asked, smiling, watching the bubbles fizz and rise to the surface of her drink.

Lachie pulled a small box from his pocket and opened it to reveal a beautiful diamond solitaire ring. 'You've made me the happiest man in the world since you came into my life. I never thought I'd truly get the chance to find happiness a second time, but I have and I want to tell the world, so if you'll have me, I'd like to ask you to marry me, Cass, and become my wife.'

Cass gasped, looking at Lachie's hopeful face and then down at their daughter and Ronan splashing in the loch, and she just knew there was a very simple answer to this question. She didn't need to think about it. She didn't need to doubt. She didn't have any fears. Not anymore. She felt like she could do anything with him by her side. With the little family that they had made.

'Yes! I will!'

And he slid the ring onto her finger. Kissed. Clinked glasses and she did have a very small sip of champagne.

'Ronan?' Lachie called.

She turned to look at his son.

Ronan grinned. 'Did you ask her? Did she say yes?'

Cass raised her hand and wiggled the ring in his direction. 'I said yes. Is that okay?'

And Ronan came bounding over and gave her a hug before leaning down to place a kiss on his baby sister's face. 'It's amazing!'

* * * * *

OFF-LIMITS TEMPTATION FOR DR DAY

FIONA McARTHUR

MILLS & BOON

To my dear aunt Maurine, admired high soprano.
I was so blessed to have spent time with you xx

PROLOGUE

STANDING BESIDE THE bridegroom in black, Marco Macaluso tried to assimilate what he was feeling. It was like nothing he was used to, being part of such a gathering of people he didn't know well, but he *was* glad to be here. He would have chosen tailored cream suits instead of black for this beach wedding because fashion choices were important, but he felt honoured Henry had called on him to be the best man. Ridiculously so.

Marco's gaze swept over the man who was like the brother he had never had, seeing through the poise to Henry's nerves underneath. He said, 'You're a lucky man, Henry,' and he meant it. He'd spent time with Henry's friends and his imminent bride since he'd arrived in Queensland from Rome a week ago. The beautiful Nadia and her young daughter obviously adored Henry. But marriage? He thought of Valentina's hints. Marco shuddered internally. Non è possibile! Not for him.

The brilliant sun heated his hair, the waves crashed in his ears and a movement of colour caught his eye as the salty breeze lifted the flying red curls of the small, intense woman in blue. She herded two pre-schoolers—not hers, he knew, because he'd met Henry's specialist registrar. Dr Amelia Day was not his type, he thought and almost laughed, but something about her fluid movements and her delight in the young mischief-makers kept attracting his attention. And that red hair. Twists of unexpected disruption and mayhem when he knew the woman to be brilliant but prim, and studiously serious. Not a colour to be caught from a bottle, it would be naturally red all over her body, so…curls and colour had always stirred his libido.

'I know,' Henry murmured beside him. 'I'm a lucky man with Nadia.' He cleared his throat until Marco looked back his way. 'And I appreciate you being here for me today.'

A warning note? Marco's mouth kinked up. Perhaps he'd caught his discerning perusal of the sainted Amelia.

Marco's eyes gleamed. 'I'll be here for more than that.' His gaze drifted left again towards that hair. 'Such a year of experiences to come.'

'No, you don't. Look this way!' Henry protested in a growl. 'I need my registrar happy.'

Marco laughed. Henry knew him. Knew his ways. They'd shared a flat for several years in London together working long hours towards becoming consultant paediatricians, and even longer ones with Henry often a barely interested fourth in a double date, as Marco had caroused his way through the delightfully willing ladies of London who caught his eye. There had been those few sticky moments when Henry had had to steer away last week's paramour since Marco had moved on with the new week's temptation, but it hadn't happened that much. Really. And rarely at work.

But once Henry had left, Marco had felt oddly bored, as if his only family had abandoned him again, so that even the ladies had lost some of their lustre to him.

Strangely, the ennui had dissipated once he'd set foot on this sunny beach suburb on Australia's east coast. He'd been enamoured of the pristine sand and the sapphire skies on his first day. And the sun-kissed women.

When he'd been asked if he'd be interested in working with Henry and the senior partner, Simon, in the Rainbow Bay paediatric practice for the next year, and perhaps even seek permanent residency in Australia, it had been surprisingly easy to say yes. Apart from real estate, he had nothing in London or Rome to keep him.

He could certainly consider the move across the world to start fresh. And yes, please, to Nadia's offer of renting him her beachfront ground-floor apartment, since she and her daughter had moved upstairs with Henry, with the option to buy.

The apartment block stood above the beach and was walking distance to the hospital where he would happily take over Henry's full work commitments during his friend's honeymoon. When Henry returned, Marco looked forward to assuming jurisdiction over all paediatric emergency admissions at Rainbow Bay Hospital from then on…with Henry's red-haired registrar's help. Hence lightening Henry's workload now that he was married.

That disturbing red-haired registrar grabbed her glorious curls and held them away from her eyes while she laughed with the children, and the movement snared his attention again.

Amelia Day chuckled as her small charge headed back towards the trampoline. 'No, Sacha, Sarah, it's starting. Look, Mummy is waving to you. Time to take our seats and watch the bride arrive.'

The little girls' mouths widened in matching *O*s as they spied the wedding party on their way across the street, and they turned and scampered back towards their mother.

Amelia blew the hair out of her eyes. Why on earth had she listened to her aunt Luna about wearing it loose for the wedding? She stilled. That man was watching her again. Amelia turned her face away from him and settled in her seat. Plenty of interested ladies here he should be looking at instead of her.

Determined to ignore him, Amelia reminded herself she loved the setting she found herself in. The beach. The elegant wedding marquee on the sandy grass.

Most of all she loved that the whole child-friendly event lay open to the sparkling afternoon seascape while the sun passed overhead. White tables, blue-handled cutlery and scented flowers climbing the marquee poles made the shady space look pretty and festive. The heady aroma of roses drifting in the breeze. She knew most of the children, most of the bridal party, and a lot of the people from the hospital.

He was looking at her again. The best man. She'd been introduced to Henry's friend Marco, a ridiculously handsome Italian with an accent to die for if she was the dying type. Luckily she seriously wasn't, and apparently he was coming to work for the paediatric department when Henry went on his honeymoon next month. Oh goodie.

Amelia lifted her chin and stood with the crowd as the bride and her party gracefully arrived at the far end of the aisle. Nadia looked so beautiful, and Marco Macaluso wouldn't be starting for a few weeks, so she refused to ruin this beautiful event thinking of him. She wanted to savour the joy that kind and caring Henry and the lovely Nadia had found with their happily-ever-after.

In the year she'd worked with Henry as his registrar, she'd learnt so much and been so warmly encouraged by Henry's expanded faith in her diagnoses and decisions because she'd had serious responsibilities, but she'd also been able to rely on Henry on the rare occasions when she needed advice and backup. However, she wasn't quite so confident about the Italian Stallion being her new boss. She'd heard about the recently smitten surgical resident who'd enjoyed a whirlwind fling with Marco after meeting him at Henry's and had then been dined, danced and dropped, all before the wedding. Fast work.

The man was a flake, possibly a rake, and she didn't trust him not to take his eye off the ball when lives were at stake. Ha! That rhymes.

CHAPTER ONE

One month later

'*PAGING DR DAY. Dr Amelia Day. Please go to the emergency department.*' Amelia logged out of the computer in the children's ward and glanced at the nurse manager next to her. 'I've ordered a stat dose of antiemetic. Try that, Tara, and I'll come back after I've seen the ED.'

'No problem. Thanks, Amelia.'

Pushing her enormous new cobalt-blue prescription glasses up her nose, a fashion statement her aunt Luna talked her into this week, one she wasn't sure of, Amelia stood and strode swiftly to the exit of the ward and down the long corridor towards the ED on the ground floor. Usually, when a sick child presented, one of her residents phoned her from there or sent a message to her phone if they needed help. A global announcement through the hospital PA system meant urgency.

And darn, Henry and Nadia had left on their delayed honeymoon last night, so she had the new consultant as backup. Today, she had to work with Macaluso, and she just hoped he'd arrived because she might need him.

Within a couple minutes of brisk walking, a nurse steered Amelia towards one of the main assessment rooms. Not a cubicle for new admissions but the fully stocked resuscitation bay, also not a good indication of patient stability.

The gasping wheeze of the child as she entered the doorway quickened her heart rate and narrowed her gaze. Provisional diagnosis: severe asthma!

The small blonde girl of about six, not someone Amelia recognised from previous admissions, sat high on the white sheets, and this little one's pale cheeks almost blended into the cotton surrounds. The bedhead raised, the three pillows behind her were uncreased as her shoulders curved forward in an instinctive attempt to help her breathing as she struggled to exhale.

Amelia's gaze shifted to the monitoring equipment noting the rapid heart rate, reduced blood–oxygen percentage and high respiration rate. Respiratory distress. All that in the first second of her arrival. She pulled the dangling stethoscope off her neck as she approached the bed. Wheezing air entry. Thankfully no blue tinge to the lips. Yet. Agitation and no attempt to cry or speak. So clinically moderate respiratory distress at best.

Tom, Henry's more senior resident, spoke up. 'Thanks for coming, Amelia. Cressa is six and woke this morning with a cough that escalated quickly to breathlessness. She arrived with her parents twenty-five minutes ago by car. Jock and Grace Green, this is Dr Day.'

Amelia nodded at the worry-stamped parents. She shook their hands briefly before crossing to the other side of the bed so she was facing them across the child between them. Both were blond and fine-boned, and she could see Cressa was very like them as they held hands and leaned towards their daughter.

'I had asthma as a child,' Jock said. 'Bad for a few years.'

'But she's never had anything like this before,' Grace was saying. 'Just a cough last night, then it came on so fast. She didn't even have the breath to tell us what was wrong, so we brought her straight here.'

Dangerous with the speed of this escalation. They should have called an ambulance, Amelia thought, but didn't say yet. The paramedics could have started treatment on the way, a drip, some Ventolin, but she would make sure the parents knew before they left what to do next time. 'She's in the right place,' Amelia said. 'We've got her.'

She glanced at Tom as she took an alcohol wipe off a tray and wiped her stethoscope membrane, an ingrained essential habit before and after using it. 'You've ruled out an anaphylaxis?' Amelia verbalised the question in her mind as she went on to wash her hands. It looked like classic asthma to her, but Tom would have asked, and they needed to differentiate with treatment if there were other possibilities.

'No known allergies. No changes in diet or surroundings, no new pets, no welts, redness or swelling noted. Marked wheeze both lungs escalating, and family history of asthma, though no previous episodes for Cressa.'

She dried off and approached the bed. 'What have you done so far?'

'Six metered doses of salbutamol in a spacer on arrival and four of Atrovent. Repeated five minutes ago with minimal response. I inserted an IV but the cannula has just packed up.' His cheeks reddened. 'I paged you to replace it urgently and escalate treatment as Cressa's respirations are increasing with breath sounds decreasing. I didn't want to be left without a line in.'

'I agree.' Decreasing breath sounds were an ominous

sign, and intravenous access was paramount especially in a shut-down child. This little one was too sick to go slow with. 'Let's sort that first, and we'll get some steroids on board.' Amelia glanced at the senior emergency nurse who pushed a trolley set for cannulation towards her. 'Thanks, Gilly.'

Amelia leaned down. 'Cressa?' The little girl's eyes were wide, and she was slow to take her gaze off her parents, but when she did Amelia felt her heart grab. Yep. So, so terrified.

'I'm Dr Mellie.' The name her brothers called her, and which she used with small children to establish some rapport. 'I know you're having a hard time breathing, but we're going to help that. First, I'll listen to your chest and back.' She paused to allow Cressa to understand. 'Then I need to sting your hand again so we can give you medication into your arm that will ease the tightness in your lungs. We'll be busy and annoying, but in about ten minutes you'll begin to feel better. Okay?'

The little girl blinked and gave a tiny nod. Eyes wide and only slightly less panicked. Amelia took her hand. 'We have you. You will feel better soon.'

Before she started, Amelia listened to Cressa's chest and back, noting the wheezing and grateful there was still enough air entry to make a noise. Silence would be much worse, but both lungs were tight with secretions.

Amelia leaned down to the child. 'Thank you. Now the sting and the medicine.'

A shadow darkened the door, and Amelia looked up to see Macaluso appear. Her brows raised. He must have heard the page, and it seemed he had also come in early, maybe because it was his first day. 'Dr Macaluso. Good to see you.' Not for her but for the backup if needed. Yes, that was good.

She looked across at the Greens. 'Dr Macaluso is our consultant paediatrician. He'll talk to you about what's happening, and he is our backup if we need more help.' She smiled at them. 'Though, I believe you've brought Cressa in to us in good time.' She glanced at the younger resident doctor. 'Tom, can you do the introductions and update the boss, please?'

Then she put him from her mind as she concentrated on Cressa. Working quietly with the nurse, Gilly, and explaining as she went along, Amelia cannulated with surprising ease and little compliant from Cressa. Amelia took bloods again for further pathology assessment before connecting the line, then gave the urgently required medication. She also ensured a second cannula for emergency use, though she covered that wrist with a bandage to keep it from being bumped.

When she stepped back from the bed, the observations on the monitor had improved. More tellingly, Cressa had sunk back into the pillows and closed her eyes, and her breath came more easily. There was even a little more colour returned to her pale features. 'You okay, Cressa?'

'Better,' the little girl whispered, and Amelia carefully squeezed her small fingers. Enough breath to speak was a wonderful improvement. 'You're so brave. Thank you. I'm glad it's helping. In a minute, I'll leave you and your parents with Dr Tom. But I'd like you to stay overnight or even two in the hospital until you feel a lot better. I'll see you on the ward when they get you there. Mummy or Daddy can sleep here too if you'd like them with you.'

Cressa smiled, though she didn't open her eyes.

Amelia found Marco's intense brown gaze on her when she looked across the room. He stood relaxed against the wall beside Cressa's parents, who now looked much calmer. Now that she thought about it, she could vaguely remember his lilting Italian accent explaining about asthma and treatments and even calling an ambulance if Cressa became ill on a future occasion. Funny how she remembered that now but hadn't paid attention at the time. Seemed she had.

She caught his gaze as he raised his brows.

What? she thought. Update maybe? 'I've given methylprednisolone, and we'll repeat the dose in six hours.'

Marco nodded and moved to the bed, speaking quietly to the little girl as Amelia approached the parents.

She said, 'We've given steroids because we needed to break the escalation of her lungs' response to whatever triggered this attack. Cressa is very brave and didn't complain about the two cannulas. I added the extra in case her condition worsens again. We don't want the only cannula to fail just when we need it. But when she turns the corner properly, Gilly or another nurse will remove one of those. I've taken more bloods and would like her to stay in overnight at least, possibly longer, as you heard me tell her. We'll make sure you have a printed asthma plan and follow-up appointments with Dr Macaluso before she goes home.'

They nodded as Marco began to listen to Cressa's chest with Gillian by his side.

Amelia turned to Tom. 'Let me know when the results come through from pathology. Try for a sputum culture and admit her to the children's ward under Dr Macaluso.' She glanced up at Marco questioningly.

He nodded as he stepped back. 'Finish the third dose of Ventolin and Atrovent before transfer, and I'll see Cressa on the ward.' He smiled at the little girl, and she gazed up at him with her big eyes wide. A tiny smile fluttered on her pale lips. Of course. He could even charm children.

CHAPTER TWO

'DO YOU HAVE more questions before we transfer your daughter to children's ward?' Marco gave his full attention to the parents now as the nurse and Tom began preparing the spacer with the bronchodilators.

Mrs Green said softly, 'We'll see you or Dr Day when we she's admitted to the ward?'

'Yes. They will call us.' He glanced to check with Tom. 'You'll call after the last dose of inhalants has been given?'

'Yes, sir.'

'Then,' he added to the parents with a smile, 'arrivederci, a presto. Good-bye. I will see you soon.'

Marco shook hands with Cressa's parents in farewell and followed Amelia out of the room, glad that he'd obeyed his instincts to respond to her page over the hospital announcement system. Now he had seen Dr May in action.

As expected, she proved methodical and skilled at diagnosis, treatment and calmly cannulating children. He also liked how she'd given further orders to the junior staff concisely and confidently and was amused she'd delegated the explanations for parents to him.

As he followed the slim figure in the professional grey trousers and collared white shirt, he decided her grey boots with low heels were trendy but without much appeal. Mostly, he noticed that her hair had been totally confined, braided and pinned. Even the colour looked subdued. He suspected it had been gelled down as well and resisted the ridiculous urge to touch it to confirm its stiffness.

No idea what that nonsensical thought was about, except she looked different to the time he'd seen her a month ago. He'd even thought of her once or twice while he packed up his life.

'Well managed, Dr Day,' he said as he caught up to her and she slowed. As she turned slightly to look up at him, he was struck again why any woman would choose such outrageously ugly glasses, though the blue brought the colour out in her striking eyes, and he disliked how they hid half of her fine-boned face, so heavy-rimmed and large that she resembled a fly. Puzzling, but no matter, it was her choice.

But he couldn't help saying, 'Those glasses are…quite striking.' Perhaps he should not have paused before choosing the descriptive word. He tried not to grimace.

'Thank you.' She kept walking, and he noted again how she wore her blouse buttoned to the throat as if to keep the world out. 'I like blue.' Then she sped up again. 'I need to return to children's ward. Are you going that way as well?'

'I plan to.'

'Good. I was called away from a fourteen-year-old, Penelope Hann, with vomiting. I need to reassess her, and I'm thinking appendicitis or I would have stayed longer with Cressa.'

'Perhaps when you have completed your reassessment, you will give me an update on the other patients there as well.'

'Of course.' She glanced at her watch. 'I had planned to meet you on the ward at eight to do so.'

'Excellent. Shall we make that a daily appointment unless called away?'

'Certainly.'

She was most agreeable and yet he could feel her lack of warmth. He was not used to that from women, and a small, determined seed inside him decided he would not let it continue.

'Are you happy with the clinical progression in your residents, Tom and Sam?'

She blinked behind the lenses. Truly they did make her eyes appear larger. Quite arresting. 'Yes, Tom's reliable, quick-thinking and happy to discuss any of his concerns.'

'You think this is a good thing?' He watched her bristle at that. Did she think he disagreed? He did not. So prickly.

'Absolutely. Hive-mind respect in a team is important.'

'Just so. And Sam?'

'Sam is meticulous and sharp and considers options outside the box. He will go far.' Again, she showed that confidence and sure assessment of others as well as seeing worth.

Well. He liked that about her too. Henry had said something similar about his team, but most of his praise had been for this small woman with the ridiculous glasses. 'Henry tells me you have an excellent diagnostic grasp and that we have a diverse demographic of childhood diseases, here in Rainbow Bay. Also, you were in the team involved in government changes to encourage parents to immunise their children.'

She turned those heavy rectangles towards him as they neared the doors to the ward. Fearless Fly. He'd watched an absurd cartoon with his uncle's housekeeper once with such an insect performing as a superhero. Amelia could be such, and the thought made him smile. She was saying, 'We have a transient, lower-income population, yes. Many young families are struggling with high rents as they're competing with holiday-makers here for the surf. I have had some cases more often seen in Third World countries.'

'And childhood diseases?'

'Yes. Last year we had a rise of a virulent measles strain. Henry and the team illustrated some of those heart-breaking complications in our campaign for increased incentives for immunisation. The government listened.'

'Brava. In Italy also the childhood immunisation rate has fallen. Something I would like to discuss with you later.'

'Of course.' They walked through the door into the bright and comfortable children's ward. 'I'm assuming Henry has introduced you to Tara Taylor, the nursing unit manager and walked you around the ward itself?'

'He has.'

She nodded. A quick snap of decision. 'Let's start with Tara, then we'll see Penelope.'

Bossy little thing, he thought amused and then frowned. Normally he would lead the way, but following her felt strangely comfortable.

CHAPTER THREE

FIVE DAYS LATER Amelia could almost salute the children's ward clock. Four thirty, Friday afternoon, thank goodness. It couldn't come quick enough because this week had been extra tiring. Amelia watched the agency nurse stand dazzled as Marco smiled and left her holding her electronic tablet clutched to her chest.

Nobody received Amelia's patient orders with such dreamy eyes, she thought with reluctant amusement, proud of herself that she still felt amused after watching it all week. She caught the slight brow rise and subtle smile from Tara at the nurses' desk.

If Marco wasn't so good at his job, she might be more annoyed because it was distracting to have to wait until the staff member recovered from palpitations before they could remember their patients. Even the male staff strode more quickly to his bidding, while a cohort of the female staff had some sort of delay mechanism that seemed to short-circuit their brains.

She could just imagine the frenzy when the annual charity ball arrived next week and Marco attended in all his Italian glamour.

But on the flip side, she thought, the children decreed him terrific, and his diagnostics and cutting-edge treatments impressed even her—so for that she forgave him most things.

Except trying it on with her. Because for some reason, Marco Macaluso attempting to lay his charm in her direction just fired right up her nose like a bullet.

Her phone vibrated silently with a text as she veered away towards the nurses' station and she glanced down at the screen. Call me.

'Can I use your office for a moment, please, Tara? Family stuff.'

'Of course. Just shut the door, I'll guard it.'

'Not needed, but thanks.' Amelia smiled and wrinkled her brows. 'It will be about one of the twins.' And unusual for her aunt to text during the day especially when she knew Tara could be home within the hour.

'Hello, Luna. Problem?'

'Mellie, sorry to ring you at work. I'm up in Ipswich just leaving that herbal workshop and you know what the traffic is like at this hour. Crispin asked if I could pick him up from football training. Apparently, his knee is more painful today and he can't walk home.'

'His knee?' Her brows drew together. 'He hasn't complained to me about knee problems.'

'Hmm. It's been going on very occasionally for a month or two. You know the boys don't like to worry you.' She heard Luna snort. 'Doesn't seem to bother him when you're around. He asked me not to mention it. Since it hasn't been a problem before now, and at their age trust is important, I didn't share the small stuff.'

Amelia got that they were both trying hard to make sure communication and teenage secrecy could coexist in the family home. Her aunt Luna had come to help the family when she'd been left guardian of her brothers and they all felt Luna was a gem they were very blessed to share. Sadly, she'd going back to India soon, her time with them was coming to an end. 'Of course.'

'But,' she heard the concern in Luna's voice, 'dropping out of training isn't like him, and I thought it might be a good opportunity for you to chat about it on the way home. Otherwise, he can get an Uber if you can't get away.'

Since Crispin normally walked the three kilometres home from training, someone needed to pick him up. 'Sure, I'll get away early. Thanks, Luna.'

As she left the office still glancing at her phone, her brain worried if Crispin had damaged anything else when he'd hurt his knee. Her face bumped into something solid and warm, and her head jerked up as she stepped back. 'Sorry.'

Marco's hands came out and steadied her by the upper arms. Heat and pressure sizzled through her, his big hands seeming to squeeze the breath from her—which was ridiculous since lungs were nowhere near biceps. She took another step back until his hands fell away.

Her eyes locked on his deep brown gaze, which sparked with amusement, and seeing that expression pressed some sort of emergency bell inside her. Not quite the cardiac-arrest one, but still… 'I'm sorry,' she said again and resisted the urge to rub the tingle from her arms.

'Is everything well, Amelia?'

She blinked. Forcibly disconnected their stares. Which she should have done immediately. 'Yes. Yes, of course.' Focused on the ward clock again. 'I need to pick up one of my brothers from football training. Seems to have injured his knee. I've finished everything for the day, so I'll dash off half an hour early.'

He watched her as if confused, and she wondered if he'd understood. Of course he had. There was nothing wrong with his grasp of English. She turned to Tara. 'Lean on Tom to call me if he's worried about young Sven, Tara.' Nine-year-old Sven had a nasty dose of food poisoning, and as an insulin-dependant diabetic he'd been admitted for observation and insulin dose titration.

She spoke to Marco, wondering if she should have asked permission to leave early. 'If it's okay with you?'

'Of course. You were here at six this morning. You work long hours far too often.'

She hadn't realised he'd been aware of her schedule, but that thought stuttered into another odd concept when he continued, 'I didn't know you had a brother.'

How would he? And why would it come up? 'I have two seventeen-year-old brothers, twins.' Der, well, obviously they were twins, if they were both seventeen, she mocked herself.

His brows rose, and she glanced at her watch. 'Our parents died five years ago… I'll see you Monday unless I need to call you over the weekend.' She turned to Tara. 'Thanks for the use of your office, Tara.'

Her mother's sister, Luna, managed the day-to-day running of the parental home and had done since she'd ridden in on a white horse from India at her parents' funeral as if she knew Amelia's workload had been too much to juggle everything as well as emotionally support the boys.

Amelia had no idea how she and the boys would have coped without her kind and calm aunt. Thankfully, now that the twins had their driver's licences, again thanks to Luna's tutelage, it would be easier once they worked out where they would park the third—or, horror, fourth—car.

Coolangatta had good bus services, but once they could afford at least one more car for their independence, life would streamline.

Amelia found Crispin on a park bench, one filthy hand rubbing his knee when she pulled up next to him at the football field. His eyes widened when he saw it was her.

Hers blinked when he stood up. He'd grown! And it had rained through the night, so he was muddy and damp. She suppressed the urge to shake her head at the thought she'd have to wash her seat covers again once he'd got in and spread that delightful topsoil in her Lexus. It had belonged to her late dad and had been his immaculate baby, and she was careful with the interior.

'Mellie? I thought Luna was coming to pick me up.'

'She's held up in traffic driving back from Ipswich, and I could get away.'

He eased himself in, careful of his knees, and glanced ruefully at the smears and mud on his hands and legs. 'I'm a bit dirty to come in your car.'

'So does that mean grime is okay for Luna's car?'

'She keeps towels on her seats.'

Go, pragmatic Luna! Amelia smiled. 'I'll have to do that next time I come to footy.' And just how long had it been since she'd seen Crispin play? 'But the seat covers come off, and that's what washing machines are for.' She shrugged. 'So tell me about your knee? I've only just learned they've been bothering you.'

'I asked her not to say anything. It wasn't Aunt Luna's fault.' His face creased with worry. 'It's nothing.'

He looked upset. *Not good, Amelia. Calm down.* She thought more carefully about how she'd address this. 'That's okay. Seems a waste of resources, though, since

I'm a doctor. We could have looked at them earlier. Still, it's your choice when you mention it, of course.'

He grimaced. 'It's just that you leave so early and get home late, and we don't like to put more on your plate.'

She stopped at traffic lights and glanced across at him and down at the now-obvious swelling below both knees which she wondered how she'd missed. Mum would never have missed this. She pushed back the guilt and the common refrain that only she sang.

'You and Ryan are my priorities. I will never be too busy to hear about something you're concerned about. I'll have a good look when we get home. That is, once you've showered and I can actually see your legs.'

She smiled at him, as if it all were no drama, and his shoulders drooped with relief. Just how worried were her brothers about adding to her day? Had she appeared that wrung-out? She had been anxious about how she'd do with the new consultant recently so it might have been that. She touched Crispin's arm. 'It's nice to get five minutes with you on your own, anyway, so I'm glad I could come today.'

His smile dazzled as he looked across. 'It is nice.'

She smiled back, soaking in his dear face and seeing again how much he'd grown up. There was even a dusting of reddish facial hair across his top lip and chin. 'So how's your world?'

'Good.'

She just adored one-word answers. *Not*. She'd love to have asked if he had any ladies in the wings: Crispin had broken up with his two-year-long sweetheart, and they'd all been sad for him. But…that was his topic to bring up. 'Is your coach happy with you, apart from the knees?'

'Yep. I'm the new vice-captain since George left, and

he says the pain is probably a growth spurt and I'll be fine soon.'

'Congratulations.' Go, coach! 'You have shot up the last couple of weeks. How long have those knees been annoying you?'

He shrugged. 'About six weeks. But it's worse today. Do you know what it is?'

Her turn to smile. 'I have a suspect. Osgood-Schlatter disease, which is common after growth spurts. Usually, it's your tendons and bones growing at different rates and pulling on your patella. Gives you a lump. More often when you're a bit younger than now, but you've grown this month and you do play a lot of sport. You might need a couple of weeks less stress until it settles again.'

He frowned at that idea, though he did look chuffed she had an answer. 'Just like that? You know?'

It was common for teenage boys. No biggie. 'I suspect. But I'll have a good look later.'

'When I'm clean?' he teased, but he studied her with, maybe, awe. She felt her cheeks warm.

'Lordy, yes. Not touching them!' They both laughed, and to his delight she turned into the usually frowned-upon fast-food drive-through and bought him (and his brother at home) an upsized meal because the boys were always hungry. While they waited for the order she gestured to the glove box. 'There's hand wipes in there, before you eat.'

'Yes, Doctor,' he said smiling, but still went at cleaning his fingers. 'If it's what you think it is, what can I do to fix it?'

'The usual R-I-C-E. Rest, ice every two to three hours after use, maybe use a compression bandage and elevate. But I'll get you in to a physio for a couple of exercises that strengthen support around the ligaments and the degree of compression needed.'

'I guess I should have told you earlier?'

She nodded. 'We might have been able to reduce the severity.' She decided to joke with him but also warn him of more dire consequences. 'So make sure you tell your brother that if either of you get a sexually transmitted disease, let me know sooner rather than later before your willy drops off.'

He blushed, as horrified as she thought he might be, but still snorted a laugh. 'Gross, Amelia! Don't go there.'

She grinned back. 'Well, share sooner. Here comes your meals.'

CHAPTER FOUR

MARCO WATCHED AMELIA'S determined little stride take her through the doors quickly. His brain mulled over this new information about the enigmatic Dr Day. If her parents had died five years ago, her seventeen-year-old brothers would have been twelve and she'd just graduated with long hours of residency ahead of her.

He wondered at the commitment needed to manage a household with heartbroken boys, her own grief and her new career during that time. It would explain the seriousness of her demeanour.

He stared at the empty space thoughtfully and then turned back to the nursing unit manager. 'Our Dr Day has quite the workload.'

'Yes. I admire her very much.' Tara logged out of the computer before standing to check on a nurse. 'We're lucky to have her.' She offered nothing else. Professional to the core.

He glanced at the unit manager and resisted the urge to ask more. All the staff seemed discreet and loyal, he reminded himself and inclined his head.

If he wanted more information, he would need to ask Amelia himself. Or Henry. Not that he needed to know more. At all. No. But he could at least prevent her being interrupted in her rescue mission. 'I'll be in the hospital for the next hour if you require anything you would normally ask Amelia for. Please text me and I'll return here.'

Tara smiled at him. 'Thank you.'

He left children's ward and took himself to the cafeteria for a coffee and sandwich, something he had not had time for, drumming his fingers on the table as he nursed the cup. He could admit to some curiosity about Dr Day's home life.

For Marco, who worked daily with children and parents, he had little personal experience of real family life.

Socially he had many acquaintances, including his disinterested uncle who had raised him along with his staff, but he had no siblings and or even distant cousins. He had no idea if his mother was still alive and preferred to not wonder. The only close friend he had, and he thanked the Lord for him, was Henry.

It still surprised and delighted him that moving here had given him access to the families of Henry's friends and married colleagues his age, like Simon and his wife, Isabella; and Malachi and Lisandra, Simon's obstetrician friends, families being a demographic he'd never been interested or invited to mingle with until now. For the first time he had savoured the unusual inclusiveness extended towards him as Henry's friend. Perhaps that was why he felt such curiosity for Amelia's home life.

Even his first exposure at Henry's wedding had been a glimpse into a whole other world of warmth, relationships and, dare he say, the richness of connections he'd always lacked, despite the feverish dating scene that was his life outside work.

Now, he had learned, Amelia had sibling responsibilities usually reserved for two parents, and he wondered how she juggled that with her registrar's workload. He suspected she would be diligent as a stand-in parent, though he imagined it would leave little time for anything else. He huffed. But it was all none of his business.

His phone vibrated. Good. Something to take his mind from where it should not dwell, he thought, as he placed his cup on the discarded-crockery trolley and left the cafeteria.

Marco hailed Henry at 7:55 a.m. when he returned ten days later to children's ward, the newlywed tanned and beamingly happy. 'No need to ask how your honeymoon went,' Marco said, himself a little early and pleased to see his dear colleague so contented. Then more seriously, 'I've never seen you look so happy.'

'I tell you, Marco, there is such a thing as married bliss.'

Marco wrinkled his nose. 'Hopefully this is the only time you will tell me so.'

'One day, my friend, you will believe me.' Henry slapped him on the back. 'How did it go with the workload?'

'I can see why you needed me. I have been very busy with emergency and the wards, but your staff are excellent, and we have managed admirably.'

'Good to hear. You'll have time for patients in the consulting rooms now that I'm back. With you in emergency and me dealing with kids' ward, I'll get to have a life outside work.' He glanced around. 'Where are these wonderful staff of ours?'

'Amelia and Tom are in emergency with croupy two-year-old twins, and Sam is on his day off. So you have me and the lovely Tara for rounds this morning, unless Amelia arrives.'

'And how did you and Amelia manage together, while

I was away?' His brow lowered. 'You didn't flirt with her, did you?'

Marco held up his hands. 'I would never.' But looked up at the sudden coughing fit that erupted from the nurses' station: It seemed Tara inhaled something untoward. He raised one brow at her. 'Would you like me to pat your back?'

She tapped her chest. 'No, Doctor. Thank you. I seem to have recovered.' But her eyes twinkled. 'Good to see you back, Henry.'

Henry shook his head, but he was smiling. 'Hello, Tara. Nice to be back.' Henry glanced his way. 'Has Marco been flirting?'

Sotto voce she said to Henry, 'Amelia is impervious, but my staff are susceptible.' To Marco's relief, before Henry could ask more, Amelia arrived, looking trim and immaculate with her ridiculous glasses and her hair re-strained but not gelled today, thankfully. The red strands picked up and shone in the lights, several small twists of curls escaping and framing her face.

Their leisurely grand round of children's ward felt a lit-tle slower than his usual circuit with Amelia, and he found himself impressed again with Henry's ability to connect with parents and draw out the children.

He fell back and sent a narrowed glance Tara's way, which she ignored, though her mouth twitched. He shook his head. He enjoyed very much the easy rapport they all had in this place without the stiffness and formality of his last hospital. Henry and Amelia looked very pleased to see each other, and he began to question why *he* had not received such a warm smile in the last ten days. His brow crinkled. Perhaps he should make more effort.

When the round had been completed, Amelia asked him

to accompany her back to emergency, and Henry stayed with Tara discussing the ward patients.

Marco strode easily beside her, and he slowed when he realised she had to almost skip to keep up. 'Sorry. You are glad to see Henry back.' It wasn't a question.

'I've always enjoyed working with Henry. He's an excellent consultant and a brilliant mentor.'

'And have you enjoyed working with me for the last ten days?' Not what he intended to ask or to be so blunt, but he was strangely interested in the answer.

Amelia gave him the side-eye, but he smiled as if amused that he was the less popular boss.

Calmly she replied, 'You, too, are an excellent consultant. Now, the child I'd like you to see—'

'Before we go there, I've been meaning to ask about the problem with your brother's knees.'

She blinked, and he liked when he derailed her. It didn't happen often. 'That was more than a week ago.'

'Yes.' He waited.

She frowned but answered. 'Crispin has had a marked growth spurt in the last couple of months, and I believe it's a flare-up of Osgood-Schlatter disease. We've been nursing it, and it's less bothersome this week.'

'Ah. That can be quite painful and can interfere with his sports.'

'Yes, we've had to cut back his time on the field, but the coach is very understanding. More understanding than Crispin is.'

He smiled down at her as they walked, and her brow wrinkled as if puzzled, and he acknowledged she really was totally immune to him. Frustrating really. No accounting for taste.

She said, 'About this child—'

He cut in again. 'Of course, you know that if you wish for a second opinion for your brother, I am very happy to see him.'

Her mouth gaped, which was not something he'd seen before and was not particularly attractive but was very amusing. She closed her delightful lips.

'Thank you.' Her turn to frown. 'The child in emergency is three years old and fractured her left radius and ulna this morning. Apart from that she appears undernourished and I wonder if she has an underlying medical issue like coeliac? The father is not keen on further testing, he won't talk to me, and I'd like your opinion on how much we can push.'

CHAPTER FIVE

THANKFULLY, MARCO DROPPED the subject of Crispin: no idea where that time warp of concern came from. She'd seen him a dozen times since that afternoon, Amelia thought, as they walked into emergency. She led the way into one of the assessment rooms where a small child with one of the new purple, open-weave limb casts lay asleep on the bed.

'Dr Macaluso, this is Hetty and Bill James. Linnie fell off the baby swing onto her wrist and now has the new lightweight waterproof mesh cast, as you can see. She just needs one more X-ray to check, but the X-ray department is backlogged at the moment.'

Marco looked at Tom. 'No problem applying the new design?'

'Gillian helped, but nice and simple to apply to children.'

He nodded. Stepped up to the couple and held out his hand. 'Marco Macaluso, consultant paediatrician here in the emergency department.' The mother stepped back and the man shook hands. 'Are you happy with the cast on your daughter? Any questions?'

'Looks okay,' the man said.

'Excellent. I am sorry for the delay. The second X-ray is important to ensure Linnie's bones are perfectly aligned in the way we wish them to heal, so it needs to be done before she leaves.'

Bill nodded reluctantly.

Marco smiled. 'While we are waiting, I would like to discuss with you how Linnie's weight is perhaps less than expected for her age.'

The man's chin shot forward. 'We feed her.'

Marco smiled. 'I'm sure. Though, often disinterest in food can be due to a food allergy or disease that prevents growth rather than just being a picky eater.'

Bill glared. 'We're not having one of those mamby-pamby I'm-allergic-to-everything children.'

'Of course.' Marco's pleasant voice remained friendly and level and seemed to calm the man. Amelia wanted to squeeze the man's throat.

Marco shrugged. 'Though, sometimes it is not so simple. Hmmm?' He paused and waited until Bill gave a reluctant nod. 'More importantly, Linnie is at a crucial time for bone and brain growth for children.' He held the man's gaze. 'I'm sure you do not want to see lack of such growth affect Linnie all her life.'

He paused, and the father didn't comment. 'If there is an underlying medical issue and it is missed now, no matter how nutritional the food you give her, she would be unable to absorb the building blocks for growth should there be a problem.'

Bill opened his mouth, and Marco looked at the child's mother. 'Does Linnie have loose stools?'

'Yes. Creamy ones.' She glanced at her husband. 'You said she stinks.'

Marco smiled all around, and Amelia felt the tension ease just a little. Offensive pale stools was a sign of coeliac disease. A time when his charm came in handy, she thought and could have hugged him for managing the situation so well.

He went on. 'For how long has this been so?'

The mother said quietly, 'Pretty well once she got off the breast. Two years?'

Bill glared. 'There's nothing wrong with my daughter. Her mother is small. She picks at her food.'

The petite woman beside him compressed her lips and studied the floor.

'Perhaps. But there is a disease called coeliac which is often discovered at this age since the introduction of cereal and breads is most common after breast milk. Diarrhoea, constipation, tiredness and abdominal pain are all symptoms.' He looked directly at Hetty. 'Does this sound like Linnie?'

Hetty looked up and said firmly, 'Yes.'

Amelia admitted again to admiring his handling of this. She could do that much, anyway. In fact, maybe she had been somewhat unfair in her judgements. This wasn't the first time she'd seen him defuse situations with parents, which was why she'd asked him to accompany her this morning.

Marco nodded and smiled at Bill. 'We can test for this allergy to gluten easily, because the longer the food is given the more damage to the intestine now the antibody has formed. If it is so, then Linnie will absorb less food, affecting her growth going forward.'

Bill said nothing.

'Bill.' Marco straightened and held the man's gaze. 'Would you allow us to test for this antibody in your daughter, while we wait for the X-ray? It is a blood test, so that we may help you both choose food that will allow Linnie to grow as needed.'

'And if I say no?'

'That is your right.' Said with precision. No sign of the long, drawn-out court consequences that would follow from Marco.

The lack of threat was impressive, Amelia thought, as she forced her own face to remain neutral.

'Go on, do it—and she better not cry,' he snapped, and Hetty sagged beside him with relief.

Marco smiled calmly. 'Excellent. Dr Day is very good with young children. I will leave the taking of blood in her capable hands.'

Amelia nodded to Gillian, and the nurse slipped out and very quickly returned with the required equipment.

To Bill he said, 'If the test comes back positive, I would like your word you will both see me in my appointment room so I can make sure you all have the information needed for Linnie to grow well in the coming years. There will be no charge for this service.'

Oh, well done, Amelia thought, because perhaps the possible cost had been a factor of concern for the parents, and with that reassurance Marco had removed a potential stumbling block. Bill let out a beaten sigh. 'Yes. All right.' He glanced at his wife.

'Then, I have your word?'

'I said all right.'

Marco held out his hand. Bill shrugged. Shook. 'Yes.'

Marco offered one of his spectacular smiles, and Bill almost smiled back. 'Tom and I will leave you now so that there are less people when Linnie is woken for the test. I thank you both for your time.'

He inclined his chin at Bill and smiled at Hetty who surreptitiously nodded in gratitude. 'I hope I will not see you again,' he smiled again, 'but if even if I do, be aware you have done a good thing today for your daughter.'

When Amelia stepped out of the screened consulting area twelve minutes later, she blew out a breath of relief. No crying from Linnie. No complaints from Bill. *Phew.*

The local anaesthetic patch she'd applied and left for ten minutes while Linnie was sleeping had taken away the sting of the needle. The donated teddy bear for children undergoing procedures that Gillian had brought as well meant the little girl hadn't even noticed the drawing of blood amidst the excitement.

Amelia had taken the time waiting for the patch to work to explain to Hetty about the types of foods she could try to avoid and, while they waited for the results, a list of all those which were easily digested.

'Well done.'

Amelia lifted her head in surprise. Marco smiled, and she sucked in a breath at the unexpected impact of white teeth and crinkled eyes.

'I heard no crying.' Marco rested, one long, immaculate trouser leg crossed over the other as he leaned against the wall.

Her brows drew together. 'Are you waiting for me?'

He straightened and closed the distance to her side as she turned back towards children's ward.

'Indeed. In case there was an issue with the delightful Bill.'

'Thank you. Your intervention worked perfectly. You've been very helpful.'

'I am pleased. Now, if you are finished and about your business, I shall attempt to sway the emergency charge nurse about some extra paediatric equipment I would like to see available in the ED.'

Which left Amelia free to return to children's ward alone.

To her surprise, Henry had settled in Tara's office and waved Amelia towards the tea tray on Tara's desk, and one of the spare cups. 'Take a seat, Amelia. Join us. We're talking about a table at the hospital gala next week.'

She stifled a groan. Not that she hadn't enjoyed the company last year. She'd survived being the lone single at the table, and it was almost compulsory for the doctors to attend. Simon, their principal paediatrician, and his wife, Isabella, would share their table again, she expected. Their obstetrician friend Malachi and his wife, Lissandra, would be there too, with Henry and Nadia, children's ward's Tara and her husband, Nelson, plus now Marco and whoever he brought. And her. She would be the single one again, but it was only one night.

'I can do on call,' she offered.

'Tom and Sam will be on call, and I've arranged a pae-diatrician from another hospital to be consultant on call Friday night. Nadia and I are away until Monday. None of us will be needed during the ball. You and Marco are on call after that for the weekend, though.'

She guessed there would be no getting out of being the only single again, then. The phone rang at the nurses' desk, and Tara stood up and left the room to answer it.

Henry looked up at her. 'Were you thinking of bring-ing anyone, Amelia?'

Her brows rose. As if she had men to choose from. Un-less she brought a brother. She smiled at that thought. 'Uh, no. Not this year.'

To her surprise, Henry looked relieved. 'That works out, then. The tables hold ten and with Marco we're full.'

'Oh, I'm sure he'll find someone he wants to take… I could sit somewhere else.'

Henry waved that away. 'Marco can flirt with other tables from there…unless it's a problem sitting next to him?'

Her boss gave her a piercing look. Not something she'd been the recipient of often. She chewed her lip. 'No. Of course not. No problem at all.'

'Good,' Henry said, leaning in and lowering his voice. 'While we're alone,' he said and glanced towards the open door and Tara dealing with the inquiry on the phone, 'how've you been doing working with Marco, Amelia?'

Good grief. Still agitated by the idea of spending the ball hours seated next to Lothario, she found herself repeating what she'd told the man on the way to ED. 'He's an excellent consultant.' She thought about the stellar job Marco had done at wrangling Linnie's dad and added, 'And he's very skilled at defusing difficult situations. In those cases, he's a real asset.'

Henry looked surprised by her praise. 'I'm glad. I think he'll bring a lot to the department.' Henry sat back. 'Good. How are your brothers?'

She let out a breath, glad to be on a safer topic. Though, why the topic of Marco Macaluso felt like a dangerous discussion she didn't know. Or want to think about. 'The boys are good. Crispin's had a problem with Osgood-Schlatter disease, but it's settling this week with physio and rest.'

He nodded. 'I had that as a teen. It's a pain. And your aunt Luna?'

Amelia smiled. 'She's good. Now that the boys are older and looking at getting their own vehicles, she's making travel plans again. We've been very fortunate to have her for the last five years, but it's time for her to do her own thing.'

Henry dipped his chin. 'You'll miss her very much.'

'I will.' And she didn't want to think about how much. 'How was Lord Howe?' Nadia and Henry had flown to the island to spend a week for their honeymoon and Amelia had always wanted to see that remote isle sitting in the Pacific Ocean between Australia's east coast and New Zealand.

'We were lucky with blue skies and did all the mountain treks as well as the beach swims. We loved the place. I know Nadia would like to go back for a week every year in school holidays with Katie. We even tried scuba diving and the cliff climb.'

'So, what was the best part?'

His eyes twinkled, and she blushed and hurried on with, 'Apart from time with Nadia.'

'Knowing the phone wasn't going to ring. There was no mobile phone service because it's out of signal range and there's not much Wi-Fi.'

Amelia laughed. 'I heard they don't have mobile coverage.'

Henry sighed blissfully. 'A whole week without phones.'

She laughed. 'You make me want to move there.'

CHAPTER SIX

MARCO COULD HEAR the laughter as he reached the office door and Amelia saying she wanted to move. The thought sent a strange chill through him. Tara put her hand over the phone and whispered, 'Henry and Amelia are inside.'

His first sight was a different woman to the one he'd seen in any of the scenarios they'd shared. A beautiful woman. Her face alight. The skin around her eyes crinkled with amusement and her mouth tilted delightfully up. She even had her glasses off as she wiped her eyes.

He said, 'Move where?' And just like that, at his voice her mirth froze. Disappeared. Dissolved into a frown line as he stared at her. She slipped her glasses on.

Marco's gaze remained fixed on her for some reason.

'Lord Howe. No phone coverage,' said Henry. 'But she's joking. No paediatric jobs to be had there.'

Marco shifted his gaze to Henry for a second and saw Henry's raised brows at Amelia's drastic change. His own dropped into a puzzled expression. Marco flicked back to Amelia.

She frowned at him. She didn't say *Stop staring out loud*, but it was there in her look. She said, 'Did you talk Gilly into the new equipment?'

He could not believe the change in her from one instant to the next. As if she'd tasted something bad. Him? He answered absently while he processed. 'I think so. She has donation money to spend.'

'Which equipment?' Henry said.

'An infrared vein-finder for cannulation. I think one in each observation room would be useful for preventing unnecessary trauma for children when junior staff are required to cannulate.'

'Great idea.' Henry looked at Amelia and smiled. 'Though, Dr Day seems to have no problem with IV access. She's our star.'

Amelia stood. 'And on that high note I'll leave you to it. I want to check on Linnie's repeat X-ray.'

Marco held up his hand. 'I have done. The alignment is excellent. They've been discharged.'

'Oh good.' Yet she appeared…disappointed? He wondered why. She glanced at her watch.

Henry stood as well. 'Before you leave, Amelia, we're having drinks at our place before the ball on Friday. Nadia asked if you'd like to join us. Say six?'

She stared at Henry. Chewed her lip, the plump, soft skin creasing with the pressure. He wished she wouldn't misuse that tender flesh so cruelly. 'Lovely. Thanks.'

Marco wondered if she was being truthful, not sure why he searched for nuances that shouldn't interest him at all. She added, 'One of the boys can drop me off in my car and pick me up when we move to the ball. They'd enjoy the practice. They don't get much chance to drive at night.'

Marco almost offered to pick her up when Henry nodded and said before he could, 'See you then.'

Which meant that this was his time to either leave them to it, or add some kind of clinical contribution that Amelia could not—but of course that was a no.

Therefore, he was now officially the ED and consulting rooms paediatrician only, with Henry returned to consultant for children's ward and a greater presence in the consulting rooms like Simon.

He supposed he should go to the office himself and move into his rooms.

The following Friday Marco, running behind after a late paediatric consultation, had only been home half an hour, a busy time in which he'd showered, dressed in his silk and twill tuxedo with the peak lapel jacket and pleated trousers in blue—the same colour as Amelia's ridiculous glasses—and wondered briefly what colour dress she would wear tonight. And more whether, he hoped, she would leave her hair free.

He'd found a decent Italian delicatessen in Tweed Heads and assembled swiftly the antipasto sticks he'd promised Nadia, glad he'd bought his mini bocconcini and green olives, prosciutto and cherry tomatoes yesterday. The first thing he'd added to his kitchen had been a thriving pot of basil, and a leaf or two of that at each side of the tomato finished the sticks off nicely. The potted herbs and his patio garden should be finished this week. The contractor Tara had suggested had turned out to be excellent.

Stepping out of his ground-floor flat backwards with his tray of skewers, he leaned to lock the door and almost bumped into the woman waiting for the lift.

He heard an indrawn breath and several quick steps before he turned.

A flash of vibrant blue with an intricate floral pattern shimmered in front of him, and Amelia's pale shoulders glimmered like porcelain in the light. Most delightfully, her glorious red coils were a siren's call falling to the off-shoulder design like a writhing, flaming curtain. He had a sudden intense desire, which he curbed with too much difficulty, to twirl a ruby strand around his finger and kiss the shoulder beneath.

His gaze dropped to the straight line across her gently swelling breasts and glanced down the length of her to the floating hem that caressed her slim ankles. Silver heels lifted her height to near his throat.

'Bellissima, Amelia.' His breath caught as his gaze rose to embrace the feminine whole. 'Questo vestito ti sta bene.'

'Thank you, I think. I missed the last part.' She gestured to his platter. 'You live here? And you cook?'

'Sì. I said the dress is good.' He waved his new abode away. 'I prepared antipasto only. And sì, this is where I live. But you? You make me feel very Italian tonight. Not some laid back Australian dude, when I see you like this.'

'*Dude*?' This time she smiled as if she couldn't help herself. Just a small one, but he counted that as a win. 'You look very fine yourself.' Before he could take her hand to kiss it, unfortunately still occupied with the platter, the lift arrived.

He stood back to allow her to step in first, ruing his missed opportunity, and followed. He pressed the button for the top floor. 'Did your brother bring you here safely?'

'He did. And his twin will pick me up.' She shrugged, a smile in her eyes, perhaps for her siblings. Certainly not for him. 'They may even become handy when they have wheels of their own.'

He smiled at that. 'For all the times you go out on the town?'

Her eyes narrowed. 'Life will become less hectic. Soon.'

'This is good. When was the last time you went with a man to dinner?'

Silence until she smiled at the light above the doors, not him, as the lift stopped and opened. 'Here we are.' She stepped out and across to the door where she knocked without hesitating. Without answering. That was the last time she looked at him until they sat down together at the ball.

CHAPTER SEVEN

MARCO PULLED OUT her chair at the stylishly decorated table at the ball, and Amelia placed her evening bag behind her back as she sat.

'Thank you.' When he pushed in her chair and sat beside her, she tried not to edge away. She'd known she would end up sitting next to Marco, Marco of the glamorous tuxedo that fit like a second skin to his wide shoulders and long legs. Marco of the expertly tousled hair and sexy smile and some divine aftershave that made her want to sniff his sleeve. Or his neck. Which of course she wouldn't do.

Thankfully she had Henry on her other side to keep her sane, and Marco had Malachi's wife next to him. Lisandra could hold her own without being dazzled. Amelia wasn't so sure she could, not with that white shirt fitted to his broad chest as if by a smoothing hand and the blue bow tie drawing attention to his strong throat. It all felt far too disconcerting.

Hopefully, the man would become distracted with someone else soon and flirt far, far away.

She hadn't been prepared to run into him in all his Italian glory immediately on the ground floor of Henry's building, having forgotten he lived there, but of course right on the beach was a nice place to live. He had everything. And probably took it all for granted.

She frowned at her pettiness. *Stop it.* This wasn't like her. She needed to get over whatever had wound her up. Or whoever. She forced herself to turn to *him* and smile. 'Your antipasto at Henry's was delicious.'

'Grazie mille. My uncle's housekeeper ensured I knew how to at least create something I could eat before I drank too much alcohol. Of course, that was in my foolish days before medicine.'

'Ah. I'll pass that recipe on to the boys when they reach legal age at eighteen.' She glanced at the tables around them and several elegant women had their eyes firmly on Marco. Situation normal. 'Do you know many people at the other tables?'

He didn't look away. 'Unlikely.' Apparently not at all interested in greener pastures just yet. He turned sideways in his seat and studied her face as if fascinated by her. He felt far too close. Her heart rate picked up, and with a touch of agitation she stroked the napkin the waiter had placed in her lap.

His teeth were white as he gave her the full force of his smile. 'Tell me, Amelia'—that damn Italian accent so smooth and delicious—'how do you manage two teenage brothers and a house while attending long hours at the hospital?'

She shifted her own chair a little farther to the left from his, hoping Henry wouldn't mind her crowding him. Moistened her dry lips. 'My mother's sister, my aunt Luna, offered to move in after my parents' funeral and has stayed with us. I don't think I would have managed without her.'

That was true. Luna should have been called Solis because like the sun she'd risen every day to the occasion and just been there warming and mothering them with the lightest but most loving touch.

He quirked a brow. Just one. Cute. She'd always wanted to do that eyebrow trick but couldn't. 'Perhaps you would have managed, but it would have been much harder.'

She shrugged, unsure where he was going with this. 'I'll never know, and I'm glad I don't. We've been blessed with her for five years so far. But Luna loves to travel. Now that the boys are grown, she'll be leaving soon and they and I will have to take over the things that she does until they leave too.' She was babbling. She shut her lips and stopped. Forced her shoulders to relax. No. She could do this calmly. He was just a man.

'Then, you will be alone?'

She frowned at him. *Gee, thanks. Rub it in, why don't you?* 'We're not there yet. The twins don't finish high school until the end of the year. They might even stay on the Gold Coast for university.' She could hear the forlorn hope in that last utterance, and he didn't need to know any of this stuff. He had to find it boring compared to his social life. To other women's lives.

She was about to ask about how he was enjoying Australia when he said, 'I find this very interesting.'

'You do? Why?' She hadn't meant to say it, but that was her mouth tonight.

As if happy to find a topic of conversation, he said, 'I was an only child who spent my childhood with an uncle, cared for by his staff. Families such as yours are a mystery to me. Except in our work.'

Okay, then. That was unexpected. Maybe she should be a little sympathetic for his loss. 'I'm sorry. Can I ask what happened to your parents?'

A tiny shrug of those massive shoulders. 'I was seven

when they both went. My uncle ensured I was cared for. Later, in London, Henry became my closest friend, and it is strange,' he said as he flashed that wicked grin, 'and a pleasure to be included in his close circle here.' He shrugged. 'My first real experience of warmth and families.'

And she found that interesting, too. *Darn it.* And even a little poignant. Her gaze drifted around the table. Malachi and Lisandra had three children. Isabella and Simon had two. Nadia had one, and she doubted it would be long before Nadia and Henry thought about extending their family.

Here was this single man who clearly loved the high life and women, saying he had no experience of warmth and love. Something, despite the loss of their parents, that she, the boys, and Luna shared so strongly. She had to admit this insight lent her a small shift in her thoughts towards the man.

Tonight he appeared honest and open, and perhaps she could lower some of the barriers between them briefly. Just for tonight.

'This table does hold a lovely group of people. Though, I'm more comfortable with Henry and Nadia, since I know them the most. They're a wonderful couple.' She smiled. 'Perhaps you'll find yourself a partner on the Gold Coast and create your own family.'

His face grimaced as if she'd just asked him to lick a discarded piece of chewing gum. She almost laughed at his expression, such was his horror. Her mouth did curve.

He replied, 'Unlikely.' He lifted his glass to his lips and took a sip. Put it down. Shifted his chair back. 'Very kind of you to say, but not me. If you'll excuse me…'

He stood and walked away. Amelia blinked and shook

her head ever so slightly. Gave a little puff of amusement. Yep, that was the guy she remembered. The one she didn't understand. And didn't want to.

She shifted her chair back to its original position and turned to Henry who sat back to sip his wine. He smiled at her. 'How are you getting on with Marco? Haven't stabbed him with your fork yet?'

Another puff of amusement, and she felt herself fully relax, at last. 'Certainly not, Henry.' But what a great idea if he caused her a problem. She could feel the crinkle around her eyes. 'Thanks for the invitation to drinks tonight, Henry. It really was a fun start to the evening.'

His smile was easy. 'Glad you enjoyed it.' He glanced at the empty seat next to her. 'Marco gone to check out the room?'

'I imagine so. Lots of lovely ladies here tonight. He did say you two lived together in London.' Couldn't imagine it, but there you go. 'You both worked at Great Ormond Street children's hospital?'

'Yes. Excellent place to finish for experience. Marco's a good antidote for homesickness.'

'I can imagine he would be diverting,' she said dryly.

Henry laughed. 'He does have stamina.' He paused thoughtfully. 'Don't get him wrong, Amelia, he's a player, but the man has a good heart. I count myself lucky he's my friend.'

She was surprised Henry had felt the need to say that. She'd always had the impression he'd frowned on Marco's flirtatious lifestyle. 'That's a nice endorsement, Henry. I'm glad for you both. Do you think he'll stay?'

Henry smiled, and there was true pleasure in it. 'He's already put his deposit on Nadia's flat downstairs.' He patted his wife's hand. 'Says he's going to learn to surf.'

Nadia leaned across her husband, joining the conversation. 'You're a local, aren't you, Amelia? Do you and the boys surf?'

'A long time ago. When I was younger. They still do. A lot of us did at school.'

Henry laughed. 'And you're so old now?'

Nadia tutted at her husband. 'She's younger than you, darling.' She smiled at Amelia. 'Our grandmother taught my sister and me to surf when we were kids.' She looked at her and said nonchalantly, 'Maybe you should teach Marco to surf?'

'As if,' she blurted out before she could stop it, and both Henry and Nadia laughed. Her eyes met Nadia's, the shared knowledge that Marco would look great in swimmers. That had been a moment of such truth she probably should have held it in. They grinned at each other.

The topic left Amelia with a disturbing visual of Marco in designer swim trunks bobbing on the board next to her in the waves. 'I mean, no, I don't think so. Plus, who has time for that stuff with our workload, anyway?'

'Henry will,' Nadia said firmly. 'With Marco here, he will have loads of time of not being on call.'

'That's the plan,' Henry said calmly. 'Where do you think you'll be looking for your consultancy, Amelia, when the time comes? Can we entice you to stay here with us?'

It was only another year away. But very nice to think there might be an option of joining a group of men she respected so highly. Except for Marco, of course; though professionally, the man was excellent. 'I guess it depends where the boys go to uni. Luna is about ready to go back to her travels.'

'Big changes.' Henry took his wife's hand in his. 'The twins finish school at the end of this year, don't they?'

'They do. I could be an empty nester by December.'

'You might find you'll enjoy some time to yourself. It was your parents' nest, really, and you haven't even started yours.' He smiled as the musicians took their instruments up again. Henry glanced at Nadia. 'Excuse me. I need to beg my wife for a dance.'

Amelia smiled, loving their romance, and resisted the urge to say *Awww* at the cute couple, until a dark shadow appeared beside her.

'Will you dance with me, Amelia?' Dulcet tones lifted the hairs on her arms, and she slowly turned to see Marco holding out his hand towards her.

The low rumble of his voice seemed to vibrate right through her chest, settling somewhere dangerous near her throat. Which closed. She'd been trying not to watch him from the safety of her seat beside Henry, noting how every woman in the room seemed to lean toward him like silly moths hoping he'd wave his light at them.

The way he moved with that unconscious grace, the way his dinner jacket fit his broad shoulders perfectly, the way he threw his head back when he laughed—all of it had been difficult to ignore in her periphery.

Now he was back. In her space. He loomed. 'You want to dance? With me?' The question came out sharper than she'd intended. She couldn't help it. Men like Marco Macaluso didn't dance with women like her. They danced with stunning creatures like Sybyl, an agency nurse she didn't know well, in her scarlet silk or sophisticated beauties who knew how to tilt their heads just so and flutter their lashes with practiced ease.

'This is a ball, is it not? Dancing is required.' His elegant hand remained. Waiting. The music swelled around them, a tune she at least recognised.

Patiently he said, 'You should say *Yes, thank you* and stand.' He lifted those dark brows, and she caught the hint of amusement in his eyes. 'No?'

No, she thought wildly. Absolutely not. The last thing she wanted, or needed, was to make a fool of herself in his arms while half the hospital staff watched. But something in his expression, something gentle, made her defences waver. Before she could think better of it, she lifted her fingers to his, that grip warm and strong, as he helped her from the chair.

The contact sent shivers shooting up her arm. His hand, sure and strong, completely engulfed her smaller one.

Oh heck, she thought as he led her toward the dance floor. Thank goodness for dance lessons even if they were from more than ten years ago for her high school formal. Please don't let me step on his feet. Please don't let me trip. Please don't let me—

But one turn into the dance she discovered she probably didn't need dance lessons when she had Marco Macaluso holding her firmly in his arms. There was no hesitation in directing her where he wanted her, no uncertainty in his movements. The heat from his fingers soaked into her bare shoulder, and the firmness of his press at her waist, warm through the thin silk of her dress, directed her easily.

She'd forgotten how tall he was until she had to tilt her head back to meet his gaze. This close, she could see the flecks of gold in his dark eyes and catch the scent of his cologne, that something expensive and masculine that made her want to lean closer.

The music lifted her, and she followed his lead with astonishing ease, so much so that she could have closed her eyes and just drifted after him. Her body seemed to know instinctively where he wanted her to go, anticipating his turns, matching his rhythm as if they'd done this a hundred times before.

It wasn't too bad, actually. Almost…magical.

The thought terrified her.

'You dance well, Amelia.' His voice was lower now, intimate, meant only for her ears. She could feel the rumble of it where her hand rested against his chest, could feel the steady beat of his heart beneath her palm.

'Hmmm. No choice. I'm just following your strong lead.'

It was easier to deflect than to acknowledge how perfectly they moved together, how right this felt when everything about Marco Macaluso should feel wrong for someone like her.

'You are like a bluebell in the breeze, bending and swaying, beautiful like a nymph in that dress.'

The words hit her like cold water. Bluebell. Nymph. Pretty words, practiced words—the kind of flowery compliments he probably scattered like confetti to every woman who caught his attention. She stumbled, reality crashing back as she remembered exactly what this was: Marco being Marco, charming and smooth and utterly superficial.

He lifted her back into step before anyone could notice, his hold tightening protectively, but the spell was broken.

She looked up and glared at him, anger at herself replacing the dangerous warmth that had been building in her chest. 'Stop flirting with me.'

He smiled broadly down at her, seemingly unbothered by her sharp tone. 'You don't trust me. You never have. But we dance well together.'

The observation stung because it was partially true. She didn't trust him but didn't dislike him, though, not really—that was the problem. She disliked how he made her feel, how easily he could scatter her thoughts with nothing more than a smile.

'I think I've had enough.'

For a fleeting moment she panicked, needing distance and to get away from the heat of his hands and the way he was looking at her like she was something precious instead of just another conquest.

'But to walk away in the midst of the music will not happen, I think.'

He was right, of course. She had been raised better than that, and besides, creating a scene would only give people more to gossip about. The hospital grapevine was vicious enough without adding fuel to the fire.

'Really?' She did not make scenes. She made do. 'True. It will be over soon enough.'

But even as she said it, part of her wished the music would go on forever. Wished she could stay here in his arms, pretending for just a little longer that she was the kind of woman who deserved fairy tale moments.

She had overreacted. That had been childish because the man couldn't help himself, and she knew she should have let it pass. She just didn't want to be one of those women he picked up and put down like those on the wards, collected like pretty shells on Coolangatta Beach before moving on to the next shiny thing. She would have to apologize. Darn it.

The final notes of the music hung in the air between them, and she stepped back immediately, breaking the spell completely. His hands lifted, reluctantly she noticed, as if he'd been in no hurry to let her go.

'I apologise. I did not mean to annoy you.' The sincerity in his voice caught her off guard. She'd expected smooth charm, easy dismissal—not this quiet acknowledgement that suggested he actually cared about her reaction.

She felt the ease of tension beneath her fingers, forcing herself to relax. 'I overreacted. I apologise too.' She glanced very briefly up at him, noting the way his dark eyes seemed to search her face. Her chin lifted as she gathered her courage. 'Just don't flirt with me, Marco.'

It wasn't a request. It was a repeated plea out of self-preservation. 'Thank you for the dance.'

Let him be confused. It was safer for both of them that way.

CHAPTER EIGHT

SO THE FEARLESS Fly really was fearless. Marco looked down at the vibrant red of Amelia's hair so close to his chest before she stepped away and wondered what he'd said to annoy her. It was so easily done with this woman, but disconcertingly he wanted her closer.

Of course, those ridiculous glasses would probably catch on his shirt buttons…and she would stamp on his toes if he tried to hold on. He'd never had someone take such an active dislike to him before. Except perhaps his mother. He frowned the thought away.

This was disappointing when she felt so good in his arms.

He should've savoured the last of the dance because he doubted she'd accept again, anytime soon.

She glanced very briefly up at him, and her beautiful eyes were firm. Her chin lifted briefly as she stepped away.

Just don't flirt with me, she'd said. It was her right, of course. But why not? he wondered. Flirting was fun. Usually, though, he was standing there like some lovesick fool watching her weave through the crowded ballroom with that brisk, efficient, yet feminine walk of hers. Normally he didn't have a problem with women saying no to him: their choice. But with Amelia he didn't like it. The question lodged in his chest. Why didn't she want him to flirt with her?

She was beautiful—not in the obvious way of the women who usually caught his attention but in a way that had crept up on him. The way she moved with unconscious grace, the way her eyes sparked with intelligence when she was arguing a point in case discussion, the way that stubborn chin of hers lifted when she was about to deliver one of her decisive observations.

Even the way she'd felt in his arms just now, perfectly sized and surprisingly pliant despite her prickly exterior.

But there was something else, something that made his usual smooth confidence feel clumsy and inadequate. She looked at him and saw not the man other women seemed to find pleasing. She saw something that clearly offended her.

Him? The realisation stung more than it should have.

Then, as he turned, his eye caught the smile of a woman in red, welcome in her eyes, and there was no doubt about the warm interest being offered. Warmer than the woman walking away, certainly. Sybyl—that was her name. An agency nurse with obvious assets and even more obvious intentions. She had been his companion last week for a few nights.

With a very strange reluctance he followed the woman in red's invitation, allowing himself to lead her back onto the dance floor, and pushed away all thoughts of Amelia Day. Or tried to.

Sybyl pressed against him with practiced ease, her conversation light and flirtatious, her laughter tinkling at all the right moments. Everything a man could want in a dance partner. So why did he find himself scanning the room over her head, looking for a flash of ruby hair and wide-rimmed glasses?

'You're distracted tonight,' Sybyl purred, her fingers trailing along his lapel. 'Something on your mind?'

'Not at all,' he lied smoothly, forcing his attention back to the woman in his arms. But his gaze kept drifting toward the tables, searching for Amelia's familiar figure.

This was ridiculous. He didn't pine after difficult women who made it clear they wanted nothing to do with him. He moved on. He always moved on.

Marco returned to his table when the entrées arrived, sliding into his chair with practiced ease. Amelia had slipped back to her own seat from where she'd taken his to chat with Lisandra, and now sat with her back slightly turned toward him. Professional courtesy kept her from being openly rude, but her body language spoke volumes.

She smiled when he sat down, so polite, and so distant, but her gaze appeared fixed over his shoulder, as if meeting his eyes directly might be physically painful. The careful way she avoided looking at him was almost insulting. He was used to women stealing glances, fluttering their lashes, finding excuses to catch his attention.

Not this one. This one acted like he was invisible. Or repulsive.

The salmon was perfectly prepared, but Marco found himself picking at it absently, far too aware of the woman beside him who seemed determined to pretend he didn't exist. When she laughed at something Nadia whispered about Henry, a genuine, warm sound, he felt an unexpected stab of envy. What would it take to make her laugh like that with him?

The thought was so foreign, so unlike his usual confidence with women, that it left him slightly off balance.

He left when he'd finished his appetiser and danced

with Sybyl again, who flirted outrageously with him, pressing against his chest and whispering suggestions that would have made a seasoned playboy blush. It didn't upset her when his responses were less than enthusiastic; if anything, she seemed to take it as a challenge, her hands wandering in ways that should have been arousing but only made him feel restless and irritated.

This was what he was good at, so why did it all feel so hollow tonight?

When Henry and Amelia passed on the dance floor, his brows drew down to hear Amelia chuckle at something Henry had said. The same warm, genuine laugh she'd shared with Nadia, her face transformed from merely pretty to beautiful. Henry spun her with expert ease, and she threw her head back with delight, her glowing hair catching the ballroom lights.

Something dark and possessive twisted in Marco's chest. Henry was newly married, for saints' sake, and yet she responded to him with an ease and warmth she'd never shown Marco.

What did his colleague have that he lacked? Respect, a treacherous voice whispered in his mind. He has her respect.

Sybyl squeezed his shoulder suggestively, murmuring something about dessert being served at her place later, and he found himself vaguely annoyed rather than intrigued.

He was glad when the dance ended, and he could return to the table again for the main meal. Which had to be a first. Tonight, it all felt like empty theatre.

Amelia said goodnight as soon as dessert was removed, rising from her chair with that efficient grace that somehow managed to be both businesslike and utterly feminine.

No doubt one of her brothers had arrived to pick her up. She gathered her small purse and wrap with quick movements, said her polite goodbyes to the table and headed for the exit.

He didn't miss her at all, he told himself firmly. The woman was prickly and difficult and seemed to take genuine pleasure in deflating his ego at every opportunity. Her absence was actually a relief.

Though, he found himself watching her progress toward the door, noting the way she seemed to have somehow shed the ball from her. As if she'd wrapped a practical cardigan around her shoulders, covering the elegant line of her dress, transforming herself back into the no-nonsense registrar he was used to seeing in the corridors of the hospital.

Even her exit was efficient: no lingering farewells, no dramatic gestures, no backward glances. She simply… left. Leaving the ballroom feeling somehow less vibrant, less interesting.

He forced himself to turn back to the table with a casual smile, as if he hadn't been watching at all.

'What happened there?' Henry asked in a low voice, settling back into his chair with a knowing look that made Marco's jaw tighten. There was something almost paternal in his friend's tone, protective in a way that made Marco's chest clench with an emotion he didn't want to examine too closely.

He shrugged, reaching for his wine glass with studied casualness, grateful for something to do with his hands. 'Nothing. A compliment that drew an unexpected response. Your registrar is odd.'

Even as he said it, the word felt wrong on his tongue. *Odd* wasn't right. *Complicated*, perhaps. *Intriguing*, definitely. But not odd.

'My registrar is perfect just the way she is.' The warning in Henry's voice was unmistakable, the message clear: hands off. As if Marco were some sort of predator circling innocent prey.

Was Amelia perfect? The word echoed in his mind as he took a careful sip of wine, trying to look unaffected by the rebuke. Perfect, prickly, and completely immune to his charm.

Which should have been a relief, he told himself. He didn't do complications in his life, work was enough. He didn't need to add a prickly woman to the mix. Especially one who worked under him, one who could make his professional life hell if things went wrong.

Instead, Henry's protective stance only made him want to try harder. Made him wonder what it would take to crack through that professional facade and find the woman underneath—the one who laughed so freely with Henry, who moved like that bending flower in his arms when she forgot to be defensive.

The one who'd felt so right against him that he was still thinking about her hours later.

CHAPTER NINE

At ELEVEN O'CLOCK ON SATURDAY, the night after the ball, Amelia's hands trembled as she reached for her phone. *Marco.* The name blazed through her mind like a lifeline. Fifteen-year-old Braelynn Wild was dying, and she needed help to save her.

The emergency department admission had shattered Amelia's pleasant evening at home with the boys like glass. Sam's urgent call still echoed in her ears—a young girl spiralling into critical condition. Braelynn had woken with what seemed like a simple sore throat that morning.

By afternoon, nausea and headache had crept in, and now exhaustion had claimed her so completely that her terrified mother had rushed her to the hospital.

Now Amelia's blood turned to ice as she pressed the petechial rash with her fingertip. The pink pinpricks refused to blanch, refused to fade to healthy skin colour. Every fibre of her medical training screamed one conclusion: *meningococcal disease.*

Her mind raced through scenarios as the phone rang.

'Marco.' Just one word yet his voice poured through the phone like warm honey, languid and sexy. Music drifted in the background, but Amelia's world had narrowed to this single moment, this need for help.

'It's Amelia. New admission, fifteen-year-old female.

Critical on admission. I'd like to rule out meningococcal disease, but I can't.' The words tumbled out, each one holding the gravity of Braelynn's young life hanging in the balance.

'Ah. I will be there immediately.' The line went dead.

Thank heaven. Relief flooded through her like a tide. She was already organising the chaos around her, nurses scurrying to prepare equipment under her rapid-fire instructions to be ready, when Marco swept through the emergency department doors.

Ten minutes. He'd made it in ten minutes—he must have driven. The sight of him stopped her for a moment: cologne trailing behind him, crisp white shirt stretched across his broad shoulders, dark trousers and black shoes. His hair stood dishevelled, but those intense eyes, they burned with the same determination that she needed to see.

Together they could do this. Stop a girl from dying.

'Her parents are outside. The nurses are setting up for a lumbar puncture, and the on-call anaesthetist is on his way for intubation.' The words came automatically, her training overriding the way her body responded to his presence.

He nodded, and she felt that annoying flutter in her stomach at his commanding presence.

'I've put two cannulas in and taken bloods. We're waiting for the lumbar puncture before we start antibiotics. I'm considering isolation procedures.'

'Begin them.' Two words, but they carried the weight of absolute authority.

'We're going into isolation procedures. Masks everyone,' her voice rang clear through the department. The familiar ritual began—masks, gloves, yellow gowns that crinkled like paper. Even through the chaos, she was aware of Marco beside her, his gaze roaming the read-outs of the equipment. Assessing the patient. Efficient and practiced.

She followed him to the sink, words spilling out as he scrubbed. 'Braelynn had a sore throat this morning, nausea and headache at lunchtime, photophobic, stiff neck and exhaustion this evening. Her parents brought her into emergency twenty minutes ago and she has a petechial rash. Nonblanching. Temperature forty degrees Celsius, blood pressure eighty over forty, heart rate one fifty.'

His eyes met hers as he dried his hands, and she saw her own fear reflected there. 'These observations on admission?'

'Correct. She's had immunisation for the four meningococcal strains but not type B.' *Please don't let it be type B. Please.*

'Merda,' the Italian curse slipped out under his breath, and her heart sank. He caught himself, glanced at her with something like dread. 'My apologies. This is not good.'

Not good was medical understatement for *this child might die tonight.*

'Do you wish to do the lumbar puncture, or shall I? We're ready now. The consent has been signed by parents. I'm happy to, but you might be faster since antibiotics is our essential aim.' Her words tumbled together, professionalism wrestling with the desperate need to save this girl.

'Sì, naturalmente.' The Italian rolled off his tongue like music, even in crisis. He looked at the nurse. 'Size eight gloves.'

Amelia's chest tightened as she watched him dress in sterile clothes, his movements swift and sure. This is why she had called him, why she wanted his support. The load already felt lighter in the shared space with Marco.

While Sam and the nurses positioned Braelynn, Amelia forced herself to face the parents, to explain with calm authority that antibiotics would begin the moment the lumbar puncture was complete. Inside, she tried not to think *What if we're too late? What if we can't save her?*

She couldn't tear her gaze away as Marco worked. His hands moved with surgical precision, each gesture speaking of years of training, of lives saved and lost. When he drew out the cerebro-spinal fluid—far too cloudy—her stomach clenched. The ominous lack of clarity told a story neither of them wanted to see.

A nurse whisked the sample away to pathology where a technician had been called in to test it immediately.

The moment Marco withdrew the needle, Amelia's hands were ready, injecting the first of the multitude of antibiotics into the IV line. Please let it be the right ones. Please let it be in time.

Neisseria meningitidis: The name of their invisible foe repeated through her thoughts as she worked.

By two in the morning, stress weighed on Amelia's shoulders. Braelynn had stabilised—thank heaven she'd stabilised—and now breathed through a ventilator in the care of intensive care, two specialist nurses in the room with her.

The battle had been intense: antibiotics against infection, medications against crashing blood pressure and soaring temperature, intravenous fluids flowing, supportive ventilation keeping breath moving in and out of Braelynn's lungs.

Now came the hardest part: the waiting.

Amelia's hands trembled as she checked Braelynn's circulation, searching for signs of the blood clots that could steal fingers, toes, even limbs from this fifteen-year-old girl who should be worrying about homework and first dates, not fighting for her life.

Please, no amputations. Please let her keep everything that makes her feel whole.

For now, she was critical but stable, so while Marco discussed doses of medication with the nurses, Amelia found Braelynn's mother and father hunched in the family consultation room, their hands wrapped around cold cups of tea that someone had brought them hours ago. The woman's eyes were red-rimmed and desperate, and Amelia's heart clenched at the terror etched on her face. The father looked shut down.

How do I explain this without terrifying them more than they already are?

'Mr and Mrs Wild?' Amelia settled into the chair across from them, keeping her voice gentle. 'I wanted to talk to you both about what we're dealing with and answer any questions you might have.'

The woman's head snapped up. 'Is she… Will she…?' The words fractured before they could form.

'Braelynn is stable right now,' Amelia said quickly, watching relief flicker across their features. *Start with hope. Always start with hope.* 'But I want to help you understand what meningococcal disease is so you know what we're fighting.'

Mrs Wild nodded frantically. 'Yes, please. I don't understand how this happened. She was fine yesterday morning, just a normal teenager complaining about getting up for school.'

That's how it worked, swift and deadly. Amelia leaned forward slightly. 'The pathogen that causes this disease is specific to humans. It's a bacteria called neisseria meningitidis, and it causes infection in the lining of the brain and spinal cord—that's the meningitis part—and it can also get into the bloodstream.'

'But how?' Mrs Wild's voice cracked. 'How did she catch it? We're careful about hygiene, we eat well, she's had all her vaccinations...'

The guilt. It was always about the guilt. 'This isn't your fault,' Amelia said firmly. 'Ten to twenty per cent of young teenagers carry this bacterium in the back of their nose or throat without any symptoms at all. They're perfectly healthy carriers.'

Mrs Wild blinked. 'You mean other kids at school might have it and not even know?'

'Exactly. They can carry it for weeks or months without getting sick themselves.' Amelia watched understanding dawn in the woman's eyes. 'It spreads through close contact—coughing, sharing drinks, kissing.'

'I knew she shouldn't have gone to that party.' Mr Wild shook his head.

His wife sighed. 'That was two weeks ago.'

Amelia said quickly, 'Two weeks would be a stretch. Unlikely. But now your household is at risk, which is why we'll need to give preventive antibiotics to you and your family members.'

They both stared. 'Our resident doctor, Tom, will organise that.'

She knew Braelynn had two brothers. 'But it's not as easily transmitted as something like the common cold. You can't catch it just by breathing the same air in a room. It requires closer contact than that.'

'So her friends...her boyfriend...' Mrs Wild's face paled.

'Yes. We'll need to track close contacts and provide preventive treatment where needed,' Amelia assured her. 'That's standard protocol.'

Mrs Wild's hands trembled around her teacup. 'But she had her immunisations. The school nurse made sure all the kids were up to date before they started high school.'

Amelia chose her words carefully. 'Braelynn did have immunisation for four strains of meningococcal disease. Unfortunately, there are five main strains, and she hadn't received the vaccination for type B yet.'

'Type B?' The mother's voice was barely a whisper.

'That one is a newer vaccine. Not all teenagers have received it yet, though we're working to change that. South Australia has it on their free list and we're hoping all of Australia will have it soon, too.'

'So this could have been prevented?' The accusation in Mr Wild's voice cut through the room.

The question every parent asked. Marco appeared at the door. Entered and sat beside Amelia, and she felt some of the tension ease from her neck. Solidarity well-timed.

Marco said, 'The vaccination would have significantly reduced her risk, yes. But, Mr Wild,' he said and held up his hand, 'right now, our focus needs to be on fighting this infection with everything we have. Braelynn is getting the best possible care.'

The father nodded. Dropped his face in his hands. Mrs Wild's shoulders sagged. 'I just keep thinking, what if I'd brought her in sooner? What if I'd known about that other vaccine?'

The eternal torment of parents, Amelia thought, but before she could answer, Marco leaned forward.

'You brought her in as soon as you recognised she was seriously ill. That quick action may save her life.'

His voice was steady and professional, but his face was sympathetic as he directed his attention to Braelynn's mother's pain. 'The symptoms can develop very rapidly, sometimes within hours. You did exactly what you should have done.'

'Will she…' Mrs Wild couldn't finish the question, but Amelia heard it anyway.

Will she live? Will she be the same? Will she keep all her fingers and toes? 'We're cautiously optimistic. She's responding to treatment, and we caught it early enough that we're hopeful about preventing the worst complications.'

The silence stretched between them, filled with all the fears none of them wanted to voice.

'Can I stay with her, here?' Mrs Wild finally whispered.

'Of course. Though, not both of you in her room. Perhaps you could take turns. But remember, she's sedated right now, in an induced coma, so she won't respond to you. That's normal. We're keeping her comfortable while her body fights the infection.'

As they stood to return to Braelynn's room, Amelia felt the familiar weight of carrying another family's hope in her hands, which made her appreciate Marco had stayed this long to help carry the load. He could have left once the treatments had been decided on an hour ago.

Another hour later Mr Wild finally agreed to go home, exhaustion winning over parental terror to allow alternate shifts in the morning. His wife had curled into a chair, dozing fitfully in the corner.

'I'll stay in the unit overnight,' Amelia had promised the father. 'If anything changes, I'll phone you immediately.' The words were both professional duty and personal oath.

The unit settled into the quiet rhythm of machines— the steady beep of heart monitors, the rhythmic hiss and puff of the ventilator breathing life into sedated lungs.

The tick of intravenous calibration. Sounds that meant there was hope.

Marco's hand touched her shoulder, and she turned as unexpected warmth spread through her tired body. 'Come, Amelia, we will have coffee and sandwiches in the nurses' tearoom and discuss our options now that she is reasonably stable.'

Coffee. Food. She blinked, suddenly aware of her own exhaustion.

Before following him, she reached out with her gloved hand, pressing gently against Braelynn's toes. Warmth heated her fingertips, and she exhaled a breath she didn't know she'd been holding.

'Okay.' The word came out smaller than she intended as she followed Marco, discarding the isolation clothes, mask and gloves at the door, and washing at the sink before walking toward what felt like the first real break in a night that had stretched forever.

As soon as she sat at the bare wooden table, she said, 'Did we do everything? Is there something we missed?'

He turned around from where he was spooning instant coffee into cups. She hadn't realised he'd moved straight to making the coffee, and she looked away. She actually didn't care enough to take over.

'We have done all we can. Stop for a moment. Take a five-minute break. What were you doing when the call came in?'

She blinked. Answered after a few seconds of thinking. 'The boys and I were finishing a movie.' Did that mean she had to ask him? She'd already guessed. 'What were you doing?'

'I was dropping a friend back to her house.'

Of course he was. It could have been worse. 'Good timing, then.'

He smiled wickedly at her. 'She didn't think so.'

Oh my heaven. This man and his love life. 'Spare me. Marco, please. TMI.'

He handed her a coffee. 'White. No sugar.' As if he made her coffee all the time. How had he known that? When she took it, frowning at him, he said nonchalantly, 'TMI?'

She sipped. Perfect. Not extra milky or extra strong. *'Too much information.'*

'But you asked.'

'Only because you did.' She fluffed a tired hand at him. 'This is why I only talk about patients with you.'

The smile he gave her would quite possibly keep her awake if she ever went to bed. It was all white teeth, sculptured lips and warm crinkled eyes. A smile that said he cared how she felt and wanted to help. She tried to ignore it, but she needed the confirmation of support too much.

She decided he must have combed his hair sometime, on a bathroom break. Because apart from the five-o'clock shadow on his face, he looked pristine. Why didn't he look like the cat had dragged him in? Because that's how she felt.

'You need to relax for just this moment. Ask me something not related to tonight.'

She rubbed her forehead with the heel of her hand. A brief break from Braelynn's myriads of possible poor outcomes might be nice. 'Was your uncle good to you?'

He tilted his head, his brows high. 'This is what you ask?'

She frowned back at him. Shrugged because she was

still tired, but if she had one question she did want to know, that was it. She'd thought of the orphaned seven-year-old too much since he'd mentioned his childhood. She pushed for an answer. 'You said you were seven?'

'I was cared for well by my uncle's staff until I went to school in London. I stayed for university.'

He shrugged. 'You look distressed.' A slight smile. 'Perhaps we should discuss our patients.'

CHAPTER TEN

MARCO WATCHED HER FACE, studied the way her eyes widened. For a heartbeat, he thought she might believe he was joking, that somehow this night of hell could pause for coffee and conversation, because a break made brains clearer.

Then the alarm sounded from intensive care.

Before he could even process the sound fully, she was moving. Hair flying behind her as she bolted through the door. *Brava, dottoressa.*

The admiration hit him unexpectedly, warming something deep in his chest that had nothing to do with professional respect. The alarm wasn't from Braelynn's room—*grazie a Dio*—but watching Amelia's instant response crystallised something in his mind. She would stay the night. Of course she would stay. It was who she was.

And if she stayed awake all night, burning herself out on vigil and worry, she'd be useless tomorrow when they might need her most.

He needed to think strategically. To preserve resources.

The decision settled in his mind, clicked into place. If he went home now, grabbed some sleep, he could return at eight and relieve her. Let her rest while he took the day shift. It would be a long weekend, and having both of them exhausted served no one, least of all their young patient.

He caught up with her outside Braelynn's room, where

she was already pulling on fresh protective gear with the efficient movements of someone who'd done this a thousand times.

The sight of her made his chest tighten with something he didn't want to examine too closely. 'I will leave you. She is stable. Until you need me.' He touched her shoulder, felt the slight tension in her muscles, the fine tremor of exhaustion she was trying to hide. 'Phone me. Do not hesitate. I return at eight and relieve you.'

She turned, and he caught the flash of something vulnerable in her eyes before her professional mask slipped back into place. 'You don't have to do that. I'm the person on call.'

Stubborn woman. But wasn't that exactly what drew him to her? 'But I will. You will be needed many times over the weekend. Some sleep is essential for good management and decisions.'

'Your choice.' She lifted her mask.

He added, 'I need you sharp. I need you at your best because we don't want to lose this one.'

She closed her eyes briefly, and her breath released. 'You're right. That makes sense. Thank you.'

He turned to leave, every step requiring more effort than it should. Strange. He'd worked hundreds of cases, saved dozens of lives, lost others despite his best efforts. But something about leaving her here, standing guard over a fifteen-year-old girl…

She'd done well tonight. The thought followed him down the corridor. Done everything perfectly. But he'd seen that flash of relief when he'd first arrived, the way her shoulders had straightened when she wasn't facing this alone anymore. *Bene.* She was right to call me.

The satisfaction of that, of being needed, of being the one she turned to in a crisis, stayed with him all the way home.

When Marco returned at eight the next morning, his sleep had been broken, but he had gained more than his registrar would have had, and the ICU felt different. Quieter, but not in a peaceful way.

More like the tense quiet before a storm. There had been no calls through the night, which meant Braelynn's condition had remained stable. But the same could not be said for the family dynamics.

He could hear raised voices before he even reached Braelynn's room, and his pace quickened. The father had apparently replaced his wife as the on-site parent, and from the sound of it, he wasn't the sit-quietly-in-the-corner type.

It wasn't quite an altercation, not yet, but Marco was relieved to see they were having this conversation outside the patient's room rather than at her bedside. Still, the father's back was rigid with anger, his voice carrying that particular edge of a man who'd spent the night imagining worst-case scenarios and was now looking for someone to blame.

Sam stood to the side and looked relieved to see him.

Amelia's acknowledgement when she spotted him over the man's shoulder, plus her pale face and dark circled eyes, made Marco's protective instincts flare to life. Without conscious thought, he stepped immediately to her side, close enough that his presence would be felt, his support unmistakable.

'Good morning, Dr Day. Mr Wild. Sam.' He kept his voice professionally neutral but let his accent thicken slightly—a trick he'd learned years ago. Something about his Italian inflection seemed to defuse tension, made people pause and recalibrate.

'What is Braelynn's condition this morning, Dr Day?'

And what exactly is the problem here, signore? The thought burned, but Marco kept his expression neutral. Years of dealing with distraught families had taught him that anger, however justified, served no one, least of all the patient.

'Still critical. I was explaining to Mr Wild that we would not be extubating Braelynn yet. That her condition would not benefit from straining her resources.'

Bene. Marco felt a familiar surge of professional admiration. Of course, Amelia understood that pushing too fast could be as dangerous as doing nothing at all.

'I want to talk to my daughter. What if she's brain-damaged? I want a second opinion.'

Marco felt Amelia stiffen beside him at the words, even though he wasn't looking at her. There it was: the barely controlled panic of a father who'd spent the night imagining the worst outcomes. Marco had seen it a hundred times before, but it never became easier to witness. Still, panic was no excuse for attacking the woman who'd probably saved his daughter's life.

He caught and held the man's gaze, letting his own steady presence fill the space between them. 'Of course, you are concerned. Your daughter is very sick. Critical. So much so that one of our senior medical officers has remained the whole night with her.'

Choose your words carefully, Marco. This man needs education, not confrontation.

'It's her job.' The man cast an almost disparaging look at Amelia, and Marco felt his brows rise with arctic precision.

Enough.

Heat flared in his chest—not the professional irritation he'd expected but something far more personal and protective. How dare he dismiss her sacrifice? The intensity of his reaction caught him off guard. When had Amelia Day become someone he felt compelled to defend with such fierce determination?

'You are mistaken.' Marco's voice carried the quiet authority he'd learned from one of his mentors in Roma—firm but not aggressive. 'Dr Day is not on night shift. She does not get to go home and sleep after eight hours until tonight when her shift starts again. She is on call all weekend. Forty-eight hours of critical decisions on call for all paediatric patients in this hospital. She is consultant to resident doctors who cover the night or day hours. Like Sam here.' He gestured to the silent Sam.

Look at her. Really look at her. 'Yet to her, last night, your daughter's treatment was paramount, so she stayed. Yes? She remained diligently above and beyond her duty.'

The words came out with more passion than he'd intended, and he felt a moment's surprise at himself. *When did I become her champion?* But even as the thought formed, he knew the answer: the moment he'd heard the relief in her voice when she'd called him.

'It's fine, Dr Macaluso. Mr Wild is naturally concerned and upset.' Amelia's voice was steady, professional, but Marco caught the slight thread of exhaustion running through it.

Madonna. She's defending him after he insulted her? The man had the grace to redden at her response, but he didn't apologise. Marco's jaw tightened.

'Sì. But I-I thank you for your diligence, Dr Day.' The

formal words carried warmth he hoped she would hear. 'Perhaps now is a good time to give handover, before I go in to see Braelynn.'

As Amelia began her succinct and precise recitation of the night's events, Marco watched Mr Wild's face change. The man took a step back, his head lowering as the clinical details washed over him. *Now you see.* Every medication adjustment, every vital-sign change, every nursing observation that Amelia had been present for, all consulted on, remembered and repeated.

She is extraordinary. The thought whispered through his mind as he listened to her professional summary. Not just competent but extraordinary. And he was not the only one recognising it. Mr Wild's head lowered as he realised the scope of expertise that had been devoted to his daughter.

When the handover was complete, Marco felt a deep satisfaction settle in his chest. *Now you understand what you dismissed so carelessly, signore.*

The three doctors donned protective outerwear—a ritual Marco had performed so often—but today he was acutely aware of Amelia beside him, her movements efficient despite her exhaustion. Inside Braelynn's room, he assessed his young patient with fresh eyes, noting the subtle improvements that Amelia's vigilant care had made possible.

'Brava, piccola,' he said quietly to Braelynn. 'Keep fighting.'

Mr Wild declined to enter, instead staring through the observation window with the haunted expression of a parent confronting his own helplessness. Now you are beginning to understand, Marco thought without malice. This is not about blame. This is about hope.

* * *

When they emerged from the room, Amelia removed her protective gear with quick, practiced movements. She nodded politely at Mr Wild—such grace under pressure—washed her hands at the sink and left the ward with her head held high.

As she should. Marco's chest swelled with an admiration so fierce it tightened his chest.

Marco forced himself to smile at Mr Wild after washing his own hands. The man's worry was genuine, even if his expression of it had been unacceptable. He was a frightened father, not an enemy.

'I am hopeful, as you must be, to see that your daughter is slowly improving. This is good news.' He extended his hand, offering the man a chance to salvage some dignity. 'Now, I will see you later. The nursing staff know to contact Sam first and then me with concerns, but I will return in two hours if they have not called me sooner.'

As he strode from the ICU, his mind was already racing ahead. If he hurried, could he catch Amelia before she drove away? The thought propelled him. She was exhausted—bone-deep, soul-weary exhausted—and the drive home could be dangerous. Accidents were common. People relaxed when they thought they were almost safely home.

His pace quickened as he headed for the underground car park, his heart beating faster than professional concern alone could explain. Perhaps one of her brothers could collect her car later.

Perhaps he was in more trouble than he realised. But as he hurried toward the elevator, Marco found he didn't care.

CHAPTER ELEVEN

AMELIA FELT LIKE CRYING, the emotion in her throat threatening to spill over in hot, silent tears. She didn't cry—wouldn't let herself—but the urge sat there, heavy and persistent. Was it because of that terrified father's conflict and cutting comments? Or the relentless stress of the night and the accumulated fear that Braelynn would die or lose fingers, toes, maybe even limbs?

Or was it the way Marco had stood up for her, his voice carrying a fierce protectiveness that made something deep in her chest ache?

Maybe it was simply that she'd barely slept after the ball the night before either. Two nights of little sleep, and now this.

She was too exhausted to work out which emotional thread was pulling at her the hardest. That crushing tiredness was probably the real reason tears pressed behind her eyes. She felt like a dam about to break.

Her car beeped open with a cheerful sound that seemed obscenely bright in her grey world. She slipped into the driver's seat, the leather cool against her back; she hadn't replaced the seat covers yet and must do that. She closed the door with a soft thunk and pressed the lock button to let herself exist in this small, protected space.

Her head fell forward onto her hands where they rested

on top of the steering wheel, the leather grip a small, hard pillow.

She let her forehead rest there, felt her shoulders finally drop from the rigid line they'd held all night. Her eyes drifted closed. Just for a moment. Just to breathe in and out, in and out.

So good. So quiet.

Knocking. Someone was knocking on her window.

Amelia's eyes flew open, her heart lurched. She must have had a microsleep. Best not to do that on the way home, she thought, her brain still thick with the remnants of the unplanned nap. How long? Seconds? Minutes? Her mouth felt numb, and she quickly wiped at it, hoping desperately she hadn't been drooling.

She turned her head and saw Marco looking at her through the glass, concern etched across his handsome face. Those dark eyes held something she couldn't quite read. She did not have the energy to battle him at the moment. Not when her defences were this low.

'Open the door, Amelia.' His voice was muffled by the glass, but she could hear the authority in it, the doctor voice that expected compliance.

'Why?' Her brain was still foggy, but she wasn't stupid. Why was he here? How had he found her so quickly?

'Because you're in no fit state to drive. I will take you, and one of your brothers can drive your car home. This is much more sensible. Sì?'

The logic was sound. Infuriatingly sound. She was too tired to mount a proper fight, something she'd probably regret later when her pride recovered. With a sigh that puffed out of her, she unlocked her door.

He pulled it open immediately, like he'd been waiting for that tiny click, and his hand came down to help her out. His gesture was automatic, but it sparked a flicker of irritation in her tired mind. Now she couldn't get out of a car by herself?

When had she become so pathetic that strong, competent Dr Marco Macaluso felt the need to rescue her from her own vehicle?

Resigned, she placed her hand in his. His fingers were warm, and they closed around hers with a steadiness that felt too good.

He pulled her upright with easy strength, and suddenly she was standing too close to him, close enough to catch that faint cologne.

Much too close. She stepped back against the car, her spine pressing against the cool metal, and he stepped away too.

'My car is here,' he said quietly, his voice pitched low like she was some frightened deer that might bolt at any sudden movement. Or stamp on his toes—ha! The tone made her shake her head in frustration. What was she doing? She'd driven home more tired than this before. Hadn't she?

'This is crazy. I'm fine.' The words came out with less conviction than she'd hoped for.

'Humour me.' He smiled at her, and it was an expression she didn't recognise. Not the practiced charm he used on countless women. This was something else—amused exasperation mixed with something warmer, more genuine. It made her stomach do a small, unwelcome flip.

She threw her hands up in defeat, too drained to maintain an argument. 'Okay. Whatever.' The words came out grumpier than she'd intended, and she felt a flush of embarrassment. Here he was doing her a favour, and she was acting like a petulant child.

She looked in the direction he'd pointed and couldn't mistake which car had to be his. A very expensive, very low, blindingly bright yellow Italian sports car sat gleaming in the parking garage like a beacon of excess. One she knew the boys would fall head over heels in love with and drive her absolutely mad talking about for the next six months.

She groaned. It had to be Sunday—they'd be home and bored—so this would not be missed. She muttered under her breath, 'Spare me. And so subtle.' She looked up at him. 'What is it?'

He smiled, and this smile was completely different from the previous one. Boyish and delighted, ridiculously attractive and it made her belly do more flips. She shut that flutter right the heck down before it could take root.

'A Ferrari 360 Modena.'

'A Ferrari.' Of course it was. Because regular, sensible cars were apparently beneath Dr Marco Macaluso. She was awake now, fully and completely awake, adrenaline cutting through her exhaustion like caffeine. She said gloomily, 'You'll have to show the boys. You won't be able to drive off straightaway.'

'*Nessun problema.* Braelynn is stable. No problem. I have my phone. I like to show her off.' His voice carried such genuine pleasure that despite herself, despite her exhaustion and irritation and the way he'd steamrolled her into this situation, her mouth twitched.

Imagine that, Marco Macaluso, paediatric consultant, was just like every other man when it came to fast cars. But somehow, instead of annoying her further, the revelation made him seem more human. More real. Her mouth twitched again, and then she was grinning tiredly despite herself.

He helped her into the luscious leather seat like she was some sort of princess, his hand steady on her elbow as she settled into luxury that probably cost more than she made in three years. The leather was butter-soft against her legs, and she had to admit it felt amazing after the night she'd had.

Not how she'd expected this night to end. Not even close.

Driving with Marco down a beachside street in a bright yellow convertible Italian sports car with the top down caused everyone to look at them. Who knew?

The wind whipped through her hair, probably destroying what was left of her professional appearance, but for the first time in hours she felt like she could actually breathe.

The salt air filled her lungs, the rumble of the perfectly tuned engine vibrated through her bones, and despite everything—the exhaustion, the embarrassment, the way this man had completely disrupted her careful control—she felt oddly peaceful.

Amelia was still shaking her head, though she couldn't hide the smile tugging at her lips, when they pulled up at the big old white-brick home where she'd lived for most of her life. The house was slightly run-down, refurbishment not being on the agenda, but it had a fabulous view of the ocean and was only one street away from the beach.

The boys were waiting on the kerb, eyes wide, mouths hanging open in pure, undiluted delight. At this moment they didn't look like the academic high achievers they were, bound for university scholarships and bright futures. They looked like kids at Christmas, staring at the best present they'd ever seen.

She'd texted Luna from the car that she was being dropped off by her Italian boss in his Ferrari. The response had been a string of question marks followed by This I have to see.

Now came the hard part. The invitation she knew she had to extend, the polite thing to do after he'd gone out of his way to drive her home. The words that would let him into her private world and her family. Unless he declined. Maybe he'd decline.

She crossed her hidden fingers and hoped that he would politely excuse himself and drive away.

'You're invited for Sunday breakfast.' The words felt thick and awkward on her tongue.

'Thank you. I accept.' Of course he did.

'So you are the lovely Luna, Amelia's aunt who saved the Days.'

Amelia shook her head at the pun on her surname as Marco took Luna's hand and kissed it with old-world charm. Luna accepted the gesture with aplomb: She'd lived in Italy for six months at some stage in her wandering youth. She'd lived nearly everywhere, collecting experiences like other people collected souvenirs, Amelia had always thought.

Luna's eyes twinkled with mischief. 'I miss Italy.'

'I am sure Italia misses you, bella donna.' The endearment rolled off his tongue, and Luna actually giggled. Giggled! Amelia had never heard Luna giggle in her life.

'Oh yeah. Enough flirting. Please sit, Marco.' Luna gestured him to the table laden with plates of bacon, eggs, tomato and mushrooms—the full Sunday breakfast spread that had been a tradition in their house for as long as Amelia could remember. 'I understand the boys are in love with your car. You'll have to take them both to pick up Amelia's vehicle.'

Marco settled into the chair with easy grace. 'She does not have a back seat. I will have to take one brother for a short drive and then return for the other.'

'They would appreciate that.' Luna glanced at Amelia with sharp eyes that missed nothing. 'Were you up all night?'

Amelia blinked away from the fixed stare she'd had on her glass of juice. The conversation flowed around her, warm and comfortable, but suddenly the tiredness crashed back after the brief adrenaline high of the car ride. Her eyelids felt scratchy. 'I'm still on call.'

'Except,' Marco pointed his chin at her with casual authority, 'I will take your calls until this afternoon, cara. Sleep.'

Cara. The endearment slipped out so naturally she almost missed it. Almost. Judging by the way Luna's fork clattered against her plate, she hadn't missed it either. But thankfully Luna didn't say anything. She would later, though. Oh, she definitely would.

Amelia sighed, feeling like she was watching her carefully ordered life slide into chaos. This man was causing waves in her home's peaceful waters. But he'd be gone soon, wouldn't he? Back to his world of expensive cars and casual endearments and women who probably knew how to handle such things.

'Eat.' Luna waved at the table with maternal authority, and the boys appeared as if summoned, sliding into their usual chairs. Conversation flowed around Amelia hazily—Marco charming Luna with stories about Italy, the boys peppering him with questions about the Ferrari's engine specifications, Luna regaling him with tales from her own Italian adventures.

Amelia managed two poached eggs, toast and a grilled

tomato before sitting back, her appetite satisfied for the first time in what felt like days. The familiar comfort of Sunday breakfast, even with this unexpected addition, settled something restless in her chest.

Luna looked up from her plate, her eyes zeroing in on Amelia's exhaustion. 'Go shower, Mellie. Then hit the bed. We've got this. You'll excuse her, won't you, Marco?'

He nodded, his own heaped plate now empty. How did the man eat so much and stay so lean? 'Of course. I'll see you this afternoon, Amelia. Shall we say three in ICU?'

And just like that, her day was planned for her. By him. In her own kitchen. With her family's approval.

As Amelia headed toward the shower, she wondered when exactly she'd lost control of her life and why the thought didn't bother her quite as much as it should have.

CHAPTER TWELVE

MARCO WATCHED AMELIA walk away with her shoulders straight but her head bowed like a flower after a storm. The metaphor twisted something in his chest. Thinking of flowers made him think of her in his arms two nights ago—how she'd been a flower then, swaying and relaxed against him, trusting him with her softness until he'd ruined it all with his careless words.

The memory burned. He'd learnt since then that Amelia did not do careless. Everything about her was deliberate, considered, protective. No wonder she thought him a playboy.

'She looks like she's had a hard night.' Luna's voice carried the kind of warmth Marco had only heard in other people's lives, genuine concern and unconditional love. The kind of voice that caught you when you fell, that asked about your day and actually listened to the answer.

His throat tightened unexpectedly. Perhaps his life would have been different if he'd had a kind aunt like this family possessed. If someone had cared enough to notice when he was struggling, to put their own life on hold for his well-being.

Basta. He pushed that useless thought away before it could take root. Poor little rich boy indeed. Self-pity was a luxury he'd abandoned years ago, along with fairy tales about loving families.

He turned back to the table and smiled, the expression as practiced as breathing. 'She cares for her patients very much.'

'Always has.' Luna's knowing look suggested she saw right through his deflection. 'But I suspect you do as well.'

The simple statement hit harder than it should have. When had anyone last acknowledged that he cared?

Henry, perhaps? His friend had always seen more. In Marco's world, caring was weakness, emotion avoided. Yet here was this woman, recognising something in him that he'd almost forgotten existed. 'True. But in the last ten years I've learned we don't have as much control over outcomes as we think.'

The words tasted bitter. How many times had he stood beside beds with tiny patients, watching hope drain from parents' faces? How many times had he delivered news that shattered worlds? And yet…watching Amelia with her patients, seeing her refuse to give up even when logic said otherwise, had reminded him why he'd chosen medicine in the first place.

He turned to the boys, needing to escape the weight of Luna's perceptive gaze. 'So, Crispin, what do you plan to do when you leave school at the end of the year?'

The question felt safer, more familiar. Career advice he could manage. It was the closeness of this family that left him floundering.

Crispin glanced at his brother, and a look passed between them—the kind of wordless communication Marco had never experienced. Something else he'd never had. 'Something in medicine, like Mellie, but I'm more into the research side.'

Ryan nodded, that same easy consideration. 'I've been looking into forensic science or clinical engineering, but possibly the same degree as Crispin until third year when we'd diverge.'

Clever boys. And considerate ones, keeping their options flexible, their futures intertwined. Marco found himself genuinely interested. 'Having choices is good.'

Crispin drummed his fingers, his eyes faraway with the dreams of his age. 'There's a university open day on Monday at the local campus. All the unis are offering information stands. We're both going.'

The enthusiasm in his voice reminded Marco of himself at that age—before cynicism had crept in. 'Excellent. I also have some knowledge of universities overseas if you wish to discuss those options.'

Both boys' eyes widened with the kind of excitement that made Marco wonder when had he stopped feeling that spark of possibility. Ryan leaned forward eagerly. 'Thanks. We might do that, though we're probably looking at Melbourne.' He glanced at Luna with an awareness that spoke of deep family loyalty. 'But that'll depend on Mellie, of course.'

Of course. Because in this family, no one got left behind. No one made major life decisions without considering how it would affect the others. The concept so foreign to Marco it might as well have been from another planet. In his world, you looked out for yourself because no one else would.

Luna's smile held a world of sacrifice and love. 'Or if you both get full scholarships. That would help.' She observed the table with an amused expression that reminded him startlingly of Amelia. 'Clear the table, boys. I think everyone's finished.'

Marco watched both young men jump up and begin clearing without complaint, without the sullen resentment he'd have expected from teenagers. This was a family that functioned well, each member knowing their role, caring for the others.

When he went to rise, Luna motioned him to stay. 'It's their turn.'

He settled back, oddly touched by the casual inclusion. When had anyone last told him to relax, to let others take care of things? 'Grazie per la colazione.'

'Thank you for breakfast,' she repeated. Luna's smile was warm, genuine. 'My Italian is rusty but still there.'

The easy acceptance in her voice made something tight in his chest loosen fractionally. Here was a woman who'd made choices based on her heart rather than her bank account. 'Amelia says you're almost ready to begin your travels again. Do you have a first destination?'

'I'll be waiting until after Christmas, but yes, I have plans.' Her voice carried the excitement of someone half her age, and Marco found himself genuinely curious about this remarkable woman who'd helped shaped Amelia into the fierce, caring person she was.

Luna side-eyed the boys laughing at the sink, and Marco followed her gaze. They kept glancing toward the window, clearly fascinated by his Ferrari. The sight should have amused him; instead, he felt vaguely uncomfortable and didn't want to think about why.

'I fly out to India on the twenty-eighth of December,' Luna continued. 'There's an ashram there I'd like to re-visit for a couple of months before I head back to Europe.'

'Europe in the spring. Nice.' The words came automatically, but something in her wandering spirit called to a part of him he'd long buried. The part that had once dreamed of travelling for adventure. 'I inherited a villa in Rome and an apartment in London, both left to me by my departed uncle,' he said shrugging, the gesture hiding complicated emotions about his uncle's legacy. 'I have no wish to dispose of them. You are very welcome to stay in either if you wish to visit those cities and spend some time. Both have housekeepers who would be happy to have someone to care for.'

The offer surprised him as much as it seemed to surprise her. When had he last made such a gesture without expecting something in return?

'A little different to my usual accommodation.' Luna's eyes sparkled with mischief. 'I'd like that. Amelia said you were a rich Italian playboy. It's true, then?'

The direct question should have amused him. Instead, it stung. Because, yes, that's exactly what he was—or what he'd allowed himself to become. But sitting here, in this kitchen filled with love and laughter, the label felt hollow. 'I would rather have had an aunt who cared enough to put her life on hold for her family.'

The words slipped out before he could stop them, carrying more truth than he'd intended to reveal. Luna's expression softened with understanding that made his throat tight.

'And now you're a caring paediatric consultant. I can see you're more than the sybarite Amelia suggests.'

Sybarite. The word hit like a slap, even though he'd known that's how Amelia saw him. Knowing and hearing it confirmed were different things entirely. 'I am well aware of her thoughts. Your niece is an intriguing woman.'

Intriguing was a safe word. It didn't reveal how she'd slipped under his skin, how her passion for her work had rekindled something he'd thought dead. Didn't hint at how her smile could make him forget his cynicism or how her tears had made him want to slay dragons—or desperate parents—on her behalf.

'It will be good for her to have time to be a woman, even though she'll miss the boys.'

Luna's words carried meaning that made Marco's pulse quicken. Amelia needed time to be a woman? With him, perhaps?

His phone vibrated against his chest, a sharp reminder of the hospital waiting beyond this warm kitchen. Time to return to his real life, to being on call, to the endless cycle of work and empty social obligations. 'And she will miss you.'

'And I, her.' Luna stood, and Marco rose as well, the moment of connection ending. 'She's been amazing with the boys, but she has no life apart from here and work. I love the idea of her getting out more.'

The hope in her voice made Marco's lift his head. Luna saw futures he didn't dare imagine. He leaned forward and kissed her on both cheeks, the gesture carrying more emotion than he'd felt in years. 'Addio a una donna straordinaria.'

'I'm an extraordinary woman, am I?' she translated.

The Italian had felt right on his tongue, carrying the weight of his gratitude for this glimpse into what family could be, what love looked like when it was unconditional.

As he walked toward the door, Marco caught sight of Amelia's empty chair and felt her absence.

'Do come and visit us anytime, Marco.'

CHAPTER THIRTEEN

AMELIA WALKED INTO the intensive care unit at three o'clock, her body finally feeling human again after four hours of deep, dreamless sleep. The first person she saw was Marco, looking just as uncreased and debonair as he'd looked this morning when he'd charmed her entire family over breakfast. She'd really like to know how he managed that trick. Both the clothes and the family-charming.

Seriously. Did the man ever look rumpled? Ever show a hair out of place? Even after working till the early hours, he looked like he'd stepped out of an advertisement for a medical journal.

Meanwhile, she'd needed a good swipe of concealer and carefully applied make-up to hide the signs of the night.

'Good afternoon, everyone.' She smiled and nodded at Braelynn's parents, deliberately keeping her expression warm and professional. She could feel Marco's quick examination of her appearance, no doubt ensuring like some sort of medical mother hen that she'd had adequate rest. The thought almost made her lips twitch. Dr Marco Macaluso, worried about her!

Marco gestured to Tom, the resident medical officer on duty today. 'Tom, please commence the update on Braelynn's condition.'

Amelia listened intently, her mind automatically cataloguing each detail. Some concern with renal output, not unexpected with meningococcal disease. The febrile body temperatures were still a problem, but that too was part of the body's fight against infection. But the rash had lessened, and that was wonderful news. Her heart lifted with relief. The petechial haemorrhages fading meant Braelynn's circulation was improving, that the devastating blood clots they'd all been fearing weren't developing, as yet.

'Good news. Thanks, Tom.' Marco's voice carried the same relief she was feeling. He turned to Braelynn's parents, and she watched his face soften with compassion. 'Do you have further questions?'

This time it was Mrs Wild who spoke up, her voice trembling with barely contained hope. 'Do you know when our daughter will wake up? It won't be weeks, will it?'

The fear in that question made Amelia's chest tighten. She'd heard it so many times before—parents terrified that their child might never be the same. The awful uncertainty that came with critical illness.

Marco replied, 'If she continues to improve as she is, then tomorrow around this time the anaesthetist will reassess her intubation. She is heavily sedated at present, and the sedation will be decreased until we can see she is able to breathe for herself.'

'Oh. That's good news.' Mrs Wild reached out for her husband's hand like a lifeline, and they leaned into each other. This was why she did this job, for moments like these, when hope began to replace terror.

Marco continued gently, 'It can be frightening for her, the transition from the tube in her throat to breathing, which is why we do not want to push too fast if her body is too weak for the extra effort.'

Mrs Wild glanced at her husband and nodded. He remained silent, but Amelia could see the tension in his shoulders beginning to ease. This morning's angry, demanding father was being replaced by a man who had finally allowed himself to believe his daughter might be okay.

'That's quicker than I expected,' Mrs Wild whispered, as if speaking too loudly might jinx this news.

'Once she's conscious and still improving, we'll be able to give you an idea of her possible readiness for discharge.'

'Oh.' Mrs Wild's hand lifted to her throat. 'In days, you mean?'

'Plan for a week, if all goes well. If earlier, then good. But tomorrow we should be able to give more of an idea if she continues to improve like she is.'

Amelia felt her own shoulders relax. A week before Braelynn would go home, but she would be whole, healthy, ready to slowly get her energy back from this edge-of-death experience and return to the normal teenage life that had been so brutally interrupted. No amputations, no long-term complications. Just a young girl who'd fought a terrible infection and won.

Amelia and Marco left the intensive care unit together, their footsteps echoing in the quiet corridor. While she was still on call, she didn't need to remain in the hospital specifically for Braelynn: The girl was stable, improving and in excellent hands.

She needed to say it. 'Thanks for the lift this morning, Marco, and for putting up with the boys. They're both over the moon having ridden in a Ferrari today.' She could still picture their faces reliving the experience for her. Heck, they'd probably tell this story for the rest of their lives.

His smile was genuinely warm. 'They admire you very

much, and your aunt also sings your praises. You have a lovely family, Amelia.'

The compliment settled around her. Family had always been her anchor, but hearing Marco say it—seeing how easily he had fit into their Sunday morning—made her feel proud in a way she hadn't expected.

'Well, thanks for getting me home safe to them, anyway.' She paused, suddenly uncertain. 'I'm going to children's ward now, and then I'll go home.'

'Would you like a coffee? I thought I might walk down to the café at the beach. Perhaps you would join me after you check the ward?'

The invitation hung in the air between them, casual but somehow weighted with possibility. Sunday afternoon coffee. Just coffee. With her boss.

It was a beautiful day outside, and she'd missed most of it sleeping. 'You mean you'd wait for me, here?' The question came out smaller than she'd intended.

'No, I will check the emergency department, then come back here to wait for you to finish. Then we can walk together.'

Unless someone came in and needed her or Braelynn took a turn for the worse, she was free until tomorrow morning when she was back in for her week of day shifts. A walk in the sunshine with an attractive man who'd gone out of his way to be kind to her sounded harmless.

When was the last time she'd done something like that? Something spontaneous and pleasant and completely unrelated to work?

'Sounds nice.' The words surprised her as much as they seemed to surprise him, but he just nodded and strode off toward the emergency department with that confident walk that made the nurses' heads turn.

* * *

Everything was good in the children's ward. None of the patients needed extra tests or medications, and she was satisfied all would continue to improve until tomorrow morning unless something unexpected cropped up. The routine check took less time than usual, a blessing when she'd spent so much time in the hospital the last twenty-four hours. And with someone waiting for her.

By the time she walked back out of the ward, Marco was leaning against the wall, checking his phone. He'd changed out of his formal shirt into something more casual, and the sight of him in the afternoon light through the hospital windows made her anxious in a way that had nothing to do with medical emergency.

Umm… Was this dangerous territory? Coffee with her boss, who happened to be devastatingly attractive and had just spent the morning with her family like he belonged there? But as she approached him, watching his face light up when he saw her, Amelia shut down the second thoughts and decided some risks were worth taking.

They walked out the front door together and up the street towards Marco's apartment building, warmth on the back of her head as the sun slipped towards the horizon. Amelia found herself matching his stride naturally, something that surprised her because when she'd first met him, he'd walked too fast, leaving her feeling hurried. She realised he didn't do that anymore when they walked the corridors now. He'd adjusted to her speed.

There was a slight breeze coming across from the ocean, the bay would come into view very shortly, carrying with it the salty scent that always reminded her of weekends at the surf club.

As they approached the familiar café, her heart sank slightly at the sight of a sign: *Closed for Repairs on Sunday*. She'd been looking forward to neutral territory, somewhere public where she could maintain her composure but enjoy the company.

'Ah, disappointing,' Marco said, shooting a glance at her. 'Would you be offended if I offered the use of my own espresso machine?'

Her stomach fluttered. His apartment. Alone. The thought made her pulse pick up speed, not all from nervousness, a touch of excitement, which worried her more than she cared to admit. 'Offended?' She wouldn't be offended. Nervous maybe, just a bit.

Marco offered, 'Perhaps if I promise the flirting doctor Macaluso will not be in residence this afternoon?'

She had to laugh. No doubt that was from the ball when she'd had her little tantrum during the dance. 'I apologised for that.'

'Sì, as did I. I make a very good cappuccino, and there is a lovely shady garden. It catches the sea breezes very well.'

Despite her reservations, the offer did sound genuinely appealing. And she was curious about how he lived, what his private space could reveal about the man. 'That does sound pleasant, and I do have to walk past your door to get back to my car.'

Even as she spoke, she recognised the excuse for what it was, a way to say yes, while pretending she hadn't really chosen to. She wasn't usually a devious person. She lifted her chin. 'Thank you. I'd like that.'

He gave her one of those dazzling smiles that seemed to light up his entire face and waved toward the street entrance of his home. Yup. That smile was dangerous.

As they climbed the steps together, Amelia couldn't help be aware of his height, his confidence and, again, that darn cologne as he held the door.

When he bypassed the elevators and opened the door to number one with a key, she remembered the night of the ball—was that only two nights ago?—and could almost see him there in his tuxedo holding the platter of antipasto. Another memory burned into her brain.

But this apartment would be convenient for everything, the beach, his work, the lifestyle, like the rest of his life seemed to be.

Stepping into his apartment felt oddly intimate, as if she were crossing a threshold into something more personal than she'd intended. The first thing that struck her was the garden visible through the windows opposite: unexpectedly lovely. She liked that he'd drawn all the curtains back, allowing light to flood the space. So many people seemed to prefer caves to come home to.

The room itself surprised her. She'd half expected the bachelor pad, all black leather and modern art. Instead, while unmistakably masculine, it felt warm and lived-in.

The leather was a rich burnt-butter colour, and the settee and spinning recliners looked as inviting as the seats in his Ferrari. The ceramic-topped dining table caught her eye immediately—suspended on curved metal wings that made it appear to float. It was unlike anything she'd seen, unmistakably expensive, and absolutely beautiful. 'Wow,' she said, and he grinned.

The bookshelves lining the walls intrigued her most. She found herself wanting to examine the titles, to understand what he read in his private moments. The paintings were another surprise, gentle impressionist works that spoke of someone who appreciated beauty for its own sake, not just as status symbols.

'It's beautiful.' The words came out more heartfelt than she'd intended, and she watched his face light up with genuine pleasure at her approval. It struck her how much her opinion seemed to matter to him. 'I love your dining table.'

He shrugged, looking almost sheepish, an expression that transformed his features in a way that made her stomach flip. 'An extravagance that caught my eye.'

She couldn't help but laugh. 'This from a man who owns a Ferrari? I shudder to think.'

His answering smile made her feel clever and appreciated in a way she hadn't experienced in years. 'Come through to the kitchen, and I will make us coffee.'

Seated on the travertine bench, Amelia watched him work the impressive coffee machine with practiced ease. Everything about his movements spoke of competence and care, qualities that, she realised with a start, she found deeply attractive. The familiar aroma of Byron Bay coffee beans filled the air, and she sighed happily despite herself.

'If I phone first, do you do takeaway in the mornings?' The teasing words slipped out before she could censor them, surprising her with their playfulness.

His laugh was rich and warm. 'Perhaps for you.'

The simple words, the way he looked at her when he said them, sent heat through her chest. This was dangerous territory—the kind of intimacy that could make a woman forget her personal rules. Not her, though.

'So I assume you're happy in the apartment? Henry said you've signed a contract to buy it.' Safe ground. Acquaintance territory.

'Sì. The location is everything. Good parking below, the

beach to the front, walking distance to the hospital, and now the opportunity to entertain you as well.' He looked up quickly. 'Fact, not flirting.'

She spluttered, caught between laughter and something warmer, more unsettling. The ease with which he could make her laugh, the way he seemed to genuinely enjoy her company—yep, it was intoxicating and terrifying in equal measure. 'I'll take that on advisement. Sounded flirty to me.'

'Yes,' he said mock seriously, 'we need to talk about your paranoia.'

The unexpected response made her splutter again, and she realised with shock that she was having fun. Actually enjoying herself with a man for the first time in longer than she cared to remember. 'Who are you? You're making me laugh at the most inappropriate times.'

'The greatest gift in my life at this moment.' He placed a magnificent, frothy cappuccino in front of her, complete with a heart design in the foam. The casual words, combined with the careful artistry of the coffee, made her stop and sit back.

He held up his hands. 'The heart is not flirting,' he added with mock solemnity. 'It is the only design I can create in my coffee.'

She needed to change the subject before she did something foolish like believe that the man could be genuinely interested in a woman like her. 'Thank you again for taking the boys in your car.'

'They are most welcome.'

'And for this morning. I think we're all feeling a little lighter with Braelynn's improvement.'

He nodded seriously. 'It could have gone either way, and that is the challenge of our work.' He placed a small plate of biscotti on a tray along with some nuts and dried fruit and his own mug. 'Shall we take these outside?'

She followed him to the patio door, followed directions to unlock and open it for him, and let him go first with the tray. She noticed when he put it down on the stylish white wrought iron furniture how perfect the garden was. Terracotta pots of red geraniums, dozens of herbs, a fountain, obviously solar-driven, splashing water into the bowl a slender nymph stood in, and squares of planted greenery. Even a lemon tree bearing fruit in a square pot. 'It's beautiful.' So Italian, she thought, like the gardens she'd seen in magazines and smiled.

'It's a miniature version of a garden I loved in Rome. I have a landscaper who has agreed to maintain it. He comes when needed.'

He shrugged, his shirt shifting and pulling in a play of muscles she tried not to stare at. 'I informed the apartment management body I would prefer to have it done my way instead of them being responsible for the upkeep. They were happy to save expenses.'

Outside on the patio, surrounded by the garden and soothed by the sea-breeze, Amelia felt her last defences slip away. The conversation flowed easily between local tourist spots and practical matters like first cars for young men. Ferraris were not in the mix.

It struck her how long it had been since she'd sat somewhere beautiful with an intelligent man, talking about everything and nothing.

When he offered her another coffee and she declined, she weakened and agreed to iced water when she knew she should leave. The smart thing would be to thank him and go, before this dangerous sense of contentment could take deeper root.

But as she watched him gather the empty cups with economical grace, she found herself reluctant to break the spell.

For the first time in years, she felt like herself again: not just a big sister or needy niece, not just a professional, but a woman, one who could even be worthy of this kind of attention.

The realisation should have scared her. Instead, as she watched Marco disappear into the house with promises to return *presto*, she found herself hoping he would take his time coming back, giving her a few more minutes in this sun-warmed bubble where anything seemed possible.

Her phone buzzed in her bag, and she answered the call with resignation. This was who she was. Tom with another admission, this time the young girl with asthma from weeks ago, from Marco's first day actually, and wasn't it strange how she could pinpoint a patient with that time marker? 'I'll be right there.'

'You are called in?' Marco had reappeared with her glass of water.

'Yes.' He proffered the crystal tumbler, and she took it, drank half and handed it back. 'Thank you. Our little asthma girl from your first day is back.'

'Cressa?'

She smiled at him. 'Good memory. Tom says she's not as severe as last time, thankfully.' She picked up her cross-body bag. She had this. 'I'll see you tomorrow.'

'You will. Or earlier if you need me.' He led her inside, crossed the room with her and opened the door. 'Would you like me to drive you?'

'I imagine that would take as long as it will for me to

walk. I'm fine. It would have taken longer from home. Thank you for the coffee.'

'Thank you for the pleasant company, Amelia.'

As she walked swiftly along the footpath towards the hospital, Amelia played those words over in her head. *Pleasant company.* It had been more than pleasant. It had been fun and a little exhilarating, which she needed to damp down quick smart. But she had felt more relaxed than she would have believed possible in Marco's company, and she would consider returning another time if he were to ask her. Not something she would have thought a week ago. She just wasn't silly enough to think anything could come of it.

Monday saw the lessening of Braelynn's sedation and her slow return to consciousness in the intensive care unit. Each curl of Braelynn's fingers felt like a small miracle to Amelia, proof that their desperate fight through the weekend had been worth every sleepless hour.

But they had other patients too. She really had judged Marco harshly, without good reason. The thought hit her as she and Marco sat with Cressa and her worried mother, going over the little girl's new asthma plan. Watching him explain the medication changes with infinite patience, seeing how he crouched to Cressa's eye level to make sure she understood which symptoms should trigger action, this was who he really was. Not the shallow rich boy she'd dismissed but a doctor who cared as fiercely as she did, just with better funding.

As Cressa had settled well overnight and her symptoms had improved, they'd made the changes to her plan for earlier intervention. The relief on her mother's face when Cressa was cleared to go home after lunch made Amelia's throat tight with familiar emotion. These moments—this was why she'd gone into medicine. She was glad that at Marco's request, Cressa was scheduled for an extra follow-up at his consulting rooms in a week's time. She'd need careful watching.

Another thing she liked was Marco's suggestion that he, Henry, Amelia, Tom and Sam meet for a lunchtime case conference to re-examine Braelynn's test results, treatment and observations. The proposal caught her off guard. The idea of systematically reviewing their care, looking for improvements for next time was exactly what she'd been thinking they needed but hadn't had time to voice. Not when they were always so stretched, always just trying to keep their heads above water. It was a good thing Marco was here for all of those reasons.

Amelia relished the chance to reconsider all angles while Braelynn's struggle was so fresh in her mind, every decision still pressing on her. The *what-if*s that had kept her staring at the ceiling last night finally had somewhere productive to go.

She knew Henry would agree wholeheartedly with Marco's suggestion for weekly meetings. The whole concept, while not revolutionary, was new to their understaffed hospital where survival often outweighed reflection.

But now, Amelia found herself appreciating Marco for his professional passion. This wasn't the playboy passion she'd envisaged, late nights with socialites and expensive toys. His commitment to the same excellence made her re-examine him with a dawning recognition.

All in all, Amelia decided as she finally allowed herself to breathe properly for the first time in days, it had been a satisfying weekend. The kind that reminded her why she loved what she did, despite the chaos and lack of sleep. She even found herself singing along with one of Crispin's endless rotation of songs when he came to pick her up—some indie rock number he played over and over until she knew every word despite herself.

He and Ryan had borrowed her car for the day to attend the information day at the Gold Coast Campus, and she could see the excitement radiating from him even before he spoke. The kind of barely contained energy crystallising in his brilliant brain.

'So any of the unis make you want to dash off tomorrow?' she asked, though her heart was already bracing for the answer. 'Or have you changed your mind about your choice of study?'

Sitting in the car with Crispin behind the wheel, looking more grown-up than she was ready for, with a line of traffic waiting for a Learner plate driver to master parallel parking, he risked a glance at her, eyes bright with possibility. 'University of Melbourne has a bachelor in biomedicine that we're keen on. When I'm done with that, I can diverge into research and discovery if that's where I want to.'

Melbourne. The word hit her like a physical blow, even though she'd been expecting it. Of course it would be Melbourne—brilliant boys deserved brilliant opportunities, and Melbourne University was about as brilliant as they came. The sad tug at her heart felt disproportionate to the single word, but it carried the weight of empty bedrooms and quiet dinners and no one to worry about but herself. 'Sounds amazing,' she managed, proud that her voice stayed steady. 'And what about Ryan?'

'He likes that one too, but more for the forensic science angle.'

Both of them. The double blow shouldn't have surprised

her, but somehow it did. They'd always been a matched set, her brothers, making decisions together, supporting each other through everything. Of course they'd leave together too. 'If you both went the same way, at least you could share a flat together.'

The practical words hid the sudden panic. Luna would be gone too. Who would she be without them to care for? Who was Amelia Day when she wasn't sister/niece/provider?

Crispin's eyes shone with dreams she'd helped nurture. 'That course is on fire. It's an amazing uni.'

'I've heard that.' She had to hope, in those moments when she'd allowed herself to imagine their futures, that they'd have choices she'd been given before their parents died. And they did have those choices. Well done, her and Luna, and well done, them!

The traffic lights turned red, and Crispin looked across at her with an expression that made her heart clench—part little boy seeking approval, part young man ready to take on the world. 'You wouldn't mind if we went away?'

Mind? The question was so loaded she didn't know where to start. Mind that they'd be living their dreams? Mind that some of her sacrifices had led to this moment of possibility? Mind that her heart was breaking even as it swelled with pride? 'Watch the road,' she said instead, deflecting because the truth was too raw. 'Of course, I'd miss you both.' She added dryly, though her chest felt like it might cave in, 'And I'd miss all the washing so much.'

His laugh was pure joy, the sound she'd been chasing since the day she'd become responsible for two traumatised young boys. 'Really?'

'No.' The admission slipped out before she could stop it. 'And, yes, I'd miss you both horribly.' The understatement of the century, but she kept the smile plastered on her face.

'I want you both happy, and the work you guys are putting in at school means you get to choose where you want to go.'

It was true, every word, but it didn't make the prospect of their departure any less horrible. She'd still have her own career. One she had thanks to Luna who had helped keep it possible through her sacrifices as well.

'Would we be able to afford a flat in Melbourne?'

The truth sat heavy in her stomach: probably not—Melbourne rents, living expenses, university fees for two brilliant boys who deserved every opportunity. Maybe they could sell the family home? House prices were high, and it had the view, but it was the only security she'd ever known. Still. They could buy something small and practical down there. She could find a tiny flat here, somewhere well back from the beach for a reasonable price.

The thought of rattling around alone while her boys lived their dreams made her throat close, but she forced her voice to stay light. 'We'll have a look tonight at the costs and see.'

Change was coming and coming fast.

Amelia stepped carefully out of the Indian restaurant with her takeaway box far too full of divine aromas and delicious naan. Luna's birthday dinner had fallen on a torrentially rainy day. Cyclone Cindy was off the coast, but Amelia couldn't hold an umbrella and the box, so she hunkered beside the passenger's door being pelted as she slipped the box onto the seat before dashing around to the driver's side. Luckily the air still held the summer warmth.

Once seated she took stock. Her hair felt saturated, her clothes stuck to her, and water ran down her neck. At least she had the seat covers back on and they were soaking up some of the rain. She reached for the small towel she kept in the centre console and scrubbed her head, wincing as the pins stabbed her scalp.

Scowling she began unpicking them from the semicircle of restraint she needed to keep her hair under control. It was even worse in rainy weather with curls and frizz in a riot of disarray. Once her hair was free she scrubbed with the towel until it stopped dribbling all over her. Of course now it would look like an exploded spring mattress, but at least felt drier.

Her phone rang and she cursed. Not something she did often or well, the boys often teasing that her swearing sounded lame.

'Amelia?' Her glasses still too fogged to see the caller's name, she jammed the phone into the crook of her neck to hold while she removed her glasses to wipe them on the towel. Better.

'It's Sam. Sorry. I know you've just left, but we've a new admission in emergency. Eighteen-month-old boy. Febrile convulsion. Dehydration. I need a second opinion, and Henry and Marco are in the consulting rooms today.'

'I'll pop back.' She glanced sadly at the Indian food. They could reheat it. Not for the first time. 'I'll be there in ten. Ask one of the nurses to find me a gown to wear over the top of my clothes.' She shivered at the discomfort, not the cold. 'I'm saturated.'

Ending the call, she made a careful three-point turn and drove back to the hospital car park reminding herself she wasn't as upset as the poor mother must be with a sick child.

CHAPTER FOURTEEN

MARCO NOTICED AMELIA'S vehicle arrive in the car park just before he hit the ignition to go. He'd left the consulting rooms at five and decided on an unscheduled drop-in to the intensive care to check on Braelynn. She'd looked so improved he'd suggested a move to children's ward in the morning and had actually been smiling at nothing as he'd returned to the car park and slid into his vehicle.

When he saw Amelia stop, his day improved even more. Why was she back? He watched in his rearview mirror as she climbed out and slung that ridiculous bag across her shoulder. Her wet clothes stuck to her: She must have been caught in the recent storm they'd just had, and while it would be uncomfortable for her with the extreme dampness, for him it was a pleasure with every curve outlined, curves he'd enjoyed so much the other night with her dancing in his arms.

Even more delightfully, her riot of thick red hair bounced unrestrained in every direction, such energetic springs of disarray, and the sight lifted his mouth and made him shake his head in wonder. Even in the dim car park her hair was glorious. He'd only seen it loose twice before, once at Henry's wedding and once at the ball, but he'd never seen hair so wet and wild and frizzed to the max like hers was now. He suspected she'd be unhappy, but his hands itched to run the crazy strands through his fingers and play.

'Bellissima,' he murmured as he climbed back out of his car to follow her in like a needy puppy. As if she felt his gaze, she paused, stopped and turned, and he knew when she found him in the dimness. She waited and he lengthened his stride to catch up.

'I thought you were gone,' she said. 'Sam has a new admission in emergency.'

'Buonasera, Signorina Sirena.'

She raised her brows at him. *'Sirena?'*

He waved his hand at her hair. 'Mermaid.' He couldn't help his smile. Gestured down her body at her damp clothes. 'You have been swimming?'

She huffed a laugh, and he enjoyed that she behaved much freer with him since Sunday. 'Feels like it.'

'Perhaps I could see the needy Sam and you could go home to shower and change.'

Her gaze jumped to his. He could see indecision and possibly hope. 'Well?'

'Would you see Sam?'

'Certainly. I do not wish you to fall ill with the cold.'

She huffed. 'It's twenty-five degrees. Unlikely.'

'Still… Go.' She looked torn for a moment, and he frowned at her. 'Am I not as good as you?'

She laughed at that. 'Hardly. You have my full confidence in your magnificent paediatric skills, Marco. Never doubt that.' And now his chest warmed, and he could not help bowing slightly.

'Grazie mille, Amelia.'

'Anyway, what I was going to say… I have Luna's birthday dinner in the car growing cold, so accepting your kind offer would be wonderful.' She lifted her chin as if the decision were made. 'And afterwards, if you haven't eaten, you are welcome to enjoy a meal with us. We're having Indian takeaway tonight and birthday cake. We have plenty. Though, please don't feel obliged if you have other plans.'

'You are sure I would not be intruding?'

She raised her brows at him. 'You didn't care last time.'

Never easy, his Amelia. 'So harsh, but I will say yes before you change your mind.'

She smiled at him. 'I won't change my mind. See you when you're done.'

Marco turned up an hour later while the rain still fell, but he used an umbrella as he strode from the car to the front door of Amelia's house, so he felt barely damp. He'd acquired a sheaf of pink birthday roses for Luna from a supermarket, as the florists were shut, and a bottle of fine Prosecco he wouldn't mind a glass of. This all required some juggling with the umbrella.

Crispin opened the door, and an aromatic wave of spices and curry swirled out of the house and made Marco's belly growl.

Ryan craned behind his brother, no doubt to see if Marco's car was parked in the street.

He smiled. 'Sì, the Ferrari will be fine. The top is secured. Please take the umbrella.'

Both boys grinned at him. Crispin stepped forward and took the umbrella and folded it. As he leaned the dripping hook against the wall outside, Ryan said, 'We wondered about your car. Come in.'

On entering the house, his gaze slid to Amelia, and he blew out a small breath of pleasure, pleased she had left her hair out and wild. He hoped to get closer to that whirl of colour before the evening was done, but he was mindful of the birthday girl in the room and crossed the room to Luna first. 'Bon compleanno, signorina.' He handed her the roses and kissed both her cheeks.

She laughed. 'Indeed it is a happy birthday, Marco. Thank you. These are beautiful, and I'm so glad you could make it.' She tilted her head to look at the Prosecco's label. 'Very nice. Is it cold?'

He ran his palm over the bottle even though he'd taken it from the fridge in the shop, to check. 'Sì.'

'Then, hand it to Ryan. He's our best sommelier and won't spill.' She looked at her nephews. 'Get the special glasses, Crispin.'

'Such a shame you boys aren't eighteen yet,' Amelia teased, as she added another plate and cutlery to the table and lifted the lids from the warming dishes. His gaze settled on her too much like coming home. 'Hello, Marco. Welcome.' She looked happy and at ease, and his world felt right. Things were changing for him very fast. Sadly, not so fast for her, he decided.

'They can have a sip of my wine,' Luna said. 'The boys need to acquire a taste for good wine before they're ruined for life by the cheap stuff.' She gestured. 'You're Italian. When did you first taste wine with meals, Marco?'

He smiled, aware she wished for endorsement. 'I was seven.'

'See!' Luna placed both hands on her hips, satisfied.

Amelia smiled at him, but her eyes appeared troubled as if worried the discussion would upset him. 'Was that when you moved in with your uncle?'

'Sì. It was the time of day I shared with him.' The only time, but he ignored that thought and just smiled. 'Look at this wonderful food. And cake.' A round, uneven birthday cake with many, many candles stuck into the lurid pink of the icing held pride of place.

'Crispin made that,' Ryan said. 'I iced it.'

'That's a lot of red food colouring!' Amelia teased. 'Did you know they used to make it from squashed scale insects?'

Ryan blanched. Marco laughed. And Luna patted the boy's shoulder as she went past to sit at the table. 'Eat, everyone.'

Happily, Marco found himself seated next to Amelia, though he suspected that was the work of Luna who appeared to be avoiding her niece's attempt to catch her eye. Crispin carried over the glasses that Ryan had filled, and when everyone was seated, and the boys had soft drinks until Luna allowed a sip of hers, Amelia stood and raised her glass. 'To the best and calmest aunt any family could wish for.'

'Hear, hear,' cried the boys, and Luna laughed.

'To Luna. Buon compleanno,' Marco added, and they all drank to her health.

Marco had sampled Indian food many times, as he and Henry had practically lived on the cuisine in London, but he couldn't remember when he had last enjoyed a meal so much. A family meal of teasing and fun. Lots of random discussion and respect for all who offered opinions. He'd never seen the like.

The boys began to explain to Marco how they had been trolling the rental market in Melbourne near the university, so he assumed they must have decided which campus they would move to. 'I hear that is an excellent university for biomedicine.' He looked to their sister.

'How will you get on here, Amelia, once Luna has

flown to India in December and the boys to Melbourne? It seems a large house for one person.'

She glanced around the table and then back at him, and he wondered if she hadn't thought or perhaps spoken of this before. He should not have asked.

He watched her draw a deep breath, and his chest tightened with a bad feeling, and suddenly he hoped he had not precipitated something they were all not ready for.

She passed her tongue over her lips before speaking. 'I wondered if it might be useful to put this house on the market, so the boys could buy a place in Melbourne, instead of renting. I could get somewhere smaller a little farther away from the beach but still close enough to work.'

There was a collective gasp, though he made no sound. He didn't know why he hated that idea so much. It would not be a painless transition, and he disliked the idea of her losing the home of her parents' memories. The boys stared open-mouthed at their sister as if she'd blasphemed, and Luna's brow had furrowed.

Amelia waved her hand. 'But that's all for later. There's no rush to do anything. We'll all decide together.'

Gradually, after the shock settled, everyone relaxed. He sat back in his chair and considered what he'd just witnessed.

Amelia selflessly offering to provide for the boys, and he'd seen the boys back off from their dreams at the idea of their sister having to sell the family home.

Luna had sat still, not happy yet not offering any comment, and he realised she'd most likely been like this the whole time she'd lived here. Allowing Amelia and the boys to verbalise ideas without putting pressure on anyone by disagreeing. A family caring and in tune with each other. So unlike his own. So special. So wonderful. So strange.

CHAPTER FIFTEEN

AMELIA PUT DOWN her glass, the wine barely touched. She couldn't blame the two sips she'd had for blurting that out—the words had escaped before she could catch them.

The idea had been burning in her chest for days, and at least it was out in the open now. Though, she probably could have waited for Marco not to be here.

Speaking of Marco, her brows drew together as she considered what he'd said. He'd known that Luna was leaving in December. She knew she hadn't told him that. Or that the boys were considering biomedicine.

The pieces clicked together with uncomfortable clarity. 'Just how long did you stay on Sunday, when I went to rest, Marco?' Her voice came out sharper than intended. How dare he collect information about her family like some kind of—what?—sticky beak? The thought made her stomach flutter in a way that only confused her more. What else had he discovered? What other secrets had been shared while she'd been vulnerable, sleeping?

Luna interjected calmly. 'Marco was only here another fifteen minutes. Then he was called away as well by the hospital.'

And that shut her up completely. Shame washed over her, hot and immediate. If he'd been called away, then she wouldn't have had the peaceful sleep she'd desperately needed, because he'd taken her call. Like he'd promised he would. He hadn't mentioned it. Hadn't tried to make her feel guilty or indebted.

But he had been protecting her rest.

'Thank you all for my lovely birthday celebration.' Luna's calm acknowledgement redirected Amelia's scattered thoughts.

Yes, this was her aunt's evening, and there was no doubt Luna was glowing under Marco's attention. The way her cheeks had flushed when he'd presented those roses, how animated she became practicing her Italian with him. The wine really was delicious too.

Amelia forced herself to let her suspicions of Marco ease. Later. She could dissect her reactions later.

It would be okay. She wasn't stupid. He'd leave after dinner. Men like Marco didn't linger for family game nights.

Except he didn't leave. The rain came down heavier, drumming against the windows, and the boys brought out the Monopoly board, and the game seemed to stretch on for ever.

Luna rose after losing all her fleeting wealth—too generous with her property deals, just like always—and made a jug of hot chocolate to put on the table, along with the leftover cake. The kitchen filled with warmth and laughter, and Amelia found herself stealing glances at Marco when she thought he wasn't looking. The way he threw back his head when Crispin made a joke. How his eyes crinkled at the corners. How he fit into their little family circle as if he'd always belonged there.

Dangerous thinking.

When she threw a six and groaned, 'Nooo.'

'You owe me twelve hundred dollars.' Marco's words

were deceptively soft and amused, but she caught the predatory gleam in his dark eyes.

She huffed a sigh and handed over her last five hundred dollars to Marco, nowhere near enough to meet her commitments from landing on his expensive hotel.

Her fingers brushed his as she transferred the bills, and the brief contact sent an unwelcome jolt up her arm. 'I'm out. Bankrupt. I should never have sold you that property and let you complete that street.'

'Business is business, cara.'

'I'm not your cara.' The words snapped out before she could stop them, sharper than the situation warranted. She glared at him, hating how easily he could rattle her composure. She hated losing at Monopoly, but this felt like losing something much more important.

'She hates losing,' Crispin whispered to Marco with the conspiratorial glee of a younger brother, and she turned on him.

'I was doing fine until you boys put the Get Out of Jail money and all the fines into the middle for whoever lands on Free Parking. It makes the game drag on forever.'

'I see she does,' Marco whispered back, not quietly enough, and his accent made the teasing sound like silk.

Luna laughed—a sound of pure delight that Amelia hadn't heard enough of lately—and despite herself, her cheeks began to ache from trying not to smile. Which meant they were all too comfortable with each other, too easy in this domestic scene.

She seriously hoped she wouldn't regret asking him to join them tonight. Already, she could feel herself softening more toward him, and that was a luxury she couldn't afford.

Luna and Amelia had both been too good-natured when

it came to selling their unwanted game properties, especially when faced with pleading from scheming men. 'Next time, I'm going to be ruthless. No mercy, no matter how much anyone begs. That's the only way to stop these calculating types from winning.'

She pointed her finger at Marco, who had easily accumulated the largest pile of money and the most valuable property collection. 'You didn't sell a single one of yours when we asked.'

He flashed her a smile that made her pulse stutter with charm and unapologetic confidence. 'Business is business.' His eyes showed only mischief as Crispin picked up the dice. 'And now Crispin will join you in bankruptcy. Pay up, Crispin.'

Her brother threw down his assorted change and stood with exaggerated drama. 'I'll get you next time, Marco.'

After several more rounds, Ryan landed on Marco's most expensive property, and the game finally ended with Marco's decisive victory.

By then Amelia had cleared the kitchen, rather grateful for the familiar routine that gave her hands something to do. Luna had said goodnight and retreated to her room to shower, and both boys packed up the board game with the efficiency of long practice.

Marco came to stand beside her at the sink, close enough that she could feel his warmth, smell that combination of soap and something uniquely him—cedar, maybe, or sandalwood—that made her want to breathe deeper.

Tension ramped inside her. Please don't let the boys abandon her now.

'Night, Amelia. Night, Marco.' And they were gone. Just like that.

She was alone with Marco, and he had a very strange

smile on his face when she finally risked a glance. Heat and something that made her mouth go dry. 'It was a very enjoyable night.'

He looked so tall and dark and unfairly gorgeous standing in her familiar kitchen, making the space feel smaller, more intimate than it had any right to be. 'I've wanted to do this all night.' He reached out and twirled one of her rebellious curls around his finger, his touch gentle but deliberate. Those dark eyes held hers with an intensity that made her pulse skip. Every nerve ending seemed to come alive under that steady regard, as if he could see straight through to all the things she was trying not to feel.

She pulled her head sideways, and her hair unravelled from his finger, springing back to join the rest of her unruly mop. 'Bad hair day.' The words came out breathless, despite her attempt to sound casual.

'Glorious hair day,' he corrected. 'Do you have family nights like that often?'

She told herself to focus on his question not on the compliment or on the way her scalp still tingled where his fingers had been. Not on how her traitorous body had wanted to lean into his touch instead of pulling away like any sensible woman would. 'Yes.' The single word was all she could manage.

His smile was hard to read. Not sad exactly, but not amused either. Something deeper, more complex. 'Then, you are blessed. Thank you, Amelia, for a wonderful family night.'

'You are very welcome.' Her politeness felt thin but necessary.

'Am I able to kiss your cheeks in the Italian fashion, like I do with your aunt?'

Every instinct screamed no. This was how flirting

worked, small intimacies that led to bigger ones, the casual touches that became anything but casual. Still, she said, 'Yes.'

And then he was closer, invading her space with his big body. His male scent surrounded her, that haunting cologne. Soft lips brushed her cheek—how could such a brief caress send heat racing through her veins? Then he kissed the other cheek, his mouth warm against her skin. She was certain he lingered at her neck, inhaling as if memorising, and the intimacy of it made her knees weak.

She stepped back quickly, her hands shaking.

'Buonanotte, bella Amelia.' The words in his native tongue felt like a caress all its own.

She forced herself to move toward the entrance, each step toward the door a small win over wanting to ask him to stay.

Mentally, she dragged him in her wake, desperate to get him safely outside before she did something too stupid for words.

She opened the door to rain still falling, though not as heavily now, and glanced around with relief when she spotted his umbrella leaning against the wall.

'Good night, Marco.' Her voice sounded almost normal. Collegial, professional. Go, her.

He nodded as he moved past, collecting his umbrella with efficient movements. The brief brush of his body against hers in the doorway sent another jolt through her system.

He snapped the umbrella open and strode to his car with that confident stride, and her hand lingered on the door-handle. She should close the door and start the process of forgetting how good he'd looked sitting at their kitchen table. Instead, she found herself watching.

Only when the street was empty did she finally close the door and lean against it. Her heart still bumped from a simple goodbye kiss on the cheek.

CHAPTER SIXTEEN

'WHAT'S GOING ON with you and Amelia?' Henry's flat tone carried an edge that Marco hadn't heard before, definitely protective. It was 7:50 a.m., and they were waiting for the woman who'd been occupying far too many of his thoughts to appear in the children's ward before starting their Wednesday round.

'Nothing.' The word tasted bitter as he spoke it, and Marco felt his jaw tighten with familiar frustration. Because it was true, wasn't it? Despite the evening at her home and the way she'd looked at him when he'd touched her hair, the way her breath had caught when he'd kissed her cheeks—she was still a master at keeping people at arm's length. Especially him.

He'd had such hopes yesterday morning after the night's breakthrough. For a few hours, he'd allowed himself to believe something had shifted between them. But she'd been as cool and collected as always since, managing to keep that maddening distance between them with an ease that left him wondering if he'd imagined the entire evening. Had he imagined the way she'd trembled when he'd touched her curl? The way she'd watched him from the doorway as he'd driven away.

Madonna, how did she do it?

'Well, she's acting strange around you,' Henry said, his

frown deepening. 'I noticed that yesterday.' Another quick, suspicious glance. 'Have you done anything to upset her?'

Marco's fingers tightened at his sides. The accusation in his friend's voice rankled more than it should have. Did Henry really think so little of him? 'Certainly not. We have shared coffee. And,' he paused, unable to resist needling his overly protective friend, 'I have eaten at her family home for the lovely Luna's birthday.' He tapped his chin thoughtfully, enjoying the way Henry's eyes widened. 'Oh, and Sunday breakfast before that.'

'You went to her house? Twice?' Henry's voice climbed an octave, and Marco had to bite back a smile. His friend's agitation was almost comical.

'Sì.' Marco felt a surge of dark amusement. He would never hurt Amelia—the very idea was repugnant—but he wasn't above rattling Henry's cage. 'Although really, it is more times if you count taking her brothers in the Ferrari just for a spin.'

Henry's mouth fell open, and Marco had to struggle not to grin outright. 'You talk to her brothers? You're that much in her life?'

The question hit closer to home than Marco cared to admit, wiping away his amusement. 'Not as much as I wish, my friend.' The admission slipped out before he could stop it, raw and honest and unwelcome. This dissatisfaction, this constant awareness of her troubled him more than he wanted. When had he become the kind of man who pined after a woman who clearly didn't want him?

But even as the thought formed, he remembered the way she'd looked at him in her kitchen. The way her pulse had fluttered at her throat when he'd leaned close. She wasn't immune.

'But,' Henry shook his head, his voice that earnest tone

that meant he was about to deliver unwanted advice, 'I told you in the beginning, Amelia is not someone you play with.'

The words hit Marco like a physical blow. Play with her? Is that what Henry thought he was doing? Heat flared in his chest, sharp and defensive. He met Henry's intense gaze head-on, raising one eyebrow in challenge. 'What if I am not playing?'

The question hung in the air between them, loaded with implications that Marco hadn't fully intended to voice. But now that the words were out there, he accepted the truth. This wasn't a game to him. Hadn't been for some time, if he were being honest with himself. No other man should look at Amelia as their future—except him.

Henry grimaced, clearly uncomfortable with the direction of the conversation. 'I wouldn't believe you.'

The dismissal stung, but before he could respond, Amelia appeared from the direction of the emergency department with Tom beside her, speaking intently.

Marco's breath caught as it always did when he first saw her each day. She moved with that efficient grace he'd come to associate with her, her dark hair pulled back and secured with many pins, and her crazy glasses did somehow make her look both professional and achingly beautiful.

The round went smoothly, though Marco found himself stealing glances at her profile as she examined patients and spoke with parents. She had such gentle hands with the children, such patience with their fears. It made his chest ache to watch her give so much of herself to others while keeping herself locked away.

They stopped briefly when Henry took a call from Nadia, which had him moving away from them with an apologetic gesture. Marco used the moment to step closer to Amelia, close enough to catch that subtle scent of jasmine, uniquely her.

'You're very good with her,' he said quietly, nodding toward the little girl they'd just examined.

She looked up at him, and for a moment her professional mask slipped just enough for him to see the warmth beneath. 'She's scared. An extra minute or two costs nothing.'

'But it means everything to the children and their parents.' He held her gaze, trying to convey how much her compassion moved him. 'You have a gift, Amelia.'

Colour rose in her cheeks, and she looked away quickly. 'It's just my job, Marco.'

No, it wasn't. It was so much more than that, and they both knew it. But before he could press the point, Henry returned, and the moment was lost.

They completed the circuit only a little late, which worked well now that Marco was only being called back for complicated emergency admissions. Both he and Henry held complete confidence in Amelia's triaging and treatment skills; she had a mind that cut straight to the heart of a problem. Sam and Tom deferred to her naturally, and she decided when the consultants needed to be called in for cases beyond their scheduled rounds.

It was an efficient system, and it meant everyone had more time, except Amelia and the residents, of course. Marco had heard that their principal partner, Simon, now had his own neonatal registrar, which meant Amelia no longer had to cover the neonatal unit as well. A small mercy, since she was already carrying more than her share of the load.

Rainbow Bay Hospital's patient load and staffing levels were growing rapidly, and Marco couldn't help but wonder how long Amelia could maintain this pace without burning out.

The thought of her exhausting herself troubled him.

Before Marco could leave the ward, Henry caught both his and Amelia's attention, drawing them aside with that slightly awkward expression he wore when he had to ask for favours.

'Nadia would like me to ask you both to dinner on Friday. I was on call but have booked another paediatrician to cover, so I know you're both free, and...' he looked genuinely embarrassed now '...it's my birthday, and I was supposed to organise this earlier.'

Marco felt his pulse quicken. An evening with Amelia outside the hospital, away from the professional boundaries that she wielded so expertly. Even with Henry, this could be exactly what he needed.

'Anyone else going?' Amelia asked, and Marco noticed with a stab of disappointment that she didn't so much as glance his way.

'Malachi and Lisandra are away, and Simon and Isabella have a prior engagement. So I'm in trouble for not organising this sooner, and I need you both. It would be just the four of us. Katie is going downstairs to her great-grandmother for the night.'

'I'd love to come.' Amelia touched Henry's arm with that easy affection she showed everyone except Marco. 'I'm looking forward to it, and I will phone Nadia later to ask what I can bring.'

Perfect. Marco's mind was already racing ahead, planning. 'I could pick you up from your house, Amelia.' The offer came out more eagerly than he'd intended, and he saw her stiffen slightly. Cazzo! Too much, too fast.

'That's very thoughtful of you, but not needed. You live in the same building as Henry.' She raised her eyebrows in that way that made him feel like she was humouring him. 'One of the boys will drop me off and pick me up.' Then she smiled at him—actually smiled—and Marco felt his world tilt on its axis. 'You know they love to drive my car.'

That smile. Madonna, what it did to him. He couldn't do anything but smile back, even as disappointed as he was. 'Not as much as they'd like to drive my car.'

'You'd let them drive your car?' Henry's voice cracked with disbelief.

Amelia's grin widened, and she laughed, that sound that Marco felt in his very bones. 'Of course not. Not the Ferrari.'

The sound of her laughter was the sweetest thing he'd heard all day. He wanted to make her laugh like that again, wanted to be the cause of that joy lighting up her face. But when he looked at Henry, his friend's expression had shifted to something that wasn't sweet at all.

More suspicion. More disapproval. And from his friend. This was not London. He'd been much better behaved here, mostly because his fascination with Amelia directly increased the disinterest he now had in other women.

Marco pushed down his frustration. He'd proven himself as a colleague and as a friend. Henry would soon see he meant no harm to Amelia.

Marco arrived at Henry and Nadia's apartment at six fifteen, running late because of an unexpected phone call from Valentina, a former colleague and friend with benefits, in Rome. She'd been persistent, fishing for information about his plans, hinting at possibilities that no longer held the appeal they once had. He'd found her surprisingly difficult to discourage, her voice carrying undertones of assumption that grated against his nerves.

The conversation had left him feeling unsettled, reminded of a version of himself he was no longer sure he recognised.

The man who'd lived for the chase, who'd collected beautiful women like fine wines, that man felt like a stranger now.

Nadia met him at the door, and he kissed both her cheeks before presenting her with a bouquet of pink roses—similar to the ones he'd given Luna. He was saving red roses for someone special. Someone whom he hoped would one day be ready to receive them.

He shook Henry's hand and passed over another bottle of that Prosecco he'd enjoyed at Amelia's house, remembering the way she'd looked that night with her hair loose around her shoulders, her defences temporarily lowered.

And then she rose from the lounge to greet him, and Marco felt his breath catch in his throat. She was wearing a lilac summer dress with shoestring straps and a faint floral print that faded and returned. It cut straight across the swell of her small breasts and tiny waist, and the colour brought out lavender tones in her eyes that he'd never noticed before. The dress skimmed her curves in a way that made his mouth go dry, while her glorious hair was half-up and half-down in a style that left twirls and scattered across the elegant line of her neck.

Bellissima. *Absolutely breathtaking.*

'Buonasera, bella Amelia.' He leaned forward, close enough to catch that intoxicating scent of jasmine that seemed to cling to her skin, and asked quietly, 'May I?'

She inclined her head and turned her face each way, allowing him the brief contact of lips against her cheek.

Even that innocent touch sent heat racing through his veins, and he had to force himself to step back before he did something foolish.

'None of that on the ward, I hope,' Henry muttered, barely audible, and Nadia immediately shushed him.

'You don't complain when he does that to me.'

'I trust him with you,' Henry replied, and Marco felt the sting of the implication: *but not with Amelia.*

Marco ignored the exchange because Amelia's eyes seemed guarded tonight as she greeted him, more shuttered than usual, if that were possible. 'Hello, Marco. We wondered if you'd been held up somewhere.'

'A phone call from Rome. It is their nine a.m. and our six p.m. My apologies.' He waved his hand dismissively, not wanting to think about Valentina's presumptuous questions or the way she'd tried to make him feel guilty for leaving Italy.

'We're all here now.' Nadia moved to the coffee table laden with glasses and appetisers. 'Let's have a toast to the birthday boy with your lovely wine. Amelia brought cheeses and homemade fig jam, which I for one am dying to try, and I made miniature arancini balls and bruschetta. My specialty.'

As Henry popped the cork and filled the glasses, Marco watched Amelia settle onto one end of the large lounge.

Of course he sat beside her, perhaps a little closer than she would have expected, judging by the way she shifted slightly away. But she'd chosen the far left of the couch, leaving herself only a little room to escape, and he found that both amusing and encouraging, especially when she didn't move farther or as far as she could.

The warmth of her body so close to his was intoxicating. He could smell her perfume, could see the delicate curve of her collarbone where her dress crossed at the neckline. It took all his willpower to focus on the conversation flowing around them.

They toasted Henry, and Marco found himself more attuned to the woman beside him than to Nadia's animated description of their honeymoon on Lord Howe Island. Every time Amelia laughed or leaned forward to ask a question, he felt the brush of her arm against his, felt the way her dress shifted to reveal another inch of creamy skin.

Dio, he was losing his mind over this woman.

When they moved to the dining table, Marco made sure to sit across from her rather than beside her, partly for his own sanity, and partly because he wanted to watch her face as she talked. She was animated tonight in a way he rarely saw at the hospital, sharing stories of growing up in this beachside suburb, of her time with the surf lifesaving club.

'So you paddled out on a board to save people?' he asked, fascinated by this glimpse into her past.

'We took turns on duty, and I loved it, but that all stopped when I went away to university.'

The image of her cutting through the waves to reach someone in distress stirred something deep in his chest. Of course she'd been a lifesaver and spent her weekends risking her own safety to help others. It was so Amelia that it made his heart ache.

'Have you seen Marco's flat?' Henry's question came out of nowhere, and Marco felt his attention snap back to the present.

'I've seen the coffee machine in the kitchen and the patio garden, yes.' Amelia glanced at Nadia with a calm smile. 'It's in a lovely location. You must have been very happy there.'

Marco's chest tightened. She had been in his home, and he wanted her back there. Other places he wanted to show her than his kitchen and garden. Alone.

'I was happy there,' Nadia replied, smiling at her husband. 'Though, Katie and I love the view up here.'

Henry raised his eyebrows with mock indignation, sliding an arm around his wife's waist. 'Is that all you love up here?'

She patted his cheek affectionately. 'And you. So needy, my husband.'

Marco watched the easy intimacy between them with a mixture of envy and longing. When had he started wanting that for himself? When had the idea of someone who would tease him about being needy, who would look at him with that kind of fond exasperation, become more appealing than all the sophisticated women in London or Rome?

He knew the answer, even if he wasn't ready to admit it out loud. It had started the moment a certain brilliant and impossibly spectacled doctor had walked into his life and turned everything upside down.

When it was time to go, Marco's pulse quickened as he followed Amelia to the door. The evening had been torture and pleasure in equal measure watching her relax and laugh with Henry and Nadia. She'd been animated and comfortable in a way she never was at the hospital.

They said their goodbyes. Of course, she'd already texted Crispin, her phone showing the efficient message that summed up her approach to everything. 'He'll be here in a couple of minutes,' she said, and Marco felt his disappointment at how eager she seemed to escape.

Amelia stepped into the lift, and he pressed the ground-floor button without asking, his decision automatic. 'I'll wait with you downstairs.'

As if she'd guessed he would never leave her standing outside alone at night—and perhaps she had learned to read him better than he'd realised—she answered easily, 'If you like.'

If you like. Such casual words. Yes, he liked. He more than liked. He also would have liked a few more precious minutes of opportunity to stand alone with her in the darkness, perhaps with Crispin meeting every red traffic light between here and her home. He willed it. A man could hope.

The lift descended in silence, and Marco found himself noting the way she stood just far enough away that their arms wouldn't brush and the careful way she kept her eyes fixed on the floor numbers rather than looking at him.

When the doors opened at ground level, he followed her out and held the door as she stepped into the night air. The sound of waves crashing on the beach below drifted up to them, and the sea-breeze was cooler than it had been during the tropical storm a few days ago. She shivered slightly, and every protective instinct he possessed roared to life.

'Are you warm enough?'

'Yes, thank you.' She pulled the delicate scarf she'd brought around her shoulders, but he could see the goose bumps rising on her arms. Without thinking, he slid his jacket off, covered her shoulders and stepped closer, close enough to share his body heat, close enough that if she swayed even slightly, well… He could hope.

'I had a nice night,' she said, and there was something softer and less guarded in her voice.

'As did I.' A truth. Watching her tonight, seeing glimpses of the woman he knew lay beneath, had only made him more aware of her. More determined to risk a refusal on one honest question. 'Would you consider coming to dinner with me, Amelia? Just the two of us. I would like to spend more time with you outside of work.'

The words hung between them in the salt-tinged air, and Marco held his breath as he watched her face. Eyes widened with what looked like surprise, and something that might have been panic flickered across her features.

'Are you offering a fling, Marco?'

The assumption stung more than it should have, but he forced himself to answer calmly.

'I am offering honesty and a genuine wish to spend more time with you. It's difficult to prove my sincerity when we're always surrounded by colleagues and patients and professional boundaries.' He took a closer look at her, letting her see the truth in his eyes. 'I'd like that chance to know more of you, Amelia. Not a fling, as you call it, or a one-night stand. The chance to show you who I really am.'

'And who are you?' she said, her voice quiet.

'I am just Marco, who thinks you are the most fascinating woman he has ever met.'

The vulnerability in his own voice surprised him. He wasn't used to this anxious need for someone else's approval. With other women, the outcome had never mattered this much. But with Amelia, everything felt more important.

She studied his face in the soft glow from the building's entrance lights, and he could practically see her weighing risks and benefits like a medical decision. For a moment he thought she was going to refuse and leave him standing there like a fool.

Then her expression softened fractionally. 'I think I'd like that, too, Marco.'

The simple words sent triumph surging through him. She'd said yes. *Madonna!* Now he had to make sure he didn't ruin this chance, didn't let his eagerness overwhelm her natural caution.

'Is tomorrow night too soon?' The question escaped before he could stop it, driven by the fear that if he waited, she'd change her mind. 'Henry is on call this weekend apart from tonight, and I have no idea when we'll both next be free.'

She was quiet for a moment, and he could almost hear her mental calendar flipping through to check for obligations and responsibilities. 'I have nothing planned.'

He licked suddenly dry lips. 'Then, I will pick you up at seven.'

A car swept around the corner, its headlights cutting through the darkness, and he recognised it instantly as Amelia's distinctive sedan.

Acting on pure instinct, he stepped back into the shadow cast by the building's overhang and gently tugged her hand so that she came with him, out of the glare of the approaching headlights. 'Goodnight, Amelia.'

And this time he kissed her on the lips. Just as gently as he had her cheeks, but with all the tenderness he felt for this amazing woman concentrated into that one intense contact. Her lips were warm and incredibly soft, and she tasted faintly of the wine they'd shared at dinner. He wanted more but stopped.

For one perfect moment she didn't pull away or stiffen or even retreat. Instead, she seemed to melt slightly against him, her fingers curling into his jacket as if she needed something to hold onto. Him.

When he finally drew back, her eyes were wide and dark in the shadowy alcove, her lips slightly parted. He wanted desperately to kiss her again, to deepen the contact, to lose himself in the sweetness of her response.

But Crispin was already pulling up to the kerb, and he could see the practical part of her mind reasserting itself even as they stood there.

'Tomorrow,' he said quietly, a promise softly in the night.

She nodded, slid his jacket from her shoulders into his hands, and the spell was broken as her car stopped beside them. Marco went forward with her and opened the door to the vehicle. She glanced over her shoulder at him, an odd expression he couldn't read on her face. But all she said was 'Thank you' and slid in.

He raised a hand to Crispin, then closed the door and stepped back, his chest ridiculously tight. Tomorrow.

CHAPTER SEVENTEEN

'MARCO LOOKED SERIOUS,' Crispin said as they drove away from the apartment building, his voice carrying that teasing note that meant he was fishing for information.

'Did he?' Amelia could still feel the phantom pressure of Marco's lips against hers. Her mouth tingled with the memory, the taste, and she raised and then dropped her hand. She absolutely did not want to go into that conversation. 'How were your knees after football training tonight?'

Nice deflection, Amelia. She winced, but she needed time to process what had just happened. That kiss—so gentle, so careful, yet still so hot—had reverberated right through her. She'd wanted to lean into him, go with whatever this was between them, and that thought terrified her more than she cared to admit.

'A lot easier. Coach is happy to see me back into full training this week.'

'That's great.' And it was. Grateful for the familiar territory of her brother's recovery. Much safer than thinking about the way Marco had looked at her in those last moments, unsure of himself.

Crispin flicked her a sideways look as they waited at traffic lights. 'How was your night?'

'Watch the road.' The automatic big-sister response

bought her a few seconds to gather her thoughts. 'Very pleasant.' And it had been more than pleasant, if she were being honest. It had been a revelation. Sitting across from Marco at dinner, watching him laugh with Henry and Nadia, seeing him relaxed in a way she never witnessed at the hospital. The man was a completely different person wearing the same handsome face.

She'd enjoyed the view, certainly. What woman wouldn't? But it had been less overwhelming than sitting beside him where she'd been constantly aware of the heat radiating from his body, the way his cologne mixed with something essentially him to create a scent that made her want to bury her nose in him.

Thankfully, at the dinner table, she'd been able to observe him safely, to catalogue the way his eyes crinkled when he laughed. Notice how his hands moved when he spoke. Hear the genuine warmth in his voice when he'd asked about her life-saving days.

Dangerous observations. The kind that led to stupid decisions like agreeing to dinner dates with Italian doctors who kissed like they meant it.

'It was good to spend time with Henry's wife without lots of people around,' she added, partly because it was true and partly because she needed to focus on something other than Marco. She suspected she and Nadia could be good friends in the future, if Amelia didn't completely spoil things by falling for her husband's colleague.

'You're not on call tomorrow night, are you?'

The question made her mouth dry. She left a list of her call dates on the fridge so the family could organise their lives around her schedule. *No, I'm going out on a date.*

'I'm not. Why?'

The thought sent a fresh wave of anxiety through her.

She still didn't know how she felt about that decision, except nervous. What did one wear to dinner with an Italian surgeon who drove a Ferrari and looked at her like she was the most fascinating puzzle he'd ever encountered?

'Can we borrow your car tomorrow night, please?'

We meaning him and Ryan. The twins did everything together, had done since they were small. 'Sure. What's on?'

'Great. There's a band we want to see up in the hills, so it's hard to get there with public transport.' He tapped his fingers on the steering wheel in that restless rhythm that meant he was building up to something. 'Sure you won't need it?'

'I won't need it.' The words came out steady enough, but her heart rate picked up as she prepared to voice the reality. She took a breath, steeling herself. 'I'm going out for dinner with Marco tomorrow night. So he'll pick me up.'

'In the Ferrari?' Crispin's grin was immediate and infectious, lighting up his whole face as he glanced across at her.

Despite her nerves, she had to smile at his excitement. 'I think it's his only car,' she said dryly, but who knew. The thought of climbing into that sleek, expensive machine again made her palms sweat. She was more of a practical sedan kind of woman.

Crispin laughed, the sound pure delight. 'That's crazy. Who owns a Ferrari?'

'Marco, apparently.' The conversation felt surreal. Six weeks ago, the most exotic thing in her life had been Luna's occasional stories about her travels. Now she was discussing Ferrari rides with her teenage brother as if it were perfectly normal. But she had to smile at her brother's infectious enthusiasm.

'So crazy. Anyway, that's great. Really great.'

Something in his tone made her study his profile. 'Because you can have my car for the evening?'

'No, though that's good too.' He glanced at her as they stopped at another set of lights, and his expression was suddenly more serious, more adult than his seventeen years. 'Because you don't go out much, and he'll take you somewhere really special.'

The observation stung a little, mainly because it was true. When had her social life become so narrow that her teenage brothers were worried about her? 'And?'

'And we like him. Not just his car.' Crispin's voice carried a sincerity that made her chest tighten. 'He's good people. We like the way he looks at you as if you're the most amazing thing he's seen all day.'

The words hit her, unexpected and devastating in their sweetness. Did Marco really look at her that way? She'd thought she'd imagined the intensity in his gaze, the way his attention seemed to focus on her with precision whenever they were in the same room. But if her brothers had noticed...

The cars in front of them shimmered as her eyes filled with unexpected tears. She blinked rapidly, trying to clear her vision before Crispin noticed.

'Thank you, Crispin. That's lovely of you to say.'

'Thank you, Mellie.' He cleared his throat, and she could hear the emotion he was trying to hide. 'We know you've given up a lot for us.'

The words made her throat hurt. 'Oh, no, you don't.' This was not a conversation she was prepared for tonight, not when her emotions were already scattered from Marco's kiss and the prospect of tomorrow's date. 'You boys have pulled your weight. Been dream teenagers. We've had none of the drama other families have had.'

So far. She mentally crossed her fingers, hoping she wasn't tempting fate. But it was true. Somehow, through the worst tragedy of their lives, the twins had remained steady, dependable, awesomely mature for their age.

'You and Ryan have behaved responsibly, way above your years ever since we lost Mum and Dad.' The familiar ache settled in her chest, duller now than it had been five years ago but still there. Still real.

Crispin started to speak, but she held up her hand. She needed to finish this, needed him to understand. 'I know you could have made bad choices along the way, but neither of you did. Didn't get mixed up in anything you shouldn't have.' She gave him the side-eye that had served her well over the years. 'Not that I found out about.'

He laughed at that, the tension breaking slightly. 'Aunt Luna's been amazing, but you've been the best big sister anyone could have.'

The sincerity in his voice made her want to cry all over again. Or hug him, though that would be dangerous while he was driving. Maybe this was about more than just her going on a date. Maybe the reality of them leaving for university was hitting them all harder than she'd expected.

'Well, you guys do things for me too.' Her voice came out slightly rough, and she cleared her throat. 'It's very nice to have my own designated driver, thank you. And thank you for your thoughts about Marco.'

'You mean *end of subject*?' He laughed, but she could hear the understanding in it.

'Yes, please.' She wasn't ready to examine her feelings about Marco with anyone else, not when she barely understood them herself.

CHAPTER EIGHTEEN

AMELIA STOOD AT the bathroom mirror and straightened her glasses, studying her reflection with the critical eye she usually reserved for X-rays and lab results. She hadn't really thought about clothes for the last couple of years, had built a capsule wardrobe that covered most situations and that mixed and matched efficiently.

Professional blouses, well-cut trousers, a few dresses suitable for hospital functions. Everything designed to project competence and authority while remaining practical for twelve-hour shifts.

But the glasses. They were different. The frames really did take up a lot of her face, didn't they? And they were very blue, a practical choice when she'd bought them, but now she wondered if they were too bold, too attention-grabbing.

Or maybe she needed different coloured glasses to go with different outfits. Or she could look into laser therapy and ditch eyewear altogether. Which was a strange thing to think about while getting ready for a date, but then again, everything about tonight felt strange and unfamiliar.

Her gaze drifted to the glasses again, and she felt that familiar knot of uncertainty twist tighter in her stomach. Oh heavens, the glasses. The bright blue frames seemed to mock her in the mirror, gaudy and juvenile in the evening light filtering through her curtains. What on earth had she been thinking? She could practically hear Marco's voice again from that first encounter in the corridor. *Those glasses are...quite striking.* The way his mouth had curved just slightly, not quite a smile, not quite a grimace. The diplomatic pause before *quite striking* that had spoken volumes about what a sophisticated Italian man really thought of her eyewear choice.

Heat crept up her neck at the memory. She'd walked on feeling like a schoolgirl who'd raided her mother's make-up bag, trying to look grown-up and failing spectacularly.

She lifted them off with a frown as the memories flooded back. That rushed afternoon at the opticians so many weeks ago—heavens, had it really been that chaotic? Luna insisting the blue was *So you, Amelia!* while Amelia's eyes had darted to her watch every thirty seconds, anxiety building with each tick. The boys had a match across town, and she'd had exactly twenty minutes to choose frames that would supposedly suit her for the next few years.

Twenty minutes. For something she'd wear every single day.

Luna had been enthusiastic, so certain, her face glowing with the pleasure of helping her niece with something that felt almost...sisterly. It had been nice. And Amelia had been too harried, too focussed on the ticking clock and the boys waiting in the car, to properly consider whether her aunt's taste—however well-intentioned—aligned with what a thirty-year-old registrar should wear to work.

'These ones show off your eyes,' Luna had insisted, as she held up the blue frames. 'And they're fun. You deserve fun, darling.'

Fun. Amelia's chest had tightened at the word, guilt

and defensiveness warring inside her. When had fun become a priority in choosing eyewear? When had her aunt started seeing her as someone who needed rescuing from her own boring choices? But Luna had looked so pleased with herself, so eager to help her niece with something, anything, that felt like the kind of shopping trip Luna probably thought they should be having more often.

So Amelia had swallowed her doubts, nodded quickly and said yes. Paid without really looking at the total, rushed the boys to their match and tried to ignore the way her reflection looked like she was playing dress-up in someone else's life.

Now, many weeks later, she couldn't shake the feeling that Marco saw her as the woman who'd had some sort of crisis in the opticians. The competent, reliable Dr Day who'd suddenly started sporting bright blue frames that belonged on someone with Luna's natural confidence and flair for making statements.

Her throat felt tight. Someone who wasn't her. Maybe she just needed to admit that she'd made the choice for Luna's sake, not her own. That rushing nonimportant decisions had become such a habit she didn't even recognise when she was doing it anymore.

Yup. Made her wonder how many other choices she'd made this way.

She could wear her contacts tonight. Her hands moved toward the contact case almost without conscious thought.

But something about that felt like pretending to be someone she wasn't, as well. She hated contacts. Though, maybe the someone she wasn't, included making questionable eyewear choices under pressure from the demands of everyone else's needs. She'd wear her glasses tonight, and perhaps the first chance she had she'd find another pair to alternate with. Ones she felt comfortable in. Enough.

She needed to let go of these destructive thoughts that kept circling through her mind.

The glasses were fine. The dress was fine. She was fine.

It was just… Tonight, she wanted to look more than just competent. More than professional. She wanted to look… beautiful? The *bella* Marco kept calling her. The thought made her stomach flutter with nerves. When had she last cared about looking beautiful for someone?

No, what she had on was fine. The black dress was classic, well-fitted without being too revealing. The pearl earrings her mother had given her for her eighteenth birthday added a touch of elegance. She looked professional, put-together. Her hair half-constrained with a clasp on top, half-loose. Safe.

But as she stared at her reflection, she couldn't shake the feeling that *safe* wasn't what Marco saw when he looked at her with that intensity Crispin had mentioned. Maybe safe wasn't what she wanted to be tonight. With a sigh she took out the clasp in her hair—that she could change.

She just hoped this whole thing wasn't a massive mistake, because she still had to work with the man if it all went sideways. If he turned out to be the player Henry worried about. What if she let herself fall for him only to discover she was just another conquest? What if the morning after brought awkwardness and regret instead of whatever romantic fantasy her silly imagination kept conjuring?

Though, she'd managed to navigate through some awkward situations in the last weeks, hadn't she? The coffee encounters, the family dinner, the way he'd looked at her after touching her hair. And she did seem to understand him more now, to see past the charming exterior to the dedicated physician beneath. She admired his work ethic and his genuine care for their young patients.

One date couldn't change everything, could it?

But as she touched up her lipstick, she couldn't help remembering the soft pressure of his mouth against hers, she had the sinking feeling that everything had already changed. The only question now was whether she was brave enough to see where it led.

'He's here.' Luna's voice came through her bedroom door, and Amelia's stomach immediately twisted. She glanced at her mother's watch—a nervous habit she'd developed since inheriting the delicate timepiece—and felt her eyebrows lift in surprise. Not quite seven. He was early.

She wasn't ready. But then a different realisation settled in, one that made warmth spread in her chest. Early meant he really wanted to be here, didn't it?

The man wouldn't bother showing up at all if he didn't want to be seen with her. For heaven's sake, he could have any woman in the hospital—probably on the entire Gold Coast—and yet he was here, outside her modest family home, waiting for her.

The thought should have been reassuring, but instead it sent a fresh wave of insecurity through her. She just hoped this wasn't some elaborate game where she was playing hard-to-get without meaning to, where her natural reserve had somehow made her more appealing simply because she was a challenge.

The idea made her feel sick.

But there was no backing out now. She lifted her chin in the gesture that had got her through medical school, through the worst days after her parents' deaths, through every difficult decision she'd had to make over the past five years. She picked up her handbag, that practical black leather piece that went with everything, and opened the door.

She sucked in a breath. Hopefully silently.

A god stood outside. He wore dark pants that moulded to his strong thighs with a precision that should have been illegal, and a fitted jacket that caressed his broad shoulders like she wanted to. Yep. Hold that thought.

Even his pale blue shirt and darker tie proclaimed quality rather than shouting it. Apparently, Italians loved ties. Every line of his clothing spoke of a man who understood that style was about fit and fabric rather than flashy labels. Didn't go for his cars, though, and the amused thought eased her tension and allowed her to smile a greeting.

He and Luna were laughing about something when she appeared, but his eyes tracked to her instantly, as if he'd been waiting for that exact moment. The intensity of his focus made her freeze. 'Buonasera, bella Amelia.'

'Good evening, Marco.' Her voice came out steadier than she'd expected, though her heart rate wasn't so steady.

He was holding a box of artisan chocolates and crossed the room with that fluid confidence she'd noticed from their very first meeting, stopping directly in front of her. He offered his now-usual cheek salutation, so soft and gentle, until he changed up and leaned forward to kiss her more firmly on the lips. The contact was both brief and definite, his mouth warm and sure against hers, and the scent of his cologne, a different one this time, something sophisticated with notes of cedar and bergamot, swirled and seduced her.

He smiled at her confusion and handed her the chocolates while her mind went completely blank. Except for a brief *Thank you for the chocolates*, the careful conversation topics she'd rehearsed simply vanished under the assault on her senses. When he stepped back, his gaze locked on hers as if he could see straight through to all the uncertainty she was trying so hard to hide.

'You look very beautiful.' The simple words sent heat rushing to her cheeks, and before she could form a coherent response, he took her hand. She found it tucked securely into his elbow as he drew her toward the door, his touch both possessive and protective in a way that made her feel cherished rather than controlled.

Her mind whirled, still trying to process the fact that he'd kissed her mouth in front of Luna, that he'd made this evening feel significant from the very first moment. This wasn't casual. Whatever was happening between them, however terrifying it might be, it wasn't casual.

'Buonanotte, Luna.'

Luna stepped forward. Took the chocolates from Bella's limp hand with a smile and said, 'Good night, you two.' Luna's voice carried a warmth that spoke of approval, maybe even happiness for her. 'I'll be in bed if you come back for coffee. I'll leave the chocolates on the table.'

The suggestion that the evening might extend beyond dinner sent another flutter of nerves through Amelia's stomach. She wasn't sure if Luna was being optimistic or simply practical, but the genuine warmth and mischief made Amelia smile at her aunt. And she caught Marco's twitch of the lips as well. Oh yeah, he hadn't missed the innuendo.

As Marco guided her toward the door, his hand warm and steady against her arm, Amelia realised that all her careful planning and mental preparation had been utterly useless. Whatever happened tonight, she was already in far deeper than she'd intended to be.

And the most terrifying part was that she wasn't entirely sure she minded.

He took her to the Coolangatta Breeze Rooftop Bar and Restaurant, and when they were seated, Amelia had to catch her breath at the view. Their table looked out over the beach from thirteen floors up, the ocean stretching endlessly toward the horizon where the last traces of afternoon light painted the sky in shades of rose and gold.

The height made her slightly breathless—or was that Marco's presence across from her, the way he seemed to fill her vision even when she was trying to focus on the scenery?

'I've never been here before.' She was genuinely awed by the elegance of the space. Crystal glasses caught the soft lighting, and the gentle murmur of other diners created an intimate atmosphere that made her aware of how alone they were, despite being surrounded by people. A special table, perhaps. Just like Marco to have arranged such a thing, and who was she to complain?

'Sam recommended it, and I'm impressed with the view.' He was looking directly at her when he spoke the words, his dark eyes holding hers with an intensity that made her stomach flutter.

She gestured toward the spectacular panorama laid out before her and behind him. 'You have your back to the view.'

'Al contrario.' The Italian rolled off his tongue, and she couldn't help the clench in her stomach, she so loved his accent. But…

She smiled and shook her head, falling back on the

safer territory of gentle teasing. 'What have I told you about flirting, Marco?'

His eyes sparkled with mischief. 'Sì, so I am not. But I could if you wish.'

Despite herself, she laughed—a sound that felt surprisingly good.

He smiled back at her. 'What would you like to drink?' The waiter approached with perfect timing. Marco picked up the wine list with the casual confidence of someone accustomed to fine dining. 'A cocktail?'

The suggestion made her pause. She could imagine herself sipping something sophisticated and colourful, letting the alcohol blur the edges of her anxiety. But that was exactly why she shouldn't. 'I think just a Prosecco.'

'Not just…' He scanned the list with the focussed attention she'd seen him bring to patient charts, pointing to his selection. 'And sparkling or still water, Amelia?'

'Sparkling, please.' The waiter nodded and disappeared, leaving them alone in their strange intimacy.

The bubbles would help, she thought. Something to occupy her hands, something effervescent to match the strange lightness in her chest. She was absolutely going to make sure she had a full glass of water between every glass of wine.

However the night ended, she would be doing it with her wits fully about her.

He smiled as if he'd read her mind, that knowing look that suggested he understood her better than she was comfortable with. 'Would you like to order now or wait?'

She didn't want to rush. Refused to. 'Let's just wait until we've had our first drink.' She needed time to find her footing in this forgotten territory. So long since she'd been out with a man. She smiled at herself. Well, she'd never been out with a man like Marco. 'I don't go out much, as my brother informed me.'

'Crispin?'

'Crispin,' she confirmed. 'Thank you for bringing me. I'm going to savour this, soak it up.' The admission felt naive, like showing him a piece of herself she usually kept hidden, but it was true. To her surprise his face lit up with such genuine pleasure her anxiety eased just a little.

'This pleases me,' he said, leaning back in his chair with a satisfied tilt to his mouth that made her pulse jump. The relaxed posture should have made him seem less imposing, but instead it highlighted the breadth of his shoulders, the easy confidence that was such a part of him. She should be so easy. 'The more I learn of you, Amelia, the more I value your company.'

The simple statement sent warmth to her chest and probably her cheeks, followed immediately by a spike of panic. This was exactly what she'd been afraid of—that he would be charming and sincere and completely impossible to resist. That she would start believing this could be real.

But looking at him now, seeing the genuine warmth in his dark eyes, she found herself wanting to believe it anyway.

'I enjoy your company too, Marco.' The words felt like stepping off a cliff. Or the balcony outside. She was so not used to this. But she would enjoy herself. 'Thank you for asking me out tonight.'

'My pleasure.' His voice dropped to that lower register and she had to resist the urge to stare at his mouth. Or his throat. Or…

Instead, she reached for her now-filled water glass, grateful for the cool touch of crystal against her fingers, and smiled.

CHAPTER NINETEEN

MARCO HAD BEEN many things, but he'd never been in love. Lust, yes—many, many times. Affection, yes, sometimes: He'd had some affection for his colleague Valentina, until she'd pushed for more, but despite himself he'd felt nothing like the delight and warmth and eagerness to please that he felt for Amelia.

He wanted her to enjoy his company as much as he enjoyed hers, but first she needed to relax. As always, the best way was through work. 'I saw Cressa this week. She looked well and her mother more confident in handling an episode.'

He watched her face light up, and his own pleasure increased. 'I'm so pleased. They're a lovely family, and it must have been terrifying that first time.' He watched as she eased back in the chair, and that beautiful smile made his chest ache as it appeared and stayed.

'They send their regards. And Cressa's mother is full of praise for Dr Mellie.'

She shook her head. 'That is sweet, but we're all a team.'

'Except,' he said and shook his head as if sadly, 'calling you Mellie is such an aberration of your beautiful name.'

She smiled. 'But easier for children. The boys always called me Mellie, and it works well for the younger ones.'

He held up his hand, a stop sign low to the table, just for her. 'I will never call you Mellie.'

She copied him teasingly, her hand up. 'And I will never call you Markie.' The ridiculous parody of his name, delivered in her drawled Australian accent, caught him completely off guard. Laughter burst from his chest so suddenly he nearly choked on his Prosecco, coughing and sputtering like a schoolboy. He laughed and coughed, and she laughed with him because he almost spilled his drink.

'Nice to see you can lose your composure occasionally, Dr Macaluso.' He shook his head. This was the woman he could not resist. The one he needed to discover.

'With you, Amelia, there is always the possibility.'

She smiled at that, and so he moved on to find out more. 'Will you tell me what happened to your parents?'

She took a moment, sipped her wine, glanced at the view and then back at him. 'Yes. Five years ago, they were killed in a car accident on the Gold Coast Highway. One minute the boys were carefree kids, I was fancy free and focussed on my career, and the next our wonderful parents were gone. Our world was in shambles. It was terrible and traumatic, and then Luna appeared, and it was like we'd found the rudder to our broken ship.'

She stared at the darkening view, and he knew she wasn't seeing it.

He said quietly, 'Your aunt is steady, yet she does not force her will.'

Amelia looked up at him. 'You noticed that?'

'Sì. She is a listener and, through her listening, guides.'

'Thank you for saying that.' The smile she gave him took his breath. 'She does. I find it interesting you see her so clearly.'

'Interesting how? Because I am a man or because I am the man you think I am?'

She raised her brows. 'Cryptic.'

He put down his glass. Amused. Remembering the way she would not answer his smiles when he first came to Rainbow Bay. 'Truth. You judged me on my clothes.'

'And your women,' she teased.

Gently he said, 'I wish I'd had someone like your Luna in my life when I was younger.'

She studied him, and it was his turn to stare into the distance and not see. He'd said too much. The waiter came, filled their glasses, and enquired, 'Sir, Madam. Would you like to order?'

Marco blinked and smiled. 'Amelia?'

'Sure.' She picked up the menu and chose decisively. 'I'll have the tempura zucchini flower entrée and the lobster thermidor, please.' Marco smiled at her. Swift and sure. Like her work when she made decisions. Always good ones.

'Sir?'

'The seared scallops da Costa and the lobster as well.'

'Would you like a different wine with that?'

Marco raised a brow at Amelia, and she shook her head. 'We may have dessert wine later.'

So they would have a later. His chest eased now he knew. She took a sip of the Prosecco and waited until the waiter was gone. Then lifted her chin. 'Your turn. How did your parents die?'

If he must…but he supposed it was fair. They were here to know more of each other, after all. Where to start? 'My father was older, a wealthy businessman, pharmaceuticals. He was fit and healthy until his heart gave out unexpectedly. Or so I was told. He was fifty-two. Not long after, my mother, twenty years younger than he, dropped me off at my uncle's—my father's brother—for the day and never came back.'

Amelia blinked. He saw her shock. Had known it would come. This was not something he shared with people for this reason. 'What do you mean *never came back*? How did she die?'

He grimaced. 'As far as I know she has not died.'

He watched her put the glass down carefully, his decisive Amelia now taking her time. 'I'm sorry. You were seven years old and your mother left you at your uncle's house and never came back?'

'Sì.'

'Oh, Marco.' Her beautiful eyes glittered with emotion, and her hand reached for his, but he moved his fingers back. Not pity. He wanted none. He wanted her to stop. Instead, he cloaked himself in the shell that played the part so well for so many years.

'That is the end of the story.'

'You haven't searched her out?'

He said coldly, 'Why?'

Her brow furrowed, and angry at himself for the destruction of their ambience, he wanted to call his words back.

'Why?' she said slowly. 'Compassion. Closure. At least curiosity?'

'Compassion for a woman who left a bereaved child?' He snorted. 'Closure for whom? I am already finished with her.' He lifted his chin. 'Curiosity as to why she did not want me?'

'Marco—'

'Amelia. Enough of this topic.'

She narrowed her eyes at him, and he saw the topic might be finished, but it would return at a later date. She would keep the agreement for now. 'So who was the female figure in your world? Surely you had someone except for an uncle who only saw you at dinner time.'

He stared at her. She had remembered that comment and divined the truth. The lonely years with his uncle he did not talk about. But he'd known she had a brilliant mind. 'I am a man who has many girlfriends.' He shrugged, but she just raised her brows at him as if she would keep waiting. He sighed. 'Perhaps you mean my uncle's housekeeper.'

She smiled. 'Thank goodness. The one who taught you about antipasto sticks. Is this housekeeper still alive?'

'Sì. Now my housekeeper, though she has more help to run the house than when my uncle was alive. This is in Rome.'

Her quick mind calculated. 'She must be elderly now?'

He thought of Maria. Her work-worn hands never idle, despite his requests for her to slow. Brushing him away when he remonstrated with her. 'Her place is secure, and she has help.'

'Of course. You are a caring man. You would have made sure of that.'

He blinked. She thought that of him, and his chest warmed, but he forced a shrug. 'So now you know. My distrust of women has a long tail.'

Her lips curved slightly. Teasing again. 'I can see that. This is the Marco I'd like to know. The one who still cares for a woman who was kind to him as a child. He's a little different from the one I first met.'

He sat back. 'The one you despised.' Held her gaze and thought again how he could lose himself in her beautiful eyes.

'Not *despised*. But I may have judged.' Pursed her beautiful lips. 'A little.'

'Amelia?' His turn to tease. 'A little?'

'A lot.' She smiled. A gorgeous open smile such as he'd

dreamed of. 'But your professional knowledge and expertise and the way you managed difficult parents has always had my admiration.'

Her admiration. Good. But he wanted more. 'You held me at arm's length.'

'I was just the quiet mouse in the corner, and your world is a different world to mine.'

She was no mouse. Or perhaps she was a pretty mouse with sharp teeth and a brilliant brain. 'And yet we are the same when we care for the Braelynns or Cressas or any of the other children who need our skill. We have the same drive, the same passion and dedication to saving children's lives. Our love of our work connects us.'

He savoured the way she listened. As if his words mattered. It was new and precious to him. Being truly heard. She sat, her eyes on his, her face composed as she focussed fully on him, and for the first time in a long time, he felt perhaps he might be worthy of the attention.

Finally, she said, 'Yes, it does make me feel connected to you.'

The shock of her words closed his mouth as something inside him unfurled, slowly, carefully, as if testing the outside world.

The meal arrived, and the diversion was well-timed. He admired Amelia's zucchini flowers as most attractive and, as she said, delicious, then they tasted slowly through the mains, the lobster tender and succulent, while he kept the conversation to more general topics.

He spoke about his time in London with Henry, making her laugh at his attempts to convert his friend to the sybaritic lifestyle, which hadn't worked, and she shared anecdotes about the boys and their friends and sports.

By the time dessert had arrived he felt an ease with

her unlike with any other woman. Yes, he wanted her, her mouth, her body, her crying out his name under him more than ever, but he also wanted her respect and understanding and, he suspected, her future very much entwined with his.

He also understood enough about Amelia to know that there was no rushing her, that trust needed to build, or he would risk losing her to his impatience. That would not happen. He would woo her. Slowly. And together they would see what the future would bring.

By the time they left the restaurant and were back in the car she'd allowed herself to relax properly. Had even come to the conclusion that Marco's fear of commitment could have come from the damage left from his mother's desertion. Was that why he had so many lovers, no special someone? Had he seen safety in numbers? Protecting himself from more abandonment by not allowing a woman too close?

And yet, he was asking that of her. To be closer. Sharing his past.

That thought ignited the caring woman inside her. Could she take a risk on a relationship with him if he couldn't trust her not to leave?

She suspected he was capable of great love. She could see it in his compassion for his patients, his care and consideration for her, his ease with Luna and the boys. Marco deserved a family, and she wanted him whole with a strange desperation she didn't understand.

Was it the doctor in her who wanted to help Marco heal or the woman who wanted him whole?

'Let's not go home yet. Will you drive to the breakwall at the end of Rainbow Beach?'

'Sì. I am in no rush to lose you.'

Her cheeks heated, and she slid her gaze sideways to see a small smile on his beautiful mouth. He caught her gaze and smiled more widely. Lifted one elegant hand from the wheel and stroked her knee before putting it back again. 'I like your idea of driving elsewhere.'

The noise of the waves seemed to fill the car when he turned the engine off. They were parked looking out over the ocean towards the skyline of Surfers Paradise in the distance, and the breeze twisted her hair into flyaway coils that she had to keep pulling out of her eyes. But she felt relaxed and happy. Glad to be alive.

'I'm taking you parking, Marco.'

'Parking?' The question in his eyes made her smile.

'Australian teenagers love parking at the beach for the privacy of what they call *submarine races*.'

'Ahhh. Amore.' His teeth gleamed in the dark. 'Such a spectator sport, this watching of submarines underwater.'

'True.' She smiled and turned in her seat to study his strong features and chiselled jaw. The cut of his cheeks and the curve of his lips. She was far too relaxed with this man. That dessert wine had a kick.

She turned to the waves. 'I love this view but rarely come here.' Funny how being here with Marco felt right.

He shifted and frowned. 'My car is very pretty but not built for submarine races. Would you like to sit on that seat over there. I would hate to miss a…' He completed his thought with satisfaction as if he'd found the word *periscope*.

She laughed and thought about her black ensemble and dubious park benches. As if reading her thoughts he said, 'I have a blanket to throw over the wood and protect your lovely dress.'

'Too kind.' It was a beautiful night with the moon not yet full but shedding enough light to brush the waves with liquid gold, while the breeze felt playful but not cold.

And she felt very safe here with Marco.

In moments he appeared at her door and held out his hand. Finding her fingers entwined in his was becoming more common, she thought, and when she was safely standing he reached behind her seat to extract a small blanket.

He drew her across to the park bench, his hand now resting warmly at the small of her back, possessive and filled with promise. Anticipation flared, and she didn't wrestle it down. She was on a date. She was allowed to be exhilarated.

She knew this seat. 'There's a memorial plaque of someone I knew here.' She reached over and touched the small square of metal attached to the wooden backrest as she sat down. 'A sweet friend of my mother's loved sitting here.'

His head turned as his gaze followed the distant lights. Then he looked down at her. 'Now you are sitting here. It is a wonderful view. Also, very beautiful and sweet.'

Marco lowered himself until his hip rested against hers and his strong thigh seeped warmth against her own. His arm came around her shoulders and casually he pulled her in against him more firmly. The weight of his shoulder made his heat sink into her like the waves sank into the sand.

She smiled. It was a compliment and not flirting. So there, she told herself. Her gaze swept the familiar rocks and trees and distant lights. 'I love this beach.'

'We should come one weekend soon, for breakfast, walk the beach and those paths I would like to follow towards Coolangatta.'

'I'd like that. When I'm not on call.' She snuggled in a little. 'I don't get down to the beach enough these days and never at night.'

'You can see the ocean from your home, though.'

She could, yes. The house had been built on a rise that gave an almost unobstructed view across the road and down the hill to the water. Which made her think about her busy life.

How little she stopped to enjoy the view, but if she sold the house, she'd miss it horribly. 'My parents used to have a sundowner every evening out on the front porch. They'd sit on the swing and hold hands as they sipped their gin and tonics. Watch the ships pass by. Talk about their day.'

She felt him shift beside her, lift her hand and place it in his. 'I like very much the picture of that.'

She leaned into him more as she visualised the past, could see them smiling at each other, so clearly. 'Yes. Me too. I wish they were still here.' She sighed, and he shifted and kissed her cheek.

Comforting. She nodded her head, having made a decision. 'I need to sit on the front veranda more often.' She turned her face to his and surprised herself by saying, 'You're welcome to join me when you're free at sunset.'

He smiled. 'I will set the timer on my phone for every night.' She smiled at the light-hearted promise. But he went on, 'I would like to share those moments with you very much, Amelia.' Her name on his lips sent goose bumps pebbling her skin, that rolling Italian pronunciation of who she was, something she'd begun to savour more and more. He added softly, 'I would like that for many, many sunsets.'

'That doesn't mean you get dinner every night.'

'What if I come to you, have one drink and go?' His

eyes dancing. Full of questions and promises and desire. He lifted his free hand and removed her glasses, and his features blurred to her as he folded and slipped them into his pocket with one-handed skill. Blurry or not, she knew exactly where she was, and who with, as he whispered, 'Now we have Amelia unhidden.'

She soaked in the feel of his hand on her cheek as he held her face and stared into her eyes, his own dark and warm. And not quite in focus.

One long, elegant finger traced her cheekbone, up her nose and around her brow as if he'd wanted to do that for such a long time, and the sensation sent heat flooding her body. Her skin tingling where he touched. 'Your face is so beautiful. Your eyes I could lose myself in.'

'Flirting.'

'Truth, not flirting,' he whispered and settled his mouth on hers with a press of his lips that was soft and warm, firm and a little demanding. Suddenly his mouth was searing with heat that fluttered her blurry eyes shut. The tease of his tongue swept her into a world of taste and texture. Heat and need, a place where want and wantonness curled her fingers as she clutched at his shirt and returned the kiss with a passion and enthusiasm she hadn't known she had. Until her foggy brain grumbled about whose idea this stupid park bench had been. They needed a private settee or, even better, a bed.

Marco didn't take her to bed, but he held her tight and kissed and adored her until she felt as if she were the most beautiful woman he'd ever seen. Until her heart raced and her thoughts were hot and bothered and needing. When they drew apart, both were breathing heavily, and she thought hazily about those waiting chocolates on the way to her room and how she could get him there, but before she could form the words, he lifted her glasses from his pocket and placed them gently back on her face.

His smile flashed clearly as her vision stabilised. 'I think, la mia bella Amelia, I need to take you home before we rush something too special, something between only us, that I refuse to rush or share with others.' He stood, drawing her up from the bench, sweeping the blanket up yet keeping one arm around her as he ushered her back to his car.

Which was how she found herself transported home, standing alone at her door, leaning into the frame as if her legs wouldn't hold her, as Marco waved before he drove off into the night.

CHAPTER TWENTY

ON MONDAY THE emergency department had been mercifully quiet for paediatrics, and children's ward busy enough to keep her mind occupied, though her Marco-packed weekend was a distracting folder of feelings and warm memories that kept intruding.

Only Henry had come for the morning rounds because he'd been the one on call and was perfectly aware of his patients' status, so there was no need for Marco's handover. The rhythm had felt familiar, without an Italian paediatrician to unsettle her carefully maintained composure at work. But she did wonder about tonight's sundowners.

An hour before sunset, Amelia opened her door and found Marco on the doorstep, a bottle of expensive gin under his arm and two bottles of tonic water in his hands.

She stared at the sight of him standing there with his shirt pristine but open at the collar, and for the first time his sleeves were rolled, not cuffed, exposing strong forearms that she just might dream about later. His dark hair was actually mussed from the ocean breeze, and the relaxed man in front of her made her heart skip in a way she was beginning to recognise as *the Marco effect*.

'You came prepared.' She tried to keep her voice light despite the anticipation in her chest.

His smile was slow and devastating as he leaned forward and kissed both her cheeks…and then her lips. Softly, gently, with a promise for later that weakened her knees. 'I keep my word.'

Indeed he did, and she couldn't help the warmth in her chest that rivalled the evening heat outside as she stepped back. 'Come in. Put those down. Let's create our sundowners.'

He glanced around as if looking for her family. 'Luna and the boys will be home soon from footy.'

'Ahh.' He followed but soon took over once she put out the glasses, so she leaned against the bench and enjoyed the show as he measured and poured. His face intent, his body fluid as he moved.

'I see you're an experienced barman,' she quipped with amusement as he produced a perfectly ripe lime from his pocket and requested a knife and board. She laughed, complied and very quickly accepted her professionally presented beverage.

He inclined his head towards the front of the house. 'Shall we?'

She guessed they should, a little blown away by this different-again version of Marco as he followed her outside to the porch, and with a silly trip of excitement she put her drink on the side table and sat on the swing, pretending nonchalance as she waved him to the seat beside her.

When they were settled on her front porch, hips together on the same swing her parents had swung in all those years ago, the sun painted the ocean in shades of amber and rose in front of them, and the breeze drifted across like a blessing. Surprisingly, conversation felt easy as they spoke about their respective days at work.

Nothing big. But not unimportant. Updates that one or the other had on a certain patient. Little wins. A less than successful outcome that could perhaps be reassessed and new direction tried. Colleagues at the hospital. All things she didn't usually speak about at home and were pleasant to unload.

It felt amazing.

But as the light disappeared, Amelia became acutely aware of how Marco's presence filled the space around her. The way his fingers brushed hers when he reached for his glass. How his voice dropped to that intimate rumble that made her skin tingle. The careful way he watched her, as if she were something precious, or *amazing* like Crispin had said, or that he was afraid to break.

When their glasses were empty and he reached for her, she went willingly, her hands finding the solid warmth of his chest through the soft material of his shirt. She could feel his heart beating beneath her palm, as quick as her own. The first touch of his mouth was gentle, as if he were giving her time to change her mind. But when she sighed and melted into him, something unleashed between them. His hands slid into her hair, tilting her head to deepen the kiss, and she thought dimly that she might have been waiting her whole life for this moment.

He tasted of gin and possibility, of laughter and something darker that made her want to discover all his secrets. When his tongue traced the seam of her lips, she opened for him eagerly, her own hands fisting in his shirt to pull him closer.

Time seemed to slow and speed up—the solid strength of his body pressed against hers, the way he seemed to surround her with his warmth, the soft sound he made when she nipped at his lower lip.

'Bella Amelia,' he breathed against her mouth, and she felt the words like a physical caress.

She wanted to tell him that she felt it too, this wild, wonderful thing blooming between them. Something she'd never experienced, the way he made her feel cherished and desired, yet safe and reckless. She pulled him closer for another kiss, pouring all her confusion and longing and hope into the press of her lips against his.

He responded with heat, his thumb tracing the curve of her cheek as if memorising the feel of her skin.

When they finally broke apart, both breathing hard, time had passed, and she had to remember where she was. Marco rested his forehead against hers, his hands still framing her face, and she could see the desire reflected in his dark eyes.

The sun had gone. When he stood to leave, she felt the sharp pang of disappointment. Too soon. Funny how she was now thinking *too soon*. 'The sun is down now. I should definitely go,' he said, his voice rough with restraint.

'Thank you for tonight,' she said. The flash of car indicator lights in the street heralded the arrival of her family, and she was happy to take his hand to help her stand steady. Her back found the door-frame, and he pressed closer, one hand braced against the wood beside her head, the other cupping her face with tenderness. He kissed her one last time before he paused at the top of the steps, turning back. 'Amelia?'

'Yes?'

'Sogni d'oro. Sweet dreams.' The simple words, delivered with that slow smile sent warmth lingering long after his car had disappeared down the street. She touched her lips, still tingling from his kisses, and wondered if she would sleep at all.

On Tuesday, Amelia became so buried in children's ward paperwork that she missed Marco entirely when he'd gone through to emergency to help Tom with a difficult case. She looked up from a medication chart to find the ward strangely quiet, that particular energy that accompanied his presence nowhere to be found.

Worryingly, the disappointment felt sharper than she expected, perhaps because she knew she wouldn't see him that evening because of the senior-school farewell ball for the boys.

That night at the event, she and Luna discreetly wiped their eyes as they watched Crispin and Ryan dance with beautiful young women like the gentlemen they were. Her brothers—young men moving with confidence and grace she remembered teaching them in the living room when they were gangly fourteen-year-olds stepping on her feet.

'Oh, Luna. They're grown.'

Lunna patted her hand. 'And beautifully, my love.'

Time was moving too fast toward changes she wasn't ready for, and that included a certain doctor she wasn't sure of.

On Wednesday, Amelia waited outside the children's ward for Marco to arrive from emergency, and yes, she was tapping her foot with barely contained impatience. The anticipation was eating at her more than her desire for lunch. She hadn't seen him yet this morning, though they'd texted several times. The last had been a voice message, when he invited her to walk with him down to the beach café.

She didn't really have time to eat, but she had to fuel up or risk the headache that always accompanied skipped meals. And Marco had been very persuasive that they could at least walk to the Beach Café for a quick sandwich. The memory of his voice, warm and slightly pleading on the message, had swayed her.

She glanced at her watch again. One fifteen. She needed to be back by two, which meant if she actually wanted to eat rather than just order and scoff it down, it would be better to meet him at the ED in case he couldn't get away.

She knew how emergency worked—how a simple lunch break could vanish into thin air the moment an ill child rolled through the doors. If he was stuck, at least she could grab something quick from the cafeteria.

Decision made, she headed toward emergency, her sensible shoes clicking against the polished hospital floors with purpose. But as she rounded the corner, she stopped so abruptly that a passing nurse had to swerve to avoid her.

The sight in front of her knocked the air from her lungs in one devastating rush.

Marco stood in the embrace of a tall, slender and chic woman with dark hair that fell in perfect waves past her shoulders. The woman wore a red dress that probably cost more than Amelia's monthly salary—the kind of sophisticated European elegance that made Amelia conscious of her practical hospital attire. As she watched frozen, the woman leaned in and placed her mouth on Marco's.

He didn't fight her off, though he didn't exactly lean into the woman either. Nor did he step away. Either way she couldn't stand here and watch.

Amelia's stomach heaved, bile rising in her throat as the carefully constructed hope she'd been nurturing since their fair-tale weekend and their sunset drinks turned foul. She spun on her heel and walked back the way she'd come, her movements mechanical, autopilot taking over while her mind replayed the scenario.

So blatant. Right there in the emergency department where anyone could see. And the woman had been beautiful with the kind of effortless, continental sophistication that Amelia would never have.

She shook her head, trying to fit the pieces together. The Marco who had sought her out, who had kissed her so passionately, who had looked at her like she was something precious—how did that reconcile with the man currently in another woman's arms? Maybe he'd just saved the woman's child? Maybe she was a relative? Sister? Cousin? No—he'd told her he had none of those.

Ex-girlfriend, then. Her stomach twisted. Had to be.

She felt like smacking her forehead for her own stupidity. How had she let herself believe that a man like Marco would genuinely want someone like her without women on the side?

And yet, the logical, analytical part of her mind insisted that he'd seemed so sincere on all occasions these last few days. So genuinely affected by their kisses, by the times they'd shared. The sunset drinks. There had to be a reason for this.

Her footsteps slowed as professional curiosity warred with personal devastation. She glanced at her watch again. One twenty. Whatever was happening in emergency, she had just as much right to be there as Marco did. And infinitely more right than the woman in the expensive red dress.

Resolutely, she turned and walked back down the hallway, her spine straight and chin lifted in the posture that had carried her through every difficult moment of the past five years.

They were still standing in the same spot, but now there was a good shoulder width of space between them. The woman was gesticulating with elegant hands while Marco watched her with an expression Amelia couldn't quite read.

Then he glanced up as she approached, and his face transformed into that same warm, genuine smile he gave her every time he saw her.

The smile that made her believe she might actually matter to him.

'Hello, Marco.' The words came out as a question, carrying all her confusion and hurt.

He stepped around the woman immediately, moving to Amelia's side with an urgency that made something tight in her chest ease just a bit. Though, she did find herself stepping back slightly—a defensive gesture she couldn't quite control—and caught his quick, concerned glance. His brows furrowed as if he were reading distress in her expression that she'd tried to hide.

'Amelia.' Her name on his lips sounded like relief. 'Dr Day, this is Dr Valentina Forelli from my old hospital in Rome, who has surprised me with a visit.'

The dryness in his tone was unmistakable, and Amelia found herself glancing at him sharply. He didn't look happy: If anything, he looked like a man dealing with an unwelcome complication. All of a sudden, Amelia felt just a tad sorry for the woman in red. A minuscule amount. So small a person would barely see it between their fingers if they squinted.

Okay. She could do benefit of the doubt. 'How do you do, Dr…?' For some reason—probably Freudian, as her subconscious was clearly rebelling against this entire situation—she could not remember the woman's surname, though Marco had just said it.

'Forelli. Valentina Forelli.' The woman's slight accent caused more angst. She sounded like Marco. 'And you must be the Amelia Marco has told me about.'

'I'm sorry I haven't heard of you, but I'm sure I can catch up, but sadly not now.' She glanced at her watch with pointed efficiency. 'I'm guessing lunch is off, Marco, and I need to eat before a very busy afternoon, so perhaps I'll see you both later. Where are you staying, Valentina?'

'Why, with Marco, of course.'

The casual assumption in Valentina's voice hit Amelia like a slap, and she didn't look at him. Of course she was staying with him. Of course she'd simply assumed she'd be welcome in his life. The easy intimacy implied by those five words almost made Amelia's careful hold on her temper crack.

'Do get him to make you a coffee. He's good at that.' She smiled with a fierce glare at Marco, who opened his mouth and shut it again, no doubt aware he would only sink deeper. She strode away on her so-sensible shoes with no intention of eating. Damn Marco. No wonder she'd been cautious. Shame she'd let herself down at the end.

'You offer her my coffee, cara?'

She stopped, turned to find Marco right behind her. Before she could open her mouth, he said, 'Valentina will not be staying with me. I did not know she was coming. Nor did I ask her.'

He lifted a hand towards her, and she glared. He dropped his attempt to touch her, but his dark eyes narrowed as he held her gaze. 'Valentina is a friend and an ex but not one I have given my heart to. It is your trust and your heart I wish to hold into the future. May I call on you tonight? At sunset. To answer your questions and talk about us, not other women.'

And that stole the wind right out of her furiously flapping sails. Amelia closed her eyes and then opened them to see him watching her. His eyes were a touch remote but still gentle. She'd have her family around her. He would come. They would talk. And Valentina would go. If that all happened, she could deal.

Amelia didn't see Marco for the rest of the day, which was a good thing. She had to admire his spot-fire technique, and his obvious fast catch-up pace, and she couldn't help wonder if he'd had a lot of experience at separating women fighting over him.

Of course he had. But he did ask for her trust, and except for the punch to the chest she'd felt to see him in that woman's arms, she was doing okay.

But it had hurt. So she did care. A lot.

The highlight of the day was the discharge home for Braelynn with no long-term sequalae. That was, except for the trauma of her induced coma and visit to ICU, though the young teen would see a paediatric psychologist to help with that. Braelynn did suffer a lingering exhaustion that might last for weeks if not months, but she would eventually return to normal as her body and brain fully recovered.

Amelia smiled and waved, but inside she shuddered at how much worse it could have been and wished Marco had been there for the farewell.

Marco arrived before sunset with roses. Red ones. An enormous sheath of twelve long-stemmed, incredibly expensive and perfect roses with a huge red bow.

Amelia opened the door, and when she saw him standing on the step with the roses in his arms, his broad shoulders straight in his well-tailored jacket and that broad chest encased in the crisp button-down shirt—well, his presence felt overwhelming. What had she been thinking? She didn't fit with him. She was a fool. She sighed and leaned against the door. Because he was the prince she wanted, and right this moment she didn't believe in fairy tales.

CHAPTER TWENTY-ONE

Dio, the way she had looked when she opened the door. Stiff and uncompromising and…sad. 'Whatever you are thinking, cara, stop, please.' He lifted his elbow laden with roses. 'May I come in?'

She stepped back. She had no option really with him standing there. But still he felt relief when she said, 'Of course.'

He opened the screen door with his free hand and waited for her to precede him into the house, feeling her warmth in front of him. Her subtle jasmine scent drifted back to him. But most of all he felt his need to make things right.

Once inside she stopped and turned to face him, and he lay the roses in her arms before she refused them. They were perfect, like her. But she barely looked at them. 'Thank you.'

'May I kiss you?' His eyes searching hers for permission, for a need in her eyes like he had in his. He searched her expression. Nothing. But no refusal.

When she didn't answer he leaned forward and went straight for her mouth. Brushing his mouth across her soft lips, inhaling the scent of her, he kissed her more firmly, trying to tell her he was hers. But she broke the kiss and stepped back. The roses between them. A red guard. Still she didn't say anything.

So he must then. 'I have wanted to bring you roses

since the beginning, and there is no apology in this. Not a request for forgiveness. They are a gift to a woman I admire very much.'

She looked from them to him. 'The roses are beautiful.'

'You are more beautiful.' She turned her face away, and he stopped her with his fingers on her cheek. 'To me you are the most beautiful woman in the world, bella Amelia. And I am yours if you would have me.'

Her eyes flashed at that. There was the fire. At least she cared that much. 'She kissed you.'

His pulse rate jumped. How had she seen that brief embrace before he'd stepped back? No matter. It was true. 'Sì. She kissed me. My friend.'

'Ex lover.'

He shrugged. 'That too. But not current. I have had no lovers since we began this dance.'

'Speaking of dances, what about the one at the ball?'

He smiled at that. She remembered. 'The ball is where I fell in love.' He shrugged. 'I went to Sybyl's house, yes. But the moment she kissed me, I knew.' He touched Amelia's face gently. 'I knew I felt nothing. Nothing but the need to come home to you. We had coffee because I owed her that courtesy, but I was already walking away in my head.'

He smiled. 'The old me would have stayed, would have taken what was offered because it was easy. But you have changed me, Amelia. You have made me want more than easy. Though I would have gone home with you—and stayed, if you'd asked.'

The truth was harder to admit, that he'd gone to Sybyl's expecting to feel something, anything that would prove Amelia hadn't completely captured his heart. Instead, he'd sat across from his former lover feeling like a stranger to himself, counting the minutes until he could leave.

He glanced around at the empty room. 'Where is your family?'

She sniffed. 'They deserted me in my hour of need. Luna refused to be here.'

He smiled at that. Bless. 'They left you because of their love for you, Amelia.' He stroked her cheek. 'Luna is wise. And I am trying to tell you to listen to me. Hear what I am saying. Valentina has gone to a hotel, and yes, I paid for that. She does not love me, never has, but I am rich enough for her to follow to Australia and hope that I am homesick.' He smiled. 'I am not homesick. Because for me, now, you are my home. Yes, I have houses in Italy. But only you are here. If you will have me, then we could look at the future before us, together.'

She lifted her head at that, and some of the awful rigidity fell away.

He took the roses from her and laid them on the table. 'Come sit on the swing outside with me.' He drew her to the door and out onto the patio that looked out to the golden hues of evening over the sea. 'Let me plead my case.'

Her face softened at that, and then she released a small breath as she followed and then sat, looking out over the ocean, and he next to her.

He moistened dry lips. 'My life has changed because of you, Amelia.' He gestured back at the house. 'Because of your beautiful family. Because of your depth and caring in your work that calls to the same I have in me. You know I love your determination and fierceness, but I also love the softness and kindness that you give to the young and, hopefully, one day, to me. I want your heart, my love, and I vowed I would not rush you.'

He shrugged. So continental of him, but pah! 'Perhaps I would have rushed more if I'd known she was coming.'

She smiled at that, and his dread lightened. There was no use trying to protect himself from the truth he needed to speak. 'For a time now, I have known you are the one for me.' He watched her beautiful eyes widen. 'I want you in my future if you will have me. Please, la mia Amelia.'

Her gaze travelled over his face. 'What are you saying?'

'I'm saying I'm not patient anymore. I am not risking any further women intruding between us. That I need to proclaim myself to you.' He took both her hands and slid slowly to the floor on one knee.

'When you are ready, marry me, Amelia Day. Please.'

She gasped, but he surged on. 'Take me as your husband, and carry my children if we are so blessed.' Her lips parted, and he wanted to kiss her so badly, but he was not finished.

'Be my partner, my friend, my lover, my everything. Because I love you.' He squeezed her hands in his as he saw the tears well, the change in her dear face, the moistening of her lips, and he prayed. Dio, he prayed that she would say yes.

She squeezed his hands. 'I did not expect this.'

He smiled ruefully. 'Nor did I tonight, until this moment, or I would have brought the ring that sits in my bureau at home for you.'

Her eyes widened. 'You have a ring?'

He nodded, with pretended solemnity. 'Sì. It is very expensive.' He grinned at her enjoying her shock now that he saw the softness for him in her. 'Quite vulgar, really, three point five carats, but I wanted something that told everyone how much I love you.'

Her eyes narrowed as if she didn't believe him. 'I'd like to see this ring.'

He laughed, relief bubbling through him like the Prosecco they enjoyed so much. 'Only if you give me an answer.'

She drew him back up beside her and took his face between her soft and so capable hands, until her nose almost touched his. Her eyes, deep pools of lavender blue, showed him her love. 'You are incorrigible. Incredibly handsome. Disgustingly rich. A fabulous paediatrician that I love working with, and worst of all, I've fallen for you head over heels, and it's most uncomfortable with all the other women who want you.'

'I do not want them.' His heart filled and he closed his eyes as he vowed, 'I will keep you comfortable, my love. I will keep you more than that. And your answer?'

'This has been so fast. If we take time to make sure. No rush for a wedding. Then, yes. Please. We can make plans.'

His heart leapt. 'And what plans would we make?'

'Future ones. To spend my life with you. Share my family and make our own family…eventually.' She completed the tiny distance between their faces and sealed her lips against his, leaning into him with her body soft and willing, and he wanted nothing more than to carry her off in his arms and show her how much he loved her.

He stood. 'Come with me now, to my home, and I will show you this ring.'

Her eyes were warm and knowing. 'Will you show me your bedroom too?'

'Sì. It is where the ring is.' His body surged. 'It is there I will show you just how much I love you in all the ways.'

And he did.

CHAPTER TWENTY-TWO

THE WEDDING RECEPTION would be held later upstairs at Rainbow Bay Surf Club, where Amelia had friendships, deep roots and warm affection, something he was learning from her.

But their ceremony would be here by the water, on the beach that had become so special to him since that first night she brought him here. The night everything changed between them.

The beach wore not a towel to dry oneself, but a large red carpet, wide enough to hold four abreast, leading down to a small knoll above the waves, and Marco felt his chest tighten with emotion as he watched the tall white flags flutter in the salt breeze, the scene of his wedding to come. Those flags surrounded the Italian wrought iron table and chairs he'd brought from his own garden, now transformed into symbols of a home and a future with Amelia.

Potted orange and lemon trees lined the wedding aisle, their familiar Mediterranean scent mixing with the ocean air to create something entirely new.

Their life together would be like that. New and wonderful. Full of love and family. With the woman he trusted with his heart.

The white chairs arranged in neat rows held the guests who had assembled in a chattering crowd, and Marco marvelled at how their voices carried so much warmth and friendship. These people, Amelia's colleagues, her surf club friends, neighbours who'd watched the twins grow. They were here because they loved her, and somehow, impossibly, they'd come to welcome him into that circle.

Marco stood in his cream Brunello Cucinelli suit, the fabric blown tight against his skin, his Christian Louboutin suede boat shoes a concession to the beach setting that made him smile. He cared not.

This Marco cared only that Amelia would smile when she saw him waiting for her.

How had he been so fortunate? The question whispered through his mind with gratitude.

Henry stood beside him in matching cream, solid and dependable as he had been when Marco had stood for him less than a year ago. The symmetry felt profound—these two men who'd found their hearts in this coastal town, both discovering love.

It had taken six months for his Amelia to agree to a date, determined not to rush, but happy to wear his *vulgar ring* as she called it. It looked so beautiful on her, especially in those quiet morning moments when that was all she wore, when she belonged completely to him and he to her.

Madonna, his new life. The conversations over breakfast, the lazy Sunday mornings, the sundowners of conversation now a staple in their days. He had become part of her, just as she had become part of him.

Marco had never been this happy. Never felt so completely at home, so encased in protective arms that weren't just physical but emotional. Her family's loving acceptance of him still caught him off guard sometimes. The way Crispin and Ryan had seamlessly included him in their plans, the way Luna consulted him about household decisions as if his opinion mattered, as if he belonged there. And on their honeymoon, he would take his beautiful Amelia to Italy. To Rome. To Maria for her blessing. He couldn't wait.

He had made plans here, of course. Careful, considered plans that reflected this new life he was building. After some stubborn resistance that he'd eventually circumvented with what Amelia called his *Italian wiles*, he'd purchased a beautiful three-bedroom apartment in Melbourne for the twins. Close to the university, with two parking spaces and a spare room designed specifically for their sister or aunt to visit.

It had given him such pleasure to hand them those keys, to see their faces light up with possibility and independence.

Other plans were already in motion: the renovation of Amelia's family home into their primary residence, the installation of a pool and cabana in the spacious backyard, the long-needed refurbishment and expansion that had both women practically glowing with excitement as they pored over design magazines and paint samples.

Under Luna's vocal protest, though he had caught the tears in her eyes, he'd signed the apartment he'd purchased from Nadia over to Luna. A permanent base in Australia to return from her travels to. Pah! What was the use of having money if you couldn't use it to lighten the burden of the family that had claimed you?

Now he stood with Henry, his back to Surfer's Paradise in the distance across the waves, watching for the bride of his dreams. As his gaze swept over the assembled guests, he felt that familiar swell of emotion—wonder, really—at the smiling faces of people he'd come to know and respect and genuinely enjoy the company of. He was still surprised by how happy they all seemed for him and Amelia, how readily they'd accepted this Italian stranger into their tight-knit community.

He savoured this sense of belonging, this feeling of being woven into a larger community.

Then his breath caught.

Ahhh, here she comes. He drew in a breath. His heart pounded.

Amelia, his Amelia, floating across the sand in a long, sweeping white dress that brushed the ground below her silver sandals, each step bringing her closer to him. Her new white glasses, not quite so large and so much better suited to him admiring her face, perched on her sweet nose.

Her glorious hair flew free and flowing around her face, and he smiled, knowing it was probably annoying her with its unpredictability, but she'd worn it loose as a gift to him because she knew how much he loved to watch it dance in the breeze.

The gesture made his throat tight with love. With gratitude. With awe.

In her hands she clutched red roses—not white, not pink, but deep crimson blooms reminiscent of the very first flowers he'd given her when he'd been trying so desperately to find a way into her guarded heart. The bouquet choice had been hers, another gift, another acknowledgement of their shared history, and his throat threatened to close.

'You okay?' Henry's voice said quietly beside him, grounding him. He nodded and breathed.

He smiled as he watched Luna walk beside her niece, radiant in her role as matron of honour, while Crispin and Ryan flanked them both, guardsmen in a wedding party configuration he'd never seen before but was perfectly fitting for this woman who'd always done things her own way. Four abreast they strolled down the carpet towards him.

He embraced this freedom of choice in his new country, this Australia that lay across an ocean from everything he'd once thought he wanted.

As Amelia drew closer, her eyes meeting his across the distance, Marco felt the last piece of his carefully constructed defences crumble away completely. He was home. Finally, completely, home.

This place that had become his world, his heart, his home—not because of its beaches or its sunshine, but because it held his love, his family and his future. With Amelia.

* * * * *

If you enjoyed this story, check out these other great reads from Fiona McArthur

Falling for the Single Mum Next Door
Healing the Baby Doc's Heart
Father for the Midwife's Twins
Taking a Chance on the Best Man

All available now!

MILLS & BOON®

Coming next month

THE PARAMEDIC ROOMMATE PACT
JC Harroway

'Sometimes life doesn't make much sense,' he said, his gaze lingering on her mouth for a few exhilarating seconds during which Kaia became increasingly convinced that he wanted her too.

'It makes no sense to me that a guy would walk away from you.'

A thrilling gasp sounded in her head. 'You're just saying that because you're my friend,' she pointed out, almost from habit, clinging to her last shred of willpower.

Their jokes often bordered on flirtation. But Levi's expression wasn't friendly. It was intense and searing and raging with need.

'I *am* your friend,' he confirmed, the look on his face and the few cryptic words he'd spoken, flooding her pelvis with liquid heat that slid down her legs so she feared she might actually collapse.

Drunk on the excitement pounding through her body but safe in the knowledge that he cared about her, that she trusted him, she slowly raised her hands to his shoulders.

'Well on that note, happy birthday,' she whispered.

She rose onto the tips of her toes and pressed her lips to his. Brief. Forbidden. And so tempting she couldn't breathe.

Continue reading

THE PARAMEDIC ROOMMATE PACT
JC Harroway

Available next month
millsandboon.co.uk

COMING SOON!

We really hope you enjoyed reading this book.
If you're looking for more romance
be sure to head to the shops when
new books are available on

Thursday 26th February

MILLS & BOON